Tales of Southeast Asia's Jazz Age

Tales of Southeast Asia's Jazz Age

Filipinos, Indonesians and Popular Culture, 1920–1936

Peter Keppy

NUS PRESS
SINGAPORE

© 2019 Peter Keppy

Published by:

NUS Press
National University of Singapore
AS3-01-02, 3 Arts Link
Singapore 117569

Fax: (65) 6774-0652
E-mail: nusbooks@nus.edu.sg
Website: http://nuspress.nus.edu.sg

ISBN 978-981-3250-51-2 (paper)

National Library Board, Singapore Cataloguing in Publication Data

Name(s): Keppy, Peter.
Title: Tales of Southeast Asia's jazz age: Filipinos, Indonesians and popular culture, 1920–1936 / Peter Keppy.
Description: Singapore: NUS Press, [2019] | Includes bibliographic references and index.
Identifiers: OCN 1078335752 | ISBN 978-981-32-5051-2 (paperback)
Subjects: LCSH: Popular culture--Philippines--History--20th century. | Popular culture--Indonesia--History--20th century.
Classification: DDC 306.09599--dc23

Cover image: A publicity picture of Luis Borromeo taken in a Manila photo studio with Luis's printed autograph, c. 1922. Courtesy of Alice Marvin.

Typeset by: Ogma Solutions Pvt Ltd
Printed by: Mainland Press Pte Ltd

For my father
Etus Keppy (Bondowoso, 1930–Amsterdam, 2011),
who loved popular music so much

Contents

List of Illustrations

Acknowledgements

A great number of people contributed enormously to this book. They inspired me with thoughts on popular culture, fed me with source materials, connected me to others working in similar fields, offered me their hospitality or encouraged me in one way or another. My thanks go to:

Henk Schulte Nordholt for teaming me up with Bart Barendregt and for his enduring support for the joint KITLV-NIOD-Leiden University project *Articulating Modernity: The Making of Popular Music in Twentieth Century Southeast Asia and the Rise of New Audiences.*

Bart Barendregt for his crash course on popular culture, our hunting missions for vintage popular music, his cooking skills and his positive vibes in general.

Jaap Erkelens, who remained down-to-earth and sceptical from the start about my intellectual interpretations of popular culture in colonial Indonesia; a critique that kept me humble and sharp. His collection of rare 78rpm gramophone records, including those of Miss Riboet, photographs, and newspaper articles from colonial Indonesia proved a treasure trove and a crucial asset, without which this book would have been impossible.

Richie Quirino, musician, jazz aficionado and writer was helpful in suggesting people I should contact in Manila. He showed me Filipino hospitality and served me his infamous homemade squash salad served with fish and rice. His wife Cherry was so kind to help me with translations from Tagalog and Ilongan.

Research assistant Karl Poblado, introduced to me by historian Ricardo T. Jose (UP), took up the time-consuming task of surveying Philippine historical newspapers, paving the way for my in-depth newspaper research. Karl also translated part of the Tagalog- and Spanish-language materials. Our pilgrimage to the Black Madonna [Señora de la Paz y Buen Viaje (Our Lady of Peace and Good Voyage)] in Antipolo, helped me to navigate my way through this ambitious project.

Hope Sabanpan-Yu, director of the Cebuano Studies Center of the University of San Carlos in Cebu City, and her staff are praised for their hospitality and for giving me generous access to the institute's rare Cebuano newspaper materials during the institute's transfer to a new premise. Hope translated texts from Cebuano (Sugboano) into English, offering me a perspective on culture and history away from central Manila. In addition, Hope and Raphael Polinar's kindness during my unfortunate, but luckily brief, hospital visit in Cebu cannot go unmentioned.

The Borromeo family in the Philippines and the US, for their generous help in reconstructing the history of their illustrious relative Luis Borromeo: John Borromeo, Jack Borromeo and Mary (Milal) Borromeo Requilman in Cebu City; Vincent Borromeo in Manila; Amparito Borromeo Guilatco and her husband Amando Guilatco in San Francisco, California, and last but not least Luis's sole remaining daughter, Alice Marvin, in White Salmon, Washington, D.C., USA.

Fritz Schenker for sharing his insights on music and Filipino materials with me and as liaison to Alice, Luis's daughter. Particular mention must be made of Fritz's piano recordings performed from original scores. These recordings allowed me to listen to and enjoy the hybrid Filipino foxtrots and tangos from the 1920s and 1930s, very difficult to find on original records or even as digital reproductions.

The staff of the Special Collections Division of the National Library of the Philippines in Manila for their patience and help in accessing the original published compositions of Luis Borromeo and his contemporaries.

Mario Quijano for sharing with me his knowledge on Spanish *zarzuela* theatre in Mexico and the Philippines, and for his translations from Spanish in the bilingual English-Spanish Philippine print press.

Eveline Buchheim for patiently going through individual chapters and the entire manuscript at different stages of the project and for collecting materials in the Library of Congress, Washington, D.C.

The anonymous peer reviewers for the painstaking work of going through a messy manuscript.

Anna Yeadell-Moore for the copy-editing.

Many thanks also to:

Jan van der Putten for his hospitality during my research in Singapore; Freddy Irawan Keppy for his translations of Javanese poetry into Indonesian; Basil Triharyanto for retrieving some of the newspaper materials at the National Library and the Pusat Perfilman in Jakarta; Naqiah Binte Mohamad Sumri in Singapore for translating Jawi texts from Malay newspapers into English; Tristan and Jude Reignier for their hospitality during my research in London (Jude's bicycle proved a crucial asset for reaching the National Library after the capital's subway personnel went on strike!); Fe Susan Go for generously assisting me with research at the library of the University of Michigan, Ann Arbor; Cora and Ed Yee for hosting me at their home in Ann Arbor; Betty Litamahuputty for her hospitality after I was forced to evacuate my guesthouse during a severe flood (*banjir*) in Jakarta, January 2013; Hugo Strötbaum for providing me with information on the German recording engineer Max Birckhahn, who recorded Miss Riboet in Java and Luis Borromeo in Cebu; Philip Yampolsky for information on Javanese *ketoprak* theatre; Edwin Jurriens for reading the manuscript at a very early stage; Tjalling Bouma for helping me out with microfilmed newspapers from Jakarta; The NIOD Institute for War, Holocaust and Genocide Studies for support throughout the project.

Thanks also to those who encouraged me somewhere along the journey:

Michael Peletz, Otto van den Muijzenberg, Michael Cullinane, Els Bogaerts, Marije Plomp, Ariel Heryanto, Brent Luvaas, Matau van Wijk, Michael Hawkins, Tim Barnard, Heather Sutherland, Djohan and Anilo Keppy.

Without a subsidy of the Netherlands Organization for Scientific Research (NWO), this project would not have been possible. Needless to say, I bear full responsibility for the imperfections in this book.

Chapter 1

New Cultural Landscapes

In 1922, Luis Francisco Borromeo, an educated Filipino from a wealthy provincial family, took the Manila stage with a new form of vaudeville. Within a few years this pianist, cultural business entrepreneur and self-proclaimed Filipino "King of Jazz", was tremendously popular in the capital city, setting a new trend in vernacular theatre in the Philippine islands.

Three years later, in 1925, a similar cultural breakthrough occurred in Java, the Netherlands East Indies. The newspapers on the island reported that a young Javanese woman, Miss Riboet ("Ribut" in modern Indonesian and Malay spelling), electrified the multi-ethnic urbanites of the port city of Surabaya with a modernised form of Malay opera. Within two years, in 1927, she was dubbed the "darling of tens of thousands in all cities along Java's North Coast".[1] By 1930, her fame had travelled to both sides of the Strait of Melaka making her the first female translocal popular culture star in the Malay world to date.[2]

Tales of Southeast Asia's Jazz Age tells the story of a new culture taking shape in the 1920s from the rarely taken perspective of two colonial subjects: Luis Borromeo and Miss Riboet.[3] In the 1920s, a time of profound social and political turmoil, a brief but dynamic cultural transformation occurred that slowed down in the mid-1930s. Borromeo and Riboet stood at the cradle of this new culture associated with modernity, cosmopolitanism and nationalism. They, their professional companions and their audiences are central to this story.

---

[1] "Het een en ander over den Stamboel", *De Locomotief*, 18 June 1927.

[2] Here "Malay world" refers to the places where one or another form of Malay was used as the vernacular. For contesting notions of "Malayness", see Barnard (2004). For a critical discussion of Malayness in relation to Filipinos and the Philippines, see Curaming (2011).

[3] Another fascinating protagonist of this new culture is Po Sein, the Burmese actor-singer who transformed and modernised Burmese theatre from the 1910s to 1930s, as documented and narrated in the late 1960s by Po Sein's son, in collaboration with an American co-author and Burmese art lover (Sein and Whitney 1998). Po Sein's tale raises several social issues relevant for a discussion of an emerging popular culture in Burma and Southeast Asia, such as his attitude towards British colonialism, politics and religion (Buddhism).

The two protagonists deserve attention for three, closely interrelated reasons. Firstly, they revitalised local theatre and music, merging Western and local cultural genres into something that local audiences perceived not only as novel and exciting, but also as socially meaningful. Secondly, they were the first secular stars of a new culture that drew mass audiences. And thirdly, Borromeo and Riboet pioneered and embodied a popular, but "in-between" culture that remained awkwardly situated between high art and vulgar entertainment.

The making of this new culture occurred at a time when the Filipino and Indonesian emancipation and nationalist movements regained new confidence. It would, however, be misleading to assume that nationalism was the single and dominating driving force behind the new culture. For Luis Borromeo and Miss Riboet, the many artists they collaborated with and for their fans, modernity and cosmopolitanism were equally important signifiers. To capture this new culture in the making, three deceivingly simply main questions are posed: How were Miss Riboet and Luis Borromeo able to rise to stardom? What did they and their cultural products mean and to whom? And, how could this new culture wax and wane in a relatively short period?

Popular Culture and Historiography

Popular culture rarely serves as an object of historical scrutiny, and even less so in non-Western contexts. This is a pity, as a critical examination of popular culture can do more than reveal exotic forms of entertainment; it can expose mentalities and ethics within and across societies. *Tales of Southeast Asia's Jazz Age* aims to take popular culture as a prism of societal change.

Popular culture is often taken for granted as something that might be defined along the lines of commodification, entertainment, mass consumption and also media technology. Although these could be considered quintessential elements of popular culture, we would still be at odds with what these characteristics mean to people living in societies dissimilar in social, economic and political respects. The position chosen here is therefore different: popular culture is seen as a contested and contradictory social phenomenon. It is an elusive realm or space where meaning is disputed, something long argued by exponents of Cultural Studies. This struggle over meaning is a process that is specific to time and place.[4] In short, in order to understand popular culture we need to contextualise and historicise it.

---

[4] For an overview of critical theory on popular culture from a Cultural Studies perspective, see Middleton (1985); Pinches (1999) and Storey (2003).

A handful of experts on performing arts in Indonesia acknowledge Miss Riboet's role as a novel entertainer.[5] She however, does not feature in Indonesian, Malaysian or Dutch cultural history as a socially relevant cultural pioneer. Luis Borromeo shares a similar fate in Philippine historiography. Riboet and Borromeo have fallen victim to a process that narrowly recollects the past and rewrites history, which Priti Ramamurthy, in her study on modern female film actors in colonial India, phrases as an "all-consuming nationalism".[6] The fascinating transnational histories of border-crossing cultural activity of the two artists simply do not fit smooth nationalist narratives of cultural heroes who unambiguously contributed to anti-colonialism and nation-building.

The tale of Borromeo and Riboet should however not be read as a hagiography of two gifted individuals, nor is it a response to all-consuming nationalist histories or amnesia. It is a critical account of the making of popular culture under influence of nationalism, modernity and cosmopolitanism in two different yet, in many ways, similar colonial societies. Rather than simply focusing on modern or cosmopolitan practices and enthused by anthropologist Frederick Cooper, I searched for a "discourse of modernity". That is, I explored and interpreted discussions about modern life as documented in a wide variety of historical sources.[7] In a wealth of largely unexplored material, including short stories, poetry, letters, theatre and film reviews, advertisements and sheet music published from the 1910s to 1930s, I was able to track moral debates on issues like modern fashion to new forms of social dancing. Rare visual and audio source materials, the popular consumer items produced in the period under consideration, were also used: photographic images, cartoons and vernacular songs and theatre plays recorded on phonographic shellac discs.[8]

Comparing two popular artists and their audiences in two different colonial societies positioned me to question the (alleged) uniqueness of historical

---

[5] On Miss Riboet, see Sumardjo (1992: 114–7); Biran (2009: 80–4); Cohen (2010: 180–1, 183–4, 225), and, more recently, Hutari (2017: 129–39). A concise overview of the history of Riboet and Tio Tek Djien Jr. and their Malay opera company Orion is found on Wikipedia, the free encyclopedia. See https://en.wikipedia.org/wiki/Miss_Riboet's_Orion, accessed 28 Aug. 2015.

[6] Ramamurthy (2008: 151) defines this "all-consuming nationalism" as "a historical process that provided a dynamic space for some Indian women to be modern actors in the 1920s and 1930s but eventually shored up a hegemonic nationalism, and as a continuing tendency in popular film histories to eclipse these alternative and more complex stories about gender, nationalism, and modernity".

[7] Cooper (2005: 130–1).

[8] The majority of these sources were found in the national libraries of the Philippines and Indonesia, in the library of the University of the Philippines and, to a lesser extent, in private collections.

processes. Comparison also forced me to rethink the ways cultural histories have been cast in the past. For example, culture in the Philippines tends to be presented in terms of a clash between a Spanish colonial legacy and a new American culture. Another central theme in the historiography of the late colonial Philippines is the appropriation by Filipinos of American cultural institutions as a form of resistance to American cultural imperialism.[9] In contrast, cultural appropriation and resistance is hardly central in discussions on popular culture in colonial Indonesia. The emphasis tends to lie on cultural hybridity, the merger of the alien with local culture. So, why not take cultural hybridity in the Philippines more seriously? And why not examine more thoughtfully cultural appropriation and resistance in the case of popular culture in colonial Indonesia? I frankly admit that the academic exercise of comparing and connecting different historical trajectories through the common thread of popular culture was ambitious and, at times, also rather arduous. By and large, though it was a fruitful journey, it offered me a fresh view on the cultural histories of two neighbouring colonial societies.

Of course, we are not completely in the dark about the social and cultural meanings of "popular culture" during the colonial period and about how Indonesians and Filipinos attempted to reconcile cosmopolitanism and modernity with nationalism. For example, William Frederick focused on debates among Indonesian intellectuals, who, in the late 1930s and early 1940s, struggled with new models for a modern national culture, including whether to adopt modern, popular hybrid musical styles as national music.[10] More recently, discussing music and national identity in the colonial (and post-colonial) Philippines, Christi-Anne Castro observes that the drive for a national music led to the obscuring of musical origins and, as a result, the blurring of the boundaries between folk, popular and art music.[11]

In this book, I move in a related yet slightly different direction, looking at a short-lived cultural renaissance in the 1920s. To understand this cultural revival, I will begin with a discussion of the notion of in-between culture. To get a deeper understanding of meaning in popular culture, I will subsequently turn to three other key concepts: popular cosmopolitanism, popular modernity and participatory pop.

---

[9] See for instance Enriquez (2008) on broadcasting in the Philippines.

[10] Frederick (1996).

[11] Castro (2011: 6, 10, 32, 34–5).

"In-between" and "Popular" Art: A Century of Intellectual Debate

Throughout the 20th century, the concept of in-betweenness has appeared and reappeared in different guises. In 1909, anthropologist Arnold van Gennep was the first to introduce the notion of a symbolically marked transitory or in-between stage that people enter before acquiring a new religious status or social identity. Independent of Van Gennep's anthropological concept, a similar idea of cultural in-betweenness, rather than liminality as a temporary and transitional social state, took on a different life in the United States, when Afro-American dance music like the foxtrot and the Charleston divided American intellectuals on the issue of whether such dance music contributed to American national culture and identity. Where to place the modern dance music in aesthetic terms? Was it akin to refined European classical music or simply unsophisticated music for mass consumption? Jazz's hybrid European and Afro-American origins, the involvement of both Afro-American and white musicians who appealed to both "black" and "white" audiences, evoked debates and controversies from the late 1910s to 1930s, a period generally known as the jazz age.[12] Modern dance music, such as the Charleston, the foxtrot, but also the Argentinean tango, the dance venues and the audiences, induced people to question and reconstruct the boundaries of race, class, national identity, gender and the modern. These debates continue to this day and are helpful in assessing popular culture in the Philippines and Indonesia in the age of jazz.[13]

According to jazz studies scholar Nicholas Evans, a very early example of suggesting an alternative to the binary opposition of low versus highbrow art came from the American writer Gilbert Seldes in 1924. In defence of jazz, Seldes attempted to define the music in three distinct aesthetic categories. "Throughout Seldes's writing on popular songs, ragtime, and jazz, there is an effort to articulate how these musical forms manifest something neither high nor low, something interstitial, which sometimes veers towards a broader, Boasian sense of *culture*."[14] In the 1920s, the American anthropologist Franz Boas regarded culture as a set of values developed and shared by people that should be understood on its own

---

[12] On discussions about culture, race and nationalism in the US, see Evans (2000) and also Garrett (2008).

[13] The separate field of "jazz studies" can be regarded as the intellectual offspring of these long-lasting debates in the US. For a brief discussion of social issue-driven studies on jazz and the jazz age in the US, see Gennari (1998). Jazz studies remains an American-Eurocentric biased scholarly discipline. Notable exceptions are Jones (2001) on China, Atkins (2001) on Japan, and more recently Schenker (2016) on the Philippines.

[14] Evans (2000: 110).

terms. In short, Boas acknowledged the possibility of cultural variation and thus challenged notions of cultural homogeneity.[15]

In the early 1930s, discussions on low versus highbrow culture also occurred in Germany, albeit under quite a different social and political constellation compared to the US. Building on Marxist ideas, German intellectuals, from what came to be known as the Frankfurt School, theorised about capitalism as a force in shaping fleetingness in popular culture. Deeply concerned with capitalism and the contemporary political system, that is fascist authoritarian rule and its mass appeal in Germany, they discussed consumer manipulation, through elites and the media. In sum, the Frankfurt School assessed popular culture in distinctly negative terms.[16] After the Second World War, the Frankfurt School evoked criticism, particularly among British scholars, who would become pioneers of what came to be known as Cultural Studies.

In the 1960s, the scholarly discussion on popular culture was revitalised in Great Britain and this without reference to earlier debates on "mid-brow" art. At that time, concerns arose about the alleged debasement of British youngsters by the new mass media technology of television and that of beat music. In opposition to assumptions about these corrupting influences, cultural theorists Stuart Hall and Paddy Whannel (1964) fervently argued that a distinction between the "serious" and "the popular" was misleading. They instead advocated use of the term "popular art", arguing that some forms of apparently mass consumed culture carried artistic qualities of their own, setting them apart from "popular culture" and high art alike—"a popular art, for the people".[17] Hall and Whannel took the history of the British music hall as an example. This vaudeville type of theatre moved from a folk roots theatre in the 19th century to urban commercial entertainment at the turn of the 20th century.[18] As will be demonstrated, Filipino vaudeville and Malay opera would go through similar processes, with the difference that these latter forms of theatre were urban-centred from the start, and that they originated in Southeast Asia's cosmopolitan port cities.

Another 30 years had passed, when, in 1994, a scholar of English and American literature, Homi K. Bhabha, like Seldes, and Hall and Whannel before him, questioned the simplicity of binary models in analysing cultural dynamics

---

[15] Evans (2000: 28, 110–1, 256).

[16] In their critique of mass consumerism, exponents of the Frankfurt School consistently used the term "Culture Industry" instead of "popular culture" emphasising its commercial and manipulative nature. Particularly the work of Theodor Wiesengrund Adorno has been influential. On the intellectual history of Adorno and the Frankfurt School, see Leppert (2002: 1–82).

[17] Hall and Whannel (1964: 59).

[18] Ibid.: 56.

by introducing the idea of "in-between space". As Bhabha stated: "These 'in-between' spaces provide the terrain for elaborating strategies of selfhood—singular or communal—that initiate new signs of identity, and innovative sites of collaboration, and contestation, in the act of defining the idea of society itself."[19] As I will show throughout this book, this Bhabhian "idea of society itself" is highly pertinent in relation to a burgeoning "popular culture" or in-between culture in the colonial Philippines and Indonesia in the 1920s.

Pop Cosmopolitanism, Popular Modernity and Participatory Pop

Let us now move on to three key concepts useful for scrutinising meaning in popular culture and for seeing the often-underrated active role of consumers or audiences in shaping it. The first two notions, pop cosmopolitanism and participatory pop, have been developed by fandom guru Henry Jenkins. Anthropologist Joel Kahn has used the third, popular modernism. Jenkins and Kahn challenge older, yet persistent Frankfurt School ideas about elites being the architects and guardians of cosmopolitanism (receptiveness to alien cultures) and of modernity (ideas and practice associated with progress and individual freedom). Both see roles for non-elites in actively shaping and engaging in cosmopolitanism and modernity without associations of high culture and elite manipulation.

In 2006, when discussing a Japanese type of fandom, *otaku*, among American fans of Japanese anime, Jenkins introduced his concept of "pop cosmopolitanism" arguing that:

> We tend to apply the term to those who develop a taste for international food, dance, music, art, or literature, in short, those who have achieved distinction through their discriminating tastes for classical or high culture. Here, I will be using the term "pop cosmopolitanism" to refer to the ways that the transcultural flows of popular culture inspires new forms of global consciousness and cultural competency [...].[20]

Using the term pop cosmopolitanism, I will examine what these cultural flows and competency meant in the case of the careers of Luis Borromeo and Miss Riboet and their audiences.

Like Jenkins, Joel Kahn takes issue with older theories about the fleetingness of popular culture and its escapist nature, as developed by the Marxist-inspired Frankfurt School. Exponents of the Frankfurt School view political elites,

---

[19] Bhabha (1994: 1–2).
[20] Jenkins (2006a: 155–6).

intellectuals and *avant garde* artists as the true bearers of modernity. In contrast to assumptions about elite cultural domination, Kahn asserts that people outside these highbrow groups equally contributed to modernity. These non-elites assumed a cultural brokerage position within society "[…] reworking the modernist meanings and texts of the elites on the one hand, and constructing meanings for the masses on the other". And Kahn argues that these agents were "[…] of pivotal importance in the emergence of the broad modernist sensibility that I have called popular modernism".[21] To avoid confusion with modernism as a specific art style, and to connect it more firmly with the popular culture realm, I prefer to use the term "popular modernity", rather than Kahn's "popular modernism".[22] I argue that Luis Borromeo and Miss Riboet were pivotal actors, who helped to create a pop cosmopolitanism and popular modernity in their respective colonial societies, but whose social cultural positions and significance were misunderstood and ignored by contemporaries in the metropolises of America and Europe.

Let me end the conceptual tool kit with another of Henry Jenkins's original notions: participatory culture. I have taken the liberty of transforming it into the term "participatory pop".[23] Jenkins critiques the often implicit and misleading divide between passive consumers and active producers, and the way the latter have control over media. He shows that popular culture consumers can turn into active participants, even become cultural producers themselves. "Fandom studies", to which Jenkins has contributed significantly, paved the way for taking consumers seriously and removing them from the moral condemnation often associated with fanatic consumers, that is fans, of a banal popular culture.[24] Hence, the notion of "participatory pop" is particularly helpful for capturing the fluid boundaries between consumer and producer and to seek for meaning in popular culture that goes beyond banality. In other words, and as far as the

---

[21] Kahn (2001: 19).

[22] Modernism itself is generally understood as an aesthetic response to mass consumerism and popular culture, leading to an eponymous artistic style of music, architecture, painting, sculpture and so forth.

[23] "The term participatory culture, contrasts with older notions of passive media spectatorship. Rather than talking about media producers and consumers as occupying separate roles, we might now see them as participants who interact with each other according to a new set of rules that none of us fully understands. Not all participants are created equal. Corporations—and even individuals within corporate media—still exert greater power than any individual consumer or even the aggregate of consumers. And some consumers have greater abilities to participate in the emerging culture than others" (Jenkins 2006b: 3).

[24] For pioneering work on fans and fandom, see Lewis (1992). For a critical assessment of the state of fandom studies in the early 2000s, see Hills (2002).

historical sources allow me, the audiences of Borromeo and Riboet will be made visible as active participants of a popular culture in the making.

The Philippines and Indonesia in the Early 20th Century

The careers of Luis Borromeo and Miss Riboet in professional entertainment are the chronological threads that weave together my narrative of pop cosmopolitanism, popular modernity and participatory pop.[25] This making of the popular did not occur in a social and political void. To fully gauge the social cultural meaning of the new culture and its agents, it is imperative to briefly consider the social and political conditions of the respective colonies in the first two to three decades of the 20th century.

In 1896, Filipinos rebelled against the Spanish coloniser, the first revolution in colonial Southeast Asia to date. The uprising was followed by the Spanish-American war. The Treaty of Paris, signed in 1898, officially terminated the conflict, stipulating that the Spanish possessions of the Philippines and Puerto Rico ceded to the Americans. In the Philippines, however, peace was forestalled. Filipinos pursued their aspirations for political freedom and subsequently fought the American occupier in what became known as the Philippine-American war (1898–1901). Official pacification of the islands followed in 1902. The Americans pursued a policy of "tutelary colonialism" with the purpose that Filipinos "assimilate American ideas and American institutions".[26] Moreover, already one year after the signing of the Treaty with Spain, the American authorities promised Filipinos political freedom. The educated Hispanicised Filipino upper class, also known as *ilustrado*, many with a landholding background, proved susceptible to this prospect and, as the Americans intended, chose to collaborate with the new American regime.[27] Luis Borromeo originated from this ilustrado milieu.

It took another 17 years before American President Woodrow Wilson signed the Jones bill in 1916, granting the Philippines increased political and administrative autonomy. The Act provided for a Senate and House of Representatives, to be staffed completely by Filipinos. The same act acknowledged the right to political

---

[25] It was the work of Filipino writer Nick Joaquin, for decades the unofficial and inspiring chronicler of popular culture in the pre-Second World War Philippines that put me on the track of Luis Borromeo, see Joaquin (1978). It was during my previous research on popular female singers in pre-Second World War Indonesia that Miss Riboet drew my attention. See Keppy (2008).

[26] William Howard Taft to Elihu Root, 18 Aug. 1900, as cited in Go (2008: 1). Pockets of guerilla resistance continued after 1902. See Cullinane (2003: 73).

[27] Go (2008: 109–10).

freedom, but without a fixed date and on the condition that Filipinos had to prove that they were fit for independence. The American reluctance to grant independence unconditionally caused disappointment and resent among Filipinos, leading to domestic political tension and cultural confusion for the next two decades. The 1929 Wall Street Crash and the worldwide economic recession that followed in its wake, combined with staunch Filipino political lobbying for independence in Washington, D.C., eventually turned the political tide in favour of Philippine freedom. In the early 1930s, facing the economic slump, American agricultural industries actively lobbied for protective measures against Philippine imports, primarily sugar cane. Independence would imply a reordering of economic relations between metropolis and colony, including the lifting of American preferential treatment for Philippine exports. In March 1934, President Franklin D. Roosevelt approved the Tydings-McDuffie Independence Act, which paved the way for a phased-out trajectory from autonomy under a commonwealth in 1935 to full independence of the Philippines in 1946.[28] In 1935, Manuel Quezon, leader of the dominant Partido Nacionalista and senate president, was elected commonwealth president of the Philippines. Since the early 1910s, he had actively lobbied for independence. The prospect of independence in the early 1930s did not halt domestic social and political tension; in fact, tension between capital and labour increased. In the early 1930s, Manila cigar workers and harbour workers in Iloilo organised strikes.[29] Moreover, dissatisfied with the way Quezon had handled the terms of independence with the US, a new radical political movement, the Sakdalista Party, was born in response. In 1935, the Sakdalistas launched a revolt in Manila's rural hinterland that was curbed by the Constabulary, a native-staffed military force with a policing mandate.[30]

In sharp contrast to the Philippines, an educated locally rooted elite with political and economic power was absent in the early 20th-century Netherlands East Indies. The absence of such an economically powerful class was the outcome of Dutch policies since the times of the Dutch East India Company (VOC), which prevented the accumulation of capital by natives. In spite of promises to uplift the native, made since the turn of the 20th century, the colonial government did little to promote education at all levels for wider sections of the population. Thus, in 1934, one Filipino observer compared the favourable educational opportunities under the American regime in his country to that of the Netherlands East Indies: "[...] with this rigid feed-the-stomach-and-not-the-head principle adopted by the Dutch, the flames of national consciousness instead of being extinguished

---

[28] Golay (1998: 303, 333, 343).

[29] McCoy (1981).

[30] Golay (1998: 340–1).

continue to rise in ever-increasing grandeur. They have rallied to a grand awakening of the east!"[31] This awakening referred to the emancipatory movement (*pergerakan*), which had emerged around the turn of the 20th century, under the influence of Chinese nationalism and the Dutch tutelary policy known as the "Ethical policy", aimed at uplifting natives. The awakening movement targeted social rather than political reform. Among the greatest obstacles for colonial subjects and a bone of contention for the awakening movement was the Dutch colonial legal classification system based on race. It was simply impossible for colonial subjects, such as locally rooted Chinese (*peranakan*), native Indonesians or Eurasians without Dutch citizenship to obtain access to higher education, to attain high official positions in government and to break Dutch dominance and monopolies in trade and industry.[32] Demands by the emancipatory movement to end social injustices based on the racial classification system fell on deaf Dutch colonial ears.

By the 1920s, frustrated by the half-heartedly implemented tutelary policy of "uplifting the native", the emancipatory movement transformed into a nationalist movement, demanding political reforms in the form of increased autonomy from the Netherlands. Apart from creating a pseudo-parliament, the Volksraad (People's Council) in 1918, whose members were appointed and not elected, the Dutch did very little to meet the Indonesian nationalists' demands for representative politics. In addition, the nationalist movement was weakened by party rivalry and a division between those who compromised by collaborating with the Dutch and those who stubbornly refused cooperation. In 1926, the Indonesian Communist Party (PKI), established in 1920, moved to militant action. The rebellion was crushed and Dutch colonials remained in shock. The communist insurrection offered the Dutch authorities a pretext to move against the Indonesian nationalists and to step up colonial surveillance. Government repression and policing of political activity in print and speech increased. The PKI was outlawed. By the early 1930s, leading nationalists had been trialed and exiled under the excuse of criminal intent, weakening further the already divided nationalist movement. Many nationalists and communists ended up in the first political prisoner camp established in 1926 in an archipelago outpost, Boven Digoel, in what is currently the province of Papua.[33]

---

[31] "Between Two Giants. Japan North and Dutch South Squeeze P.I.", *Philippine Free Press* (*PFP*), 7 July 1934.

[32] Peranakan Chinese, also known as *baba* in British Malaya, are of mixed Chinese and Indonesian descent and developed a creolised or hybrid culture distinct from Chinese and indigenous society. See Skinner (1996).

[33] On the history of the political prisoner camp Boven Digoel, see Shiraishi (1996).

It is in these times of political turmoil that Luis Borromeo and Miss Riboet came to the fore and that a "popular culture" emerged. They were admired and supported by people who remain confined to the backdrop of most historiographies. Here, I will attempt to highlight them as people who co-developed and questioned the new in-between culture and its stars. These consumers originated from social groups situated in Southeast Asia's urban centres of commerce and industry that, since the late 19th and early 20th centuries, had benefitted, in different ways, from economic changes, but, rather paradoxically, had faced very limited political freedom and experienced the pain of institutionalised racism.

New Social Groups, Audiences, Cultural Consumption and Media Technology

There is little dispute among historians about seeing Southeast Asia's commercial urban hubs as sites of cultural diffusion, borrowing and adaptation. Cultural hybridity was the norm rather than the exception. Cross-cultural encounters between members of multi-ethnic communities made these cities distinctively cosmopolitan and modern in their own right.[34] Up to the 17th century, the courts of Southeast Asia's royal cities, or city-states, remained the dominant cultural, religious, political and economic centres. State ceremonies included public festivals accompanied by entertainments that drew masses. According to historian Anthony Reid, this situation made it impossible to distinguish between court and popular culture. At the same time, he notes that, at least in 17th-century Siam, a more "urban and rational mentality" developed, suggesting a process of separation between a semi-divine court culture and secular popular culture.[35]

What transpired in the cultural realm over the next three centuries, from the 17th to the 20th century, is largely open to educated guessing. The general and accepted reading would be that, by the late 19th century, the colonial powers, and along with them imperialism and capitalism, had penetrated more deeply into Southeast Asian societies compared to previous centuries, drastically altering cultural, political and economic conditions for the majority of the colonised.[36] In the 1920s, most of the royal courts either had ceased to exist, or had been effectively subjugated by or allied with Western colonial powers

---

[34] Nas (1986: 23–33); Reid (1988: 205, 209–21); Harper (1999: 15, 18); Irving (2010: 51–84); Bosma and Raben (2008: 3–8); Montesano and Jory (2008: 34–6); Lewis (2016).

[35] Reid (1988: 179, 202); Nas (1986: 21).

[36] See for example Lewis (2016: 27–46) on Yangon, Bangkok and Penang from the late 16th to early 20th century.

under systems of indirect rule. Some of the harbour cities, like Melaka, Makassar or Ambon, had declined as significant commercial nodes in the previously lucrative spice trade.[37] During the late 19th century, other cities benefitted from the expanding colonial agricultural export economy and the service sector that developed in tandem. It is exactly in port cities like Batavia, Surabaya, Singapore, Penang, Manila and Cebu that urbanites shaped a novel, modern cosmopolitan popular culture that transformed, and as I and others suggest, fully blossomed in the 1920s and 1930s.[38]

Historians working on the late colonial Philippines and Indonesia have noted that a process of increased social differentiation occurred around the turn of the 20th century. Although the majority of the rural population and city dwellers belonged to the working classes, "new" groups emerged, interchangeably referred to as "middle class" and "petty bourgeoisie". The social and political homogeneity of these groups in both colonies has been critically questioned and remains the subject of ongoing debate.[39] What I am particularly concerned with is how these emerging groups participated in popular culture, and how the new modern culture of the 1920s shaped new social identities.

The new social groups that emerged in the Philippines have alternately been referred to as the "middle sector", "urban aristocracy", "planter aristocracy" and "upper class".[40] The arrival of these new social formations should be understood against the upsurge of commercial agriculture during the American period. The sugar industry especially brought wealth to the Hispanicised provincial landowners-cum-planters, who diversified into other economic activities.[41] In addition, the active American policy of promoting Filipino participation in the civil service, particularly after 1916, and of providing public education at all levels, primary to tertiary, were two significant factors in enhancing social mobility and opening up white-collar employment to larger segments of the

---

[37] See Nas (1986: 30–3) on the decline of the city-state in 18th- to 19th-century Indonesia.

[38] Keppy (2013); Lewis (2016: 68–71, 227–46).

[39] For an overview of demography and social composition of Southeast Asia's urban populations in the first three decades of the 20th century, see Elson in Tarling (1999: 164–8). On social structure and class in colonial Indonesia, see Shiraishi (1990: 27–40). On social structure in the Philippines, see Doeppers (1984: 64). In his study of the emergence of the Filipino political elite in the early 20th century, Michael Cullinane (2003: 8–10) argues that the term "middle class" oversimplifies the very complex social structure of 19th- and early 20th-century Philippine society. He prefers the term "urban middle section" over "middle class". For a more recent debate of new urban classes in colonial Java, see Hoogervorst and Schulte Nordholt (2017).

[40] Stanley (1974: 47); Doeppers (1984: 59–60); Cullinane (2003: 21).

[41] Larkin (1993: 81).

population, including women.[42] Despite definitional problems and the political and social differences between and within the two colonies under consideration, there is also scholarly consensus that newly emerging social groups displayed a cosmopolitan orientation and a modern, consumer lifestyle. For instance, in his study of sugar planters in colonial South Luzon and in Negros in the Philippines, John Larkin notes that, by the second decade of the 20th century, the Filipino upper classes in these two provinces were driven by the cultural ideal of "blending of American culture with native refinement".[43] What this blending meant and how it was reflected in the terrain of popular culture is the subject of this book.

As previously said, a native or locally rooted landholding elite with political power and in favour of independence was virtually absent in the Netherlands East Indies. In the first two decades of the 20th century, however, a new generation emerged of educated native Indonesians, local-born Chinese, Indo-Arabs and Eurasians. This generation included several journalists, many of whom publicly questioned the social injustices created by Dutch colonialism. They spearheaded the emancipatory movement that paved the way for what would become the Indonesian nationalist movement. Like the new social groups in the Philippines, this group has long been studied predominantly from a political perspective and this leaves much of their cultural orientation and lifestyles in the dark.[44]

Contemporaries only occasionally referred to the cultural orientation of this "social group", as reflected in their modern lifestyle. A rare and early example in the early 1930s was the Dutch expert in Javanese culture and language, Theodoor Pigeaud. He recognised a connection between newly emerging social classes in Javanese society and their novel ways and forms of cultural consumption. Pigeaud found it difficult to use the older and, by then apparently oversimplified, binary opposition between Javanese commoners, the majority, and the Javanese aristocratic elite with its high-cultured lifestyle ideal of chivalry, as represented in the *wayang* puppet plays and in Javanese literature.[45] This expert on Javanese culture and society preferred to speak of "urban- or semi-urban workers and petty entrepreneurs who have become detached from the old Javanese way of

---

[42] Doeppers (1984: 59–64).

[43] Larkin (1993: 109).

[44] Obviously, exceptions to this rule exist, such as Rudolf Mrázek's (2002) work on the Indonesian middle class and cultural consumption during the pre-Second World War era. More recently, Schulte Nordholt and Hoogervorst (2017) have been concerned with lifestyle and middle classes in colonial Java.

[45] Pigeaud (1932: 164).

life and arts".[46] In other words, cultural transformation and social differentiation had gone hand in hand. The new social group neither followed the ways of the Javanese court, nor those of the Javanese peasant. A group of "in-between people" had emerged with a hybrid "in-between culture" drawing from multiple cultural sources, foreign and local. We encounter them in different guises, for example as young native Western-style educated Indonesians, *kaum muda*, in Takashi Shiraishi's history of the pergerakan, the Indonesian emancipation movement:

> The emblems of kaum muda were the Dutch words sprinkled in their daily conversation in the vernacular, their wearing of Western-style clothes and shoes, their habit of going to restaurants and drinking lemonade, seeing movies, enjoying music and not gamelan, in short doing the modern things that the Dutch did.[47]

In contrast to this image, the tale of Miss Riboet will demonstrate that, rather than taking Dutch modernity as a model and mimicking Dutch-style consumerism, colonial subjects proved significant cultural producers of "modern things" themselves. Moreover, Dutch culture proved a rather poor model. Instead, colonial subjects, native Indonesians as well as locally rooted Chinese, and Eurasians tapped from a wide variety of sources: alien and local. One of the nexuses of the new homegrown popular culture where people interacted was the vernacular theatrical stage. It is there that we see most clearly cultural dynamics at play and how different arts, that is theatre, dance, music, literature, cinema and even sports, drawn from local and alien cultural repertoires connected and converged into a new popular culture with modern and cosmopolitan features.

The popularity of Borromeo and Riboet can hardly be understood without taking into consideration media technologies, particularly the significance of the phonograph and motion pictures. In early 20th-century Southeast Asia, theatre and music were inseparable twins; by the 1920s, theatre had closely connected to the recorded industry and started to interact with, first, the silent and, in the early 1930s, the sound motion picture. Around the turn of the century, not long after the introduction of the phonograph, Anglo-American and European record companies dispatched sound engineers on "expeditions" to the "Orient" to record local popular music on shellac disc for commercial purposes.[48] Without exception, and whether in Burma, British Malaya, Indo-China, Siam or the Philippines, these engineers turned to the vernacular theatre

---

[46] Pigeaud cited in Groenendael (1995: 19–20).
[47] Shiraishi (1990: 30).
[48] Tan (1996–97).

as a source for commercial recordings.[49] It was exactly in the 1920s, as I will show, that commercial recording of local popular music gained momentum in the Philippines and Indonesia, and it did so in close relation to developments in vernacular theatre. Radio broadcasting and the burgeoning sound film industry of the mid-1930s boosted this development in recorded sound as artists and playwrights from the vernacular stage entered the local film industry.

Tales of Southeast Asia's Jazz Age

Starting with Luis Borromeo as a guiding figure, the book's first four chapters are devoted to the emerging popular culture in the Philippines, with its distinct modern and cosmopolitan flavour. The second part and final four chapters follow the ascendency of Miss Riboet as a modern Malay opera star in colonial Indonesia paving the way to a new culture.

Chapters 2 and 3 offer the social cultural context in which to situate Luis Borromeo. As will be demonstrated in Chapter 2, he originated from the elite that was rooted in older, cosmopolitan Hispanic traditions. In the mid-1910s, Borromeo was tested and trialed in American vaudeville, before re-entering the Manila stage in the early 1920s. His American journey, a genuinely cosmopolitan and transnational experience, proved a crucial asset for innovating and revitalising vernacular theatre in the Philippines. These developments would contribute to transforming the older, elitist Hispanic cosmopolitanism into a Filipino pop cosmopolitanism for the masses. In Manila, Borromeo created his own vaudeville for a Filipino middle- to upper-class audience, infusing it with Filipino patriotism. His loyalty to Philippine nationalism was, however, riddled with contradictions. As an important backdrop of Borromeo's new vaudeville, Chapter 3 highlights tension and resistance within Philippine elite society against alien cultural influence and modern popular culture, particularly modern social dancing in the institution of the dance hall. Chapter 4 shows that Borromeo did not simply innovate vaudeville single-handedly. How his version of vaudeville developed is closely examined from the perspective of cross-border roots and artistic connections. In Chapter 5, the focus is on the blurring of the boundaries of low- and highbrow culture in music and theatre and the cultural confusion and controversies this evoked. Borromeo, and a host of respected Filipino classical music composers, created popular hybrid dance music, jazz with a Filipino tinge,

---

[49] For a sample of these recordings see, for instance, *Longing for the Past: The 78 Era in Southeast Asia*, a CD series containing recordings roughly from the period 1920 to 1950. See also https://www.youtube.com/watch?v=4EaTsnECtHw&list=PLWkrJW0zArcZt4iZJfERO V32kZb2lwb1v. Philippine music is, however, conspicuously missing from this collection of digitised vintage music.

an "in-between genre".[50] Controversies over modern popular culture are also addressed looking at three issues: the popular institution of the Manila Carnival and elite participation, articulations of the modern Filipina and the search for upper class acceptance of the new style vaudeville. Chapter 6 tells the story of the end of the dynamic cultural climate of the 1920s Philippines; the transformation of Filipino vaudeville from a form of popular art to light entertainment in the early 1930s.

Chapter 7 opens with the socio-political landscape of colonial Indonesia, with an emphasis on the emancipatory and nationalist movement. As I will show in subsequent chapters, prominent members of the nationalist movement took popular culture seriously as a realm for discussing and articulating some of its social, not necessarily political, aims. From this general socio-political introduction, the story takes us to the development of a modern form of Malay opera, as pioneered by Miss Riboet and her husband. Having set this socio-political and cultural backdrop, Chapter 8 looks closer at forms of participatory pop, that is how fandom around Miss Riboet evolved and which social groups were involved. The chapter also introduces us to Miss Riboet's first self-confessed fan, a young local-born Chinese journalist, Kwee Thiam Tjing. Like Borromeo, Riboet could have never emerged as a star without the support of journalists, actors, playwrights, and specific audiences, some of whom, as indicated, were outspoken fans. Chapter 9 highlights the social relevance of Malay opera and Miss Riboet, also from the perspective of rival opera company Dardanella. Both companies became the yardstick to measure artistic standards and social relevance of Malay opera. A particular social significant form of participatory pop by Malay opera fans is also discussed: charity. The final chapter starts detailing how new notions of society and community related to the popular culture realm. The relation however between society and popular culture proved fragile. In the context of unspoken political loyalties and shifting audiences of the mid-1930s, Miss Riboet and Dardanella lost their social potency. The epilogue deals briefly and tentatively with post-colonial developments in popular culture and the ambiguous legacies of Luis Borromeo and Miss Riboet.

---

[50] Without claiming to offer a musicological or social analysis, Richie Quirino (2004) was the first to call attention to the fact that Filipinos had made jazz their own in the colonial period.

Chapter 2

Luis Borromeo and Filipino Pop Cosmopolitanism

This chapter will start by situating Luis Borromeo in the turn-of-the-century, elitist, high-cultured, Hispanicised cosmopolitan environment into which he was born. Luis adapted smoothly to the new American regime. Having visited the 1915 Panama Pacific International Exposition, he made a radical career shift, moving from a position of high-ranking government official in the Philippines to that of a professional entertainer on the US vaudeville stage, performing Chinese jazz act. American middle-class vaudeville audiences appreciated orientalist "yellowface" acts that stereotyped Chinese, as well as Japanese, as exotic and alien. As we will learn from the section on his career move, Borromeo was struggling with, rather than resisting, such American orientalist and racist stereotypes and racial hierarchies. He seems to have been caught between the commercial demands of the American entertainment industry, his own genuine Filipino patriotism and, paradoxically, his political loyalty to the United States. This contradictory in-between position is also reflected in the popular music Borromeo produced, the subject of the two closing sections of this chapter. His "oriental jazz" will be discussed from the angle of American racial hierarchies, Filipino nationalism and Henry Jenkins's critical ideas on cosmopolitanism and cultural borrowing.

Hispanicised Elites

Born around 1879 in Cebu City in the southern Philippines, Luis Francisco Borromeo was the fourth in line of a family of 16 children of Juan Borromeo and Paulina Veloso y Rubi.[1] In 1920, Cebu City was the second largest city after Manila, and the third biggest commercial centre and harbour in the

---

[1] Personal communication with Michael Cullinane, 10 Sept. 2011; unpublished interview, Fritz Schenker with Alice Marvin, Luis Borromeo's youngest daughter, 25 Feb. 2013, White Salmon, WA. Courtesy of Fritz Schenker.

Philippines after Iloilo and the capital.[2] Cebu was, and still is, an important Catholic pilgrimage site in the Philippines. Devotees pay homage to the Holy Child Santo Niño, the city's patron saint, whose statue is kept at the San Agustin Church, currently known as the Basilica. In the 1920s, the city's 65,300 urbanites annually welcomed tens of thousands of pilgrims from across the archipelago. The Basilica is Luis Borromeo's final resting place.[3]

The Borromeo extended family was, and still is, regarded as "prestigious" in terms of social status and wealth. They belong to the urban merchant and landholding elite of Cebu, with origins in the 17th-century Chinese and Chinese-*mestizo* (people of Chinese-Filipino descent) community of Parian, Cebu City.[4] Luis's father and first music tutor, Juan, was a music teacher in Cebu and Manila, a composer of sacred music and an organist at Cebu's Cathedral and San Agustin Church. His mother, Paulina Veloso y Rubi, who was a teenager when she married Juan, also came from one of Cebu City's wealthy Chinese-*mestizo* families.[5] In brief, the Borromeos could be ranked among the ilustrado, "a small segment of the indigenous elite that came to be recognised for their intelligence and educational attainment".[6]

In the early 20th century under the American regime, members of the Borromeo family moved into the expanding colonial bureaucracy as high-ranking civil officials. They also successfully took on white-collar professions as lawyers, priests and medical doctors, producing several professionals of note. For instance, Maximo Borromeo, first cousin of Luis, was a physician and politically active for the Democrata party, and Andrés Borromeo was a judge.[7] Luis himself and his first cousin Florentino Borromeo moved from official government positions into the burgeoning entertainment industry. In the 1920s and 1930s, cousin Florentino combined activities as a playwright for vernacular *zarzuela* theatre and locally-made cinematic films with official positions in Cebu's administration.[8] Luis would radically break with officialdom and embark on a full-time career in popular entertainment.

---

[2] By 1930, Cebu had surpassed Iloilo as an economically significant harbour in the Visayan Islands.

[3] "Patron Saint of the City of Cebu", *Progress*, 16 Jan. 1931; unpublished interview, Fritz Schenker with Alice Marvin, 25 Feb. 2013, White Salmon, WA. Courtesy of Fritz Schenker.

[4] Cullinane (1982: 257–620); Briones (2000).

[5] Briones (2000: 14).

[6] Cullinane (2003: 2).

[7] "Si Dr. Max Borromeo pilionon sa pagka-Gobernador", *Bag-ong Kusog*, 19 Dec. 1924.

[8] Camasura (1932: 328–30). According to Yeatter (2007: 15), Max Borromeo financially supported the cinema venture of his cousin Florentino.

The Borromeos enjoyed an education according to the standards of the Hispanicised provincial elites. Although fluent in vernacular Cebuano, Spanish was spoken at home. After studying at Cebu's San Carlos University, Luis was sent to further his knowledge of commerce and trade at the esteemed Santo Tomas University in Manila.[9] His formal education and initial professional career indicate that neither he, nor his parents planned a career for him in popular entertainment. After his studies, around the turn of the century, Luis entered government service as a judge for the duration of ten years.[10] In 1905, he married Clementina Atillo, from another prominent Cebuano Chinese-*mestizo* family. Clementina passed away somewhere between 1905 and 1915. Luis remarried around 1920.[11]

Illus. 2.1   Four of Luis's younger brothers, two academic graduates and two priests, with their father Juan Borromeo, Cebu, early 1920s. Courtesy of Joaquin (Jack) Borromeo.

Luis was raised in a distinctly religious and elitist cosmopolitan environment. The bilingual Spanish-Cebuano newspaper, *Nueva Fuerza*, published in Cebu,

[9] One of Luis's elder brothers studied in Spain. Personal communication with Michael Cullinane, 10 Sept. 2011. Interview with John Taylor Borromeo, Cebu, 29 Feb. 2012.

[10] Luis Borromeo might have served as a Justice of the Peace in Cebu, or elsewhere in the islands. This official position did not require legal training. "Says he would rather be a vaudeville performer in America than government official in Philippines", *PFP*, 13 Apr. 1918.

[11] Personal communication with Michael Cullinane, 10 Sept. 2011. According to Briones (2000: 14), the Atillo family was of Spanish mestizo origin; unpublished interview, Fritz Schenker with Alice Marvin, 25 Feb. 2013, White Salmon, WA. Courtesy of Fritz Schenker.

gives us a glimpse of this high-cultured milieu. In 1915, for example, we find Luis's father Juan performing with two itinerant Italian opera artists in Cebu City on the occasion of the baptism of the child of Mariano Cuenco, senate representative from the province of Cebu. The child's godmother was Gerarda Veloso, suggesting that a (fictive) kinship tie had been established or reaffirmed between the Cuencos and the family of Juan Borromeo's wife, Paulina Veloso. On this same occasion, Luis's sister, Lourdes, played a violin piece, accompanied on piano by a certain Mr Jakosalem, another prominent Cebuano. That same year, Luis's mother, Paulina, was reportedly the leader (*Hermana mayor*) of a Catholic association (*cofradia*) in the city of Cebu devoted to the patron saint Nuestra Señora del Rosario. A religious procession was held in honour of the saint, which concluded with a lavish banquet, arranged by Paulina at the Borromeo residence, served for the local elite and "travellers", the latter category possibly pilgrims.[12]

Religiosity, hospitality and conspicuous consumption went hand in hand among the cosmopolitan-oriented Cebuano urban elite. Elites across the Philippines used such festive religious occasions to forge social networks, enhancing economic and political power and social status. Such social occasions sustained what historian John Larkin, in his analysis of the Pampanga landed elite of Luzon, calls a "closed society", restricted to the elite.[13]

The Panama-Pacific International Exposition

In 1915, around the age of 35, Luis Borromeo embarked on a journey to San Francisco, California, to visit the Panama-Pacific International Exposition. A world fair dedicated to the completion of the Panama Canal, the event was an opportunity for the US to display its economic power and imperialist stature to the world during a violent conflict raging in Europe, by then known as the Great War.

In 1914, the Philippine senate accepted the American invitation to participate in the fair.[14] The Philippine government earmarked funds to exhibit in San Francisco, in a specially designed pavilion, the achievements of the Philippines in the fields of commerce, industry, education, agriculture and arts (the latter including painting, literature and music).[15] The official inauguration of the

---

[12] "Mga balita", *Nueva Fuerza*, 14 Oct. 1915.

[13] Larkin (1993: 94–5).

[14] Due to the war, Britain and Germany abstained from participating in the fair.

[15] Ley que reforma la ley numero dos mil ciento sesenta y tres titulada ley que crea una comision para adquirir organizar y hacer una exhibicion de productos manufactoras artes etnologia y educacion de filipinas en la panama pacific international exposition [...] [No. 2358] *Official Gazette* 12(14) (8 April 1914): 811.

Philippine pavilion took place on 26 February 1915. The event was documented by the official chronicler of the Exposition, Frank Morton Todd, in a chapter under the tellingly paternalistic title "Progress of the Philippines". Todd was keen to legitimise empire and to emphasise America's benevolent intentions in the Philippines "to uplift rather than to merely exploit".[16]

It is important to note that the Filipino political elite had its own agenda. Obviously, the exposition offered the opportunity to lure investors to the islands and to promote export of cash crops, such as sugar. Participation in the San Francisco Fair should, however, also be seen in the framework of the campaign for Philippine independence, which would eventually culminate in the politically ambiguous 1916 Jones law. Since 1910, Manuel Quezon, one of the founders and main leaders of the Partido Nacionalista (est. 1907), in his capacity as resident commissioner for the Philippines, actively lobbied in Washington to gain support for the independence cause. By 1912, however, Quezon had moved from demanding an immediate independence to a postponed one. One of the main reasons for this shift was the ascendance of Japan as a military power in Asia. To protect the Philippines from Japan's imperialist ambitions, protection by the US was imperative. Opposition from American retentionists and the war in Europe delayed a bill on Philippine independence, drafted by Democratic chairman of the Committee on Insular Affairs, William Atkinson Jones.[17] In 1914, Quezon resumed activity to revive what would be known as the second Jones bill.[18] By that time, however, it had become a domestic public secret that Quezon had moved from demanding absolute and immediate autonomy to a conditional independence. His shift caused resentment within his own party, leading to the founding of the Partido Democrata Nacional in 1914.[19]

---

[16] Todd (1921: 376), vol. 3.

[17] The bill provided for independence eight years after the election of an upper house. It also included the provision that American troops be stationed in the islands to deter foreign powers from annexing the islands. The bill did not come to a vote in the House of Representatives due to reluctance on the part of the Democrats, opposition from the Bureau of Insular Affairs and a lobby led by two former Governor Generals of the Philippines, William Howard Taft and W. Cameron Forbes. The latter opposition was a coalition of "dignitaries of Church and state" in the US, which fiercely and effectively opposed claims for Philippine independence, advocating retention of the islands. Stanley (1974: 173–4, 184–9).

[18] Golay (1998: 184, 192–7).

[19] In March 1914, Teodoro Sandiko established the Partido Democrata Nacional. The Democratas blamed the Nacionalistas for having abandoned immediate independence and branded Governor General Francis Burton Harrison's "New Era" (in office between 1913–21) of increased autonomy an "Era of Deceit". Speaker of the House and Nacionalista Sergio Osmeña opposed a postponed independence, but gave in to Quezon as no alternative was at hand. See Stanley (1974: 214–7).

With the independence issue having become a stalemate, the Philippine senate seized the American invitation for the San Francisco Exposition to promote independence. In addition, the exposition was an excellent occasion to counter the American stereotype of the Filipino as a "wild mountaineer". The representation of the Filipino as a savage had been firmly established in the popular American imagination since the St. Louis Exposition of 1904, when a group of non-Christian Filipinos, Igorots, had been exhibited.[20] High-ranking American officials exploited the image of the tribal, uncivilised Filipino to legitimise the American presence in the Philippines, a stereotype that also had the effect of undermining rightful Filipino claims for independence.[21] Haunted by this unfavourable American image, the official Philippine delegation to the Exposition had therefore taken "pains [...] to offset any impression which may exist in the United States that the Filipinos are a race of savages and are best represented by what are known as the non-Christian tribes".[22] And the delegation wished to emphasise that "the typical Filipino dresses like an American, is intelligent and educated just like people are here, and even play baseball—[...] the Filipino young woman plays basketball and tennis, is interested in social work and doesn't scorn the 'tango' and the 'hesitation'".[23] In short, Filipinos would show the world that they were modern and civilised and thus fit for independence. The irony was that the popularity among Filipinos and Filipinas of modern popular dances like the tango and hesitation, the latter a modern ragtime inspired waltz, would lead to a public controversy in the Philippines in the following years.

In February 1915, during the inauguration of the Philippine pavilion, the Filipino delegation raised the independence issue cautiously and subtly. Chronicler Todd reports that Dr Leon Maria Guerrero, president of the Philippine exposition board, held a speech in Spanish that was simultaneously translated into English, before a big, mixed crowd of prominent American and Philippine officials. Guerrero blessed the people of America on behalf of the Filipinos, "because they hope from you with the faith of a believer their complete political emancipation".[24] Todd did not elaborate on these words and ignored or missed the deeper meaning of Guerrero's "complete political emancipation", a euphemism for Philippine independence. Significantly, Todd also refrained from mentioning the presence at the inauguration of Nacionalista leader Manuel

---

[20] On the 1904 St. Louis Exhibition and Filipino participation, see Kramer (1999).

[21] "Describes and Protests Against Igorot Exhibition", *PFP*, 1 Aug. 1914. "Igorot" is a contested term, see Kramer (1999: 83).

[22] "The Philippines at the Great Exposition", *PFP*, 16 Jan. 1915.

[23] Ibid.

[24] Todd (1921: 311), vol. 3.

Quezon. Quezon's presence and public speech had not escaped the attention of a correspondent of the Manila newspaper the *Philippine Free Press* (*PFP*), who reported: "Mr. Quezon said that the Philippines entail on the American people both 'enormous responsibility and great expense', and that the Filipino people 'want to be free and independent of any foreign domination'."[25]

Career Shift

How Borromeo experienced the Exposition and in exactly what capacity (wandering tourist, government official, professional musician) we will never know. Certain is that his journey to San Francisco would put him on the track of a professional career in entertainment and eventually lead him to pioneer pop cosmopolitanism in the Philippines.

Borromeo, along with many of the other hundreds of thousands of spectators, must have been impressed, if not stunned, by the Exposition's great number of exhibitions by business corporations, social organisations, individual countries and US federal states. In its opening week, the event drew daily throngs of visitors that fluctuated between 35,000 and 130,000 souls, who were exposed to cutting-edge technologies, lectures, musical and theatrical performances, including vaudeville.[26]

The fair's grounds were designed as a small and compact cosmopolitan city, recreated along San Francisco Bay. It was a modern interpretation of the historical city of Byzantine, equipped with an infrastructure of avenues, buildings, gardens and an electric grid.[27] This oriental fantasy was driven by imperialism as much as capitalism.[28] Musically, there would have been little for music-lover Borromeo to complain about. Music took such prominence at the Exposition that chronicler

---

[25] "Dedication of the Philippine Building at Panama-Pacific International Exposition", *PFP*, 1 May 1915.

[26] Todd (1921: 4), vol. 3, writes on the variety of items: "The scope of these affairs was broader than any exposition ever attempted before. Nations, states, cities, counties, societies, fraternities, industries, organised families, propagandas, fads, subjects of research, universities, phonograph jobbers, and Scottish clans had days appointed for their especial celebration, exploitation or divertissement. Plumbers, actors, 'newologists', Hoo Hoos, milk men and wine men, movie men, loganberries, suffragists, dancing masters, former Presidents, the Liberty Bell, tobacco, the Non-Smoker's Protective Association, the Dekes, Zetes, Pi Kappa Alphas and other primitive tribes, besides spiritualists and grapes, all had their days."

[27] See Brechin (1983: 94–113).

[28] In the words of Exposition chronicler Todd: "[...] commercialism and the higher life mingle in an exposition whose interest at all approaches the universal. And such commingling needs no apology, for commercialism is one of the greatest servants of the human race". Todd (1921: 5), vol. 3.

Todd was compelled to dedicate a separate chapter to it.[29] A host of different orchestras, bands and individual artists performed over 2,000 concerts. Well-known (military) marching bands, including that of Philip Sousa, but also the Philippine Constabulary Band, staged mass concerts; classical concerts were offered by, for example, virtuoso violinist Fritz Kreisler; hybrid musical novelties from Hawai'i and Guatemala were presented. Todd lauded the Philippine Constabulary Band as "a superbly trained organization of ninety musicians, under command of Lieut. Col. R.W. Jones, and under the musical direction of Capt. Walter Howard Loving, [...] it won the admiration of music lovers and became one of the favorite bands at the Exposition".[30] Following the official end of the Philippine-American war in 1902, the Philippine Constabulary (PC) had been established as a national police force in the Philippines, staffed with Filipinos under American military direction.[31] Apart from quelling local insurrections, particularly in the provinces, the PC engaged in music for official state occasions. In 1904, the band went on its first foreign journey, performing at the St. Louis Exposition in the US. By the 1920s, the band had adopted a wide range of musical genres, including modern dance music. As I will demonstrate in Chapter 4, its eclectic musical repertoire, and particularly popular dance music, would become target of elitist critique.

In spite of the Band's success at the Panama Pacific International Exposition, the biggest musical revelation to the American audience was the Guatemalan Marimba Band at the Guatemala Pavilion.[32] This band performed several days a week, drawing many spectators, playing an eclectic repertoire of Afro-American syncopated music, such as one-steps and foxtrots, Argentinean tangos, waltzes, operatic pieces and marches using the exotic novelty of the marimba, a wooden xylophone instrument. The Guatemalan Marimba band also benefitted commercially from the Exposition, being contracted in 1916 by American record firm Victor Talking Machine Company, releasing, amongst others, one Afro-American ragtime song dedicated to the fair: the "Guatemala-Panama March".[33] Without suggesting that he ever witnessed the Marimba band or that he listened to its phonographic records, such an eclectically musical repertoire was exactly

---

[29] Todd (1921: 404–9), vol. 2, "Chapter LXXIV. Nine and a Half Months of Music".

[30] Ibid., p. 380.

[31] Golay (1998: 93–4).

[32] Todd (1921: 21), vol. 3.

[33] "Guatemala-Panama March". Victor B-17470. 10 inch. Hurtado Brothers of Royal Marimba Band of Guatemala. Discography of American Historical Recordings. http://adp. library.ucsb.edu/index.php/talent/detail/10055/. In 1916, the Band recorded about 20 songs for Victor.

what Borromeo would produce five years later in Manila when creating his Filipino style, *vod-a-vil*, also spelled *bodabil*, both Hispanicised corruptions of the word vaudeville.

The Exposition offered the American cultural industry, phonographic record companies and vaudeville corporations an opportunity to scout for novel, non-Western music and talent.[34] In spite of its success and recognition by established composers, including Philip Sousa, there is no evidence that the Philippine Constabulary Band was approached by the phonographic industry during or shortly after the Exposition. This would come much later, around 1928, in the Philippines itself. Borromeo, however, would indirectly reap the benefits from the Exposition, in part due to his connections to the Philippine political elite present at the fair. In fact, the Exposition proved a turning point, as Luis would make a radical career shift from government servant to commercial entertainer.

During the Exposition, Dr. Francisco L. Liongson, member of the Philippine Exposition Board, and according to Raymondo Bañas "an acquaintance" of Borromeo, invited the latter to conduct a piano concert at the fair's Dutch pavilion.[35] The invitation was accepted, and possibly encouraged Borromeo to perform also outside the Exposition's premises. According to his own testimony, an American lady witnessed him playing a "Filipino piece" at the home of an American family in San Francisco. Impressed by the performance, the lady introduced Borromeo to talent scouts of the Orpheum vaudeville circuit on the US West Coast, one of the two biggest vaudeville corporations in the United States.[36]

Vaudeville, as a form of theatre, dates back to 15th-century France and, in different parts of the globe, developed into a set of dance, music, comedy sketches, "condensed opera", acrobatics, conjuring and a variety of other entertainments.[37] As early as 1908, possibly even earlier, vaudeville also reached the Philippines, where it was staged by an American vaudevillian from the Orpheum circuit at the first Manila Carnival.[38] That same year a kind of proto-vaudeville was performed by locals in one of Manila's downtown cinemas. Filipino artists

---

[34] Historian George Kanahele notes that none of the previous American expositions had a greater impact on the commercial production of Hawaiian music than the Exposition. In its wake "Recording companies such as Edison and Brunswick released a torrent of Hawaiian records", thus contributing to its worldwide popularity. Kanahele (1979: 290–2).

[35] Bañas (1975: 185).

[36] "Said to be making one thousand pesos a week on vaudeville stage in the United States", *PFP*, 18 June 1921.

[37] Slide (1994: xiv).

[38] "Carnival Notes", *MT*, 30 Jan. 1908.

alternated acrobatics and tap dancing with silent movie screenings.[39] In 1911, John Cowper, an American veteran of the Philippine-American war, ventured unsuccessfully into "Spanish vaudeville" at the Paz Theatre, Calle Poblete, Manila, as stage manager and director. Cowper and Borromeo would connect in Manila in 1921, this time productively revamping vaudeville into a form that would prove a smash hit among the Filipino middle and upper classes.

From 1916 to 1921, as a pianist in a "yellowface" act performing "oriental jazz", Luis toured the Keith and Orpheum vaudeville circuit on the US Pacific to East Coast and parts of Canada. One of the reasons he gave for his career shift was his explicit dissatisfaction of being a government official in the Philippines.[40] Other reasons, I would guess, were that he was a genuine music lover and that earnings with the Keith and Orpheum vaudeville corporations were good, even by American standards.[41]

Oriental Jazz Pianist

From the late 19th century the Keith and Orpheum, and Albee Vaudeville corporations operated a large chain of theatres, or circuits, covering the US Pacific to the East Coast and also Canada. Although theoretically separate legal entities, the two corporations entered into an alliance to control the lucrative "big-time" vaudeville market that Borromeo had become part of.[42] "Big-time" vaudeville shows offered two performances a day with at least eight acts, including a leading act (headliner).[43] Whether Borromeo made it as headliner is difficult to say. He was sufficiently known to be mentioned briefly several times in one of New York's leading theatrical magazines and to be interviewed by local newspapers in the US about his political views.

---

[39] "Orpheum Every Night", *MT*, 5 Jan. 1908.

[40] "Says he would rather be vaudeville performer in America than government official in Philippines", *PFP*, 13 Apr. 1918.

[41] Borromeo claimed to make ₱1,000 weekly at Keith's. "Said to be making one thousand pesos a week on vaudeville stage in the United States", *PFP*, 18 June 1921. By comparison, Filipino musicians in Hong Kong, Netherlands East Indies and Indo-China earned between ₱ 117 and ₱ 522 a month. A skilled labourer in the Philippines, like a shoemaker or butcher, would make between ₱ 2.31 and ₱ 13.46 on a daily basis. See Schenker (2016: 133–4).

[42] Keith and Albee decided to divide the United States into distinct geographic zones of operation to avoid further rivalry and legal disputes over the control of theatres. This alliance, which acquired the characteristics of a trust, was aimed at monopolising the profitable US and also Canadian vaudeville market. The arrangement became the subject of anti-trust investigations in the US. See Wertheim (2006: 234–5).

[43] In contrast, "small time" vaudeville offered fewer acts, headliners were infrequent and salaries and admission fees were lower. See Stein (1984: 109).

Due to its multi-ethnic casts and eclectic repertoire of classical and popular dance and music, American vaudeville was pop cosmopolitanism par excellence. In 1916, this popular cosmopolitanism caused a Filipino journalist, who happened to witness a vaudeville show in San Francisco, confusion. Correspondent of the *Philippine Free Press* in San Francisco, Mariano Reyes Revilla was struck, or likely puzzled, by the diversity of "nationalities" sought by the American vaudeville theatre owners and audiences.[44] Vaudeville line-ups were an amalgam of ethnic groups that could include native Hawaiians, Afro-Americans, Filipinos and Chinese, alongside first- or second-generation European migrants. In spite of the multi-ethnic casts, the harsh reality of racial segregation applied as much to the vaudeville industry as it did to many other public spheres in the US. Racial segregation was reflected in a separate and smaller circuit of theatres owned by Afro-American entrepreneurs, who presented Afro-American artists to Afro-American audiences.[45] In contrast, the Keith and Orpheum circuits catered for a white, middle-class audience, a spectatorship that Borromeo had to entertain.

There was another reason why Revilla, the earlier mentioned Filipino newspaperman, was bewildered by the vaudeville show he witnessed. To his great surprise, he spotted a fellow countryman on stage, but not in the capacity of a Filipino. In the Castilian section, aimed at the relatively small, Spanish-educated elitist readership of the *Free Press* published in Manila, Revilla felt compelled to reveal his thoughts on what, to him, appeared to be an odd cultural encounter.

> Already some of our intrepid compatriots dared to appear here in America. But they are mere amateurs. And the poor people had to dress as mandarins to be admitted. Currently in Oakland, three young Filipinos, a baritone, a pianist and a violinist have won applause in a vaudeville show. "The Chinese Trio" the group is called… Why conceal their Filipino names? It's mysterious.[46]

The pianist mentioned was very likely Luis Borromeo, caught by Revilla at an early stage of his American vaudeville career. Throughout this career, Borromeo appeared in an orientalist Chinese act, alternately dubbed the Chinese Trio, Imperial Trio or Duo, Davigneau's Chinese Three and, later in his career, Davigneau's Celestials.

---

[44] Revilla noted that the vaudeville theatres "accept the foreign artist more than the American. Lots of 'dilettantes' from Milan, sopranos from Paris, from Spain; Austrian violinists and pianists, Hungarian tenors, Russian musicians and dancers, filled and continue to fill American vaudeville, whose funds amount to millions […]". "Desde América. El Artista Filipino", *PFP*, 24 June 1916.

[45] Wertheim (2006: 176–80).

[46] "Desde América. El Artista Filipino", *PFP*, 24 June 1916.

While American vaudeville theatre managers discouraged or even prohibited artists from addressing politics and religion in stage shows in order not to offend and alienate audiences, racial stereotyping, in contrast, was highly appreciated by Caucasian American audiences and actively promoted by theatre managers.[47] For example, white, and sometimes even black artists, parodied Afro-Americans in blackface or minstrel shows singing "coon songs" and "plantation songs" before white audiences.

American concerns about Chinese migration to the US and about the Chinese migrant community had grown since the turn of the century. These anxieties, in turn, produced orientalist stereotypes of Chinese (and Japanese) that confirmed white supremacy, offering a pretext to halt immigration. These stereotypes found their way into popular theatre and music in what came to be known as "yellowface" acts.[48] And this was what *Free Press* correspondent Revilla observed in 1916 in a San Francisco vaudeville venue.

To Revilla's great chagrin and bewilderment, Filipinos engaged in "yellowface" acts. His distress was informed by the fact that Filipinos in the US, whether migrant workers, *pensionados* (students on American scholarships) or intellectuals, frequently complained about Americans taking them, often in a denigrating way, for Chinese or Japanese.[49] In this racialised context, Revilla was shocked to find his compatriots representing themselves as "Chinese" on the American stage, a race despised by the Caucasian American majority. Revilla preferred to see Filipino artistic potential in the US excelling in the "arts", that is, Italian opera, like the successful Filipina opera singer Jovita Fuentes.[50] Revilla and Borromeo, as

---

[47] The emphasis on decency was partly a reflection of Benjamin Keith's and Edward Albee's strong Christian moral convictions. It was also a commercial strategy to attract a conservative middle-class audience that had previously avoided vaudeville theatres due to its bad reputation. Consequently, theatre directors and managers explicitly prohibited vulgarity and obscenity in speech, dress or bodily movements in stage acts. For example, vaudevillians working for Keith's had to live with a stringent regime of moral policing by the management. See Wertheim (2006: 30–4, 104–5, 144, 167–71).

[48] According to Tsou (1997: 26–8), racial stereotypes of Chinese were informed by intellectual social Darwinist evolutionary ideas about racial difference and hierarchy, theories that, in turn, justified Americans prohibiting Chinese migration to the US.

[49] For example, in 1924, a Filipino residing in the US wrote to the *Philippine Free Press* "[…] if you walk in the streets of New York, or ride a subway car, you will hear voices from the front and rear of the car saying 'Oh, look at that yellow Chinese!' or 'Look at that yellow Jap!' […] With this inhumane treatment, […] it becomes a tradition on the part of the Filipinos here or elsewhere to marry other nationals than Americans […]". "News From Filipinos in America", *PFP*, 26 July 1924. On American racism towards Filipinos, see also Kalaw (2001: 86).

[50] "Desde América. El Artista Filipino", *PFP*, 24 June 1916. See Schenker (2016: 150), on Filipina opera singers in Europe, who were being billed as Japanese annoyed compatriots.

we will see in due course, did not question the racial hierarchy. Quite the reverse seems to have taken place. These Filipinos paradoxically affirmed the American-imposed racial hierarchy, criticising Americans for ranking them alongside the Chinese at the bottom of the racial pecking order. The position taken by Filipino opera singer and recording artist Jose Santiago Mossegeld is instructive. On the one hand, he refused to appear in "yellowface" act; on the other, he did not denounce American racism. Reporting upon his professional experience in the US in the 1920s he told a newspaper: "[...] I have appeared as a citizen of the Philippine Islands and not as a Chinese, as some other Filipinos do, just to be sure of getting contracts from vaudeville houses".[51] Mossegeld revealed the commercial requirements of the American culture industry, to which he refused to submit. Borromeo, as we will see in due course, had his own paradoxical way of dealing with commerce, racism and patriotism.

Borromeo was not the first Filipino to appear on the American stage, or the first to impersonate a Chinese. American newspapers advertisements from the early 1910s offer glimpses of Filipinos active in vaudeville and amusement parks. We find them, for example, as violinists playing Afro-American ragtime pieces or as the popular stereotype of the savage Igorot headhunter.[52] Among the earliest recorded cases of a very successful Filipino "yellowface" act on the American vaudeville stage was Policarpio Ampatin, from the town of Santa Rita,

---

[51] "Letting America Know About Filipino Music", *PFP*, 23 Jan. 1927.

[52] For instance, in 1911, the Boston *Cambridge Chronicle* reports briefly on "Trovate, the wonderful Filipino violinist", who performed at B.F. Keith's theatre in the named city. "THEATRES B.F. KEITH'S THEATRE—VAUDEVILLE", *Cambridge Chronicle*, 22 July 1911.

In 1915, a Filipino journalist mentioned the "famous Samar twins, [...] making a tremendous 'hit' with San Franciscans as headline attraction at the New Wonderland, a playhouse on Market Street". "A Chatty Letter from the United States", *PFP*, 12 June 1915. The brothers Lucio and Simplicio Godino, Siamese twins, were born in Samar. Around 1920, ship owner and philanthropist Teodoro R. Yangco formally adopted the conjoined minors to prevent their further commercial exploitation in a Carnival side show. See Stagg (1934: 274–5, fn. 1); "The Reception to Hon. Teodoro R. Yangco", *PFP*, 8 May 1920. The Samar twins made a successful career on the Philippine vaudeville stage in the 1920s, and returned to the US to perform there; see for example "Whoopee-Making Samar Twins", *Graphic*, 4 Dec. 1929.

In 1918, Feliciano N. Mariano from Tondo, Manila, was active as violinist on the vaudeville stage in the San Francisco bay area. Son of a *Philippine Free Press* advertisement agent, this Filipino vaudevillian used his earnings to further his studies at different colleges in San Francisco, see "Feliciano N. Mariano—By Juan Salazar", *PFP*, 9 Mar. 1918.

Another contemporary of Borromeo was James R. Amok from Bontoc, who was exhibited as tribal Filipino at Coney Island's Luna Park, New York. Amok was drafted for US military service during World War I. "Bontoc Igorot Fights for Uncle Sam", *PFP*, 1 June 1918; "The News of the Week", *PFP*, 16 Nov. 1918.

Samar. Around the turn of the 20th century, Ampatin had worked himself up from cabin boy on a British mercantile ship to law student in the US. From academia, he moved to the vaudeville stage. He took up a comedy act, adopting the stage character of an imaginary Chinese aristocrat by the name of Prince Hong Fong. Ampatin's story, published in the *Philippine Free Press*, suggested that American colonialism formed the right conditions for progress, even if you chose to impersonate a Chinese on the vaudeville stage. By 1915, when Borromeo was about to enter the scene, Ampatin had retired from vaudeville, had married an American lady and moved back to the Philippines, advocating before an audience of young Filipinos for the importance of education.[53] His story proved to Filipino youngsters and the *PFP* readership that progress and social mobility were possible through education, hard work and perseverance, even on the popular stage and in the "hostile" environment of the US.

In contrast to Ampatin, Borromeo's stance on progress and loyalty to the Americans was far more ambiguous. Unlike Ampatin, Borromeo felt uncomfortable with his Chinese stage image. This uneasiness is first revealed in a brief interview given in 1918 to the *Houston Chronicle*, during a vaudeville tour in Texas. Luis addressed the paper's journalist in a slightly irritated and provocative manner:

> You said in your review of my act that I am a Chinaman. Did you ever see a Chinaman like me? I guess not. Chinese are slow and sleepy. I am not sleepy. Do I look sleepy? No, I am sometimes dreaming but I am not sleepy. I am happiest when I am playing. You see me work and you say I am a Chinaman. Bad lights, I guess. I am a full fledged American citizen and I am proud of it.[54]

Aware of the American readership, the prevailing racism and the readership's relative ignorance of political conditions in the Philippines, Borromeo made bold statements. The "reverse racism" displayed by Borromeo is striking. He stereotyped Chinese in contrast to his own image of a full-fledged American citizen. His essentialist image of Chinese is ironic, as many of Cebu's urban elite families, including the Borromeos, traced their origins to the Filipino-Chinese merchant community of Parian, Cebu City. This obscuring of Chinese origins should also be placed in the wider context of sensibilities about race and social

---

[53] "Prince 'Hong Fong' and his wife. The Interesting Story of a Poor Filipino Boy Who Worked His Way Up to a Thousands Pesos a Month. Now Preaching the Gospel of Farming Among his People", *PFP*, 11 Dec. 1915.

[54] "Says he would rather be vaudeville performer in America than government official in Philippines", *PFP*, 13 Apr. 1918.

hierarchy in the Philippines, including stereotypes of Chinese that date from at least as far back as the late 19th century.[55]

The *Philippine Free Press* made Borromeo's interview available to a Filipino readership in the islands. Borromeo's racist statement backfired. One reader from the city of Iloilo responded to the newspaper, explaining: "My heart bled on reading an article in your paper published on April 13" and "[c]an Chinese be despised in any way as Borromeo said in your article? [...] In conclusion, please let me add my sincere wishes for good feeling and better relations between Filipinos and Chinese in the Philippine Islands".[56]

Borromeo's statement about being a full-fledged American citizen is puzzling. Since the Peace Treaty concluded between Spain and the US in Paris in 1898, Filipinos were regarded as subjects, not citizens of the United States. His outspoken loyalty and gratitude to the US is also difficult to reconcile with contemporary court rulings in Hawai'i and by the Federal court in 1916 and 1917. These rulings denied citizenship to Filipinos living and working in the United States.[57] And as late as 1932, little had changed; the American sociologist Paul Cressey remarked: "[...] the Filipino's legal and social status in the United States is very uncertain. He is a national of the United States, yet because he is neither white nor 'of African descent' he cannot become a citizen."[58] Borromeo's loyalty to America was riddled with contradiction and so was his "yellowface" stage act.

Cosmo Kitsch

Borromeo's bold off-stage denial of impersonating a Chinese contrasts starkly with his stage acts and his published Tin Pan Alley sheet music. For instance, in 1920, at the end of his American career, the New York theatre and film reviews

---

[55] Wilson (2004: 54, 116).

[56] "Defends Chinese", *PFP*, 4 May 1918.

[57] That American citizenship was problematic for Filipinos can be read from several contradictory court decisions reported in the print press in the Philippines. In 1916, a judge in Hawai'i decided in favour of citizenship for Filipinos, which was reversed by a higher court. See "Filipinos Cannot Become Citizens", *PFP*, 25 Nov. 1916. In 1917, *PFP* reported that "Federal Judge Vaughan has handed down a decision to the effect that Filipinos are not eligible for United States citizenship, they being neither of the white nor black races." "The News of the Week", *PFP*, 6 Jan. 1917. Almost a year later, Federal Judge W.W. Morrow of the United States district court of San Francisco, ruled "that a Filipino is eligible to United States citizenship as he is not an alien and that it was the intention of congress in accepting the Treaty of Paris in 1898 to entitle him to citizenship because he owed the United States permanent allegiance". "The News of the Week", *PFP*, 15 Dec. 1917.

[58] Cressey (1932: 146).

Variety and *Dramatic Mirror* briefly reported on Luis's success as a Chinese act in American vaudeville. His Filipino origins remained unmentioned.[59] Borromeo's musical compositions, which were published in the US, also illustrate, visually and musically, the continuing commercial significance of "yellowface" acts. He is a good example of what Kristine Moon described as "chinoiserie" in theatre, or the "codification of yellow-face in costumes, makeup, props to set the 'Oriental' mood".[60] We find Luis posing on at least three published sheet music covers, dressed as a "Chinese" in a silk dress. In 1920, he released a foxtrot advertised as an "Oriental jazz" song entitled "Jazzy Jazzy Sound in Old Chinatown", co-composed and co-published with Fred Fisher, a well-known music publisher from the famous Tin Pan Alley music publishing industry in New York.[61] The song's title strongly suggests that Fisher and Borromeo modelled this composition after the song "Chinatown, My Chinatown", a great commercial hit in 1910. If one considers Borromeo's cultural production in the US, his music was a kind of "cosmopolitan kitsch", or to use Henry Jenkins words, something "between dilettantism and connoisseurship, between orientalist fantasies and a desire to honestly connect and understand an alien culture, between assertion of mastery and surrender to cultural difference".[62]

---

[59] At least two US periodicals reviewed Borromeo's vaudeville acts. *Variety* reviewed a show at San Francisco's Orpheum theatre in July 1916, "Orpheum, San Francisco (July 16)", *Variety* XLIII, no. 9 (28 July 1916): 12. *Dramatic Mirror* reviewed a number of shows during Borromeo's troupe tour on the US East Coast, April to May 1920, see *Dramatic Mirror*, 24 April 1920, p. 822; *Dramatic Mirror*, 8 May 1920, p. 898. *Dramatic Mirror*, 22 May 1920, announced "It is a jazzy bill at the Colonial this week, ranging all the way from a Chinese conception of the popular craze to the regular, conventional Dixieland product. Davigneau's Celestials start the jazz procession with their novel act which comprises Borromeo, a pianist with thumps St-Vitus-like along the keyboard, playing notes with a veritable frenzy of muscle-shaking. He is there, as Broadway would say. And to make the Chinese representation noteworthy, there are Men Toy and Shun Tok Sethe, two of the best shimmy artists in or out Pekin[g]." About a week later, the Celestials appeared in the Alhambra Theatre in New York, and are reported as "a decided novelty [...] who gave an original twist to ragtime that took the 'gallery' gods by storm" (*Dramatic Mirror*, 15 May 1920, p. 999). The final show in New York was probably at the Bushwick (Brooklyn), on which *Dramatic Mirror* reported: "The piano playing was exceptionally good" (*Dramatic Mirror*, 29 May 1920, p. 1104). The dancer Mentoy who would also accompany Luis from the US to the Philippines in 1921 was possibly a Filipina using the stage name of Men Toy, borrowed from the Chinese female character Ming Toy in the orientalist American-Chinese love story *East Is West*, see Moon (2005: 123–30).

[60] Moon (2005: 11, 114–8).

[61] "Jazzy, Jazzy, Sound in Old Chinatown", a foxtrot composed by Luis F. Borromeo and Al Heather (also spelled Hether), lyrics by Herman Bush. For a musical analysis of this song, see Tsou (1997: 25–62). For a brief overview of some of Fred Fisher's most outstanding songs published, see Kinkle (1974: 911).

[62] Jenkins (2006a: 164).

The year 1920, however, also marks a cautious and modest move away from this "cosmo kitsch". Within the confines of the American culture industry, Borromeo cautiously began asserting himself as a Filipino patriot. That year, his composition "My Beautiful Philippines" appeared, printed in Cincinnati, Ohio. In early 1921, another Cincinnati-based American corporation released the song as a piano roll.[63] In the Philippines, "My Beautiful Philippines" would become Borromeo's signature patriotic song.

Musically, "My Beautiful Philippines" was not necessarily less orientalist or jazzy kitsch than his "Jazzy Jazzy Sound in Old Chinatown". In contrast to the latter song, however, the lyrics and the cover of the score of "My Beautiful Philippines" reveal a compromise between Borromeo's patriotism and the American publishers reliance on the popularity of "yellowface" acts. Luis is, again, portrayed as a "Chinese" artist in a silk dress, behind a piano.

His portrait as a Chinese musician is, however, placed against a hand-drawn tropical scene of palm trees and a *nipa* (palm tree) hut along a river that flows from a volcano. The song title leaves little to the imagination. It is about a tropical part of America's empire, the Philippines. The lyrics, written by an American songwriter, are in the popular Tin Pan Alley Orientalist mould. The Philippines are represented as a woman with whom a man longs to be united. The writer evokes a stereotypical exotic scenery of swaying palm trees, a jungle and moonlight. The love for a Moro woman adds to the song's orientalist as well as colonial flavour.

In spite of its orientalism, "My Beautiful Philippines" can be considered a cautious step by Luis towards a Filipinised and patriotic musical fit for an American *and* Philippine audience. The timing of publication of Borromeo's composition coincided with the renewed nationalist vigour since 1919, when the Philippine Commission for Independence negotiated for early independence in US political circles in Washington. Coincidence or not, the Commission's promotional handbook published in Manila in 1923 also took "Beautiful Philippines" as its main title.[64]

That Borromeo was on the patriotic track at what would be the end of his American career is also evident from a Kansas City newspaper of January 1921. His relative fame as an oriental vaudevillian gave Borromeo the opportunity to do what the theatre managers denied him on stage: promote Philippine

---

[63] Ad "Vocal Style Music Co", *The Music Trades* no. 12, 19 Mar. 1921.

[64] In July 1919, the Independence Mission returned from Washington empty-handed [*Rosenstock's Manila City Directory 1924–1925*, Manila (1925: 65); Stanley (1974: 256–8)]. The full title of the Commission's publication was *Beautiful Phillippines: A Handbook of General Information* (Manila: Philippine Commission of Independence, 1923).

Illus. 2.2 The cover of the score of "My Beautiful Philippines". Borromeo as a "Chinese" against an imaginary tropical landscape, reminiscent of the Philippines, 1921.

independence. The paper stated that Borromeo "[...] has made every effort to impress on the American people the interest the Filipinos have in asking their independence".[65] Given this mix of orientalism and nationalism, it is well worth echoing the words of Filipino historian Vicente Rafael to capture Borromeo's ambivalent and contradictory cultural and political position: "From its beginnings, nationalism in the Philippines has been divided and conflictual. Loving the nation has never been a simple matter."[66]

While modern dance music like the "oriental jazz" produced by Borromeo and many other Filipino composers became increasingly popular in the Philippines in the mid-1910s, it became controversial within Filipino intellectual circles. Within a few years, this controversy mounted from moral indignation about modern dance music to a crusade against the dance halls. The timing of this controversy occurred during two nearly coinciding events. The first was the American promise of Philippine independence as formulated in the 1916 Jones Act. The second event was the American entrance into the Great War in 1917, which led Nacionalista leader Quezon and the Filipino political elite to advocate for the formation of a native militia in support of the American war effort against Germany. These events evoked cultural confusion and deeply moral discussions on the alleged disturbing impact of alien culture, especially modern dance, on Philippine society.

---

[65] "The Danger of a Philippine Invasion, A Native Believes", *Kansas City Times*, 7 Jan. 1921.

[66] Rafael (2008: 9).

Chapter 3

Cabaret Girls and Legislators

In the mid-1910s, while Luis performed as a Chinese jazz pianist on the American stage, cultural change in the Philippine islands was already underway. Filipinos and Filipinas had embraced modern dance music like the foxtrot and tango and, as will be detailed in the first section of this chapter, socialised in dance halls. The chapter opens with a Tagalog poem, a straightforward lament of, if not attack on, modern popular dances and their alleged corruption of Filipinas. This poem is a prelude to the following three sections, which deal with elitist moral concerns originating in 1916 from a disappointment with America's vague promise to grant the Philippines independence. Disillusionment evoked a patriotic and nostalgic longing for and rediscovery of "traditional" Filipino dance and music from a pre-colonial past. This recovery of a lost culture was paralleled by a Philippine-government-led social sanitising campaign against modern social dances and the dance halls.

The chapter ends as it starts, with a discussion of poetry, but this time a rare and eloquently written kind that raises issues of gender and class in relation to the dance hall, sardonically sketching painful encounters between professional female dancers, *bailerina*, or cabaret girls and upper-class male patrons. One could read the poems as an ethnography of modern urban life and popular culture in the Philippines during the jazz age, a literary articulation of Filipino pop cosmopolitanism. As will be demonstrated in Chapters 4 and 5, the author, Jose Corazon de Jesus, was more than a prolific poet and active participant in the immensely popular poetic jousts, *balagtasan*; he was also a playwright who modestly contributed to Borromeo's novel vaudeville and who was active in the emerging local film industry.

Dance Novelties

Dance!...
The public embracing of young men and women to the beat of the music.
Pleasure of hearts thirsting for fun; haven for new places flowing with the tide
of "modernismo" and the ecstasy of souls in the heat of the dusk.

[....]
Oh! The dance!
You bring joy but you are a poison!
You are a rock where one trips on even if he is careful.
You bury honor in your lap, in which the coffin is also made. You are a catchment for tears of regret.
You are amusement that kills; you darken the honor of our race, you always invite Cupid; but behind it all you are the treacherous sword that pierces the last breathe of my Motherland – the Philippines
Because of you, the grace and gentleness of the Filipina is fading away and she has learned to forget her true self, much to her eventual despair. Because of you, many flowers die out of their season, and truly because of you, we are growing backward and admiring ignorance.
Oh! The dance!...
Sweet...bitter...
Sad happiness...
Enjoyable...difficult...that is dance. Dance.[1]

The poet of the Tagalog poem translated here into English, Ismael Jesus Santos, was clearly not a modern dance devotee and his lines exude his repulsion for those Filipinas lured to novel dances like the one-step, the two-step, the hesitation and the tango.[2] These dances offered new avenues for socialising, particularly in the setting known as the dance hall or cabaret. These sites of social interaction turned accepted rules of conduct between the sexes and the existing Hispanicised Filipino upper-class dance culture upside-down.

In the late 19th into the 20th century, the ball was the accepted form of social dancing among well-to-do rural and urban classes in the Philippines. The ball was a social meeting with written and unwritten dos and don'ts. The invitation-only balls served as an occasion to link economically and politically powerful families through dining and dancing. The invitees observed a dress code and would dance to selected styles considered hallmarks of cultural refinement and social distinction: square dances and waltzes that originated in Europe.[3] Social dancing at a ball was circumscribed in terms of dancing styles, bodily movements and the way dancing partners were chosen. In dances like the *rigodon*, *lancer* and *quadrille*, couples danced to a set of prescribed movements. Dancers "booked" a partner in advance, sometimes using a small notebook or dance card, containing

---

[1] "Ang Sayaw", *Liwayway*, 21 Apr. 1923.

[2] In the absence of a Tagalog term for modernity, Ismael Jesus Santos borrowed the term *modernismo* from Castilian to indicate he was not referring to older Hispano-Filipino dances.

[3] Irving (2010: 67–8), notes for instance that the contredanse genre was already current in mid-18th-century Manila.

a list of dancing styles and an overview of intended dancing companions.[4] Whereas a ball was a socially inclusive event with prearranged social intercourse and dance, in the mid-1910s, modern dances and the institution of the dance hall broke with such upper-class social etiquette.

By the mid-1910s, Filipinos were listening and dancing to new, exciting music with origins in the two Americas. Across the islands, during secular as well as religious occasions, such as patron saint fiestas, youngsters danced to "el Rag" and "el Tango", respectively Afro-American syncopated music known as ragtime and the Argentinian tango.[5] Advertisements for modern dance music recorded on phonographic discs indicate the popularity of the novel dances. In 1914, department store Erlanger and Galinger, agent of the phonographic company Victor in Manila, advertised different modern dances under the motto "Some Victor Dance Records That Should Be in Every Home". This included the Argentinian tango, the one-step (a ragtime variety), and the maxixe (also known as the "Brazilian tango").[6] Victor also released its own dancing tutorial, arranged by the leading authorities on modern dance at that time: Vernon Castle and his wife. That same year, Isaac Beck, representing Columbia Records in Manila, Cebu and Iloilo, also advertised for modern dance music and modern dance instructions.[7]

As professional dancers, the Castles acquired world fame promoting modern dances by performing, including on the American vaudeville stage, and through dance instructions in print and on phonographic records. The couples' printed

---

[4] The social rigidity of square dances is, for example, revealed in the anecdote on William Taft, the American Secretary of War, presented by Stanley. In 1907, Taft caused confusion at the inaugural ball held at Malacañan Palace in Manila in honour of the newly-established Philippine Assembly, as he, unannounced, changed dancing partners during a rigodon. See Stanley (1974: 133). Van den Muijzenberg (2009: 138) gives evidence of the dance repertoire around the turn of the century from a rare surviving notebook from the private collection of Meerkamp, a Dutch businessman and consul of the Kingdom of the Netherlands in Manila. The dance styles listed (with partners noted in handwriting) are the rigodon, lancer, marzuka, polka and the waltz.

[5] "La Moral en Negros e Iloilo", *PFP*, 29 May 1915. "La Fiesta Popular de Magallanes Isla de Sibuyan, P.I.", *PFP*, 19 June 1915.

[6] With their dance instruction manual, the Castles aimed "to explain in a clear and simple manner the fundamentals of modern dancing. In the second place, it shows that dancing, properly executed, is neither vulgar nor immodest, but on the contrary, the personification of refinement, grace, and modesty". Castle (1914: 19). https://archive.org/details/moderndancing00castgoog.

[7] Ad "Columbia", *PFP*, 10 Apr. 1915. In May 1916, Beck's department store in Manila advertised for dance music on 12-inch Double Records P2.20, released by "COLUMBIA, including the following tangos: Tango Bonita; Tango Señorita; A Mi Rosa; Amapa; Tango Argentino". Ad, *PFP*, 20 May 1916.

dance instructions were also available in the Philippines.[8] The book *Modern Dancing*, published by the Castles in 1914, was more than a tutorial on how to make the right steps; it offered concise histories of the origins of the different dances such as the tango. Moreover, the book was also a deliberately sophisticated response to reactionaries in the US who condemned modern dances as obscene and immoral and who lobbied for a ban.[9] Similar tensions evolved in the Philippines in the same period. Church authorities in the islands regarded modern dances as obscene, vulgar and immoral.[10] Within a few years of the US entering the war in 1917, moral indignation morphed into a crusade.

Dance halls or cabarets were an important challenge to the traditional balls and the social order. In the Philippines, they appeared as early as 1902 in Caloocan, Rizal province, and catered almost exclusively to Filipino patrons. In 1910, John Canson, an Italian immigrant to the US and veteran of the Philippine-American war, opened the Santa Ana Road House in Makati, also in Rizal province.[11] In 1915, the Santa Ana Pavilion, previously a building with a thatched roof "liable to blow away during typhoon weather", was renovated and turned into what was probably the largest and most luxurious dance hall in the Philippines (and probably the whole of Southeast Asia).[12] Canson reshaped his dance hall into a cosmopolitan, upper-class institution offering patrons a spacious dance floor

---

[8] "Give a Té Tango at home to the music of a Victrola. It brings the latest Tangos, Maxixes, One-Steps, Boston and Hesitations. Played in perfect time, and supervised by Mr. and Mrs. Vernon Castle, the world's greatest authorities on the modern dances." Ad "Erlanger & Galinger", *PFP*, 18 July 1914. On the Brazilian maxixe, see Castle (1914: 21, 107, 131).

[9] Castle (1914: 18). Vernon Castle died during the Great War in a plane crash.

[10] "Public Opinion in the Manila Press", *MT*, 16 Mar. 1914.

[11] Canson, born 1878 in San Polo Matese, Italy, was taken to the US at a young age and raised in New York City. He related to *The Manila Times* in 1924: "We were poor, as are almost all immigrants, and looked on America as the Promised Land […]." In 1899, Canson volunteered for Philippine service and arrived in the islands with the 41st US, stationed in Luzon. He came to like "the people and the climate" and he stayed on when he was discharged from service in 1901. Before venturing into the entertainment business, Canson served with the Metropolitan Police of Manila and the Quarter Master Department. "Who Is Who In The Philippines. Johan Canson", *Graphic*, 25 May 1929. "John Canson 'The Amusement King' Founder of the Santa Ana Cabaret", *MT*, 25 May 1924.

[12] The Santa Ana cabaret had a beautiful spacious dancing floor constructed from "fine native woods". In 1918, a second floor was added to accommodate modern dance and music acts. Canson might have exaggerated, but he reported that his cabaret had the unexpected magnifying economic effect of encouraging small-scale businesses in its direct vicinity, particularly in the service sector. He pointed out that "[h]undreds of people earn their livelihood in connection with the cabaret and have their own chapel, restaurants, barber shops, and amusement places along the road". "John Canson 'The Amusement King' Founder of the Santa Ana Cabaret", *MT*, 25 May 1924.

and special acts by foreign artists: comedies, modern dances and music. In 1918, with hardly anyone around having a clue what the new music was about, the Santa Ana was among the first venues in Manila to present live jazz.[13] It also had a permanent band, the well-known Tolentino orchestra, directed by professor of music Juan Tolentino. Canson also introduced alien cuisine at his venue "for which an excellent American chef has been engaged".[14] The Santa Ana, but also the Lerma cabaret, advertised in the major local newspapers, emphasising luxurious leisure and cultural refinement. Both institutions contributed to Filipino pop cosmopolitanism, successfully linking the modern, the popular and openness to foreign cultures, through dance, music and food. Patrons of the Santa Ana cabaret were said to come from all walks of life.

In addition to foreign artists, locals also introduced novel dances to the public. One early example, recorded in 1915, concerns Eliseo Carvajal, who performed a tango in what was called a *cabaret teatro*, at Mabromatis's Cabaret, Calle Morga in Cebu.[15] Carvajal is of interest because he was an artistic innovator who experimented with theatre, music and dance, and who would collaborate with kindred-spirit people like Luis Borromeo. Eliseo was born in Manila around 1885, from a Spanish-*mestizo*, a Filipino-Spanish family. The Carvajal family was well known across the Philippines as propagators of Hispano-Filipino *zarzuela* theatre, originally a Spanish form of musical theatre.[16] Between 1900 and 1912, as zarzuela transformed into a modern vernacular theatre, it appealed to the Filipino educated middle and upper classes. Playwrights explicitly promoted the zarzuela to counter the older and popular vernacular *kumedya*, from the Spanish

---

[13] For example, The Santa Ana announced the performance of Tod Sanborn "King of Jazz". Ad, *MT*, 3 July 1918.

[14] "Cabaret Opens Tonight", *PFP*, 18 Dec. 1915.

[15] Ad "Cabaret ni Mabromatis", *Nueva Fuerza*, 11 Nov. 1915.

[16] Eliseo Carvajal was the son of actress Ubalda Roche and the Spanish-mestizo comical actor José Maganti Carvajal. Eliseo was named after his grandmother, the Spanish zarzuela actress Elisea Raguer, who had arrived in the Islands in the early 1880s. See Hernandez (1975: 59, 70–1). See also "Eliseo Carvajal, The Last Act. The Decline of the Spanish Stage", *The Sunday Tribune Magazine*, 31 May 1931. Between 1917 and 1930, the Carvajal family, including Eliseo's (half-) sisters, engaged in zarzuela with different troupes in the theatres in the Binondo district of downtown Manila. In 1917, the Carvajal family had their own troupe, the "well-known" Carvajal Quartette. "Grand Benefit at the Cines", *PFP*, 21 Apr. 1917. "At the Lux – Vaudeville by Tagaroma-Carvajal Co", *MT*, 18 July 1918. In 1920, a new Spanish vaudeville troupe, The Iberia Dramatic Comico-Lyrico Co. debuted at the Cine Sirena, Binondo. This was the only theatre in Manila that featured a daily-twinned programme of silent movies with Spanish vaudeville and zarzuela. The Iberia Dramatic Comico-Lyrico Co. included, amongst others, Eliseo Carvajal and zarzuela stars Dumas Precious and Camille Adelina Amoros, ad, *MT*, 8 Mar. 1920.

comedia, also known as *moro-moro*. In contrast to the kumedya, which took the Christian-Islamic rivalry of ancient times as its main subject and the backdrop for romantic and exotic stories, zarzuela presented realism by dramatising current social issues. Between 1900 and 1909, the vernacular zarzuela became notorious for its anti-colonial and anti-American content. To counter this form of cultural resistance, the Americans resorted to the legal instrument of the 1901 sedition act that prohibited appeals to independence. According to Tomas Hernandez, this law proved effective in curbing Filipino cultural resistance as after 1909 no seditious plays were produced.[17] For now, it suffices to say that this development should not lead us to conclude that zarzuela or other forms of vernacular theatre became entirely politically or socially irrelevant.

At Mabromatis's Cabaret in Cebu in 1915, Eliseo offered the audience the opportunity to dance "el Tango Argentina" and, important to note, "with whomever they please".[18] In the mid-1910s, Carvajal's invitation to his audience was revolutionary as these dances abandoned social etiquette as well as prescribed dancing movements. In the dance hall, one could pick a dancing partner randomly on the spot, without prior announcement, even a complete stranger. Moreover, in some of the modern dance styles, participants would engage in close bodily contact, unknown in the rigidly prescribed dance step patterns of, for example, the square dances. As Anne Gorsuch has argued for the 1930s Soviet Union, modern dances, like the tango, challenged "civilised restraint" and were therefore regarded as dangerous to the existing social order.[19]

Sections of the Hispanicised upper classes articulated their concerns with dances such as the tango. In October 1914, Don Simplicio del Rosario, judge with the Court of First Instance in Manila, took the lead. In a letter, published in the Spanish section of the *Philippine Free Press*, he sided publicly with actions taken by the director of the Dormitorio de Señoritas from Manila.[20] The director had prohibited her students from engaging in modern social dancing. Del Rosario's public support heralds the beginning of explicit moral concerns regarding modern popular dances that were shared within broader sections of "polite society". The *Free Press* editors endorsed the moral indignation in forceful and well-chosen terms worth quoting in full:

---

[17] Hernandez (1975: 139–40).

[18] "Artistas que vienen", *Nueva Fuerza*, 4 Nov. 1915; "El beneficio Carvajal: Se dará en el 'Cabaret' el 15 del actual", *Nueva Fuerza*, 12 Dec. 1915; "Dakung kalingawan sa 'Cabaret'", *Nueva Fuerza*, 12 Dec. 1915.

[19] Gorsuch (2008: 188).

[20] "Moralidad Social", *PFP*, 24 Oct. 1914.

Those filthy, indecent, ruffianesque dances born from the slum, the tavern, the Café cantante, cultivated by men and women belonging to this social underworld cavorting in the suburban swamps; those lusty, pornographic, nauseating dances that serve as a medium for scoundrels and prostitutes in the big cities to flaunt their offensive impudence [...]. They have taken root in the social body of this country, and prevail triumphantly in the halls of the high classes. Our modest, angelical dalagas [Tagalog for unmarried young women, PK], ignore the rottenness of the environment that they are forced to breathe, deliver their virgin bodies lewd up and down, to the exciting "contra-compases" of a dance, as in the "merengaso" of Cuban blacks [...].[21]

According to this harangue, modern social dances were perceived as culturally polluting and socially upsetting. From an elitist Hispanicised Filipino perspective these dances were particularly suspicious, if not dangerous to society as they originated from the ranks of the lower classes, and even worse, from the descendants of African slaves. To the elite Cuban "blackness" was even more appalling than just working class origins of the dances, and we will return to this racial issue in Chapter 5. In 1915, judge del Rosario had taken his moral campaign to the southern provinces of Negros and Panay.[22]

It is difficult to tell how widespread the moral indignation was among the Filipino upper classes. They were most certainly divided. Some elites paid no heed to moral considerations. For example, in 1915, for the local elite on the isle of Sibuyan, in the province of Romblon, south of Luzon, local religious tradition proved perfectly compatible with modern secular entertainment. A two-day patron saint fiesta in the capital town of San Fernando was sponsored and organised by a local businessman-cum-philanthropist, who invited "all those of name and prominent strangers" (todo lo granado del pueblo y distinguidos forasteros). This included, among others, the Mayor of San Fernando, the candidate governor of the island, justices of the peace and invitees from neighbouring districts and the adjacent island of Romblon. After the conclusion of the rigodon square dance, "los ragguistas y tanguistas" [the ragtime and tango dancers] took over.[23]

In 1915, the snobbish cultural taste of the Hispanicised Filipino elite and their hostility to modern dance appears to have been sufficiently conveyed to the general public. For example, the Manila-based dairy corporation Nestle & Anglo-Swiss Milk Company mocked the elite's musical taste and moral

---

[21] Ibid.

[22] Rosario was quoted by the *Free Press* as having labelled two modern popular dances, the hesitation and the tango, "proper for pimps and prostitutes". "La Moral en Negros e Iloilo", *PFP*, 29 May 1915.

[23] "La Fiesta Popular de Magallanes Isla de Sibuyan, P.I.", *PFP*, 19 June 1915.

indignation in an advertisement for one of its products, stating that "the 'rag' [was] generally banned in polite society in the provinces". To soothe the elite, one of the dairy products promoted came with a published copy of a traditional waltz composition.[24]

Back to the *Balitaw*

In addition to moral indignation, elites made a patriotic call for cultural restoration. Indignation and restoration were two sides of the same coin; both dealt with genuine feelings of cultural loss caused by modern life. In Bacolod, the capital of the province of Negros Occidental, for example, local elites believed that modern dances would wipe out Hispano-Filipino music and dances. They promoted *balitaw*, courtship songs and *kundiman*, a Tagalog love-song genre, as fiesta dance music.[25] Intellectual support for cultural restoration also emerged in the print press. For example, the *Philippine Free Press* called attention to nearly extinct native musical genres under the headline "The Cundiman, the Cumintang, the Awit and the Balitaw Must Not Be forgotten". Moreover, native music was regarded as patriotic music.[26]

The irony of the upper-class search for an authentic and pristine native culture was that during the previous centuries of Spanish colonisation, this same group had alienated itself from a pre-colonial cultural repertoire in favour of European round and square dances and European classical music. Intellectual efforts were now being made to turn back the clock; to retrieve a native cultural stock and reintroduce it to the urban middle-to-upper classes. Another irony of this upper-class reassessment was that the "common people", normally patronised and regarded as backward and in need of education and guidance, were assigned a new role as guardians of a native cultural heritage.

---

[24] Ad, *PFP*, 20 Mar. 1915.

[25] "Ejemplejo de imitacion", *Nueva Fuerza*, 3 June 1915. On balitaw, also spelled as *balitao*, Raymundo Bañas (1975: 82–3) noted: "The music is happy and humorous and its tempo is similar to that of the Spanish *jota*." And "the word balitaw originated from the Tagalog word balitao, or news". Another love song and dance style was the *kurutsa*, also spelled *kuracha*, the Spanish word for cockroach. *Kumintang* was "an ancient native dance and melody of the Christian Pilipinos [...] [it] is an authentic example of pre-Spanish music in the Tagalog areas. Originally a war song, it was later adopted into a love song and still later into a song of repose" (Bañas 1975: 81). On kundiman, see Bañas (1975: 82–3, 91). See also Cultural Center of the Philippines (1994: 92–6), Vol. VI.

[26] "Cundiman", *PFP*, 13 Feb. 1915.

The resurrection of nativism in music is also revealed in a modest upsurge of anthropological research on "native amusements", produced between 1915 and 1920 by students of the University of the Philippines (UP, established in 1908) in Manila. The research was under the aegis of the American anthropologist Henry Otley Beyer, who, in 1914, had been assigned the professorial Chair of Anthropology and Ethnology at UP.[27] Filipino folk music and dance developed into a distinct interest of Beyer's anthropology students, many from provincial upper-class families themselves. Against the expectation that the forces of modernisation had a detrimental effect, the students discovered that native music and dances were alive and kicking across the archipelago. Between 1915 and 1919, a steady flow of unpublished ethnographic production on "traditional" music and dance appeared, the majority of a descriptive nature. Emphasising the preoccupation with native music, these writings had telling titles such as "Musical Instruments of the Tagalogs" and "Pangasinan Folklore and Amusements".[28] Of the dozen or so ethnographies produced, only two were explicitly devoted to modern popular music in the Philippines; that is, jazz, which will be briefly addressed in Chapter 5. These two studies stand out as aberrations within this modest body of anthropological work on native music and dance.

Given their background in social science, the fledgling ethnographers documented performative, rather than musicological, aspects such as sung poetry accompanied by dance, as featured in courtship rituals of the balitaw genre. The students offered typologies of native songs based on the social occasion and the song's moral message.[29] Preoccupied with cultural loss and tradition, the students

---

[27] Otley Beyer started his career in 1909 as an ethnologist with the Philippine Bureau of Science, and as part-time head of the Museum of Ethnology in Manila. Rahmann and Ang (1968: 6–8).

[28] "Native Musical Instruments of Pampanga", by Adolfo N. Feliciano (1915); "Tagalog Songs" by Paz. N de Guzman (1915); "Tagalog Nursery Rhymes and Cradle Songs" by Vicente M. Hilario (1915); "Pangasinan Folklore and Amusements" (1915); "Bisayan Songs from Samar" (1916); "A Brief Sketch of the Native Dances and Songs in the Province of Rizal" (1916); "Customs and Amusements of the Ancient Filipinos" (1916); "Iloko Songs from Rosales" (1916); "Bisayan Songs" (1918); "Folksongs in Lipa, Batangas" (1918); "A Collection of Native Songs" (1918); "A Collection of Iloko Poetry and Songs" (1919); "Pampangan Songs" (1919); "Games and Amusements of the Young and Old People of Samar [illegible] paper no. [illegible]" by Francisco A. Tan, Manila (14 Mar. 1919). H. Otley Beyer ethnographic collection, National Library of the Philippines.

[29] As in "Iloko Songs from Rosales" (1916), in which the author explained the social and moral meaning of particular song genres.

were not interested in documenting and explaining the appeal of modern popular dances with the well-to-do classes in the provinces.[30]

Also conspicuously absent in the ethnologies on music are the popular wind bands that developed out of the tradition of Spanish regimental bands.[31] From an anthropological perspective this is remarkable, as in the 1920s every *barrio* or town across the archipelago had its band, which played an important role in life-cycle celebrations, from birth to death.[32] These bands also engaged in musical contests during religious fiestas sponsored by prominent townspeople.

For the young middle-to-upper-class Filipino ethnographers, "primitive dances" like the balitaw, performed by the "labouring class" were depicted as sources of progress within idyllic rural communities.[33] Such images of harmonious rural life downplayed the hardships of agricultural labour, class tension and intra-village conflict. For example, the earlier mentioned fiesta band contests were often the source of violent clashes between fans of contesting bands from different barrios or towns. In the absence of judges, such musical contests could easily erupt into violence and often required the presence of the Constabulary.[34]

In the early 1920s, and more systematically in the early 1930s, the UP's Conservatory of Music, established in 1916, also developed an interest in "native" music.[35] The Conservatory's curriculum initially focused on European classical music, reflecting a Hispanicised cosmopolitan orientation and a stress on high culture. Jorge Bocobo, first dean and later president of UP, and conservatory staff member and composer Francisco Santiago, developed an interest in native music. In the early 1930s, Bocobo would lead a research project aimed at documenting native music and dances, a project that would serve as a basis for a national repertoire.

---

[30] Paper No. 20. "Dancing and Its Social Significance in the Town of La Carlota, Occidental Negros" by Manuel S. Sitchon, Manila (1916), p. 2. H. Otley Beyer ethnographic collection, National Library of the Philippines.

[31] Tan (2014: 79–80).

[32] Talusan (2004: 506–7).

[33] Paper No. 20. "Dancing and Its Social Significance in the Town of La Carlota" (1916), p. 7.

[34] "Band Concerts that Last Thirty Hours or More", *PFP*, 23 Aug. 1924.

[35] "Historical Sketch of the Conservatory of Music of the University of the Philippines" by Raymundo C. Bañas (Manila: [The Author, n.d.]), p. 6. Typescript. Bañas collection. Special Collections, National Library of the Philippines. On the Conservatory, see also Pagayon Santos (2005: 179–93).

The Conservatory's official disinterest in studying modern dance music contrasts starkly with the musical practices of its staff members. For example, in the late 1910s and 1920s, conservatory professors Francisco Santiago and Nicanor Abelardo, both trained in classical music, performed and composed modern popular ragtime style dance music like one-steps and foxtrots. Santiago, Abelardo, Luis Borromeo and many other Filipino composers attempted to connect or even assimilate these foreign genres into native genres like kundiman. The conservatory professors' modern hybrid compositions were popularised through commercial phonographic recordings on shellac discs. For instance, in 1923, American record company Victor released Abelardo's instrumental foxtrot "Amorosa" in the Philippines. For commercial reasons, it was not advertised as Filipino music, but as "Spanish genre". Victor also marketed the song in Mexico, placing Abelardo not simply in a Filipino-Hispano, but in the modern pan-Hispano commercial music industry of the 1920s.[36]

The discrepancy between the Conservatory's emphasis on European classical music and the popular musical practices of its staff is also apparent from Abelardo's conductorship of the Lerma Orchestra. The Lerma Cabaret was the next largest and most luxurious dance hall in the greater Manila area after the Santa Ana.[37] Abelardo's role as conductor of an orchestra engaged in popular music in a cabaret is particularly salient. Since 1915, the institution of the dance hall had come under public scrutiny. Innocuous moral indignation would intensify and eventually dominate public opinion, leading to official measures to curb the cabarets in 1917.

Highways of Perdition

Since the early days of the American occupation, hygiene reform, including the regulation of prostitution, had been central to the American civilisation mission in the Philippines.[38] In 1915, however, prominent Filipinos and Americans

---

[36] The song "Amorosa" was performed by the International Orchestra and recorded by Victor records in New York in October 1922, and released in the Philippines in July 1923 as one out of two "new Filipino records". Ad "Victor Records", *MT*, 31 July 1923. Between 1921 and 1930 the International Orchestra, working under different names such as Orquestra Internacional, the International Novelty Orchestra and also as Orquestra Pajaro Azul, recorded over 100 Spanish titles for Victor. See http://victor.library.ucsb.edu/index.php/matrix/detail/800000877/B-26947-Amorosa.

[37] Ad, *MT*, 26 Jan. 1917. The Lerma was located in Caloocan, a suburb of Manila in Rizal province.

[38] Anderson (2007: 26, 91).

linked prostitution to the popular institution of the dance hall, creating a social controversy that materialised in repressive policies.[39]

The cabarets had become a favourite pastime for urbanites. The year 1915 witnessed a boom in the number of dance halls in downtown Manila. Manileños engaged in modernity, listening to modern music and moving to the exciting rhythms of the tango and ragtime varieties like the foxtrot. The dance hall offered the opportunity to socialise with the opposite sex without the social control of parents or spouses. The municipal board was "at a loss" about what to do with the majority of these "obnoxious houses [...] not properly conducted". The board considered suppressive measures.[40] Meanwhile, civic leaders joined in the debate. In May 1915, trade union leader Hermenegildo Cruz recommended that the Philippine legislature draft a new charter for the city of Manila that would prohibit dance halls as well as the cockpits.[41] Linking cabarets to juvenile delinquency and a debasing influence on youths, the president of the Juvenile Protection Association of the Philippines gave a similar advice to the public welfare board.[42] It would, however, take another two years before measures were taken.[43]

In April 1917, two months after Quezon's patriotic call to form a National Guard, opposition to the dance halls gained momentum. Having ordered the closure of "La Insular Cabaret" in the Santa Cruz area downtown Manila, Mayor Justo Lukban, prominent leader of the Partido Nacionalista, considered

---

[39] Studies on prostitution in the colonial Philippines mention in passing that in the mid-1910s dance halls became part of sanitary reforms, see Teraimi-Wada (1986: 310) and Dery (1991: 482). Referring to the prohibition of the sale of alcohol, Andrew Jimenez Abalahin argues that attempts at reforming, or even to abolish, prostitution, should be seen as part of a wider "purity crusade" in the US around the turn of the century, which was exported to the Philippines. See Abalahin (2003: 339–40).

[40] "Salones de Baile", *PFP*, 17 Apr. 1915; "The News of the Week", *PFP*, 6 Nov. 1915.

[41] "The News of the Week", *PFP*, 29 May 1915.

[42] "After Dance Halls", *PFP*, 9 Oct. 1915.

[43] Rafael Palma, one of the three major Nacionalista leaders, and Teodoro R. Yangco, businessman, philanthropist, Nacionalista and YMCA supporter, even publicly defended the dance halls they had inspected. It is not clear which of the dance halls were the subjects of their investigations. The favourable opinion of these prominent Nacionalista proved to be minority dissent that quickly evaporated in the public debate to make way for a moral crusade against the dance halls. "Dance Halls Not So Bad", *PFP*, 6 Nov. 1915.

terminating all "breeding places of immorality for the young of the city".[44] What the term immorality implied was, for the time being, left largely to the Manileños' imagination, but, between the lines, prostitution loomed as a major issue. Lukban received support from different corners; residents from the Santa Cruz area, government officials, medical and religious institutions and the Women's Club in Manila (a catholic organisation of influential Filipino women).[45] The expert opinions of medical doctors from the General Hospital in Manila, who argued that the dance halls "were a menace to public health and morals" served to legitimise what had become a crusade.[46] The majority of newspapers, both Filipino and American, usually engaged in editorial battles and libel suit controversies, closed ranks and supported Lukban. Some doubts about the effectiveness of the policy existed. For example, the editors of *La Vanguardia*, an influential Hispano-Filipino periodical, predicted that closing the dance halls in the city would drive these hotbeds of vice to the suburbs. And, indeed, this would happen in the years to come. The only newspaper that criticised Mayor Lukban's action as arbitrary and autocratic was the American periodical *Cablenews-American*. The paper refuted the "very general allegations that the dance halls are a menace to the health and morals of the community". There was no reason, according to this periodical, for closing the dance halls, because "a few students or muchachos or cocheros or sailors lost control of themselves and spent more money than they should".[47]

Lukban's action to monitor the dance halls and later, in 1918, to close Manila's licensed prostitution zone Gardenia, Sampaloc, was to demonstrate that he held high moral standards. His firm actions were also a display of vigorous leadership vis-à-vis a municipal council generally known for internal tensions and opposition to incumbent mayors. Lukban intended to show the public, who held police and health administrators responsible for moral laxity, that he was handling matters differently from his predecessors.[48] What also might have played a role in Lukban's decision to act boldly was the Nacionalista's eagerness

---

[44] Dr. Justo Lukban was a former revolutionary who had opposed the Spanish and was editor for newspaper *La Independencia*, as well as delegate for the national assembly. On Lukban's earlier political career, see Stanley (1974: 128–30). See also Quirino (1995: 131). In January 1917, Lukban was appointed Mayor of Manila. See Rosenstock (1925: 62); "The New Mayor and the Ex-Mayor", *PFP*, 6 Mar. 1920; "The News of the Week", *PFP*, 21 Apr. 1917; "The News of the Week", *PFP*, 28 Apr. 1917.

[45] "The News of the Week", *PFP*, 12 May 1917.

[46] Ibid., 5 May 1917.

[47] "Current Opinion as Reflected in the Spanish-Filipino and American Press", *PFP*, 19 May 1917.

[48] "Alcalde Lukban", *PFP*, 21 Apr. 1917; "Official Slackness", *PFP*, 12 May 1917.

to take momentum away from the newly- established Partido Democrata, a party fiercely opposing Nacionalista power and dominance in government.

The suppression of the dance halls, and later prostitution, should be seen against the broader backdrop of three closely related aspects: the vague American promise of independence as stated in the 1916 Jones Law; America's declaration of war on Germany in April 1917; and Quezon's native militia bill, which had passed in the Philippine senate two months earlier. Quezon's call for the formation of a native militia to serve on the European battlefield made it imperative to keep up Filipino recruits' high moral standards and physical fitness. These events offered mayor Lukban and the elite both cause and the momentum to act against the dance halls and prostitution. These acts showed the Americans that Filipinos possessed high moral standards and were fit for independence.

Slight protest against Lukban's dance hall policy ensued. Assisted by Attorney Vicente Sotto, a group of bailerinas spoke of the Mayor's order as arbitrary, appealing to the municipal board to "obstruct the mayor in his action". This was to no avail. In the same month, May 1917, the municipal council amended Lukban's ban, turning it into a policy of regulating and monitoring the dance halls. It is not clear what these measures exactly entailed. On the basis of the official measures announced in Malabon, Rizal, they must have, on the one hand, boiled down to tight monitoring of existing establishments and, on the other, to curbing further expansion of the number of cabarets.[49] What monitoring meant can be read from some of a total of 17 official regulations announced for Malabon: guests should not spend the night at the establishment; guests should refrain from entering the dancers' rooms; guests should refrain from dancing "in an indecent or ridiculous manner, nor execute pirouettes or figures which are scandalous or contrary to morality and decency". A separate article even prescribed the bailerina dress code and etiquette, including the condition that the bailerina "shall be provided with a fan of the type known as *anahaw*, which shall be used during dancing to prevent contact of her bosom [...] with the dancer or subscriber".[50]

---

[49] According to *La Vanguardia*, "the measures included that the public dance halls operate only once a month, from seven to ten in the evening; that there be an interval of five minutes between dances; and that no young man less than 21 years old be admitted". "The News of the Week", *PFP*, 26 May 1917.

[50] Extracts of ordinance No. 18, regulating the administration of dancing halls and their premises at Malabon Rizal were published by the League of Nations: *Commission of Enquiry into Traffic in Women and Children in the East: Report to the Council*. Series of League of Nations Publications, IV. Social. 1933. IV. 8.493. Geneva. League of Nations, pp. 207–9.

In July 1917, the dance hall controversy entered a new phase. The American secretary of the Young Men's Christian Association (YMCA) in Manila reported that its American members had contracted diseases from bailerinas at the Lerma and the Santa Ana dance hall, suggesting that prostitution and venereal diseases were thriving in these establishments.[51] Canson and Bert Yearsley, the American proprietors of the Santa Ana cabaret and Lerma respectively, denied the truth of the charges and threatened the offending papers with a libel suit.[52] In this controversy, *Cablenews* was again the only newspaper reiterating "that the evils existing had been greatly exaggerated".[53]

Dance hall fans in Manila cleverly circumvented the repressive regulations. The *Free Press* reported on the strategy of "forming dance clubs and patronizing resorts outside the city limits and thus in large measure nullifying the effects of the reform".[54] Moreover, members of upper-class associations, such as the Masonic Temple, the Oriental Club and the Cosmopolitan Building, all within Manila's municipal boundaries, used their venues as clandestine substitutes for the dance halls.[55] Some were also used as gambling dens, another moral issue in the same period. Members of the upper classes thus continued to participate in this form of popular culture, hence maintaining double moral standards.

In the second half of 1918, the battle for decent morals shifted to Manila's suburbia, to the dance halls under the jurisdiction of the provincial authorities of adjacent Rizal province: Pasay, Caloocan, San Juan del Monte and San Pedro Makati.[56] In contrast to Manila, supervision of these suburban cabarets proved lax.[57] The moral indignation was completed in late September 1918, when Manuel Quezon, Senate President, got involved in the matter, emphasising that

---

[51] "Current Opinion as Reflected in the Spanish-Filipino and American Press", *PFP*, 28 July 1917.

[52] "Get After Dance Halls", *PFP*, 28 July 1917.

[53] "Current Opinion as Reflected in the Spanish-Filipino and American Press", *PFP*, 28 July 1917.

[54] "Get After Dance Halls", *PFP*, 28 July 1917.

[55] "Current Opinion as Reflected in the Spanish-Filipino and American Press", *PFP*, 22 Dec. 1917.

[56] "The News of the Week", *PFP*, 19 May 1917.

[57] In September 1918, the bureaucracy itself had become part of the controversy and was subject to a "moral sanitation". Rafael Palma, Secretary of the Interior, instructed the head of the Executive Bureau (holding authority over the municipalities around Manila proper) to conduct a campaign for the immediate suppression of the dance halls. Palma defended his policy referring to an alarming rise of diseases contracted by army officers and youths in the cabarets. "All Dance Halls Ordered Closed Here – (Sec. Of the Interior) Palma Also Orders Closing of Dubious Cabarets", *MT*, 21 Sept. 1918.

he had seen letters "testifying to the evil which emanated from these resorts".[58] The officials of the Interior ratified a set of new, strict regulations, largely similar to those current in Manila, to monitor the dance halls in Rizal province.[59] Again, a host of civic organisations and prominent individuals responded in support of the measures. A group of distinguished ladies from the Manila Women's Club, the chairman of the Mary Johnston Memorial Hospital, and spouses of prominent Filipino politicians, such as the wife of Nacionalista Rafael Palma, also produced a report on social hygiene in relation to the dance halls. One of the issues discussed was how former bailerinas could be turned into "respectable residents of the community" and how they could "earn an honest living".[60] These intended social measures foreshadowed Lukban's far more heavy-handed policy on prostitution in Manila a few weeks later. Between 18 and 25 October 1918, the police swept through Manila's Gardenia red-light district in Sampaloc, deporting its mainly Japanese prostitutes to Davao.[61] This marked the end of regulated prostitution organised by the Spanish colonial government in the late 1880s. The police's inhumane treatment of the prostitutes caused the newspapers to abandon their previous support for Lukban's policy.[62]

The dance halls in Rizal province, particularly in the municipalities of San Pedro Makati and Pasay, remained sources of official concern. Based on investigations by the Constabulary in Pasay in May 1919, the Executive Bureau ordered the closure of two dance halls in Pasay, as they were reported for frequent rows and it was claimed that former "inmates of the Gardenia district" [read:

---

[58] "Prohibition for Philippine Islands Is Urged By Quezon – Senate President Will Introduce Measure in Legislation. Nearby Towns Close In On Dance Halls – Towns Passed Ordinances Saturday Night and Sunday", *MT*, 23 Sept. 1918.

[59] According to *The Manila Times*, the new set of rules included, amongst others, that establishments would not have private rooms or partitions, that no woman under the age of 21 and man under the age of 18 were permitted access, that no alcoholic beverages would be served and that Sunday would be considered a holiday, see "Some Cabarets May Be Opened – Acting Governor of Rizal Gives Statement", *MT*, 24 Sept. 1918. These rules deviated slightly from those reported by the *Commission of Enquiry into Traffic in Women and Children*, League of Nations (1932: 207–9).

[60] "Submits Report on Future Of Bailarina", *MT*, 6 Oct. 1918.

[61] Abalahin (2003: 346–7).

[62] Commenting on the conflicting reports from Davao and the Mayor's Office, *El Debate* compared the *Alcalde* (mayor) to the German Kaiser, pointing out that both were wonderful propagandists for the causes they espoused. *La Nacion* warned against tolerating what the paper described as an "illegal act of the mayor". The *Cablenews-American* declared that the matter "had passed beyond the purview of the courts". The *Bulletin* declared the deportation a "stupid procedure". "Current Opinion as Reflected in the Spanish-Filipino and American Press", *PFP*, 30 Nov. 1918.

prostitutes, PK] were employed as bailerinas.[63] Prominent Filipino and American residents in Pasay effectively opposed the dance halls in their district, sealing the fate of these popular venues.[64] In the early 1930s, the negative long-term effects of the prostitution ban would become painfully clear, as prostitution went underground in the suburban cabarets.

Dangerous Dancers

Bailerinas were frequently portrayed as social outcasts. Stereotypes developed of professional female dancers as low-class people of loose morals; a reflection of the Hispanicised elite's deeply rooted notion of class distinction, gender roles, social etiquette, cultural taste and the elite's fear of the blurring of social boundaries. For instance, in 1919, judge of the Court of First Instance, Manuel Camus, unreservedly depicted bailerinas as "lowly-educated and misguided cabaret girls". He warned university students to avoid these girls, "being dangerous and full of evil consequences".[65] Many years later, in a short story "The Bailarina", published in the *Free Press* in 1927, writer Jose Garcia Villa reproduced the female dancers as socially-ostracised women.[66]

In contrast to the emphasis on the bailerina as social outcast, upper-class patronage of the dance hall was a public secret. One early 1930s observer described the often-neglected category of male patrons in a single sentence: "This modern jazzy age, which has dressed the world with multicolored garments, has brought the unscrupulous legislators, the presumptuous professionals, the tired business men and the reckless students to the cabarets."[67] If the patrons were mentioned at all in the print press, the relationship between female dancer and male patron was not explicitly conceived as one of unequal social and economic power, but one in which men succumbed to their own sexual desires and the immorality of the dancer. In brief, male dance hall patrons were seen as victims, rather than as devotees of modern dance and bailerinas. This was a strong and

---

[63] "Put Lid On Pasay Halls—Executive Bureau Orders Cabarets Closed—Get Days of Grace—Rizal Provincial Governor Begs Chance for Dance Hall Owners To Continue Revels Over This Weekend", *MT*, 15 June 1919.

[64] "Cabarets Die Next Month—Nobody Wants Them So They Must Go Says De Las Alas", *MT*, 27 July 1919.

[65] "Dance Halls A Great Evil—Many Bright Students Fell By Wayside Thru Them", *MT*, 19 Nov. 1919.

[66] "The Bailarina by Jose Garcia Villa", *PFP*, 19 Feb. 1927. On the reproduction of the bailerina as a social danger in cartoons, short stories and newspaper articles, see also Schenker (2016: 293–4, 306–8).

[67] "Their Nimble Feet. Win Money and Fame For Cabaret Girls", *Progress*, 17 Feb. 1931.

popular image. The "lure of the dance hall" and its alleged devastating social effects became a popular topic for journalistic investigation.[68]

In 1930, the dance hall in the Philippines had become notorious, to the extent that it had reached the purview of the League of Nations' Commission of Enquiry into Traffic in Women and Children in the East. On its tour through Asia, the Commission took a special interest in the relationship between unlicensed prostitution and the cabarets in the Philippines.[69] During its 17-day stay in Manila, starting 24 January 1930, the Commission members interviewed several officials and visited an unknown number of cabarets. The Committee was able to reveal some of the practices used to recruit bailerina, some of whom ended up as prostitutes, particularly in establishments in Rizal province.[70] The Committee's conclusions were, however, not alarming. This might have been different had the committee visited the Philippines a few years later, when the effects of the global economic depression had sunk in. In the next few years, as incomes dropped, the number of cabaret customers likewise dwindled. Dance hall owners economised on professional dancers, a measure that possibly pushed some of the women into prostitution. What is clear is that the economic crisis did turn the suburban dance halls into economic safe havens for local criminals engaged in all kinds of illicit activities in and around the cabarets in a bid to survive the economic downturn of the early 1930s.

The image of the bailerina as a "bad girl" was dominant and persistent; dissenting views, like that of the American reporter Walter Robb, were few and far between. Sensitive to the hierarchies of class and gender in the Philippines, Robb described the daily life, dance practices and social ethics of the professional dancers and their clientele. Around 1930, he visited the Santa Ana cabaret, giving us a rarely portrayed view of the unwritten social mores of the dance hall, the divide between the private and the public spheres and the economic survival strategies of the professional dancers. Robb wrote: "They have a code. They never speak on the streets or elsewhere, outside to men they know [from the dance hall, PK]. They like to find men who will maintain little homes for them, and may do

---

[68] See for instance "The Lure of the Dance Halls. How Charms of Bailerinas and Attractions of Gay Fast Life Amid Bright Lights Brought About Downfall of One Young Man", *PFP*, 17 May 1924; "Woman's Club Renews Campaign Against Bill Boards and Cabarets", *The Tribune*, 19 Feb. 1933. The dance hall issue was not restricted to Manila and surrounding provinces, but extended to Cebu, see for instance "Hunáhuna ug Sugyot" ("Thoughts and Suggestions"), *Bag-ong Kusog*, 29 Jan. 1926; "Mahitungud sa mga 'Salon de Baile'" ("About the 'Salon de Baile'"), *Bag-ong Kusog*, 29 Jan. 1926; "Supak sa 'Salong de Baile'" ("Debate about the 'Salon de Baile'"), *Bag-ong Kusog*, 5 Feb. 1926.

[69] League of Nations (1933: 14–5, 191, 193–6, 200, 207–9).

[70] Ibid.: 193.

so; when they've done that, the code is for them to treat their benefactor on the up and up."[71] Such relationships between benefactor and beneficiary could imply a more intimate, even sexual relationship, but there is little evidence that this was the rule in the Santa Ana. Again, Robb related his encounters with bailerinas at this particular cabaret:

> A Tagalog girl may be danced with, gayly flirted with, and ravishingly complimented, but she is not supposed to be touched intimately, even by her accepted lover, before marriage. She may, if her man is poor like herself, accept common-law marriage and cheat the altar of a fee, but it is a sacred covenant in her eyes just the same: she will quickly kill a man for breaking it.[72]

Most of the girls were driven into the bailerina trade by sheer poverty. In contrast to the elites' contempt, lower-class families simply regarded the profession as a legitimate way to support the family. It was not uncommon for parents to give their daughters permission to become a dancer; some were even chaperoned by their own mothers or fiancés while working.[73] Filipino reporter Eugenio E. Santos was another who took a genuine interest in the dancers and their social background. His investigation in the early 1930s revealed that families supported their young daughters to become a dancer, and that this decision was perfectly rational. The girls could simply earn more under better working conditions compared to, for example, working in a Manila cigar factory. And such a choice was all the more pressing if the daughter had to support the entire family if, for example, the mother was a widow or had been abandoned.[74]

A clue about the social order *within* the dance hall, as well as a hierarchy *between* dance halls in the capital is revealed in a letter by a young Cebuano studying in Manila, published in the *Free Press* in 1924.

> One night in the past we went to 'Santa Ana Cabaret', the biggest and most beautiful Cabaret in the East and to our astonishment, the majority of the dancers were Cebuanos. […] They come from the cities of Cebu, Dalaguete, Alcoy, Samboan, Ginatilan, Danao, Carcar and Bogo. Their lives here are really dancers' lives. Some of them have come into money because they managed to hook someone with money; but most have poor and wasted lives. They dance at the 'Santa Ana Cabaret' without pay and they earn if they are taken away from dancing by their male friends if not lovers. The 'Santa Ana Cabaret' is divided into two: one portion is for those prominent families, where Quezon, the Senators and famous

---

[71] Robb (1963: 32–3).

[72] Ibid.: 34.

[73] Ibid.

[74] "Their Nimble Feet. Win Money and Fame For Cabaret Girls", *Progress*, 17 Feb. 1931.

people from Manila dance, and the other portion is for those who are not famous and everyone can enter, even the American marines. This latter portion is where the Cebuana dancers are found. If you come to Manila and dance at the 'Santa Ana Cabaret', you will remember Cebu because it would seem like you were just dancing at the cabaret of Rodriguez or Tulyo at Carreta in Cebu.[75]

At one end and at the top were a few high-class cabarets, the Santa Ana and the Lerma, owned and managed by locally-rooted Americans. And, as the division within the hall indicates, the Santa Ana was socially segregated; not on the basis of race as one would expect in a colonial society, but rather on basis of class.[76] In addition to the most spacious dancing floors in the islands, establishments like the Santa Ana and Lerma offered cosmopolitan cuisines "spaghetti and steaks", international variety acts, vaudeville and other amenities.[77] For example, amidst the public agitation of 1917 and 1918, proprietor A.W. (Bert) Yearsley inaugurated his newly renovated Lerma in *The Manila Times* as "a new sensation for Exiles of the Far East, having private phones on each table".[78] To counter the image of the dance hall as a highway to perdition, the Lerma was depicted as "[a] sane place [...] surrounded by an atmosphere of refinement, Remember: To be Known as A Patron of Lerma Is to Carry the Mark of Social Distinction."[79] At the other end of the spectrum were smaller establishments of lesser repute supervised by local thugs, fortified "roadhouses", some simply brothels under such names as the Smile cabaret situated in Manila's suburbs Pasay, Parañaque and Makati. No private telephones, spaghetti or steaks available, instead young women offering their sexual services.[80]

The Lerma's renovation and its publicity campaign occurred during the time when opposition to the dance halls was at its peak. The Santa Ana and Lerma cabarets were relatively safe from government intervention, and I can only speculate as to why this was so. Already, a few years before the controversy took off, the owners had proved sensitive to decency and social etiquette in order to secure the patronage of Americans and upper-class Filipinos. For example, in 1912, Aletta Jacobs, Dutch pioneer of the feminist movement, visited the Santa Ana dance hall. She reported on her first-hand experience:

---

[75] "Napuno sa mga baylarina nang Sugboanon", *Bag-ong Kusog*, 1 Aug. 1924.

[76] See also Schenker (1916: 263–5) on the issue of segregation within the Santa Ana cabaret.

[77] Ad "Santa Ana Cabaret", *Excelsior*, 20 July 1929.

[78] Ad "Grand Opening of Lerma Cabaret", *MT*, 18 May 1918.

[79] Ad "Lerma", *MT*, 2 July 1917.

[80] "Manila's Vice-Ridden Suburbs", *PFP*, 28 June 1930.

For the sake of proper conduct the police keeps a close eye. When the sexes do not dance they must remain in their separate departments, it is strictly prohibited to drink alcoholic beverages, and when the dancing pairs move too sensually the police will separate them. Indecent behavior therefore does not occur in the ballroom, but it does engender contact between youngsters of both sexes and as a result of such encounters a follow-up often occurs outside the ballroom and from this intimate relationship the number of mestizos is considerably enlarged.[81]

Intimate and sexual inter-racial encounters outside the dance hall premises no doubt took place. We simply do not know whether many children were born from these occasional relationships, as Jacobs suggests. Her first-hand experience in the Santa Ana dance hall and her observation of the place as a relatively innocuous place for leisure was probably not exaggerated. And this situation remained the same more than a decade later, in the 1930s.

Rashes of the Times

A highly informative and original view on the social meaning of modern dance, the dance hall and bailerina in the Philippines is given in a series of illustrated satirical short Tagalog poems published in 1923 in periodical *Liwayway*, under the heading of *Mga Butlig nga Panahan* (Rashes of the Times). *Liwayway*, meaning dawning in Tagalog, was a bilingual Tagalog-English and illustrated magazine founded in Manila in 1922. The magazine tapped into the new modern culture of popular stars from theatre, literature, film and modern fashion, marking and conveying an emerging Filipino pop cosmopolitanism. By 1933, *Liwayway* probably had the largest circulation of all periodicals in the Philippines, said to be over 70,000.[82] Unlike the UP anthropology students, who avoided the dance halls as research site, the poet of *Rashes of the Times* appears to have been a first-hand witness. In a sophisticated, witty and flowing manner, the poet sketches realistic scenes of an imaginary Manila dance hall and its dance fans. He offers the readers his anxieties about modernity, second thoughts about upper-class taste and the double moral standards maintained by the male dance hall patrons. And, contrary to dominant public opinion about the professional dancer as "bad girl", this poet spared the bailerina.

---

[81] Jacobs (1915: 565).

[82] In his *History of Journalism in the Philippine Islands* (1933), pp. 149, 161–2, Valenzuela ranked *Graphic* and *Liwayway* as "modern journalism" and "non-partisan" publications, suggesting these were not mouthpieces of any of the political parties. Both periodicals were controlled by the Roces family.

The skilled cartoonist remains anonymous, but the author's name Anastacio Salagubang was one of the pseudonyms used by the well-known and prolific poet and writer Jose Corazon de Jesus. De Jesus (1896–1932) is primarily known as a poet who established his name in 1920. He wrote, in total, about 4,000 poems in his column "Buhay Maynila" (Life in Manila), published in, amongst others, the Tagalog periodical *Taliba* under the pen name of Huseng Batute.[83]

Unlike many of his contemporaries who reflected on the dance halls, de Jesus refrained from morally judging the bailerinas as women with flawed moral standards. *Rashes of the Times* can be read as a social critique of the upper classes and their decadent lifestyle. The dance hall serves as a micro cosmos representing Philippine society, where social dancing to modern syncopated music is skillfully and humorously portrayed as a painful and ambiguous encounter between different sexes, generations and classes. The central and recurring character is a bailerina by the name of Josefina (Pinang) Resistensia. De Jesus seems to have carefully chosen the dancer's Spanish name. Resistensia is caught in a contradictory process of participating in, yet also resisting, as her name suggests, to an alien and modern popular culture and to the sexual advances of her male clients. The patrons are pathetic dancing partners, men of advanced age with unattractive bodies. They are wealthy, cosmopolitan Hispanicised Filipinos from the provincial upper classes, who make social dancing literally a painful and embarrassing social activity. These men behave without dignity, openly displaying their incompetency to perform the latest Afro-American dance styles like the Camel Walk and Black Bottom.

In one poem, *Aray!* (Ouch!), a clumsy dancer by the name of Don Justo Balderrama enters the dance hall scene.[84] Balderrama is taken from the root *baldar*, meaning "crippled" in Spanish. The *provincio* portrayed treads on Josefina's toes "like a steamroller". This dance hall patron is a yam plantation owner with the honorific Spanish title of Don, and thus a prominent citizen in what turns out to be the province of Nueva Ecija, Central Luzon. Portraying these people, poet de Jesus shows his intimate understanding of the socio-economic conditions within Central Luzon, a region known for its commercial agricultural production of sugar and rice and its wealthy Hispanicised landed elite.[85] From this rural, social

---

[83] Lumbera and Lumbera (1997: 92–3).

[84] "Aray", *Liwayway*, 21 Apr. 1923.

[85] Due to the rationalisation of agricultural production in the 1920s, tenancy conditions deteriorated in practically the whole of Central Luzon causing resent among tenants, leading to organised peasant protest and, ultimately, to violence between tenants and landlords. On the landed elite and agricultural production in the neighbouring province of Pampanga, see Larkin (1993). On peasant resistance in Central Luzon, see Kerkvliet (2002).

environment, de Jesus picks his characters and places them in the modern urban context of Manila's popular dance halls.

In another poem, entitled *Naku, Loko!* (You Must Be Crazy!), de Jesus stages a character by the name of Don Simon Mantecado de Paner (Mantecado being a Spanish sweet pastry), another way of ridiculing the wealthy, Hispanicised cosmopolitan provincios. This dance hall patron is sardonically pictured as "a grandfather dancing by the lady's waist". Don Simon drips with sweat and makes "strange dance moves", making himself a fool. Ignorant of the latest jazz dance fashion known as the Camel Walk, he does the "Carabao Walk", the moves of the archetypal draft animal of the Philippines. De Jesus draws an even more pathetic picture of this dance hall patron, when Don Simon proposes to the much younger Josefina, who counts many suitors among her clientele. A similar male character is staged in the poem *Suss....Ang Taas!* (My ...You're So Tall!) with Eusebio Arboleda, another carefully chosen name and a Spanish wordplay, or "Tall Sebio, a tall and thin bamboo tree that showed up at the dance hall without discretion [...]."[86]

Josefina remains largely an abstraction as de Jesus freshly and purposely reverses the more common focus on bailerina to that of the patron, the latter often obscured from moral discussions on the dance halls. De Jesus modelled his fictitious dance hall patrons on real people from the wealthy, often landowning classes, some with political positions. Such "real" people included senate president Manuel Quezon, who, like the characters staged by de Jesus, was a *politico* and a provincio with vested interests in commercial agriculture (sugar), who frequented the dance halls in Manila.

The 1920s not only saw debates about moral corruption and a patriotic longing caused by intruding alien cultures, but, equally, a blurring of the boundaries between the arts through unprecedented collaboration and cultural cross-fertilisation. Jazz musicians, *jassistas* in Spanish, worked closely with poets like de Jesus, engaged in the literary genre of balagtasan, and collaborated with actors of the Spanish and vernacular zarzuela stage. In forging these new connections, Luis Borromeo's vaudeville became a nexus of cultural innovation, a source of a new popular art.

---

[86] "Naku Loko!", *Liwayway*, 28 Apr. 1923; "Suss ... Ang Taas!", *Liwayway*, 5 May 1923; "The Sheik", *Liwayway*, 5 May 1923.

Chapter 4

Jassistas, Balagtansistas, Zarzuelistas

When Borromeo returned to the Philippines in 1921, he entered neither an environment hostile to cultural innovation, nor a virgin cultural landscape. Manila had thriving Hispano-Filipino theatre and music, with roots in the 19th century. Borromeo tapped into this existing cultural pool and collaborated with some of the leading playwrights, composers and actors from the Hispano-Filipino stage. We see the first signs of these connections during Borromeo's debut in Cebu and Manila. Initially, Borromeo's new-style vaudeville mixed two elements: Filipino patriotism and his own interpretation of orientalist music and vaudeville acts in the form of "non-Christian tribal acts". These two elements would play a significant role in drawing a Hispanicised upper-class audience to his shows, a class that would remain divided on the new form of popular culture.

In the 1920s, artists and entrepreneurs from different forms of theatre, music, sports, and literature and the print industry started to collaborate creating something that was part of a new urban pop culture. Three broad categories of collaborators can be identified. The first is a very small, but important group of American veterans of the Philippine-American war. These locally rooted foreigners developed into business entrepreneurs with stakes in the entertainment industry. The second significant category of cultural collaborators is a socially heterogeneous group of poets, novelists and playwrights, often not seen in connection to local vaudeville or popular culture in general. Several of these figures, such as poet Jose Corazon de Jesus, had established themselves as well-known and respected publicists and literary performers. Some of them were also political activists and social advocates. The final category of cultural collaborators is a second generation of Spanish-*mestizo* artists who welcomed musical and theatrical innovations, like the earlier mentioned Eliseo Carvajal. Firmly rooted in Filipino-Hispanic theatrical and musical tradition, they enriched vaudeville by introducing artistic conventions familiar to middle- and upper-class audiences.

"My Beautiful Philippines"

In June 1921, as if his celebrity status had travelled ahead of him, the *Philippine Free Press* announced the return of Luis Borromeo to the islands. He planned to recruit local talent to form a new all-Filipino vaudeville company and take them back to the United States.[1] In July 1921, Borromeo was back in the city of his childhood, Cebu, debuting at the Teatre Oriente with a company named Borromeo Lou & Co. Teatre Oriente in downtown Cebu was the home of visiting Spanish, Russian and Italian opera companies and Hispano-Filipino zarzuela theatre, owned by a prominent local, José Avila.[2] Bilingual Cebuano-Spanish daily *Nueva Fuerza*, proudly announced Luis as a "[...] man famous for his great ability known as 'King of Jazz' [who] is one of the knowledgeable Cebuano artists who is the scion of the prestigious family of the Borromeos [...]".[3]

Reviews of the shows provide us with information on the actual performance, some of the people involved and the audience. Let us start with the important observation that the 1921 Cebu premiere was not presented as a vaudeville show. Borromeo announced the show as a "Review of the Evolution of the Classic Jazz Music, Operatic and Classical Song" and as a "theatrical novelty".[4] The emphasis on the term "classic" is a meaningful social, rather than musical indicator, as we will learn in due course. The show's title sounded sufficiently familiar as well as novel to draw the interest of the cosmopolitan audience that Borromeo knew so well from his own experience: the Cebuano middle- and upper classes.

Resembling a classical music concert, the show was divided into two parts; an eclectic musical programme, with probably some modern dancing associated with jazz.[5] The first part started with an "overture", performed by composer

---

[1] "Said to be making one thousand pesos a week on vaudeville stage in the United States", *PFP*, 18 June 1921.

[2] According to a 1924 *Philippine Free Press* report, Avila was "the diplomat and official glad-handshaker and entertainer on behalf of those in power". "Those in power" refers to the Cebuano politicians-cum-businessmen active for the Nacionalista party, Sergio Osmeña and Dionisio Jakosalem. Avila held interests in coconut plantations, was founder of the English-Spanish newspaper *The Advertiser*, one of the major Cebuano newspapers of the time next to *Nueva Fuerza*, and he was owner of the Cebu Sports Centre, a regular venue for boxing bouts and source of talent for Manila's Olympic Stadium. See, "Theatre and Newspaper King of Cebu. Some Striking Points About Jose Avila, Who Successes as Newspaper Owner is Paralleling Achievements in Theatrical World", *PFP*, 23 Aug. 1924. See also Briones (1983: 33).

[3] "Ang 'Filipino Jazz' sa Oriente", *Nueva Fuerza*, 9 July 1921; "Ang Hari sa 'Jazz Music'", *Nueva Fuerza*, 16 July 1921. From Oct. 1921, *Nueva Fuerza* split into a Spanish and a separate Cebuano weekly, *Bag-ong Kusong*. From 1922, *Nueva Fuerza* continued as a bilingual weekly in English and Spanish.

[4] Ad "Oriente Theatre", *Nueva Fuerza*, 19 July 1921.

[5] Ad "BORROMEO LOU & CO", *Nueva Fuerza*, 19 July 1921.

of classical and zarzuela music José Estella, who, at the time, happened to be director of the Oriente's Concert Orchestra. Estella was no stranger to classical music lovers and those of the Hispano-Filipino popular stage. He had enjoyed his classical musical training in Spain in the 1880s. In the 1910s, he composed and performed zarzuela music in both the zarzuela and the "Spanish" vaudeville theatres of Binondo, Manila, the area where he was born and raised.[6] As his collaboration with Borromeo's debut in Cebu suggests, and as will be elaborated on later, Estella was another contributor to a Filipino popular cosmopolitanism. Borromeo's debut in Cebu was, reportedly, a success. *Nueva Fuerza* praised his "Tio Sam music" (Uncle Sam's, thus American music, which seems to point at Afro-American syncopated music), his "patriotism" and the financial returns made in equal measure. The shows closing song was "My Beautiful Philippines", Borromeo's hybrid musical composition that had become "the object of genuine admiration of the public".[7] No doubt the result of the song's patriotic message.

In addition to patriotism, two other salient musical features mark the Cebu debut that would become part of Borromeo's vaudeville staple—opera and orientalist acts. A certain Zeleb, announced as a "Malayan baritone", performed a prologue from the Italian opera *Pagliacci*. The adjective "Malayan" indicated that he was not an Italian singer, but a local artist. Borromeo would set a trend for integrating Italian condensed opera with vaudeville, a practice likely borrowed from his experiences on the American vaudeville stage.

Without completely sacrificing "yellowface" acts, Borromeo took orientalism in a different direction. He introduced a distinctively Filipino form of orientalism that, in the context of popular entertainment and racial taxonomies in the Philippines, is best described as a "non-Christian tribal act". These special acts featured the Islamic peoples of the southern Philippines, generally labelled "Moros", and the non-Christian tribal Igorots from northern Luzon.[8] Thus, in Borromeo's Cebu debut, we find "Sali The Moro Bass", apparently a vocalist operating at the lower musical registers. In 1922, "Dudu the famous Moro banjoist assisted by his Comparsa [string band] of Moros from Jolo" appeared.[9] In 1924, we find Mathilde Salming, "an Igorot in personation only" [...] a

---

[6] Estella composed music for Spanish plays staged at the Sirena and Empire cinemas and was orchestra conductor at the Opera House "Sobre el Telón Blanco", *PFP*, 24 Apr. 1915; "Cronica teatral", *PFP*, 27 Nov. 1915.

[7] "'My Beautiful Philippines' fué objeto de sincera admiración del público 'Borromeo Lou & Co.'", *Nueva Fuerza*, 9 Aug. 1921.

[8] For a discussion on the pejorative connotations of the term "Moro", see Hawkins (2013: 147fn1).

[9] Ad "Stadium Vod-A-Vil", *MT*, 1 Feb. 1922.

native of Calamba, Laguna [...], playing "her ragtime violin".[10] On stage, Hispanicised Christian Filipino artists thus sometimes passed for "authentic" Moros or Igorots. Borromeo showed that Moros and Igorots were on the road to progress, performing European operatic and modern Afro-American ragtime music. Notwithstanding this progress, these ethnic stereotypes on the popular stage affirmed not American cultural superiority over Filipinos, but that of the Hispanicised Christian Manila-based upper classes over the tribal and Islamic peoples of the islands.[11]

Since the 1904 St. Louis Exposition, stereotypes of the savage Filipino had evoked protest among the Filipino intellectual elite; no such objections occurred when Borromeo staged his Moros. Only in 1924, when Mathilde Salming, Borromeo's "Igorot ragtime violin player", was offered a lucrative contract with Keith's Vaudeville Co. in the US, did St. Louis once again resonate painfully in the Filipino elite minds and in the print press.[12] Some leading politicians believed that if this *vodavilista* were to perform on the American stage, she "might hurt the Philippine cause"; that is, that her image of tribal savage would undermine legitimate claims for Philippine independence.[13] The political elite attempted to refurbish Mathilde's image from the "savage" of the vaudeville stage to that of civilised, clean, classical musician. In a symbolic act, rather than a conversion to classical music, shortly before her departure to the US, prominent Nacionalistas invited Salming to perform classical chamber music, and not the modern popular ragtime that she performed with Borromeo.[14] Her agent, Frank

---

[10] "Matilde Salming, 'Igorot Girl Violinist', Will Play Before American Audience for P400 Weekly", *PFP*, 26 July 1924.

[11] In his historical study on the Islamic minority of the southern Philippines, Michael Hawkins critically analysed attempts to define the Moro within the broader framework of the American colonial project in the Philippines: "Constructions of 'Moroness' frequently touched on aspects of a cherished Islamic heritage and fully distinguished Filipino Muslims from other Hispanized Christian Malays" (Hawkins 2013: 6).

[12] In 1923, general director of Keith Vaudeville Co., Albee, assigned a scout, Harry J. Mondorf, to contract Asian artists for a new exotic vaudeville show "Keith's Vaudeville Mecca of Foreign Novelties" in the newly renovated Hippodrome Theatre of New York. In 1923 and 1924, Mondorf hunted for acts in China, Japan, Korea, Siam, Burma, the Philippines, Singapore, Sumatra and Java. "Hunting Acts for Vaudeville", *The New York Times*, 16 Nov. 1924. Except for his interest in Javanese textiles known as *batik*, his trip to Indonesia proved a failure. "Op zoek naar 'Nummers'", *De Indische Courant*, 4 Jan. 1924.

[13] "Matilde Salming, 'Igorot Girl Violinist', Will Play Before American Audience for P400 Weekly", *PFP*, 26 July 1924.

[14] The hosts included former revolutionary Emilio Aguinaldo, first president of the revolutionary republic from 1899 to 1901, Nacionalista Manuel Roxas and other politicians and their wives "Music at Chamber – Miss Salming to Be Guest Wednesday", *MT*, 4 Aug. 1924; "Wives Welcome at Chamber", *MT*, 5 Aug. 1924.

Goulette, appeased the public, emphasising that Miss Salming was to appear in the US as a Filipina violinist and not as "Igorotte".[15]

After the Cebu debut, Borromeo continued his journey to Iloilo, Panay, at that time the second largest harbour city of the Philippines. In late August 1921, Borromeo had one or two shows in Iloilo City.[16] From Iloilo, it was announced that the next target was Manila, where he would "present [...] beautiful and lively jazz". He was also reported to "travel to America and stay there for the next three years to make a tour in all the big cities. When they return here, they will put up a 'Conservatory of Music'."[17]

In Manila, a city of approximately 300,000 souls, and the major administrative, political and commercial centre of the Philippines, pieces would unintendedly fall into place. Within six months, from September 1921 to January 1922, Borromeo developed, perfected and eventually consolidated the different elements from the Cebu playbill into something that would be understood as a new form of popular Filipino theatrical art: vod-a-vil. He could not foresee that what were meant as trial shows, turned into an instant artistic and commercial success, preventing his return to the American vaudeville stage.

The Manila Stage: Elitist Patronage and Business Entrepreneurs

In September 1921, Borromeo was in Manila. Pending contracts with theatres in the US, he held trial performances in the Manila Opera House to test local artistic talent with his group under the name of Borromeo Lou & Co. Scheduled for 11 and 14 September, the show was announced under the title "My Beautiful Philippines", "A Thrilling Pageant with vocal and instrumental music [...]".[18] The cast consisted of Miss Mentoy "Charming Chinese Dancer from Shanghai", a "Chinese baritone", a Chinese tenor, a Malayan Saxophonist, a Moro violinist, "one Moro Jazzer—the master of many stringed instruments—and a Moro Princess, gifted with a rich soprano voice".[19] It was as if with his "non-Christian tribal acts" and "oriental jazz", Borromeo had planned to launch an orientalist and patriotic vaudeville show in the US to "educate" an American middle-class audience about Asia but, above all, about his beloved Philippines.

---

[15] "Salming Makes Hit in States", *MT*, 8 Dec. 1924.

[16] "Noticias de la semana", *PFP*, 17 Sept. 1921.

[17] "Sarisari Balita", *Makinaugalingon*, 3 Sept. 1921.

[18] Ad "My Beautiful Philippines", *MT*, 14 Sept. 1921.

[19] Ibid.

The American-Philippine daily *The Manila Times* reviewed Borromeo's first vaudeville shows: "while all the members of the cast are excellent in their different lines, their specialties being most modifications and adaptations of American jazz in a new pleasing way […]".[20] The *Philippine Free Press*, a bilingual weekly in Castilian and English, also spoke highly of "señor Borromeo", "el celebrado músico y Jassista filipino" (The famous musician and Filipino jazzman).[21] The Philippine print press generally took vaudeville audiences for granted. Very little was said about its spectatorship and why people loved Borromeo's new innovative theatre. Indeed, we only catch glimpses of the social composition of Borromeo's audiences. For example, the *Free Press* wrote of the Manila trial performances:

> The house was fairly carried away with the catchy strains and syncopation of the "jazz", and joined with the singers and players, unable to keep its feet and hands still. Many of the young ladies present hummed very audibly. Pretty soon Broadway will be listening again to Borromeo Lou and his jazz artists, but Manila will have a last chance, at a matinee performance tomorrow afternoon, to hear them.[22]

The report indicates that Borromeo was still planning to return to the US, yet his shows unsuspectedly caught on with local audiences. The young ladies present at Borromeo's debut were certainly not Manila's female cigar factory workers or domestic house maidens. A brief chronology of events following his debut at the Manila Opera House demonstrates that Borromeo's vaudeville appealed to a middle- to upper-class audience. Two weeks after the Manila opera house appearances, the Columbian Association in Pasay invited Borromeo's company to give a benefit show for the organisation. Established in 1907, the association was initially open to Filipinos who had attended US universities.[23] By 1920, however, it was, in particular, Filipinos working at the highest government levels that took membership. The Columbian Association thus was a typical *ilustrado* organisation. Unmistaken elite patronage is also revealed when Borromeo's vaudeville company reappeared at the Manila Opera House on 2 October 1921. This particular show of "the oriental king of jazz" was publicly announced as

---

[20] "Borromeo Lou's Last Appearance Set for Tomorrow", *MT*, 17 Sept. 1921.

[21] "Noticias de la semana", *PFP*, 10 Sept. 1921.

[22] "'Jazz' Gets the Crowd", *PFP*, 17 Sept. 1921.

[23] "Patriotic Ceremonies at Laying of Columbian Association Cornerstone", *PFP*, 22 Mar. 1924; "Noticias de la semana", *PFP*, 17 Jan. 1920; "Borromeo Lou and His Jazz Wonders Give Show Tonight", *MT*, 30 Sept 1921. By the mid-1920s, the membership criteria of being educated in the US was loosened and "any Filipino citizen of good moral character" was permitted to join the Columbian Association. In 1924, Nacionalista leader and Senate president Manuel Quezon was one of the association's board members, see Rosenstock (1925: 179).

being under the patronage of Misses Paciencia Limjap, Teresita del Rosario, Virginia Puyat and Feliza Limjap.[24] These young ladies, for that is what they were, belonged to the Filipino political and economic elite. Pacienca and Feliza Limjap were daughters of the wealthy Chinese-Filipino businessman Mariano Limjap. That the Limjap family was politically well-connected is demonstrated by the fact that their daughter Esperanza, not mentioned in relation to Borromeo's show, was married to the prominent Cebuano Nacionalista leader Sergio Osmeña in 1920.[25]

Between Borromeo's appearance at the Opera House in mid-September and early October 1921, another significant event took place that would propel him into stardom and open up a mass middle-class in addition to the elite audience. In this period Borromeo for the first time staged a vaudeville show at the Olympic Stadium, Rizal Avenue in downtown Manila. This would turn into a contract with the Stadium in January 1922. In contrast to the smaller Manila Opera House, the Stadium could house thousands of spectators. Moreover they came from across the social divide, particularly attracted by boxing bouts and soon also vaudeville shows.[26] Plans for a major sports venue had coincided with Mayor Lukban signing a municipal board ordinance in April 1918 that amended the law prohibiting mixed racial boxing bouts. This allowed Filipinos and Americans to meet each other in the boxing ring.[27] By the early 1920s, boxing was extremely popular across social classes in the Philippines and developed into big business,

---

[24] Ad "Borromeo Lou the Oriental King of Jazz", *MT*, 1 Oct. 1921.

[25] Mariano Limjap (1865–1926) held interests in the San Miguel Brewery, in the Manila Jockey Club and the Hong Kong and Shanghai Bank. According to Carlos Quirino (1995: 126–7), he was "leader" of the Filipino-Chinese community of Binondo, Manila and *gobernadorcillo* of that district. I was unable to find information on Teresita del Rosario and Virginia Puyat.

[26] Between September 1917 and 1918, the Philippine government and Manila's municipal board had forged plans for the construction of a "civic stadium", one of the incentives being the prospect of having the 1919 Far Eastern Olympiad in Manila. "The News of the Week", *PFP*, 29 Sept. 1917. According to Lewis E. Gleeck, Eddie and Stewart Tait, Joe Waterman and Frank Churchill commissioned the construction of the Olympic Stadium. Gleeck (1977: 100–1, 119–20). Gleeck also asserts that Churchill and Tait were in partnership with John Canson, owner of the Santa Ana cabaret.

[27] "The News of the Week", *PFP*, 6 April 1918. For a concise history of boxing in the Philippines, see Joseph Svinth (2001), http://ejmas.com/jcs/jcsart_svinth_0701.htm [accessed 6 Feb. 2014].

the Stadium being one of the major venues.[28] Filipino fighters turned into celebrities and patriotic symbols and commodities.[29] Stadium entrance fees for boxing bouts tripled those of vaudeville shows.[30] Since the turn of the century, theatres such as the Zorilla in Manila had combined boxing, theatre and silent cine.[31] The Stadium adopted this eclectic form of entertainment, integrating boxing with Borromeo's new vaudeville.

Two American-Philippine war veterans, boxing fans and promoters, Eddie Tait and Frank Churchill, recognised and seized on the new commercial opportunities in popular entertainment.[32] They made a successful step into what was to become an entertainment industry where professional boxing, vernacular theatre, silent cinema and carnival attractions converged.[33] From owners of the Mercantile Advertising agency in Manila, Tait and Churchill moved into the position of managers of the Olympic Stadium. It is not clear who took the initiative, but Borromeo and these local-rooted American business entrepreneurs began to collaborate. Many of the Filipino fighters under Churchill and Tait's management would feature in Borromeo's vaudeville shows, particularly with training stunts, adding to the theatre's eclecticism. And this commodity was successfully exported across Southeast Asia. In 1923, Tait took Filipino fighters

---

[28] "Sports and Athletics", *PFP*, 24 Apr. 1915. For example, the funeral of Filipino fighter Gaudencio Cabanela aka "Kid Dencio" in August 1921, brought throngs of fans to the Olympic Stadium, where a farewell tribute was held. Along the roads of Manila, thousands of spectators watched the march to the Loma cemetery. The fans included high-ranking Filipino government officials. "Thousands Turned Out To Do Dencio Last Honors", *PFP*, 27 Aug. 1921. A similar spectacle repeated itself after the tragic death of fighter Pancho Villa in 1925, one of Churchill's most famous and successful fighters ever.

[29] See, for instance, a *PFP* editorial on the salary paid to fighter Elino Flores, who demanded ₱10,000 for one match and reached a compromise of ₱9,000. According to the *PFP*, this amount equalled the annual salary of a bureau chief. "Beware of the Jabberwock but Learn to Jab", *PFP*, 8 Oct. 1921.

[30] Balcony seats for a vaudeville show were rated ₱1 and ₱ 2, respectively, while the same seats were ₱5 and ₱6 for a boxing bout. See ad "Stadium Vod-A-Vil and Boxing", *MT*, 17 Oct. 1922.

[31] Del Mundo (1998: 14–5).

[32] Tait and Churchill were avid boxing lovers. Churchill was manager of the Olympic Sport Club in Manila; Tait had a background as fighter himself and was the founder of the Olympic Boxing Club of the city. "The News of the Week", *PFP*, 21 Aug. 1915; "The News of the Week", *PFP*, 20 Oct. 1917; "Eddie Tait Going Strong", *PFP*, 27 Oct. 1917. "Stadium Movie Program Opens", *MT*, 18 Sept. 1922.

[33] "Stadium Movie Program Opens", *MT*, 18 Sept. 1922.

to Singapore, in 1928 to Borneo, followed by Bangkok.[34] Filipino boxers also found their way to the Malay opera stage demonstrating, as extra attraction, their fighting skills. In 1926, Young Frisco, flyweight champion from Manila, performed with rising star of Malay opera, Miss Riboet, during her debut season in the port city of Surabaya, East Java.[35]

The fame of the Tait brothers and Churchill extended to the Netherlands East Indies and the Straits Settlements and not only in relation to boxing. From 1922 deep into the 1930s, we find travelling attractions interchangeably billed as "Tait's Manila Carnival" or as "Tait's and Churchill's Carnival" in Singapore, Sumatra and Java, and on the latter island particularly as one of the main attractions on the so-called *pasar malam* (night fairs).[36] This itinerant Manila Carnival Show offered a variety of entertainments, such as a "swaying house", or, for example, "Rosario the miraculous conjurer". These attractions originated in the annual Manila Carnival (est. 1908), in which Tait had been successfully involved, probably since the late 1910s to early 1920s. As will be discussed in the next chapter, the Manila Carnival developed into a major popular culture institution of the Philippines.

The professional experience of Tait and Churchill in advertising was crucial to Luis Borromeo's stardom. They launched a big publicity campaign for Borromeo's debut show at the Olympic Stadium, held on 5 October 1921. For the first time, Borromeo's show was explicitly announced as vaudeville; in fact, as "The Greatest Vaudeville Treat Ever Shown In the Orient".[37] Large and

---

[34] Originally prohibited by royal decree, Eddie Tait was the first to secure special permission from the authorities in Siam to have foreign boxers to perform there. Filipinos faced Siamese fighters trained in Muay Thai boxing who followed European boxing rules. See, "Malaysia Takes to Boxing", *PFP*, 14 June 1930. Some Filipino fighters were extremely successful. For instance, in 1925, the "famous and tough Young Santos from Manila" had defeated the local champions of Central and East Java respectively. Additional victories on the island of Java and in Singapore earned Santos the name "The fright of fighters in Java" (in a hybrid Dutch-Malay "'De schrik der boksers' di Java"). "Boksen di Koedoes", *Warna Warta* (*WW*), 15 Sept. 1925; "SPORT", *WW*, 22 Apr. 1927. In spite of their victories over local fighters in Java, Filipinos were refused official regional championship titles, as they were neither Dutch nationals, nor Dutch subjects.

[35] Young Frisco arrived in Java in 1924 to fight the West-Java champion, see "Olympic", *Het nieuws van den dag voor Nederlandsch-Indië*, 29 Nov. 1924; ad "Orion", *Soeara Publiek*, 30 Mar. 1926.

[36] Ad "Deca-park", *Bataviaasch Nieuwsblad*, 18 July 1922; "Pasar Gambir", *Bataviaasch Nieuwsblad*, 16 July 1924; "Speciale Pasar Malem Editie", *WW*, 28 July 1928; "De Taits te Malang", *De Indische Courant*, 16 Oct. 1930; ad "Tait's Manila Carnival", *The Straits Times*, 21 Mar. 1933.

[37] Ad "Mammoth Program by a Mammoth Troupe", *MT*, 3 Oct. 1921.

extensively illustrated ads were published in *The Manila Times*, presenting the cast as Moros. In one picture Borromeo himself was portrayed as "Moro" and in another as "Japanese" dressed in kimono. Representing an all-Filipino cast of no less than one hundred artists, the show was announced as a "mammoth programme" by a "mammoth troupe". *The Manila Times* reviewed the 6 October show, under the heading "Borromeo Lou went big at the Stadium last night". One of the main attractions was a jazz contest between the Constabulary Band, which had performed so successfully at the Panama-Pacific International Exposition in 1915, and the Ilaya Band. At this stage, Borromeo's vaudeville was artistically still in its infancy, as we learn from press statements: "Manager Churchill was requested from all sides to repeat the experiment and has a second appearance of the Borromeo players under consideration. Several additions from among the best of the local talent are promised if the plans mature."[38] It is apparent that these plans did develop.

The months that followed the Stadium appearance in October 1921 witnessed growing excitement about Borromeo's innovative vaudeville. *The Manila Times* not only continued to publish the show's advertisements on a weekly basis, it also reviewed the new vaudeville favourably. We cannot rule out that the paper's enthusiasm was biased due to financial interests, specifically the earnings it gained from advertising for Borromeo's Stadium shows; it should be noted, however, that the *Philippine Free Press*, which did not advertise Borromeo's shows, reported equally enthusiastically about the novel theatre and music. In its Castilian section, addressing the Hispanicised elite, the paper wrote that Luis Borromeo, "[…], has caused a real sensation in the artistic and theatrical circles of Manila, where its 'classic-jazz' is the topic of the day".[39] Early 1922, Borromeo's vaudeville had crystallised under the name Borromeo Lou's Follies drawing huge crowds at the Stadium. For example, on 11 January 1922, 5,000 spectators were reported to have witnessed a show, while "thousands […] had to be turned away".[40]

The making of Borromeo's local vaudeville also included a remake of his public image. This process had started in the US and was ongoing in Manila in 1922. Luis was no longer portrayed as a Chinese in silk dress or as a Moro; in a publicity picture, we find him neatly dressed in a modern black tuxedo and bow tie, situated in the environment of a Manila photo studio. A transformation

---

[38] "Borromeo Lou Went Big at the Stadium Last Night", *MT*, 6 Oct. 1921.

[39] "Noticias de la semana", *PFP*, 8 Oct. 1921.

[40] Ad "Borromeo Lou's Follies of 1922", *MT*, 12 Jan. 1922. The number of 5,000 spectators might be exaggerated as, according to other sources, the Stadium could accommodate only 3,000 souls.

Illus. 4.1 A publicity picture of Luis Borromeo taken in a Manila photo studio with Luis's printed autograph, c. 1922. Courtesy of Alice Marvin.

had taken place from "yellowface" personality to that of the self-confident and modern Filipino.

By January 1922, Borromeo was a celebrity, the first of his kind in the Philippines. And the unforeseen great artistic and commercial success was probably one of the main reasons that thwarted his plans to return to the US.[41]

New Connections

In early October 1922, in celebration of the first anniversary of his vaudeville endeavour in the Philippines, *The Manila Times* credited and praised Borromeo for recruiting, training and promoting new local talent:

> A year ago, it is pointed out, native talent was totally unknown in local amusement circles. [...] Today, no banquet, smoker or club gathering is complete without a selection of able artists whose offerings never fail to please and whose abilities conjure favorably with the best anywhere, according to competent critics. These are the result of Borromeo Lou's unceasing efforts to discover and develop new and novel effects for the local stage. His weekly "Snapshots", "Follies" and "Scandals" at the Stadium have amused hundreds of thousands of spectators eager for vaudeville of the better kind.
>
> As stage director, Lou is unquestionably capable and efficient. His musical ability is established. He has given Manila and the Philippines a new angle on how to have a good time in a clean, wholesome way. He is a discoverer, a producer and a credit to himself and his country.[42]

Such public tributes helped to establish the image of a man who had single-handedly developed local-style vaudeville. This reading eclipsed the fact that Borromeo's venture could never have materialised without the help of experienced entrepreneurs and artists from the entertainment industry and the assistance of the print press. This included Tait and Churchill, but also a host of local composers, playwrights, novelists, poets and dance instructors, some of whom will be highlighted below. Borromeo might have had a gift for scouting talent; he also had a capacity for connecting to people who could compensate for the qualities he lacked. Writing, for example, whether prose, drama or song lyrics, was not Borromeo's cup of tea. The same might have been true for the vaudeville dancing acts, for which he hired choreographers. Most of these people literally remained behind the scenes, but all contributed to innovating and shaping Filipino vaudeville into a "popular art".

---

[41] Another additional reason for not leaving for the US might have been his family situation. Borromeo had recently remarried and his wife was expecting their first baby.

[42] "Borromeo Lou To Celebrate Year As Director Of Weekly Frolic", *MT*, 1 Oct. 1922.

A search of Borromeo's published music sheets, advertisements and reviews of his shows reveal the names of some of these behind-the-scenes players. These historical materials bring to the surface veterans of the Philippine-American war and people active in vernacular literature and in Hispano-Filipino music and theatre. One of the earliest names connected to Borromeo, and another pioneer in the evolution of vod-a-vil, was John Cowper. This veteran of the Philippine-American war, like Santa Ana cabaret owner John Canson and Olympic Stadium manager Tait, had become locally rooted. Retired from the army, Cowper sought a living in Manila's entertainment industry in 1911.[43] As stage manager of the Paz Theatre, Manila, Cowper was among the first to start Spanish vaudeville shows. The shows included musical comedies, melodramas in Spanish combined with skits. Having little appeal among the majority of non-Spanish speaking Filipinos, this hybrid theatre failed to attract audiences.

How and when they met is not clear, but somewhere between late 1921 and mid-1923, Cowper acted as Borromeo's manager and press agent.[44] In early 1923, he introduced Borromeo's vaudeville company at two silent cinematographic theatres, the Lux and the Rivoli at Plaza Santa Cruz, Binondo, downtown Manila.[45] The collaboration between Borromeo and Cowper extended into song writing. Among the few known examples is a piano ragtime song composed and published by Borromeo in Manila in late 1922 or early 1923, entitled "Dodge Me Daddy". Cowper wrote the lyrics for this ragtime, likely commissioned by a local Dodge dealer.[46] Borromeo's vaudeville had become an object for commerce. In 1924, toothpaste company Colgate sponsored one of Borromeo Stadium's vaudeville. Free samples were distributed during the show.[47]

By mid-1923, Cowper and Borromeo's ways appear to have parted. By that time, Borromeo had lost his "monopoly" on local vaudeville and had to compete with, in chronological order, the Variety Stars at the Lux Theatre, and the Rivoli Amusement Company at the Rivoli. Cowper was the founder of some of these new vaudeville companies, the Rivoli Amusement Company and, later, the Savoy Nifties at the Savoy Theatre. The new companies had strong casts of local vaudevillians, some of whom would perform, off and on, with Borromeo: Elisabeth Cooper aka Dimples, Katy de la Cruz and Sunday Reantaso. Others were established names in Hispano-Filipino theatre and music: Pacita Sanchez,

[43] "Foreigners Who Become Filipinos", *The Sunday Tribune Magazine*, 20 Aug. 1933.

[44] "Impressions of the Manila Vaudeville Stage", *Philippine Magazine*, Nov. 1929.

[45] Ad "The Rivoli: Borromeo's Rivoli Revue 'The Three Kings'", *MT*, 6 Jan. 1923; ad "The Rivoli: Borromeo's Rivoli Revue on Thursdays and Saturdays", *MT*, 15 Jan. 1923.

[46] Schenker (2016: 215).

[47] "Colgate's Flowers at the Stadium", *MT*, 1 July 1924.

Illus. 4.2 Cover of the score "Dodge Me Daddy" portraying Luis Borromeo seated in a Dodge sedan, accompanied by a modern Filipina, likely his wife, on foot. The text on the tyres refers to the shows at the Olympic Stadium and the Lux Theatre, respectively, c. 1922.

Vitang Cowper, Eliseo Carvajal and Atang de la Rama.[48] Professional playwrights, composers and musicians backed these new companies with originally written plays and music. Among them we find, for example, music professor José Estella with the Rivoli Company, who had worked with Borromeo during his Cebu debut. Cowper himself had started writing English comedy sketches.[49]

In 1924, the Variety Stars and the Rivoli Co. cast would eventually merge into what was probably Cowper's greatest success in vaudeville, the Savoy Nifties, at the Savoy Theatre, Calle Echague, in downtown Manila. Frank Goulette, another veteran of the Philippine-American war and key actor in the entertainment business in the Philippines, owned the Savoy. In 1909, Goulette opened a small cinema in Manila's old walled city (Intramuros).[50] In the 1910s, he was active as manager-owner of Hispano-Filipino vaudeville troupes. In 1916, he acquired the Lyric cinema at the Escolta, downtown Manila, first in a chain of cinematographic theatres he would own across the Philippines. Around 1918, the Savoy was added to this chain, a theatre that would develop into one of the main stages of vaudeville in the capital.[51] In 1924, Goulette was the agent for Mathilde Salming, Borromeo's "Igorot" violin ragtime player.

In early May 1924, Cowper teamed up with Domingo Reantaso (aka Sunday) making the Savoy their basis.[52] Reantaso, an amateur Filipino actor-singer who had lived in New York, led his own vaudeville troupe as early as 1922 and premiered at the Olympic Stadium in April 1924.[53] As general manager and stage director, respectively, Cowper and Reantaso would make the Savoy Nifties a great success. Apart from the Nifties, Borromeo's Stadium Vod-A-Vil faced another challenge in late 1924 when another company was established at the Lux Theatre: the Smart Set. This new company lured away several of the cast

---

[48] Ad "The Lux Theatre: The Variety Stars feat. Dimples in 'A Night in Chinatown'", *MT*, 25 May 1923.

[49] Cowper was reported to be the writer of a playlet entitled "Yes! We Have No Pajamas", a word play on the popular song "Yes!, We Have No Bananas" ("Shipoff Dancers At Rivoli", *MT*, 6 Jan. 1924).

[50] "Frank Goulette, Noted Manilan, Dies In United States. Pioneer In Motion Picture Industry Of Philippines Survived By Widow, Two Children", *MT*, 20 Apr. 1927.

[51] "O'Brien Would Be Receiver. Ask Court to Take Action On Savoy Company", *MT*, 20 Dec. 1917.

[52] The debut of the vaudeville company "The Savoy Nifties of 1924" featured, amongst others, vaudevillians Katy de la Cruz, Vitang Cowper, Dionisia Castro aka Toy Toy and Annie Harris (ad "Savoy Theatre", *MT*, 2 May 1924).

[53] Ad "Manila Grand Opera Sunday Reantaso's Scandals of 1922", *MT*, 26 Feb. 1922; ad "Stadium Vod-A-Vil", *MT*, 23 Apr. 1924. On the latter date, Sunday Reantaso presented a vaudeville entitled "The Million Dollar Bibingka (rice cake)" featuring Katy de la Cruz, Vitang Cowper, Toy Toy, Annie Harris and Pacita Corrales.

of both Nifties and Borromeo's vaudeville.[54] In sum, by the end of 1924, the vaudeville scene consisted of a handful of rival companies, vying for audiences and competent vaudevillians.[55] By 1926, vaudeville's popularity had grown to the extent that it had turned into a lucrative source of municipal revenue.[56]

Cowper and Borromeo were active in the local music sheet print industry, a trade about which, unfortunately, we know very little.[57] Apart from the song "Dodge Me Daddy", they co-published "Manila Mia", and a "Novelty Waltz Fox-Trot", also composed by Borromeo in or around 1922.[58] This song, a tribute to the capital in a bricolage of musical styles, reveals another significant ingredient of a new Filipino popular art: a link between music and literature. Manuel Bernabe (1890–1960), an award-winning poet who published in Spanish and worked for the newspaper *La Democracia*, was responsible for the Spanish lyrics of "Manila Mia". In the mid-1920s, Bernabe's fame was on the rise, due to his involvement in balagtasan poetic jousts. Named after the 19th-century Tagalog poet, Francisco Balagtas, this Tagalog poetry event was first organised in 1924 at the Instituto de Mujeres, Tondo, Manila.[59] Balagtasan was a literary performance in the form of a contest between poets dealing with a variety of topics in the vernacular or in Spanish: politics, morality, modernity and so forth.[60] The balagtasan poets' literary and performance skills drew mass audiences. Balagtasan performances required the close attention of audiences, who judged the texts, their content, tone as well as performative aspects, of the competing poets. Simply put, the balagtasan format was a smash, and the genre would mark a revival of vernacular

---

[54] "New Vaudeville Company at the Lux", *MT*, 1 Oct. 1924.

[55] The competition between vaudeville troupes for good acts and vaudevillians led to a few court cases. See, for instance, the case between Luis Borromeo Lou and the owner of the Lux Theatre. "Lux Owner Asks For Injunction", *MT*, 22 Dec. 1922.

[56] John Cowper also defended the interests of cinema and theatres owners in Manila. In 1926, he successfully petitioned the Supreme Court to amend municipal ordinances that implied unfavourable taxation measures for the entertainment industry. He successfully petitioned for the reduction of tax rates for vaudeville and cine shows; see "City Board Eases Up on Vaudeville Tax", *MT*, 5 May 1926; "New Cine Tax is Declared Unjust", *MT*, 10 May 1926; "New Cine Tax Law Being Considered", *MT*, 2 Nov. 1926; "Cine License Tax Boost Held Illegal", *MT*, 29 Nov. 1926.

[57] According to Schenker (2016: 207), "Manila's popular music publishing was largely decentralized and do-it yourself".

[58] A copy of a damaged cover page of the original of "Manila Mia" is kept by the Filipinas Heritage Library in Manila. The song's score is in the Music Library of the University of the Philippines.

[59] Lumbera and Lumbera (1997: 94). On the Instituto's history, see Gardinier and Sevilla-Gardinier (1989).

[60] Almario (2003).

poetry in the mid-1920s that went in tandem and interaction with innovations in popular theatre and music, vaudeville foremost.

Borromeo recognised the popularity of balagtasan and its propagators and adopted the poetic contests as vaudeville acts, sometimes inviting the greatest among the poets themselves to perform. The verbal joust proved perfectly compatible with the vaudeville format, and they were mutually reinforcing, artistically and commercially. The poetry infused vaudeville with a modern yet distinct local cultured flavour and social relevance. For example, the modernity-tradition juxtaposition proved a fruitful balagtasan theme in vaudeville. On 20 October 1926, Borromeo held a joust at the Olympic Stadium that addressed the modern topic of "divorce", with vaudevillian Chonching Diaz defending the divorce bill and Amparing Montes opposing it "in the name of the ancestors".[61] In spite of a divorce bill drafted by the Philippine legislature in 1916, the issue of the unequal legal treatment of women in favour of men had been dragging on due to the opposition of reactionary male senators backed by Catholic organisations.[62] A week later, vaudevillians Rosa Rolda and Chonching Diaz engaged in another balagtasan, addressing the problems of modern life in the Philippines. The first vodavilista championed the "city gentleman", the second the "country gentleman". As the title infers, this joust addressed the rural-urban social and cultural divide.[63] On 3 November, a grand balagtasan was part of the playbill and the theme was the social issue of capital versus labour, in the form of an opposition between bosses (*patrono*) and workers (*obrero*).[64] In several of these poetic jousts, spectators were asked to bring in their verdict on the contestants' performances.

Another of Borromeo's literary collaborators, and one of Manuel Bernabe's main literary balagtasan rivals, was Tagalog poet Jose Corazon de Jesus, discussed in the previous chapter. De Jesus is interesting in another respect as well, as a vaudeville playwright.[65] For instance, in 1923, Borromeo Lou's Follies presented a novel musical comedy "Mga Pusa at Daga" ("The Cat and the Rat"), written

---

[61] "At The Stadium Tonight", *MT*, 20 Oct. 1926.

[62] The *Free Press* reported on the divorce bill in 1916: "The senate is receiving a large number of protests from different catholic organisations all over the islands protesting against the passage of the Guevara divorce bill." "The News of the Week", *PFP*, 25 Nov. 1916. In 1933, when writing on Filipino women, Encarnacion Alzona (1934: 89), wryly concluded on the divorce issue that "[...] no appreciable progress can be reported".

[63] "At The Stadium Tonight", *MT*, 27 Oct. 1926.

[64] Ad "Stadium Borromeo's Supreme Vaudeville", *MT*, 3 Nov. 1926.

[65] Quirino (1995: 47); "When Poet Meets Poet", *The Sunday Tribune Magazine*, 7 Mar. 1926; "Bibliografia. Cantos del Tropico por Manuel Bernabe", *Excelsior*, 20 June 1929.

by de Jesus under his pseudonym, Huseng Batute.[66] Another of Borromeo's artistic literary companions was Flavio Zaragoza Cano (1892–1965), a well-known poet and social activist from Iloilo. In January 1927, they staged a musical comedy "La Iñonguita", written by Cano as part of the vaudeville playbill. The story was taken from Iloilo life, "when a young hacendero fell in love with an Iloilo damsel".[67]

Vaudevillians, poets, music composers, playwrights and business entrepreneurs thus connected to Borromeo and his vaudeville. These people fit Joel Kahn's category of cultural brokers, who "translated" cosmopolitanism and modernity to the masses. Among these cultural brokers and collaborators of Borromeo, one significant group remains to be discussed: Spanish mestizo artists, playwrights and musical composers from the zarzuela stage. This group, with roots in 19th-century Hispanicised theatre, also helped to pave the way to a new urban culture of the 20th century.

Conocidos y afamados artistas de Manila

In the 1910s, years before Borromeo entered Manila's theatrical scene, Spanish-mestizo artists already operated across theatrical and musical genres. The stylistic boundaries were fluid between what was announced in the press as "Spanish vaudeville", "Hispano-Filipino theatre" and vod-a-vil. Since the late nineteenth century, two generations of stars of the Hispano-Filipino stage had built their own fan following, for which the Hispano-Filipino periodical *Elegancia* used the Castilian term *Liga de admiradores*.[68]

One artist moving across theatrical genres and acts, mentioned previously as introducing the Argentinean tango in a dance hall to a Cebuano audience in 1915, was Eliseo Carvajal, a kind of proto-pop star. Throughout the 1920s, Eliseo connected to different artists and companies from what became an vernacular theatre, alternately operating under the name of zarzuela, Spanish vaudeville or just vaudeville. In 1922, Eliseo and his sister Patring established firm links with the novel vaudeville scene in which Luis Borromeo was a key figure. We find the Carvajals, from October 1922 to July 1923, associated with Borromeo's Follies at the Olympic Stadium doing Spanish comic songs and

---

[66] Ad "Stadium Vod-A-Vil", *MT*, 21 Nov. 1923.
[67] "At the Stadium", *MT*, 23 Nov. 1927. For biographical details on Flavio Zaragoza Cano, see Quirino (1995: 211–2).
[68] "Srta. Pacita Sanchez", *Elegancias*, 1 Nov. 1920.

sketches.[69] In 1923, Eliseo teamed up with Pacita Sanchez, in the Variety Stars at the Lux Theatre performing a Spanish song and play repertoire.[70] Sanchez was a young and popular soprano singer, with artistic roots in zarzuela, who had been performing with the Compañía Lyric in Manila's Lyric and Sirena Theatres in the late 1910s and early 1920s. Like Eliseo Carvajal, she was crossing over to vaudeville, blurring theatrical boundaries.[71] Between 1925 and 1928, Eliseo joined the Savoy Nifties. By then, he had developed from a renowned Spanish musical and comic actor into an acknowledged vaudeville playwright, as we learn from *The Manila Times*:

> Eliseo Carvajal, the comedian at the Savoy, is an actor by heredity, that is, he has been handed down to us from a long line of thespians. […] In addition to being a comedian, a character man, tragedian and the proud possessor of a real baritone voice, Carvajal is an author and the product of his pen or, to be up-to-date, his typewriter will be presented to the Savoy fans this evening.[72]

The actor with "heredity" status obviously refers to Eliseo's parentage and their legacy in Hispano-Filipino theatre.

Another celebrated Spanish-mestizo theatre artist was Agustin Llopis, who, as a teenager, worked for Borromeo Lou's Stadium vaudeville and other troupes. In 1925, at the age of 20, he was the stage director of The Lux Peaches, the youngest ever of a new vaudeville troupe at the Lux Theatre.[73] In 1926, the *Free Press* lauded Agustin Llopis as both director of the Rivoli vaudeville company and as "veteran artist" of the islands with jazz as his pastime. [74]

Actor and singer Enrique Davila (1900–59) was no stranger to either the Carvajal family, Agustin Llopis, or to Pacita Sanchez.[75] On and off, these artists had been working together in various theatrical companies since the 1910s.[76] Like

[69] Ad "Stadium Vod-A-Vil", *MT*, 17 Oct. 1922; ad "Borromeo's Grand Concert and Vod-A-Vil Matinee at the Carnival Auditorium", *MT*, 11 Feb. 1923.

[70] Ad "Lux. Special Vaudeville", *MT*, 9 Feb. 1923.

[71] "Srta. Pacita Sánchez", *Manila Nueva*, 20 Sept. 1919. "Srta. Pacita Sanchez", *Elegancias*, 1 Nov. 1920.

[72] "At The Savoy", *MT*, 2 Sept. 1925. On Eliseo Carvajal as vaudeville playwright, see also "Nifties Shine In Good Show", *MT*, 19 Sept. 1927.

[73] "At The Lux", *MT*, 6 Oct. 1925; ad "Lux", *MT*, 6 Oct. 1925.

[74] "La historia del más joven director de escena, que buscando un amor fuera, lo halló en su misma *troupe* […]", *PFP*, 18 Sept. 1926.

[75] Written communication from Enrique Ramon Garcia Herrera-Davila III, grandson of Enrique Davila, June 2012.

[76] Pacita Sanchez, Petring Carvajal and Augustin Llopis performed "snappy Spanish songs and dances" at the Savoy Theatre as part of their vaudeville show (ad "Savoy", *MT*, 3 Jan. 1921).

Carvajal, Llopis and Sanchez, Davila was also caught by the jazz and vaudeville frenzy of the early 1920s. In August 1922, he was working with his own troupe, Bobino-Davila Co., at the Olympic Stadium. The following month we find Davila at the Lerma Cabaret with another new vaudeville troupe: the Electric Jazz Company and the Radiant Radio Girls.[77] Like his contemporary and colleague Eliseo Carvajal, Davila developed into a playwright of comic sketches.[78] Davila is immortalised in a score "Jazz Electrico", published in 1922, by composer Francisco Buencamino and Alberto Campos, the latter the writer of the lyrics.[79] The two men dedicated the song to their friends and well-known artists from Manila (*conocidos y afamados artistas de Manila*): the earlier mentioned Pacita Sanchez and Enrique Davila. Composer Francisco Buencamino (1883–1952) was a Tagalog zarzuela music composer and teacher at Ateneo de Manila and Centro Escolar University.[80]

Spanish-mestizo actors and playwrights thus fully embraced the modern vaudeville format and "jazz" without cutting their links to "Spanish theatre". For example, in 1925, the Compañia Bohemia staged "light operas in English, Spanish and Tagalog, from well-known writers" at the Lux Theatre. The Compañia's musical director was Professor José Estella, who had been working with Borromeo in 1921 and later with the Rivoli Theatre vaudeville company.[81]

Luis Borromeo and the competing vaudeville companies relied heavily on the Hispano-Filipino theatrical and musical repertoires and its Spanish-mestizo casts. Spanish comic sketches, songs and dances recurred in the vaudeville bills. For example, on 25 July 1923, Borromeo's Stadium Vod-A-Vil presented "Viva España", a show in honour of the Spanish colony of the Philippine Islands. Several

---

[77] Ad "A Musical Revue of 9 Real Entertainers", *MT*, 8 Sept. 1922; ad "Lerma Cabaret Tonight", *MT*, 9 Sept. 1922.

[78] "At The Lux", *MT*, 13 Feb. 1924. *The Manila Times* reported on Enrique Davila as "author of many funny sketches [...]", who had written a musical sketch "An unexpected legacy". In 1924, Davila and Sanchez had joined the Variety Stars at the Lux Theatre.

[79] "Jazz Electrico", dedicated by composer Francisco Buencamino and lyricist Alberto Campos to artists Pacita Sanchez and Enrique Davila, c. 1922. The artwork for this score is clearly inspired by F. Scott Fitzgerald's original cover for his short stories book, *Tales of the Jazz Age*. A copy of the score is held by the Filipinas Heritage Library.

[80] Quirino (1995: 50).

[81] The Compañia Bohemia cast consisted of, amongst others: Carmencita Llopis, Liliana Aldeguer, Nenita Farias, Carmen Metz, Manolita Rodriquez, Bebe Didiers, Agustin Llopis, Manoling Infante, Carlos Tolosa, German Quiles and Jose Lope. See "Vod-A-Vil At The Lux", *MT*, 11 Aug. 1925; "'Los Bohemios' Drawing Crowds To The Lux Theatre", *MT*, 16 Aug. 1925.

actors from the local zarzuela stage featured, including Patrocinio Carvajal, Mora Bara and Manoling Infante, performing Spanish Couplets and Duets.[82]

Sensitive to the Filipino Hispanicised elite's contradictory hostility to American popular culture, Borromeo also parodied the alleged juxtaposition between Spanish and American culture in his vaudeville shows. For instance, in early 1927, he staged a musical contest between "zarzuelistas and jazzers".[83] This topical juxtaposition was repeated later that year, this time announced as: "Kundiman, our melodious native song, will take the measure with Jazz, the so-called up-to-date music from Yankeeland."[84] In this vaudeville show, Atang de la Rama, "the recognised Kundiman Queen of the Orient" was in charge of a team of *kundiman* singers. Maggie Calloway, "the only Jazzy Jazz Girl ever developed in Manila" was leading the "jazzers". As the following chapter will demonstrate, modern music and modern women like Atang de la Rama were important contributors but also disputed markers of the new popular culture. Representing a modern Filipina, female vodavilistas challenged ideal types of the popular modern woman in the Philippines, such as the widely celebrated Queen of the Carnival.

---

[82] Ad "Stadium Vod-A-Vil Tonight", *MT*, 25 July 1923.

[83] "At the Stadium Tomorrow", *MT*, 4 Jan. 1927.

[84] "At the Stadium", *MT*, 23 Nov. 1927.

Chapter 5

The Biggest Noise

Shifting away from Luis Borromeo and his peers in theatre and literature, this chapter takes a broader view of the new popular culture, the Filipino pop cosmopolitanism in motion. I will do so from the angle of the ambiguous reception of popular dance music, from the viewpoint of elite participation in popular culture, and by looking at debates about the modern Filipina, returning, in the final section, to Borromeo and vaudeville and questions about the theatre's legitimacy.

A significant element marking the new popular culture was music. Borromeo, and a host of respected Filipino classical music composers, created hybrid dance music, jazz with a Filipino tinge. The first two sections of this chapter deal with this music and its composers, starting with resistance to jazz, followed by a section on the cosmopolitan orientation of composers, musical practice and the representation of Filipino jazzy dance music.

So far, elite participation in popular culture has been highlighted from the rather narrow perspective of Borromeo, who originated from a provincial, upper-class family. The preceding chapters have revealed that sections of the elite opposed foreign forms of popular culture; it would, however, be wrong to conclude that they had no interest in popular culture at all. If we wish to understand the scope of elite interest in popular culture, the institution of the Manila Carnival makes a good case. The elite actively participated in the Manila Carnival with official American consent, and it is here that we witness a (sometimes awkward) mix of politics, patriotism, trade promotion, commercial entertainment and a civilising mission.

It is perhaps not surprising that new and contesting models of the modern Filipina were articulated most strongly and visibly in the realm of popular culture. Competing role models emerged on the vaudeville stage and at the Manila Carnival in the guise of female vaudeville stars and beauty queens, respectively. Both the vodavilista and the Carnival Queen represented localised models of the global, modern woman of the jazz age; one frivolous and free, the other educated and cultured.

The closing section examines how, in the face of charges of presenting banal entertainment, Borromeo and other vaudeville entrepreneurs attempted to produce and claim their novel theatre as classy entertainment. These efforts involved an ongoing battle against fleetingness and a struggle for legitimacy.

Yes, We Play No Jazz

In 1922 and 1925, two anthropology students, under supervision of Professor Otley Beyer, deviated from the trodden path of researching Filipino folk music and dance. They attempted to study the social meaning of jazz in the islands. What seemed a daring attempt to examine controversial popular dance music, turned into a half-hearted effort. We thus learn little from the two small studies about how Filipino jazz fans experienced the music or for example the dance hall. The studies do however inform us about academic biases. For example, obvious research sites, such as the dance hall, where people, including students, danced the Black Bottom or the Camel Walk, remained a no-go zone for anthropological inquiry. One of the student anthropologists, presumably of American origin, also proved poorly informed about Spanish and Hispano-Filipino music and theatre conventions. He boldly remarked that "During the Spanish regime in the Islands, very little, if any Spanish music was taken up by the Filipinos."[1] This student's brash, unsubstantiated statement was simply in support of the American imperial project that denied a Spanish cultural legacy in the Philippines. He could not emphasise enough the popularity and significance of jazz among Filipinos as proof of successful "Americanisation" bringing "happiness" to the colonised.[2]

Three years later, in 1925, another student attempted a more distanced, scholarly approach to understanding jazz. To measure its social meaning, he compared jazz to the stock of folk songs used in the agricultural cycle of planting and harvesting in the Philippines. This student failed to reach any explicit conclusions on the purpose of jazz in society, but he was aware of the social tensions it evoked. He did refer to the moral condemnation of jazz as articulated by Jorge Bocobo, Dean of the College of Law, UP.[3] Bocobo, known for being a moral guardian, reactionary and nationalist, stated that "Jazz is making the

---

[1] General Paper No. 95 THE DEVELOPMENT OF POPULAR MUSIC IN THE PHILIPPINES by Edward Taylor. Manila, 1922. H. Otley Beyer collection, National Library of the Philippines.

[2] Ibid.

[3] The student likely referred to a speech held by Bocobo in 1923 at the American Chamber of Commerce in Manila. See Schenker (2016: 292).

biggest noise in the Philippines." [4] The dean related that the way people twisted and shook their bodies to this dance music was as if they were possessed by demons, thus suggesting the dance and music went against the Catholic faith. [5]

At that time, academics, whatever their research experience or status, obviously had no monopoly on discussing jazz as modern times social phenomenon. The press took its share. For example, in 1924, we find an eloquently written article "A Hymn To The Great God Jazz", by a young, educated Filipino, Mariano B. Ezpeleta, published in the *Free Press*. While the title suggests that the author was in favour of jazz, his message was a more complex mix of great concern about modernity, the loss of religiosity and laxity of morals due to materialism and commercialism. Ezpeleta explained "the jazz" in the context of modern life itself. "The modern music, the jazz, is abnormal. It typifies the riotous ecstasy of youth and spring. It is a sheer, exuberant, instinctive, unreasoning, careless joy over the satiating flatness of contemporaneous life." [6] He predicted that this "musical aberration" would fade away as society would transform. So although he assessed jazz as a token of moral degeneration, Ezpeleta remained optimistic about the direction of Philippine society.

Also in 1924, a young Filipino intellectual by the name of Raymundo Bañas, a school teacher in Sampaloc, Manila, published a book on music and theatre in the Philippines. [7] This publication is of interest for three reasons. Firstly, it was the first attempt to document the careers of contemporary Filipino artists and Filipino musical and theatrical conventions from a distinct patriotic perspective. Secondly, as a manual on proper cultural taste, the book can be read as a response to the challenges of the modern jazz age. As such, it is a perfect example to put into practice Frederick Cooper's call to look for a "discourse of modernity". [8]

---

[4] General Paper No. 96 THE UTILITARIAN THEORY OF THE ORIGIN OF MUSIC (with Philippine examples and illustrations) by Dominidor B. Ambrosio […] Manila, Oct. 1925. H. Otley Beyer collection, National Library of the Philippines.

[5] Bocobo also spoke publicly against gambling and boxing and was among those influential people who opposed the dance halls. "El Decano Bocobo contra el juego en el boxeo", *Nueva Fuerza*, 28 Jan. 1922.

[6] "A Hymn to the Great God Jazz", *PFP*, 19 Jan. 1924.

[7] Bañas's introduction reads: "As true citizens, we should be acquainted with the history of the musical developments in the Philippines. To students desirous of knowing the character and growth of Filipino music, this book, I think, will be the fountain of inspiration. The study of the lives of eminent artists is as essential as the study of the achievements of great heroes and patriots" (Bañas 1924: v).

[8] Bañas's directions for proper taste went as far giving guidelines in his Chapter 6 on how to properly conduct an orchestra.

Finally, the book became a handbook for those interested in Filipino music and theatre for decades to come.[9]

Unlike the UP anthropology students, Bañas collected scores, including some of the "jazz" music he detested.[10] He approached experts in the field of classical music and vernacular theatre: Father Eulogio Sanchez, the former Director of the Colegio de Niños Tiples (boys choir) of the Manila Cathedral; Captain Pedro Navarro and Lieutenant Alfonso Fresnido of the Philippine Constabulary Band and historian Manuel Artigas, librarian of the Philippine Library and Museum in Manila. Bañas also contacted composer and director José Estella. Estella and Fresnido are of special interest here.

Like the UP students, Bañas had implicit derogatory assumptions about jazz music. He associated jazz with noise, cultural intrusion, alienation and cultural loss.[11] As a genuine music lover and patriot, Bañas sought Estella's musical authority to canonise original Filipino composers. In the early 1920s, as active member of the prestigious Asociación Musical de Filipinas (est. in 1907), Estella was among a group of Filipino composers who attempted to revive and promote "Filipino music". The Asociación's repertoire was eclectic and included Hispano-Filipino music, such as kundiman, and European opera and classical music.[12] Drawing from what was probably a private communication between the two, Bañas related Estella's attitude towards jazz: "To the introduction of the jazz representation in the Philippines, he is absolutely against. He said that it kills the growth of our native music."[13]

Estella might have expressed himself in this way, Bañas remained completely silent on Estella's engagement with modern popular culture, jazz music, movies and vaudeville. The latter's artistic border-crossing activities could not have been a secret to Bañas, or the public. In addition to his activities for the highbrow Asociación Musical de Filipinas, Estella worked for the vaudeville stage and silent movies theatres throughout the 1920s. He was with Luis Borromeo when the latter debuted with his eclectic musical programme in Cebu in 1921. And, for example, in January 1924, we find Estella working at the Rivoli Theatre, Manila, with two Russians dancers on their tour of the Orient. On this occasion, Estella

---

[9] An illustrated updated edition was prepared as late as 1969 and published in 1975 under the title *Pilipino Music and Theater*.

[10] The National Library of the Philippines in Manila keeps this corpus of sheet music in the Raymundo Bañas collection.

[11] Bañas (1924: 16).

[12] Ibid., pp. 19–20; "Annual Concert Pleases House", *MT*, 5 Dec. 1922; "Filipinas Concert Big Success", *MT*, 8 Nov. 1925.

[13] Bañas (1924: 115).

teamed up with Harry Langum's Jazz Band, the Rivoli's orchestra.[14] As explained in the previous chapter, in the early 1920s, Estella also composed and performed modern popular dance music and was co-writer of musical comedies in Spanish and English for one of Manila's major vaudeville troupes, the Variety Stars at the Lux Theatre.[15] Moreover, Estella had outspoken views on the significance of Philippine music and musicians, quite different from Bañas. In a 1924 article "Why The Philippines is the Italy of the East" (¿Por qué Filipinas es la Italia del Oriente), published in the periodical *The Independent*, this composer imagined Manila as a musical node in the "East". In a cosmopolitan and patriotic spirit, referring to the many Filipinos musicians travelling and working abroad, he underscored the capital's transnational significance as a cultural magnet as well as a centre from which cultural energy radiated into Asia and beyond.[16]

Estella was referring to the many Filipino musicians professionally active across Asia since the turn of the 20th century.[17] Contemporary sources suggests he did not exaggerate. In the Straits Settlements, the Federated Malay States and in Medan, North Sumatra, wealthy peranakan Chinese and Europeans hired local funeral and municipal town bands staffed by Filipinos.[18] As early as 1904, Filipino musicians are mentioned in relation to one of the precursors of modern Malay opera, *bangsawan*, in the Straits Settlements.[19] In the late 1910s, Filipino opera singers performed successfully in the main opera houses in Spain, Italy

---

[14] "Shipoff Dancer at Rivoli", *MT*, 6 Jan. 1924.

[15] In 1923, Estella, for example, collaborated with Eliseo Carvajal co-writing vaudeville sketches and composing for The Variety Stars at the Lux Theatre, see ad, *MT*, 23 Feb. 1923; ad, *MT*, 29 May 1923. In 1924, Estella was responsible for the musical adaptation of a vaudeville sketch written by Antonio Fernandez, probably also by The Variety Stars at the Rivoli Theatre, see ad "Rivoli", *MT*, 8 May 1924. In 1925, Estella was director of the Hispano-Filipino vaudeville troupe, the Compañia Bohemia, at the Lux Theatre, staging "light operas" in English, Spanish and Tagalog. See "Vod-a-vil At The Lux", *MT*, 11 Aug. 1925.

[16] "¿Por qué Filipinas es la Italia del Oriente (Por el Prof. José Estella) HOJAS DE MI CARTERA", *The Independent*, 1 Nov. 1924.

[17] On this "diaspora of Filipino musicians", see Schenker (2016: 115–6, 121–6, 132–56).

[18] On the presence of Filipinos as professional musicians in the Netherlands Indies and the Straits Settlement, see for example: "Manilla-Band te Medan", *De Sumatra Post*, 9 July 1906. On the funeral bands, see "The Late Mr. Tan Keong Saik", *The Straits Times*, 6 Oct. 1909; "The Late Mr. Lee Cheng Yan", *The Straits Times*, 3 June 1911. "S.R.E.(v.) Concert", *The Straits Times*, 28 Sept. 1916; "Notes from Malacca", *The Straits Times*, 30 Oct. 1916; On the role of Filipinos as musical educators in Singapore, see "82 Years in Tune", *The Straits Times*, 9 Aug. 1982. Filipinos also staffed the Selangor State Band, see Tan (1993: 81).

[19] In 1904, *The Straits Times* mentions the "Manila band of the Wayang Kassim". "Seremban Notes: A Merry Christmas at the Negri Sembilan Capital", *The Straits Times*, 27 Dec. 1904. At the turn of the century, Wayang Kassim was one of the most famous Malay opera (*bangsawan*) troupes in the Straits Settlements and Netherlands Indies, see Wan (1988: 42–3).

and the US.[20] One of the reasons why Filipinos were in demand as musicians was that they had enjoyed musical training, often at young age in Church, could read notes and, thus, could reproduce music from scores.[21] Musicologist Fritz Schenker has pointed to two other important forces that explain why Filipino musicians appeared as professional musicians from Surabaya to Shanghai in dance halls, hotels, movie theatres and on shipping lines. The first was the global economic slump that hit the Philippines after the First World War, one that drove Filipinos, including musicians, to seek employment elsewhere. The second was that Filipino musicians operated in a competitive, yet Asia-wide expanding dance music industry in which they were willing to work for lower wages compared to European, American or other Asian musicians.[22] What Estella was trying to say was that these transnational flows underscored the musical ability and, therefore, the civilised character of Filipinos. As an explicit cosmopatriot, Estella seemed hardly plagued by notions of cultural loss and the dangers of jazz.[23] Instead, he took great pride in the musical cosmopolitanism of his countrymen. And among those "musical heralds and missionaries" he had in mind, his acquaintance Luis Borromeo was likely included.

Lieutenant Alfonso Fresnido, the conductor of the Philippine Constabulary band (PC band), conductor since 1923, was also interested in modern popular dance music. As martial march music formed one of precursors of the syncopated music that came to be known as ragtime and eventually jazz, it is not strange that the PC band performed novel dance music like "jazz" or to appear with Luis Borromeo's vaudeville at the Olympic Stadium in 1922. The PC Band's association with jazz and vaudeville came into question in 1925, when the band's eclectic choice of repertoire turned into a public controversy. In October 1925, Fresnido received the order from the commander of the Philippine Constabulary, General Rafael Cramer, to stop programming "jazz". The General had received

---

[20] A brief and random sample of Filipino musicians abroad in the 1910s and early 1920s offer the following artists: Classical pianist "Guadalupe Silvestre", toured the US in September 1917, "Guadalupe Silvestre", *PFP*, 15 Sept. 1917; Nemesio Ratia, baritone, headed for the Metropolitan Opera House of New York in 1918, "Rizal Day in New York City", *PFP*, 2 Mar. 1918; opera singer Leopoldo Brias performed successfully in Barcelona, see "Brias Scores Hit In Opera—Local Singer Acclaimed In Barcelona Debut", *MT*, 5 Apr. 1918. In 1924, Luisa Tapales performed in the European capital of opera, Milan. "Noticias de la Semana", *PFP*, 19 Jan. 1924.

[21] Tan (1993: 81). On the role of the Church in musical education in the 18th- and 19th-century Philippines, see Irving (2010).

[22] Schenker (2016: 129–30). A comparable group of competent and competitive Asian musicians originated from Goa. Their number was much smaller compared to Filipino musicians working abroad.

[23] The term cosmopatriot is borrowed from Jurriens and de Kloet (2007).

complaints from "intellectual quarters" that the band played "street music", an euphemism for jazz, during its weekly public performances at Luneta Park, in the heart of Manila. General Crame wished to prevent the band from "descend[ing] to the level of the six-piece jazz orchestra found in amusement place in and near the city". Fresnido was allowed to perform classical music and operatic selections and "other highbrow stuff".[24] Concerning the new repertoire, the general released to the *Free Press*: "Yes, We Play No Jazz." This was the General's reference to a 1923 Broadway jazzy hit "Yes! We Have No Bananas", a song that, in 1924, had led to a "Yes,-we-have-no-bananas-craze" in the Philippines and Indonesia. In the Philippines, the song's popularity was mainly due to a Tagalog-English parody performed by Natalia Morales, chorus girl of Borromeo's Follies.[25] The socially heterogeneous music-loving audience of the PC band received the general's order with mixed feelings. Some listeners were reportedly tired of listening to classical music. This group included thousands of young music fans that regularly attended the Band's weekly Luneta live performances especially to hear the band play modern popular dance music.

Focused on fixing and categorising musical genres and conventions, Bañas was unwilling or possibly unable to recognise and acknowledge the border-crossing musical practices of Filipino composers and band conductors, like Estella, Fresnido and Borromeo. While Bañas presented Estella simply as an anti-jazz protagonist, Luis Borromeo was ignored altogether as a great patriot and cultural hero. This is particularly striking as Borromeo was at the height of his career and popular across the Philippines. In 1932, seven years after his initial publication, it was difficult for Bañas to discount jazz and Borromeo altogether, given his popularity and that of jazz among Filipinos. In a piece on Filipino music published in the periodical *The Music Lover* (est. 1931), Bañas, using the past tense, stated that: "Borromeo Lou [...] was once the jazz king in the Philippines [...]." And Bañas predicted that "[t]he jazz music [...], will not have a lasting life in the Philippines".[26]

---

[24] "Wagner Ousts Irv Berlin With Constabulary Band", *MT*, 20 Oct. 1925.

[25] The song gained popularity in Manila followed by the provinces, likely through phonographic recordings. The *Free Press* reported in 1923: "Everybody is playing it, singing it, humming it, whistling it." Natalia Morales's parody ran: "Yes, we have no bananas, we have no bananas today, we have *bagong* and *hipon* and *piscao* galore. We have everything else that is found on the shore. We have *balots*, have you tried them? Live *manoks* inside them. Oh, yes, we have no bananas today." Balot is the local street food delicacy *balut*, a boiled chicken embryo, or "live manoks (chickens)" in the shell, referred to in the song. "Further Glimpses of Our Local Stage Beauties", *PFP*, 5 Nov. 1923. See also "La Vida Social en Jolo", *PFP*, 26 July 1924; "News of the Week", *PFP*, 24 Oct. 1925; ad "Borromeo Lou", *MT*, 22 Aug. 1923.

[26] Bañas (1932: 11).

Bañas thus could not accept that the masses had embraced the unpatriotic jazz, and could not see that this jazz was not simply mimicry of an American model. This is exemplified in the love of Filipinos, both cultural producers and consumers, for Afro-American syncopated music. In musical practice, artists blurred distinctions and crossed the boundaries between the classical and the modern/popular, and between the alien and the local, creating modern Filipino dance music.

Syncopation-loving Public

Amidst moral controversy about jazz and measures to curb patronage of the cabarets since the late 1910s, many Filipinos continued to enjoy modern dance music and it inspired composers. The dance halls flourished and phonographic records were in demand. A newspaper report from 1922 gives us a rare impression of the consumption of commercially recorded music and musical taste in Manila:

> Your record stands against you. Manilans, as being a syncopation loving public with a taste for 'Blues' in your makeup somewhere!
>
> [...] the greatest stilling dance record out is—anything with 'Blues' in it.
>
> [...] In fact, unless the record is jazzy, it enjoys less than 80 per cent of total sales in Manila, at least 60 per cent being enticing dance records.
>
> [...] Of the 300,000 discs sold in Manila for the entire Philippines last year, was the one you bought (there was about one per unit of population) jazzy, classical or 'Blue'.[27]

It remains unclear what percentage of recorded music was "local", even if it was labelled as "jazz" or as "blues", let alone how to situate the aforementioned genres stylistically.[28] For example, the music Borromeo claimed as "oriental jazz" was a stylistic hybrid. From the sheet music that survived, we learn that he experimented with both Filipino-Hispano genres and Afro-American syncopated music, attempting to fuse them into something novel. This practice was by no means unique to the Filipino king of jazz. A host of Filipino composers associated with classical music and Hispano-Filipino genres, such as kundiman, showed an interest in creating Afro-American dance music with a Filipino tinge. This led to

---

[27] "'All Manila Has Got the Blues' about Manila's musical tastes", *MT*, 1 June 1922.

[28] In 1927, a reporter for *Graphic* documented the sales of phonographic records by six music shops in downtown Manila for a single day. He concluded that an average of 575 pieces were sold a day, of which approximately 170 were jazz and 450 kundiman—or "classical pieces". On this basis, the reporter, not void of an outspoken anti-jazz bias, concluded that jazz was on its return in the Philippines. See "Kundiman Giving the Jazz the Air. Filipinos Surrender to Gentler Strain of Native Songs", *Graphic*, 29 Oct. 1927.

hybrid genres that, by the mid-1930s, were accepted as mainstream Filipino and not associated with Afro-American or Latin American music.

Some of Borromeo's "jazzy" songs are modelled after the commercialised ragtime style of the Tin Pan Alley popular music industry of New York City. These songs have no connection with Hispano-Filipino genres. A good example is "Dodge Me Daddy", a straightforward ragtime that Borromeo wrote with John Cowper in 1922.[29] Most of Borromeo's compositions, however, offer a more complex picture of musical assemblage, and this also counts for the music of many of his Filipino contemporaries. A closer look at Borromeo's compositions shows that the scope of his musical interest rested in Afro-American syncopated dance music, Hispano-Filipino dance music, and later, Latin American music. The genres included ragtime, kundiman, tango, waltzes and, in the mid-1930s, rumba.

Borromeo's compositions reveal that he was out to create a new style that he could present as modern as well as patriotic: the oriental jazz he was propagating. One example of such an attempt is Borromeo's celebrated patriotic composition "My Beautiful Philippines", published in 1920. In the US, the song was advertised as an "oriental foxtrot", indicating that this was different from American jazz.[30] Of all his compositions, he felt most proud of this song. Borromeo revealed to the *Free Press* that it "[…] aims to picture the languorous tropical beauty of the Philippines and its fascinating daughters". According to the weekly, Borromeo believed that "he has produced a strain of real melody and succeeded in giving somewhat realistic representation in music of the theme he chose".[31] As to the musical style of this particular song, Fritz Schenker, with some reservation, places the song in the convention of popular Afro-American ragtime compositions, as adopted by the Tin Pan Alley music industry:

> "My Beautiful Philippines" has an introduction, a minor section that transitions to a major key and then has a little trio section that goes back to the major key chorus. The first part of "My Beautiful Philippines", where the vocals first come in, might sound vaguely Filipino or exotic to listeners both because of its minor scale and because the left hand plays a repeated rhythm that is a stereotyped Native American/African drumming sound ("**One**-and **two**-and **three four**"). But then it moves into something else.[32]

---

[29] "Dodge Me Daddy" (Louis F. Borromeo). Home recording by Fritz Schenker (piano) performed from original score, 2015.

[30] Ad "Vocal Style Complete Song Rolls", *The Music Trades*, 19 Mar. 1921.

[31] "Said to be making one thousand pesos a week on vaudeville stage in the United States", *PFP*, 18 June 1920.

[32] Personal email communication with Fritz Schenker, 19 Feb. 2013.

This "something else" is Borromeo's incorporation of the Hispano-Filipino *habanera*/tango musical style, which gives the song its "Filipino" tinge.[33] Another example of musical experimentation is "Manila Mia", presented as a "Novelty Waltz FoxTrot" composed by Luis Borromeo for piano. The song starts with a brief, syncopated rhythmic introduction, typical of ragtime, followed by a waltz. Halfway towards the song's end Borromeo moves back to a ragtime rhythm.[34]

This practice of pasting fragments of Afro-American dance music with Cuban habanera, waltzes or tango was by no means restricted to Borromeo. A random look at sheet music published in the period 1915–30 reveals many Filipino composers experimenting with Afro-American dance music, particularly the foxtrot and the one-step, as well as the tango, indigenising and transforming these genres into a Filipino music. A great, yet difficult to establish, number of these songs, many written for piano, were published as sheet music. We also find them as shellac records. In the newspaper ads, we find this hybrid music categorised by the phonographic industry as "himno-one step", "Filipino Foxtrot", "tango-foxtrot" and "Filipino Tango-Foxtrot". Without exception, the composers were professionals, who had received sound musical training and who were highly regarded by the music-loving upper classes in Manila, Cebu and Iloilo. These artists earned their living from composing and publishing music, sometimes commissioned, and from performing and teaching music.

Among these composers, renowned during her time but now forgotten, was Amelia Hilado. In 1920, Hilado was an accomplished classical pianist connected to the Conservatory of Music, UP.[35] Her composition "Tristezas", labelled a "Filipino foxtrot", is likely a relatively early example of what seems to have been common practice among Filipino/a composers of the late 1910s: to alternate a habanera/tango rhythm with ragtime inspired sections.[36]

A far more famous composer than Hilado was Francisco Santiago, graduate of the Chicago Conservatory of Music and, in 1924, also a piano instructor at the UP Conservatory of Music. Santiago is remembered as one of the pioneering revivalists and champions of modernising Philippine folk music, the kundiman

---

[33] "My Beautiful Philippines" (Louis F. Borromeo). Home recording by Fritz Schenker (piano) performed from original score, 2015.

[34] "Manila Mia" (Louis F. Borromeo). Home recording by Fritz Schenker (piano) performed from original score, 2015.

[35] "Nueva Profesora de Piano", *PFP*, 20 Mar. 1920.

[36] "Tristezas" (Amelia Hilado). A copy of the score of this hybrid Filipino dance composition is held by the Filipinas Heritage Library. Home recording by Fritz Schenker (piano) performed from the original score, 2015. For a detailed musicological analysis of "Filipino Foxtrots", see Schenker (2016: 223–9) who states that "Filipino foxtrots regularly employed a habanera rhythm" (2016: 224).

genre in particular.[37] Santiago's interest in Afro-American music, however, came earlier. The year 1908 marked his breakthrough as composer of his first Afro-American-inspired syncopated dance song, a two-step dedicated to the queen of the 1908 Manila Carnival, Pura Villanueva.[38] In 1920, he published his composition "Balintawak", which was advertised as a "Nuevo Fox Trot Filipino" (A New Filipino Foxtrot) with the words written by poet and novelist Jesus Balmori. That same year, the studio band of phonographic corporation Victor recorded Santiago's instrumental foxtrot composition "Malayan" in Camden, New Jersey. In 1929, also recorded by Victor, was Santiago's one-step "Aray!" (Ouch!), a title that might have been inspired by Tagalog writer Corazon de Jesus's exciting poetry on the intricacies of modern social dancing and the dance hall.[39]

Another example of a professional, modern dance music composer is Francisco Buencamino. Otherwise known for his Hispano-Filipino compositions, Buencamino wrote a series of popular dance songs, including the earlier mentioned "Jazz Electrico", published in 1922. The latter song is a mix of ragtime and habanera, more an eclectic than hybrid composition.[40] In 1924, department store Becks advertised the latest batch of Columbia records, offering new "Filipina Dance Records". This collection included foxtrots, one-steps and waltzes, all composed by respected Filipino musicians such as Buencamino, Francisco Santiago, José Estella and several others.[41] Given the popularity of modern dance music and the upsurge of original Filipino dance compositions,

---

[37] Castro (2011: 32–4).

[38] About Santiago's early syncopated piece *The Music Lover* related: "This music, with the possible imperfection, gave the composer a little monetary success but an overwhelming popularity in the metropolis and in the provinces." "Who is Who Among Filipino Musicians", Nov. 1931, p. 14.

[39] Ad, *PFP*, 1 May 1920. For details on "Malayan", see: http://adp.library.ucsb.edu/index. php/matrix/detail/700009153/B-23958-Malayan.

[40] "Jazz Electrico" (Francisco Buencamino). Home recording by Fritz Schenker (piano) performed from original score, 2015. The published score of Jazz Electrico contains the following list of Buencamino's compositions: "Reverie—FoxTrot"; "De Mi Patria—Foxtrot"; "Bajo Los Cocoteros—FoxTrot"; "Visayas—FoxTrot"; "Mi Bandera—Himno-One-Step"; "Golden Rose—FoxTrot"; "El Collar de Sampaguita—One-Step"; "Gemidos de Mi Alma—Danza Filipina"; "La Ilonga—Valse-Canto"; "Colores y Luces—One-Step"; "¡ Amor!—Cancíon Filipina para canto y piano"; "La Princesa de Kumintang—Tango-FoxTrot"; "Patria—Danza Filipina para canto y piano".

[41] Among the records released by Columbia was José Estella's foxtrot composition, "Visayan Moon", recorded by an unknown Filipino orchestra. See ad "Filipina Dance Records", *PFP*, 29 Mar. 1924. The other composers were: Leon Ignacio; J.S. Hernandez; C. Jacobe; Ramos; Tereso Zapata; David Cruz; Jose Z. Rivera; Facundo Perez; M. Nazario; Juan Silos Jr.; J. Roxas; J.B. Balingit; Era Cervantes; C. Jacobe. See also ad "Becks", *PFP*, 22 Nov. 1924.

it is not surprising to find Borromeo featuring the dance music of these local composers at one of his vaudeville shows at the Olympic Stadium in 1924.[42]

That Afro-American dance music was in vogue among the upper classes can be inferred from the fact that social associations commissioned songs to composers. Among the earliest examples found is the "Carnival Two-Step", composed in 1908 for the Manila Carnival Association by Captain Walter H. Loving, an Afro-American and the first conductor of the Philippine Constabulary Band. This two-step was "the official piece of music to be played on all occasions in which royalties appear in public", that is, the queen of the carnival. Copies of the song were for sale.[43] In 1922, Castilian periodical *Manila Nueva* reported on a foxtrot written by Adolfo Lopez, composer and playwright of the vernacular theatre, dedicated to the Bohemian Sports Club of Manila entitled: "Llevame al Bohemian. Couplet FoxTrot" (Take Me to the Bohemian. FoxTrot Verse). Lopez also provided the Spanish lyrics.[44] In 1924, a composer by the name of H. Hocson wrote a song entitled "Foxtrot Kahirup", commissioned by the recently established Kahirup society in Manila, a Visayan upper-class association with Ilongan speaking members.[45] The song was not announced in Ilongan, but in Spanish, as a "new foxtrot of modernistic making" (nuevo fox-trot de factura modernista). Poet Jesus Balmori provided the Spanish lyrics.[46]

Let me finish this discussion of the musical practices of Filipino composers and the far from exhaustive list of compositions with the work of renowned composer Benito Trapaga and that of poet Jesus Balmori as lyricist.[47] As early as 1918, Trapaga published a foxtrot entitled "Hispano-Filipino".[48] By the mid-1920s, he had become an accomplished phonographic recording artist for Parlophone, a German recording company.[49] In 1927, Hispano-Filipino periodical *The Independent* lauded Trapaga as "Famoso compositor de varias

---

[42] "News of The Week", *PFP*, 21 June 1924.

[43] "Captain Loving's Carnival Two-Step", *MT*, 29 Feb. 1908; "Carnival Two-Step", *MT*, 6 Mar. 1908.

[44] "Llevame al Bohemian. Couplet FoxTrot", *Manila Nueva*, 11 Sept. 1920. Zarzuela singer-actress Adelina Amoros had encouraged and inspired Lopez to write this song. Like Lopez, Amoros had a background in Spanish zarzuela and, like Lopez, straddled this latter theatrical form and the vaudeville stage in Manila in the 1920s.

[45] "Kahirup Celebrates With Brilliant Dance", *PFP*, 12 Nov. 1932.

[46] "Foxtrot Kahirup", *PFP*, 9 Feb. 1924.

[47] For details on Trapaga's professional career, see Schenker (2016: 191–204).

[48] "Noticias de la Semana", *PFP*, 21 Dec. 1918.

[49] "Hay Dinero en las Placas Fonograficas", *PFP*, 11 May 1929. In 1927, Parlophone changed hands from the German Lindström company to Columbia Graphophonic Company.

piezas popularísmas en toda Filipinas".[50] Among Trapaga's recorded compositions were "Favre", "Manila Jazz Scandal" and "Seti". The latter song was advertised in 1924 as an "oriental foxtrot".[51] Responsible for the Spanish lyrics for "Seti" was, again, "Poet laureate" Jesus Balmori, aka Baticuling. Hence, Balmori was a prolific popular songwriter and in this way he also contributed to Spanish literature in the islands.[52]

These musical practices indicate different things. Firstly, as said before, they indicate that the divide between serious classical and popular dance music composer was largely illusory. The "big noise" was not that big after all, given the active participation of composers of name in modern popular music. Secondly, as argued by Schenker, these "classical" composers understood the market value of the "Filipino foxtrots", the "cheap dance music" they produced. Modern dance music was simply in demand.[53] Thirdly, these examples of border-crossing musical experimentation, as Castro observed in her study of Philippine nationalism and music, show the "fluidity of those melodies through the folk, popular, and art music realms".[54] It shows that the stylistic characteristics of the modern popular music known as jazz were flexible. Filipinos, from the literal and proverbial margins of the American empire, were also defining, discussing, composing and performing jazz on their own terms. The problem of how to categorise or label this hodgepodge repertoire of modern popular dance music variously labelled as "oriental foxtrots", "Filipino foxtrot" and so forth, was solved by the record companies who simply classified it as "Filipino dance music". This genre flexibility is exactly the type of "messiness" that Nicholas Evans conceptualised in his study on jazz in the US:

> [...] from World War I into the 1920s, the lines separating what we now call jazz, ragtime, Tin Pan Alley, vaudeville music, and other relevant forms were quite unclear. Moreover, the distinctions between 'authentic' jazz and its alleged commercial corruptions were seldom recognized. This lack of clarity was not due to a failure of analysis; rather, the current, rigorous

---

[50] "Popular Compositor. Benito Trapaga", *The Independent*, 15 Jan. 1927. Trapaga was also manager of the musical department of Parsons Hardware Company in Manila.

[51] Trapaga's songs were not necessarily played and recorded by Filipinos. "Manila Jazz Scandal", for example, an instrumental song composed in the Afro-American syncopated style and orchestrated with wind instruments, banjo and violin, was performed by the German saxophone band Orchester Dobbri who did many recordings for the Lindström concern in Germany. Side 1: "Manila's Jazzy Scandal – Foxtrot". Por Benito Trapaga. Orchester Dobbri. Parlophon, B 33594. Carl Lindstrom AG. Courtesy of Fritz Schenker.

[52] Ad "Seti", *PFP*, 1 Mar. 1924.

[53] Schenker (2016: 184–204).

[54] Castro (2011: 32).

differentiation of these musical forms is retrospective. The emergence of 'jazz', as such, was a messy, uneven, discontinuous process that itself was unclear—then, if not also now.[55]

As Bañas's opposition to jazz makes clear, notions of "messiness" or the possibility of a Filipino style jazz was not at all widely shared. And in 1923, a certain Professor Edward Damon Huff, former American military man, composer, musician and director of the Huffle's Syncopators at the Lerma dance hall, claimed to have been the first to introduce "genuine jazz" in the Philippines. He kept up with the latest popular numbers "receiving advanced scores from New York as fast as they are issued […]".[56] According to this narrow and essentialist cultural view, the one and only source for authentic jazz was and remained the United States.

Finally, and at a different level, although the new Filipino popular dance music referred to modern American popular music, its Afro-American origins remained obscure. Filipino composers, including Luis Borromeo, were silent on Afro-American composers, their contribution to ragtime and jazz and influence. If jazz was discussed by Filipinos, it was "white" jazz composers who were mentioned, praised and criticised, particularly Paul Whiteman and Irving Berlin.[57] It was as if Filipinos had no knowledge of or access to the music of influential Afro-American composers and performing musicians, for instance Scott Joplin and James P. Johnson, who published sheet music, piano rolls and phonographic records. One explanation for this bias is that the phonographic corporations released dance music predominantly performed by white bands, such as Paul Whiteman's symphonic jazz orchestra. This was the jazz received by audiences in Asia.[58] The Netherlands Indies is an interesting deviation. Due to the many Filipino jazz bands working in hotels, restaurants and other venues, and Filipinos working for Malay opera troupes as musicians and jazz dancers, jazz came to be associated with Filipinos and Manila.[59] In the Indies "Manilla jazz" was a household term indicating a certain musical genre performed by Filipinos, or simply a Filipino band, enhancing the stereotype of Filipinos as natural-born jazz musicians.

---

[55] Evans (2000: 14).

[56] "Accomplished Musician And Musical Specialist Making A Hit At Lerma Park", *MT*, 22 Apr. 1923.

[57] "Kundiman Giving the Jazz the Air. Filipinos Surrender to Gentler Strain of Native Songs", *Graphic*, 29 Oct. 1927. In this latter anti-jazz article, an anti-Semitic undertone can also be detected. The Filipino author stereotyped Irving Berlin as a "prudent Jew".

[58] Schenker (2016: 352–4).

[59] On Filipino jazz musicians in the Netherlands East Indies, see Möller (1987: 20–1).

In the case of Borromeo, ignorance of Afro-American music is difficult to imagine, as he had lived in the US and had worked in the vaudeville industry, one of the main sites where "jazz" developed. Yet, he also took white jazz performers and their music as model.[60] To uphold social prestige and to espouse the racial hierarchy, the Hispanicised Filipino upper classes avoided association with Afro-American culture. It explains why judge del Rosario, in his tirade against modern dances, was so negative about "Cuban blacks". From a Hispanicised Filipino perspective, Cuban blacks apparently represented the worst imaginable form of "blackness", due to their proximity to Spanish culture. In short, "blackness" was a very sensitive topic in the colonial Philippines, close to a taboo, and this was reflected in popular music.[61]

The Hispanicised Filipino elite did not, however, form a unified front, nor were they against all forms or expressions of popular culture. In fact, the opposite was also true, as illustrated by the active participation of the elite in the popular Manila Carnival.

The Manila Carnival

In 1925, an anthropology student from the University of the Philippines summarised the ambiguous reception of the popular cultural institution of the Manila Carnival in society:

> Some people say that the carnival is another excuse to dance in large scale, and to indulge in the pastime of choosing a "Queen". They maintain that the extreme popularity of carnivals is another product of the new culture. However, there are still some optimists who look upon carnivals as a sign of progress in a new means of enhancing the culture of the people. In other words, they believe that Carnival is of constructive, rather than destructive value.[62]

---

[60] During his Cebu debut in 1921, Borromeo performed Paul Whiteman's hit "Whispering". Ad "BORROMEO LOU & CO", *Nueva Fuerza*, 19 July 1921.

[61] In May 1920, the *Philippine Free Press* broke the taboo briefly with a discussion on social intercourse between Filipinos and Afro-Americans. The discussion reveals how some Filipinos internalised the colonial racial hierarchy in a highly contradictory manner. See "Presents a Stirring Defense of the Negro", *PFP*, 15 May 1920; "On Filipinos Marrying Negro Women", *PFP*, 15 May 1920; "The Question of Filipinos Marrying Negro Women. A Young Filipina, a School Teacher, Tenders Some Very Good Advice on Subject", *PFP*, 22 May 1920. In her study on the Philippine Constabulary Band, Talusan (2004: 519, 522) notes that while American observers represented the band as a "civilised" band of native Filipinos, the Afro-American background of conductor Walter H. Loving was never mentioned. A silence on Loving's ethnic background, or race in the contemporary context, prevailed.

[62] Tagalog report No. 563. "Filipino Amusements, Past and Present" by Nativad Zacarias, Manila, 2 Mar. 1925. H. Otley Beyer Collection, National Library of the Philippines.

As the young Filipino indicated, the carnival was a popular institution marking a "new culture" of contradictory and even conflicting meanings. This assessment, as will be set out below, was the outcome of the Manila Carnival being an in-between cultural institution, where amusement met with promoting commerce and industry, and where secular popular culture mingled with elite politics and a civilising mission.

The Carnival was the brainchild of Captain George T. Langhorn, an American who, for several years, had been aide-de-camp to several Governor Generals in the islands. Founded in 1908 as a corporation, the Carnival association's official aim was to organise an annual fair to promote the islands' commerce, industry and tourism. The Philippine assembly backed the project, granting the association ₱15,000 in its first year.[63] For the next years, the association would successfully seek private funding through stockholding. Right from its inception in 1908, the Carnival association actively promoted the fair domestically as well as abroad, inviting foreign delegations from coastal China, Japan and Southeast Asia to witness the economic opportunities offered in the islands.[64] Business firms and social clubs from the Philippines kept large tents at the fair's grounds, equipped with lounging chairs and other comforts and reserved boxes at the auditorium for the purpose of socialising and businessmen to network.[65]

The Carnival might have been a secular event driven by commercial interests, its schedule was not completely arbitrarily chosen as it kept pace with the religious calendar of Catholic Manila.[66] The fair's opening year was a direct commercial success.[67] More than a decade later, in 1920, interest in and numbers of *provincios* visiting the fair had grown to the extent that it was difficult to find accommodation in Manila in early February.[68] Another decade ahead, in

---

[63] "Carnival Now Corporation", *MT*, 17 Jan. 1908; "Fifteen Thousand for the Carnival", *MT*, 25 Jan. 1908.

[64] "To "Whoop 'Er Up" Along China Coast. Carnival Association Planning to Enliven Interest in the Big Fiesta – C.W. Rosenstock Offers Services", *MT*, 25 Jan. 1908.

[65] "The Social Circle", *MT*, 3 March 1908; "Carnival Chatter", *MT*, 4 Dec. 1924.

[66] To avoid interference with special church services and religious festivities surrounding Holy Thursday, Good Friday and Easter Sunday, the fair was held shortly before Lent in early February. *The Manila Times* aptly formulated this time framing as follows: "While carnival has been established in the Christian world to let the flesh indulge in merriment before Lent, the Manila Carnival has added to it an industrial and commercial exposition wherein may be exhibited the products of the islands as well as those imported from abroad for sale here." "Carnival and Fair Open Tomorrow", *MT*, 25 Jan. 1929.

[67] "THE FIRST CARNIVAL A GREAT SPECTACULAR AND FINANCIAL SUCCESS", *MT*, 28 Feb. 1908.

[68] "Carnival Notes", *MT*, 30 Jan. 1908; "Some Carnival Visitors Lacked Accommodations", *PFP*, 7 Feb. 1920.

1930, the *Sunday Tribune Magazine* reported that "[f]or sixteen days and nights, Manila's 400,000 cosmopolitan population will share its fun with the thousands from the different provinces and nearby countries who will make their pilgrimage this year to the "'frolic ground of the Far East'".[69]

The Carnival association was a professionally-run organisation divided into different sections, such as publicity, finance, subscriptions, transportation and buildings, alongside sections on music, decoration and sports. In the original 1908 elected association, American officers dominated the board: 39 Americans against 7 Filipinos. The latter were recruited from the political elite, particularly from the Partido Nacionalista, and included Manuel Quezon and Sergio Osmeña, who was the association's acting Vice President.[70] After 1915, the board composition changed significantly in favour of Filipino participation. This was due to Governor General Harisson's policy of promoting Filipinisation of officialdom. In 1917, Cipriano E. Unson, Secretary of the municipal board of the city of Manila, and Secretary of the 1916 Carnival, was elected Director General of the 1917 carnival. The first Filipino to hold this office.[71] From then on, Filipinos assumed leading positions within the Carnival. Between 1920 and 1930, Manuel Quezon chaired the association. And in 1922, Nacionalista and newspaperman Arsenio Luz became the association's director. These men put their stamp more prominently on the fair in terms of organisation and in the selection of the fair's attractions.[72]

From the perspective of the political elite, the carnival offered popular entertainment with a civilising potential. In 1921, conscious of their elite status and political and economic power, the board of directors explicitly and, in a distinctively patronising manner, recommended that the carnival should appeal to "the masses", not just the elite. The board announced a programme of free amusement to broaden the Carnival's constituency.[73] This generous offer of free

---

[69] "The Philippine Carnival", *Philippine Magazine*, Jan. 1930, no. 8. In 1914, attendance dropped compared to 1913. In 1919, the fair was not held on account of the First World War. In 1930, the Great Depression left its mark. On the whole, however, the fair's attendance showed a steady increase. In 1929, carnival attendance reached over 700,000 spectators, a generous sevenfold increase since 1909. "'Frolic Ground of the Far East' All About the Annual Manila Carnival", *Sunday Tribune Magazine*, 9 Feb. 1930.

[70] "The Philippine Carnival Association", *MT*, 27 Feb. 1908. The other Filipinos included: Felix M. Roxas as Assistant Director-General; Mauro Prieto, also Assistant Director-General; Arcadio Arellano (in charge of music); Dr. Ariston Bautista y Lim (board of directors); Felipe Buencamino Jr. (Assistant secretary).

[71] "News of The Week", *PFP*, 25 Mar. 1916.

[72] For an overview of all the officers elected between 1908 and 1931, see "The Philippine Carnival", *Philippine Magazine*, Jan. 1930, no. 8.

[73] "The Next Carnival", *MT*, 22 July 1921.

amusement was part of the association board's belief that the Carnival served to uplift the masses and could strengthen social cohesion. In 1927, Quezon, Luz and other prominent Filipino Carnival board members reiterated that "[...] all agreed in the view that the Manila carnival is a worthy enterprise not only for the entertainment and civilizing influence it furnishes but also for the social contact it affords to the people and the incentive it gives to business in general".[74]

The Carnival's attractions were varied and lured people from all walks of life. Recurring annual features included the fair's opening with a two-hour grand army parade from downtown Manila to Luneta Park. The annual parade usually included the US army and navy, the Philippine Constabulary, and a host of other social associations who presented artistic floats. These associations could be those of university students, of cigarette factory workers or theatrical groups, such as in 1922, when Borromeo Lou's vaudeville company joined the procession.[75] The parade was reviewed by the highest American and Filipino officials, and by the Carnival Queen and King.[76] Other frequent features were historical mock battles (The battle of Santiago de Cuba, the battle of Little Big Horn and so forth); sporting competitions and demonstrations at the carnival grounds itself (volleyball, indoor baseball, basketball, soccer); and musical performances (band contests, opera shows). There was also a number of attractions varying from year to year: magic and illusion performances, acrobatic feats, animal shows, radio and cinematographic shows, vaudeville shows, Spanish theatre and a host of other obscure features. In 1922, Luis Borromeo hired a "concession" on the Carnival grounds for his Borromeo's Palace of Jazz, a dance hall with live "jazz" performances. The following year, he performed in the Carnival's auditorium, which had a dance floor "larger than Madison Square Garden" that could cater for thousands of dancers "without the usual congestion".[77] By 1924, the Carnival had grown into such a commercial success that 20 theatre owners in Manila petitioned the Governor General, claiming that the Carnival association engaged in unfair competition.[78]

---

[74] "Over 1,000,000 Persons Visited Manila Carnival", *MT*, 6 Mar. 1927.

[75] "Opening Parade of the Carnival Draws Big Crowds", *MT*, 5 Feb. 1922.

[76] For example in 1926, Governor General Wood, Senate President Quezon, Senate Speaker Roxas and other high officials were present. "Thousands See Carnival Parade This Afternoon", *MT*, 2 Feb. 1926.

[77] "Good Crowd on Hand When Carnival Gates Were Thrown Open This Morning", *MT*, 4 Feb. 1922; ad "Borromeo's Grand Concert and Vod-A-Vil Matinee at the Carnival Auditorium", *MT*, 11 Feb. 1923; "Thousands Gather at Opening of Carnival Auditorium, Pay Court to Queen Aspirants", *MT*, 23 Jan. 1923.

[78] "News of The Week", *PFP*, 8 Mar. 1924.

Let us not overstate the elite's power or control over the Carnival and its audiences. We have little clues about how non-elite Filipinos experienced the Carnival and what it meant to them. Rare examples on participatory pop by the "people" found in the local print press do indicate that they had their own ideas. For example, in 1925, an unknown number of spectators used the event to express anti-clericalism. The following year, and in anticipation of the coming fair, Manila's Chief of Police sent out circulars warning the public that it was prohibited "by the ordinances of the city of Manila for any person to appear in masquerade costumes, simulating the garb or dress of a minister, priest or member of any religious order within or without the Carnival grounds".[79] Also fascinating is that the Carnival, so strongly associated with commerce and secular entertainment, was used by spectators to publicly display their religious devotion. Puzzled by this, one observer noted: "What many Carnival enthusiasts can't understand is how religion can mix with fun and frolic. In the portion assigned to commercial and industrial exhibits is a booth where a certain group holds nightly open air services, singing and praying."[80]

One of the most popular attractions of the Manila Carnival was the annual election of the Carnival beauty queen. As an iconic symbol of Philippine nationhood, the beauty queen featured in debates about the modern woman (*mujer moderna*), competing with alternative models embodied in female vodavilistas and flappers. In brief, the beauty queens were as much part of the new and confusing popular culture as were the stars of the vaudeville stage.

Vodavilistas, Queens and Flappers

In her study on the representation of motherhood in Cebuano literature, Hope Sabanpan-Yu points out that a significant social transformation among women took place in the Philippines during the American era: the entry of wealthy and middle-class women into the public arena.[81] This development was triggered by two interplaying forces. The first is that, under the Americans, Filipinas were offered new educational and professional opportunities leading to upward social mobility and financial independence. The second is that with social mobility and global cultural flows, new models for womanhood, like the "modern girl", spread and developed in the islands.[82] As Alys Eve Weinbaum writes in general terms: "debates over the Modern Girl always relied upon and reworked notions

---

[79] "Carnival Masqueraders Not To Mock Priests", *MT*, 29 Jan. 1925.
[80] "Carnival Sidelights", *The Sunday Tribune Magazine*, 12 Feb. 1933.
[81] Sabanpan-Yu (2011: 30).
[82] Alzona (1934: 53–94).

of modernity and femininity (and, consequently, also ideas of masculinity) in specific locales. [...] the Modern Girl was a harbinger of both the possibilities and dangers of modern life".[83] In the early 1920s Philippines, two localised and competing models of the modern woman evolved in the popular culture realm: the vodavilista and the beauty queen.[84] As a new breed of female stars they manifested themselves visibly on stage as well as in the print press.

As popular stars, the vodavilista and queen celebrities of the 1920s were preceded by Spanish-*mestiza zarzuelistas* of the Hispano-Filipino theatre of the late 19th and early 20th centuries. We find zarzuelistas frequently portrayed in the illustrated Hispano-Filipino printed press of the 1910s.[85] One of those early stars was *señorita* Pacita Sanchez, one of the "conocidos y afamados artistas de Manila", mentioned in Chapter 4, who moved back and forth between zarzuela and vaudeville. In contrast to the Hispanicised zarzualistas of middle-class backgrounds, who had received musical and theatrical training, many of the new female vaudeville stars were teenagers from working-class to middle-class backgrounds, who had enjoyed little formal musical education. In 1923, the *Free Press* reported about some of the biggest stars: "Hanasan is fourteen, Dimples fifteen, Miami sixteen, Katy seventeen, Vitang eighteen and Amanding nineteen—all in their teens!"[86] In contrast to zarzuela, vaudeville had become big business. In 1923, six leading female stars were reported to be "each earning as much as assistant department secretaries of the Philippine cabinet, and more than many bureau chiefs".[87] More significant than their earnings, and setting them apart from earlier female zarzuela stars, were associations of vodavilistas with the modern Filipina.

Like the zarzuelistas before them, we find the new vaudeville stars exposed in popular illustrated Spanish language periodicals, like *Elegancia, Manila Nueva*, and bilingual Tagalog-English magazines like *Liwayway, Graphic* and *Excelsior*. The periodicals refreshed its readership on the vaudevillian's modern and cosmopolitan fashion styles, from hair dress to smoking habits. Many

---

[83] Weinbaum et al. (2008: 8).

[84] In her study of the representation of Filipina and femininity in English literature in the Philippines, Cruz (2012: 25, 66–109) identifies four recurring icons of Filipina femininity that emerged in the 1930s: the Spanish mestiza Maria Clara, the Westernised Filipina coed, the romantic barrio girl and the pre-colonial Indian. The earlier emergence of the Filipina flapper and the Carnival Queen seems to suggest a more complicated and shifting set of partly overlapping women role models.

[85] These included Spanish-illustrated magazines such as *Manila Nueva* and *Elegancias*, and in the bilingual Tagalog-Spanish satirical weekly *Kikiriki*.

[86] "Further Glimpses of Our Local Stage Beauties", *PFP*, 5 Nov. 1923.

[87] Ibid.

of these young women resembled flappers. "Flapperism" represented a new way of femininity, of autonomous, boyish girls who engaged in a consumer-oriented lifestyle pronounced by modern Western clothing, bobbed hairstyles, cigarette smoking and jazz dancing. The image of the flapper went global thanks to American novelist F. Scott Fitzgerald's short stories, published in the early twenties. Of greater influence in terms of introducing flapper to the world were Hollywood films and advertisements for fashionable consumer items, such as soap, shoes and make-up, a package Weinbaum fittingly designated as "Modern Girl commodities".[88] By 1927, the word flapper was established in the Filipino vocabulary without a vernacular equivalent. One observer stated that flapper was frequently and wrongly equated with the Tagalog equivalent for the American term "flirt": *kiri*. A flapper, according to this contemporary, was primarily defined by bobbed hair, short skirts, shiny socks, a graceful body and an energetic aura, a lifestyle in short.[89]

Vodavilistas offer us impressions of what Priti Ramamurthy labels "aesthetic hybridity", local adaptations to globally current fashions.[90] Newspapers and magazines offer us images of bobbed-hair Filipinas in a variety of dresses: southern Spanish-style (Andalusian) attire, Malay Islamic style dresses typical for the southern Philippines, the latest European fashion or orientalist "yellow act" garb.[91] Seldom do these young women appear in the Hispano-Filipino butterfly sleeve dress, the *terno*. The terno represented femininity and respectability, reserved for the patriotic Filipina, the Manila carnival beauty queen foremost.[92]

---

[88] Weinbaum et al. (2008: 18). A good example of a motion film that defined flapper is the film *Bare Knees*, a story of "the girl of today" that was screened at The Palace Theatre in Manila, alongside a vaudeville show, in November 1929. The advertisement read:

> "*Bare Knees* specifically deals with advent of the last word in modern flappers into a small, narrow town. Naturally, at first the natives are scandalized at her actions. She does the 'black bottom', to pep up a sleepy party, she smokes cigarettes in public, she 'necks' in an open roadster on the main highway—but whatever she does in public, her private life being beyond reproach morally [...] . The flapper is not only exonerated but extolled [...]." "New Vaudeville Troupe At Palace", *MT*, 19 Nov. 1929.

[89] "Kiri Nga Kaya Ang Kahulungan Ng Salitang 'flapper'", *Graphic*, 22 Oct. 1927.

[90] Ramamurthy (2008) discusses the "aesthetic hybridity" of female Indian cine stars of the 1920s and 1930s.

[91] For this "Aesthetic hybridity", see for instance the picture of Señorita Sofia Lota, aka Miss Cotabato, modern bobbed hair and dressed in "traditional" Malay-style attire from the southern Philippines who was a member of Borromeo Lou's Stadium vaudeville cast. Lota's special act was Moro dances from Mindanao. See *The Independent*, 4 Sept. 1926. For the variety in fashion styles of other Filipina vodavilistas, see the illustrations in *Graphic*, 2 July 1927; 9 July 1927; 6 Aug. 1927; 31 Dec. 1927.

[92] Roces (2004: 45–6).

In the mid-1920s, the Carnival Queen contest had become a popular culture institution, attracting thousands of spectators who participated in elaborate welcome and coronation ceremonies, including a parade, a mass ball, all dramatised enactments of royal grandeur.[93] Without exception, candidate queens were young, single, educated and recruited from wealthy provincial families. The 1908 Queen of the Oriental of the first Manila Carnival, Pura Villanueva from Iloilo, set the standard.[94] In January 1923, Catalina "Neny" Apacible, daughter of a physician and patriot from Batangas, was elected queen. Luis Borromeo honoured her with a song "Neny Mine" (a blues), with his Grand Vod-A-Vil at the Carnival Auditorium.[95] Like the female stars of the vaudeville stage, the queen candidates were popular celebrities. Candidates were expected to present themselves to the public during parades, balls and other occasions. For example, the 1926 Carnival Queen appeared at Luis Borromeo's Supreme Vaudeville at the Olympic Stadium. The show was staged for the benefit of victims of a natural disaster in Batangas.[96] The print press also played a significant role. The publicity department of the Carnival association distributed pictures of the candidate queens that were reproduced in the newspapers and also sold separately as postcards.[97]

Fleeting Social Butterflies

Like the traditional balls and banquets of the upper classes, the Carnival beauty contest turned into a special occasion for elite social networking. After 1926, networking acquired characteristics of intra-elite rivalry when the Carnival association changed the local contest into a Miss Philippines beauty pageant of national significance. The contest encouraged competition between elite families, such as provincial Senate delegates, all eager to show or claim publicly their prominent place within Philippine society and the nation through their queen candidates. Apart from gaining social prestige, participation opened up possibilities for families to link to economically and politically powerful elites

---

[93] See for example "The Philippine Carnival—1917", *PFP*, 10 Feb. 1917.

[94] Pura Villanueva was a frequent contributor to the press in Iloilo and known as an eloquent public speaker on women emancipation. See "Queen is Here", *MT*, 20 Feb. 1908.

[95] Ad "Carnival", *MT*, 11 Feb. 1923. For an overview from 1908 to 1939 of the elected queens and Miss Philippines and their social backgrounds, see Nuyda (1980).

[96] Ad "Stadium", *MT*, 17 Nov. 1926.

[97] In 1927, the *Free Press* published a special "Filipina beautiful" pictorial album targeting the "gentlemen" audience. See "They Are All Here – Miss Province Candidates for the Title of Miss Philippines. A brief letter from director general of Philippine Carnival Association", *PFP*, 12 Feb. 1927; "Little Stories of Carnival Beauties", *PFP*, 19 Feb. 1927; ad "Forty-Six Pictures", *PFP*, 5 Feb. 1927.

in the political centre, Manila. The Carnival Queen beauty pageant transformed into an elite marriage market for provincial upper-class families.

With these economic, political and social interests at stake, nepotism, corruption and conflict between contesting families took off. In 1927, tensions over the Miss Philippines election ran so high that Carnival director Arsenio Luz was forced to cancel the national beauty contest for the next season.[98] The year 1928 did not see a contest, the carnival was skipped altogether. The year hiatus did not stop "the money route" or discussions about the purpose of the competition. In 1931, this led one law student to publicly state: "has not beauty contest in the Philippines traduced into a vulgar practice, attended by fraud, commercialism and lasciviousness?" The answer given was an affirmative, as this critical observer gave a few examples of the money politics involved, including the bribing of juries. The highly politicised nature of the beauty contests also led this same observer to emphasise the fleetingness of modern popular culture:

> [...] Is it to make women more popular? And what use is this to her mission in the world? Does a carnival queen command a higher price in the marriage market? Perhaps so—but when we go deep into the moral roots of things, we shall find that the desire to be in the limelight, is the ambition of the flappers, the ultra-modern, the jazz-lovers and the fleeting social butterflies on our modern society.[99]

In this critique, he also stated that the queen candidates served "to glorify Filipina womanhood".[100] The Carnival Queen contest was indeed what Colleen Ballerino Cohen has observed for similar beauty competitions elsewhere; namely, that the event "[...] showcase values, concepts, and behavior that exist at the center of a group's sense of itself and exhibit values of morality, gender, and place [...]. The beauty contest stage is where these identities and cultures can be—and frequently are—made public and visible."[101] Debates about "money politics" surrounding the contests and reports about the humiliation of candidates did not alter the ideal of the popular beauty queen as a model for Philippine womanhood nor as a symbol of nationhood. It was simply too strong an image, with roots in

---

[98] "Over 1,000,000 Persons Visited Manila Carnival. Annual Festival Was A Success Notwithstanding Extraordinary Expense Bill, Says Luz", *MT*, 6 Mar. 1927.

[99] This same critical onlooker also offered examples of the financial sacrifices wealthy *provincios* undertook to have their daughters participate in the contest. He also gave examples of the humiliations these girls experienced. One story was circulated of a wealthy *hacendera* from Sugarlandia who had mortgaged his estate "thus reduced to proprietary servitude, just to make her [his daughter, PK] the proud possessor of a diadem"; "The Evils of Beauty Contests Brought Out By Osmena Medalist", *Progress*, 26 Apr. 1931.

[100] Ibid.

[101] Ballerino Cohen et al. (1996: 2).

both patriotism and religion. The educated, cultured Filipina embodied in the Carnival Queen was married to what Hope Sabanpan-Yu describes as the ideal of the Filipina as the "venerated Madonna", representing "the image of love, kindness, passivity, and nurturing".[102] It should not be concluded, however, that the queen candidates were necessarily docile women confined to the home. For example, Pura Villanueva, the first Carnival Queen, a supporter of Filipina enfranchisement since 1906, was president of the Asociación Feminista Ilonga, later president of the Women's Club of Manila and, in the 1910s, editor of a leading women's magazine.[103] Moreover, it should be emphasised that the ideal of the beauty queen was predominantly a male one, and rarely challenged by women themselves.

Flapperism, as indicated above, contested these ideals of womanhood, but indirectly. This challenge became apparent, for example, in October 1924, when the *Free Press* solicited for articles on the theme of the "principal defect of modern Filipino youth". Essays poured in. The authors did not so much address the topic of youth, but gender role models. The prize-winning piece, written in a paternalistic, accusatory style, was by a young man who claimed that flapperism was "alien to a true Filipino woman".[104] The flapper as model for the modern Filipina was also questioned publicly in October 1925 in Manila's Olympic Stadium, in a grand balagtasan dedicated to the mujer moderna. A picture in the *Tribune* shows the venue packed with an estimated 8,000 enthusiastic spectators, many from surrounding provinces Rizal and Bulacan. The two contenders were among the foremost poets of the day: Jose Corazon de Jesus and Florentino Collantes.[105] *The Manila Times* summarised the joust as "De Jesus defended the girl of yesterday and extolled her modesty, while Collantes championed the cause of the flapper."[106] According to the *Sunday Tribune*, the audience voted en

---

[102] Albina Peczon-Fernandez as cited by Hope Sabanpan-Yu (2011: 6).

[103] Other suffragist were Paz Marquez and Trinidad Fernandez, Carnival Queens of 1912 and 1924 respectively. See Roces (2004: 31, 38).

[104] "What Is Principal Defect of Modern Filipino Youth?", *PFP*, 25 Oct. 1924.

[105] Collantes was staff member of Tagalog daily *Ang Watawat*. "Maria Clara or Miss de los Santos?", *PFP*, 17 Oct. 1925; "La Mujer Moderna *defiende* al *defensor* de la Mujer Antigua", *PFP*, 24 Oct. 1925.

[106] "Old Fashioned Girl Gets Decision At Stadium", *MT*, 19 Oct. 1925. The *Sunday Tribune* noted that the audience was touched by de Jesus's "melodious pulsations of his stanzas" and "irresistible beauty of his verses" and he was reported to have "the advantage of popular sentiment to his favor". "'Balagtasan'. A Debate in Poetry Without a Parallel in the Annals of Literature", *Sunday Tribune*, 25 Oct. 1925. The success of this joust possibly inspired pioneering film maker Jose Nepomuceno to produce the film *La Mujer Filipina*. Released in 1927, this silent film's plot was based on the modernity-tradition juxtaposition, see Tofighian (2008: 88–9).

masse against Collantes's plea for "the cause of the wayward"; that is, an appeal for women's autonomy from male and family control.[107] Sometimes, women themselves spoke out in public in this male-dominated discussion, and not necessarily in favour of girls' autonomy and modern fashion. For instance, in 1926, the beauty queen of the province of Misamis, North Mindanao, Ampaya M. Neri, Alumna of Philippine Women's and Scholastic College, stated that: "women suffrage is nothing more than a synonym of divorce and flapperism—cosmetics, bobbed hair and short skirts—and all that are revolting to our customs and traditions".[108] In short, socially deviant flappers, and I would argue vodavilista, were antitheses of the ideal of the virtuous beauty queen.

Reminiscent of the crusade against the dance halls ten years earlier, flapperism eventually moved from a cultural to a socio-political issue in 1927, labelled by *The Manila Times* as a "war against bobbed hair".[109] A Catholic college in Manila prohibited its female students from having the modern hairstyle. Inspired by this, some provincial authorities enacted legislation outlawing bobbed hair.[110] By the end of 1927, a small group of members of the Philippine lower house, all gentlemen from the provinces, introduced bills in the legislature to stop social dancing in schools, to prohibit bobbed hair and to regulate the dance halls.[111] One cannot help but wonder whether these *provincios* and *politicos* of high moral standards were not the category of men sardonically depicted by Jose Jesus de Corazon in his Tagalog poetry on the dance hall.

Flapper and vodavilista sometimes converged, as in the case of the example of Elisabeth Cooper, known among vaudeville fans as "Dimples", who debuted as a teenager with Luis Borromeo's vaudeville around 1922. From an early stage in her vaudeville career, controversy surrounded Dimples, blurring a distinction between her off and on stage appearance. She was haunted by rumours of affairs with wealthy but aged vaudeville patrons, the landowner types ridiculed by poet

---

[107] "'Balagtasan'. A Debate in Poetry Without a Parallel in the Annals of Literature", *Sunday Tribune*, 25 Oct. 1925.

[108] "Woman Suffrage Synonym of Divorce and Flapperism", *Graphic*, 31 Dec. 1927.

[109] "Bobbed Hair Illegal in Whole Province", *MT*, 31 Mar. 1927.

[110] For example, in March 1927 the provincial board of Occidental Negros was the first to pass a resolution, see "Bobbed Hair Illegal in Whole Province", *MT*, 31 Mar. 1927. In July 1927, Pascual B. Azanza, Democrata lower house representative from Samar, proposed a bill imposing a tax on bobbed hair. "Tax Urged by Solon", *MT*, 18 July 1927.

[111] These politicos were popularly known as "blue law sponsors", the adjective "blue" apparently referring to their moralist stance. "Blue Law Sponsors", *Graphic*, 13 Aug. 1927.

de Jesus.[112] In 1924, in defence of her honour and reputation, she filed a suit against newspaper *La Revolucion*, which had reported that she had been hugged and squeezed by an admirer.[113] In 1926, a kissing scene, the first of its kind in a local film production *Tatlong Hambog* (The Three Beggars or the Arrogant Three) produced by Jose Nepomuceno, caused the threat of court action for alleged indecency.[114] In 1930, Dimples retired from vaudeville and was reported to have married a sailor and moved to New York. Rumours circulated that she had succumbed to tuberculosis on her way to the US. In 1930, however, the public was not aware that she had become General Douglas MacArthur's secret lover, commander of the Philippine department of the US Army in Manila.[115]

The lack of any formal education or experience in music or theatre proved no hindrance to gaining entrance to the vaudeville stage or to achieving stardom. In 1927, asking what made Dimples one of the most popular and highest paid vodavilistas, the periodical *Graphic* wrote: "She cannot sing; she is not beautiful. But she is a marvelous dancer and has a strong and contagious charm and personality."[116] The *Free Press* quoted "a great authority" of the vaudeville stage, Luis Borromeo, on the recruitment criteria. He attributed "to beauty 75% of the success of a star", and "[…] that 50% of the success of a song or a singer is due to a becoming dress".[117] The skimpy attire aroused criticism from reactionary corners. For example, in 1925, the Bishop of Cebu denounced Dimples' garb and that of the chorus girls of the Savoy Nifties vaudeville troupe.[118]

---

[112] See for example "Dimples, la florecida de eterna sonrisa...", *PFP*, 14 Nov. 1925. This article stated that "she has a lot of admirers, who very much want to know her secret, particularly that of her voice, as well as that of a rich landowner in the south, who is behind this beautiful stage performer in Manila".

[113] "News of The Week", *PFP*, 4 Oct. 1924.

[114] "Local Cinema Companies Move Ahead. Ambitious Plans for Philippine Pictures Call New Crop of Stars Into Limelight", *PFP*, 24 Aug. 1935.

[115] Upon his return to the US in 1930, MacArthur arranged for Dimples to follow him to Washington. In 1934, he broke up the relationship and attempted to send her back to Manila. She refused and gained the unsuspected backing from a local reporter who had learned of the relationship that MacArthur anxiously had tried to keep secret. The reporter threatened to go public with the facts. This forced MacArthur to settle with Dimples. On this affair, see Manchester (1978: 144–5, 156); see also Perret (1996: 147–8, 167–70). Dimples unsuccessfully sought a career in Hollywood and committed suicide in Los Angeles in 1960. There is inconsistency in the sources about her age, both when she first met MacArthur and when she died. If she was 15 in 1923, as reported by the *Free Press*, then she was 22 when she met MacArthur in 1930 and 52 in 1960.

[116] "With Our Filipino Stage Stars", *Graphic*, 31 Dec. 1927.

[117] "Behind The Scenes With Our Vaudeville Stars", *PFP*, 27 Oct. 1923.

[118] "Isn't This Terrible", *PFP*, 16 May 1925; "Estan, o no, bastante des vestidas?", *PFP*, 22 Aug. 1925.

In May 1925, Dimples was a flapper in a vaudeville comedy entitled "Footloose", "built around the jazzy adventures of Gloria, a modern girl who married for fun and repented at leisure".[119] Capitalising on the success of American short-story writer F. Scott Fitzgerald's *Flappers and Philosophers* (1920) and *Tales of the Jazz Age* (1922), *The Manila Times* simultaneously started a short stories sequel in collaboration with one of the capital's major vaudeville companies, the Savoy Nifties. The paper had obtained the exclusive publishing rights for this series, a sequel to *The Flapper Wife* by the American author Beatrice Burton.[120]

Like the bailerina, vodavilistas evoked the curiosity of Filipino male writers, reflected in literature, for example in the Tagalog short-story series "Tala ng Vod-A-Vil" (Star of the Vaudeville) by Juan N. Evangelista, published in *Liwayway* in 1923.[121] Another approach to the new phenomenon was a "behind the stage" view, adopted by male journalists who took a human-interest perspective in female vaudevillians and their newly found stardom.[122] Newspapers were also keen to focus on the vodavilistas' troubled private lives: parental control, marriages and elopement.[123] The story of teenage vaudevillian Juanita Antido represents all of these issues. Her father, Victor Antido, denied her an education in favour of a stage career. In the early 1920s, she toured China and British Malaya with

---

[119] "Savoy Nifties Play To Crowds In Flapper Wife", *MT*, 31 May 1925.

[120] Ad, *MT*, 27 Aug. 1925.

[121] Juan N. Evangelista "Tala ng Vod-A-Vil", *Liwayway*, 2 June 1923; 16 June 1923; 23 June 1923; 30 June 1923.

[122] "Behind The Scenes With Our Vaudeville Stars", *PFP*, 27 Oct. 1923; "Further Glimpses of Our Local Stage Beauties", *PFP*, 3 Nov. 1923; "Vaudeville Star's Heart Won by Lowly Laborer", *PFP*, 15 Jan. 1927; "Do Acting and Marriage Mix?", *PFP*, 27 Mar. 1935.

[123] A matter drawing public attention was the elopement of vodavilistas. For example, in 1925, Carmen Salvador, stage name Miami, a minor and another "graduate of Borromeo Lou's vaudeville university", as one newspaper related, was abducted by her lover. *The Manila Times* reported on the case for months, documenting intrigue after intrigue. See "No Action Taken Yet in Abduction of Local Star", *MT*, 6 July 1925; "Driver Is Accused with Del Rosario", *MT*, 12 July 1925; "Miami Is 'Insulted' Files Complaint Against Alleged Abductor", *MT*, 29 July 1925; "Miami's Abductor Sentenced to 2 Years, 11 Months", *MT*, 25 Oct. 1925; "Dimples Touches Off Bomb Under Miami in Court", *MT*, 24 Aug. 1925; "Miami Denies Writing Love Letter to Abductor", *MT*, 4 Nov. 1924; "Miami's Wooer, Abductor, Slanderer, Banished", *MT*, 15 Nov. 1925; "Miami Abductor Gets Penalty Reduced", *MT*, 29 Nov. 1925; "Miami's Abductor's Sentence Affirmed", *MT*, 7 June 1926.

In 1928, a similar dramatic scenario of elopement unfolded for vaudevillian, and newborn celebrity of the local film industry, Naty (Natalia) Fernandez. Like Juanita Antido, Fernandez escaped from the House of Good Shepherds, with her abductor, a physician, see "Naty Fernandez Breaks. Gives a confession regarding her so-called abductors", *MT*, 1 June 1928; "Naty Fernandez Case Is Dropped Due to Willingness To Stay in Convent", *MT*, 4 June 1928; "Naty Fernandez Is Missing Again", *MT*, 9 Oct. 1928.

Antido's Vod-A-Vil Company.[124] By 1924, Juanita's fame in the Philippines had risen to the extent that she was reported as "The first Filipina to bob her hair" and "The Queen of Jazz in the Orient", rivaling vaudevillian Katy de la Cruz. Around 1924, the local authorities in Manila attempted to stop Juanita from performing. As a minor, she was supposed to attend school, and not to perform on the vaudeville stage. Detectives brought the teenager to a convent in Manila, the House of Good Shepherds, an institution for the correction and protection of "deviant" women.[125] The confinement was not to Juanita's or her father's liking. Her father appealed to the court twice. Legal intervention failed and this explains the sequence of events that unfolded. One evening in early September 1924, Juanita managed to escape from the convent with the help of "unidentified men", who took her onto a *banca* (a small boat) on the adjacent River Pasig to disappear into the dark night.[126] About a month later, the secret service arrested her and brought her before the court. Her attorney, Vicente Sotto, successfully appealed using the writ of habeus corpus.[127] In late 1924, Juanita was back in business with the debut show of the New Vaudeville Company, the "Smart Set", at the Lux Theatre in Manila.[128] What these and other similar newspaper stories suggest is that being modern, from preferring the stage before an education to choosing a partner on the basis of romantic considerations without parental consent, was regarded as socially undesirable.

The behaviour of the young, female vaudeville stars, as reported in the press, worked to portray these vodavilistas as modern yet deviant women and vaudeville as low-class and vulgar entertainment. Quite different from the sensational stories on abduction, and sensitive to the social tribulations of both bailerinas and female vaudeville stars are, again, the stories documented by the Manila-based American reporter Walter Robb, who, in the early 1930s, matter-of-factly stated that: "Elopement among Tagalogs is quite

---

[124] Ad "The Lux", *MT*, 20 Aug. 1920; "Goodwood Hall Nights", *The Straits Times*, 11 May 1922.

[125] Since the 16th century, such institutions served to "correct" deviant women, see Doran (1993: 283–4).

[126] "Juanita Antido, Vaudeville Artist Escapes From House of Good Shepherd", *PFP*, 13 Sept. 1924. Escape by women from convents and reformatory institutions was said to be common in Manila. See for example "News of The Week", *PFP*, 19 July 1924.

[127] Habeus corpus is petitioning the release of a prisoner on the basis of questioning in court whether a confinement is lawful. "Ang hari sa 'jazz' sa Silangan. Nakagawas na gayud sa Kombinto", *Bag-ong Kusog*, 10 Oct. 1924.

[128] "LUX. The SMARTSET Presents 'Face to Face'", *MT*, 6 Nov. 1924.

common."[129] He took the example of the "marriage-by-capture" of the well-known vaudevillian Katy de la Cruz, whose career had been given an important boost after she associated with Borromeo Lou in the early 1920s. At a very young age, de la Cruz eloped with a former sailor, vaudeville actor and professional boxer Rafael Cuyugan; she divorced him after a painstaking legal process and remarried. She raised four daughters during her career, which since the 1910s spanned more than a decade. Robb not only reminded the reader that elopement was common, he also showed that the flapper, at least in the case of celebrities such as Katy de la Cruz, was merely an image or public facade. Beyond her image of a cigarette-smoking, boyish girl, who occasionally exchanged kisses with male fans during her performances, vodavilista de la Cruz was a caring and hard-working mother.

Classy and Clean

Against the backdrop of the elite's condemnation of jazz and vaudeville, Luis Borromeo and others active in the vaudeville business sought consciously to "uplift" the theatrical genre, to present it as a legitimate art form. There are indications that even Luis's own kin attempted to disassociate themselves from vaudeville. The evidence comes from the occasion of Luis's parent's 50th wedding anniversary, held in Cebu in 1924, covered in local newspaper *Bag-ong Kusog*. The paper reported that all the children of "[t]he blessed Borromeo-Veloso couple [...] have their respected careers and this is the mark of good parenthood of the old couple".[130] A set of pictorial postcards commemorating the anniversary portrays Luis's father and his male children as "The Biggest Family in the City of Cebu". While his brothers are noted as respected white-collar professionals, such as priests, judges and physicians, Luis is simply noted as an "ex-judge". In order to avoid the family public embarrassment, the profession of vaudevillian was simply omitted. And this deliberate erasure is all the more remarkable as Luis was already a celebrity and at the summit of his professional career.

One strategy to make vaudeville classy and thus acceptable to the upper classes was to adopt European opera and Spanish musical comedies, both associated with high-class culture. A journalist and vaudeville fan stated that an operatic

---

[129] Robb (1963: 41–2) went on to elaborate on this social phenomena: "If an elopement is frustrated, the girl, moved by filial piety, may deny her guilty part in the innocent plot; and when she persists in this, even to the point of testifying in court—which she does only for her father's sake—the unlucky young suitor receives a sentence that may keep him in prison the remainder of his life. The records would probably show hundreds of such cases at Bilibid [the state prison] today."

[130] "Ang bulahang magtiayong Borromeo-Veloso", *Bag-ong Kusog*, 21 Nov. 1924.

selection was necessary to please "those of artistic or pseudo-artistic temperament" against "a touch of vulgarity for the edification of the moronically-minded".[131] It has been noted by different authors, including contemporary composers such as José Estella, that the Filipino upper classes adored opera. Since the turn of the century, they patronised visiting foreign and local opera companies.[132] In the 1920s, the popularity of opera was also sustained through the sales of published sheet music and consumption of phonographic recordings. In a review about the state of phonographic consumption in Manila, it was noted that: "Considerable classic music is […] sold in Manila. Educated Filipinos are its patrons, many of them purchasing the records of the artists, while the less expensive records of classical music are popular with them. Operatic selections find their sales in this class."[133] Late 19th-century modern operas were especially popular, for example by Italian playwright and composer Giacomo Puccini.[134] The craving of upper-class Manileños for operatic as well as classical music is also evident from the radio broadcasts of Station KZKZ of the Radio Corporation of the Philippines. This included live broadcasts of Constabulary Band Concerts, such as the one announced to take place on Wednesday, 16 April 1925. The concert featured different guest artists performing the work of European opera and classical music composers: Edvard Grieg, Fransz Joseph Hayden, Giuseppe Verdi, Charles Gounod and Giacomo Puccini.[135]

Given the popularity of opera within Filipino elite circles, it is no surprise to find opera as part of Borromeo's vaudeville playbills. Italian opera songs, condensed or cut-down (Italian) operas and musical comedies became integral and would contribute to what Borromeo promoted as "classy vaudeville". The concept of incorporating condensed opera within vaudeville itself was not new. Since the turn of the century, Keith's vaudeville theatres in the US had staged cut-down opera successfully. Possibly inspired by this practice in American vaudeville, and familiar with the practice of his own family to invite itinerant opera singers to perform at private parties, opera became a special attraction at a very early stage of Borromeo's novel vaudeville. During his first appearance in Cebu in 1921, he staged the prologue from Ruggiero Leoncavallo's *I Pagliacci*. And, for

---

[131] "Impressions of the Manila Vaudeville Stage", *Philippine Magazine* XXVI, no. 6 (Nov. 1929).

[132] De Leon (1978).

[133] Parson Hardware Store in Manila offered piano scores of Bizet's *Carmen*, Gounod's *Faust*, Wagner's *Lohengrin* and Verdi's *Aida*, see ad "NUEVA TEMPORADA DE OPERA", *PFP*, 3 Apr. 1915; "All Manila Has Got the Blues' About Manila's Musical Tastes", *MT*, 1 June 1922.

[134] "All Manila Has Got the Blues' About Manila's Musical Tastes", *MT*, 1 June 1922.

[135] "Listen In On This", *MT*, 16 Apr. 1925.

Illus. 5.1 "Classy and Clean". An off-stage, dandy-style image of Luis Borromeo, performing modernity in a studio somewhere in the Philippines; dressed in a white suit, surrounded by two bobbed-haired young women, likely his sisters, wearing delicately embroidered *terno*, Spanish-style fans in their hands, c. 1925. Courtesy of Vincent Borromeo.

example, in 1922, two foreign opera artists appeared with Borromeo's Follies of 1922 at the Olympic Stadium: Paul Grey, lyric baritone and S. Anfimoff, bass. For the next four weeks, the two singers rendered songs from several famous and mainly Italian operas, such as Puccini's *La Bohème* (1896), Gounod's *Faust* (1859), a prologue from *I Pagliacci* (1892), and the British musical comedy *The Geisha* (1896).[136] The practice of hiring itinerant foreign opera stars as special attraction continued in subsequent years.[137] Other local vaudeville troupes in Manila borrowed Borromeo's practice of adopting cut-down operas. Among these companies was the highly popular The Nifties at the Savoy Theatre. In 1927, this company presented condensed versions of *Aida* (Guiseppe Verdi, 1871) and *Tosca* (Puccini) featuring local singer Nazarina (Nenita) Farias. Farias had a background in zarzuela, and moved back and forth between the vod-a-vil and zarzuela stage.[138]

Another important way to enhance vaudeville's status as a legitimate form of theatre was to engage respected performers from the Hispano-Filipino stage. The best example is singer-actress Atang (Honorata) de la Rama. She started acting at a young age in the 1910s.[139] Unlike the image of a flapper, she represented respectability and patriotism without being elitist or highbrow. The musical film *Dalagang Bukid* (Rural Maiden), produced and released in the Philippines in 1919 propelled her to stardom. The film would lend her the name of the "Rural Maiden" and that of the "Queen of the Kundiman".[140] In 1920, Atang de la Rama's star had risen to the extent that *The Philippines Herald* nominated

---

[136] Ad "Stadium Vod-A-Vil", *MT*, 27 June 1922; "Will Stage Geisha Tonight", *MT*, 28 June 1922; ad "Stadium Vod-A-Vil", *MT*, 10 July 1922.

[137] Borromeo's Follies of 1923 featured as special attraction Italian soprano Tamara Postova assisted by Mario Padovani (baritone) in operatic songs. See ad "Stadium Vod-A-Vil Tonight", *MT*, 1 Aug. 1923; ad "Stadium Vod-A-Vil Tonight", *MT*, 15 Aug. 1923. Padovani separated from Anastacia Shaboturoff, a Russian opera singer who was left penniless in Manila by the Italian Grand Opera Company on a tour that had started in March 1923. Anastacia took up permanent employment as a singer with the Savoy Nifties in 1925. In late 1923, Miss Effie Barton, prima donna of the Chicago opera company, appeared in Borromeo's show. Barton toured Asia in the early 1920s with an opera group operating under the name of the International Stars, "At the Stadium—Effie Barton", *MT*, 19 Dec. 1923; Barton reappeared with Borromeo Lou's Follies of 1924, when she did a "miniature song recital". Ad "Stadium", *MT*, 9 Jan. 1924.

[138] "Nifties Strut Their Stuff", *MT*, 7 May 1927; "Nenita Farias Scores at Savoy", *MT*, 20 June 1927.

[139] "Por Rizal y Cervantes", *PFP*, 26 June 1915.

[140] "La Odisea de 'Atang'", *PFP*, 1 May 1920; Yeatter (2007: 18); Tiongson (1998).

her among 15 great Filipino women for a proposed Hall of Fame.[141] It is easily forgotten, but her ascendency as a star of the popular stage was also largely due to her association with Luis Borromeo's vaudeville. In January 1922, she is first and explicitly associated with vaudeville through her association with Borromeo's Follies of 1922 at the Stadium, performing his compositions.[142] In September 1923, she traded Borromeo for the Variety Stars at the Lux Theatre.[143] Throughout the twenties, we find de la Rama working sporadically with Borromeo and other vaudeville troupes. She would straddle zarzuela, vaudeville and cinema, performed on the radio and was recorded on phonograph.

Some clues to de la Rama's significance in uplifting vaudeville can be gauged from a review of a vaudeville sketch "Blue Diamonds", written by Adolfo Lopez and staged by the Variety Stars in 1923. Her appearance in the sketch solicited the following comment from the *The Philippines Herald*:

> Modest, unassuming, never stopping to vulgarity to win the favor of audiences, and gifted with a voice of thrush like sweetness—that's Atang de la Rama, prime favorite among the Lux Variety Stars [...]. The Tagalog 'Kundiman' particularly interests this young singer, and she presents songs of this type in the authentic Filipino style, singing them in the beautiful Filipino costume that is unfortunately passing out of vogue. Jazz has come to Manila variety theaters, apparently to stay; but it has not entirely displaced the old native airs as the enthusiasm of Lux audiences for Miss de la Rama attests. Moreover, her singing draws to the theater many musical people whom the ordinary vaudeville program would not interest. [144]

Atang thus represented a female patriot, presenting Tagalog music and fashion on stage, giving vaudeville legitimacy. She also took Filipino vaudeville abroad. In 1926, she toured the Hawaiian Islands together with Filipino dancer and comedian Vicente Yerro. They staged vaudeville before the large migrant Filipino community, among them many plantation workers.[145] The *Free Press* announced

---

[141] "Who Are Prominents. Choose Fifteen Great P.I. Women. Opinion Is Solicited", *The Philippines Herald*, 21 Sept. 1920.

[142] Ad "Stadium Vod-A-Vil", *MT*, 8 Jan. 1922. Throughout 1922, Atang de la Rama appeared with Borromeo performing a repertory of American novelty and Spanish songs (ad "Stadium Vod-A-Vil", *MT*, 1 Feb. 1922; ad "Stadium Vod-A-Vil", *MT*, 26 Feb. 1922; ad "Stadium Vod-A-Vil", *MT*, 13 July 1922; ad "Stadium Vod-A-Vil", *MT*, 17 July 1922; ad "Stadium Vod-A-Vil", *MT*, 25 July 1922).

[143] The Variety cast included, amongst others, Katy de la Cruz, Vitang Cowper, Pacita Sanchez, Enrique Davila, Planing Vidal, Richard Reynolds, Sunday Reantaso and Augustin Llopis. Ad "Lux Theatre", *MT*, 7 Sept. 1923.

[144] "Kundiman Queen Popular At Lux", *The Philippine Herald*, 14 Oct. 1923.

[145] On labour conditions of Filipino plantation workers in Hawai'i, see Bruno Lasker (1931).

the trip as "The rural maiden who goes on a mission to promote the art of her country."[146] Given de la Rama's artistic flexibility, the question was, of course, what art she was promoting. Filipinos in Honolulu, Hilo as well as in Maui warmly welcomed her and her vaudeville troupe. The Filipino Young Men's Club in Maui offered her a banquet. Moral condemnation of vaudeville had, however, also travelled, as we learn from a letter sent by a Filipino migrant in Hawai'i to the editors of the *Maui News*:

> Of Madame Atang de la Rama it is said that she is a first class prima donna, but does not help her standard of dignity by appearing in vaudeville. She is beautiful in her Filipino dress, her voice is skeet, and her acting is graceful. She would receive more appreciation in her concert vocal numbers if she did not couple these with vaudeville.[147]

For most Filipinos in Hawai'i and in the Philippines itself, de la Rama remained a popular theatrical star. For them, a distinction between the vernacular zarzuela and vaudeville stage was unproblematic. What likely enhanced de la Rama's popularity was that she spoke out in public on the ill social conditions under which Filipinos laboured in Hawai'i.[148]

As vaudeville impresarios balanced between offering banal entertainment and sophisticated attractions, the struggle for respectability was ongoing. In 1923, *The Philippine Free Press* examined the state of the vaudeville in Manila posing the question: "Does Simple Stupidity Characterize Local Shows?". The paper wrote:

> Director Puig at the Savoy is also doing his best to elevate vaudeville. At the Lyric, the performances are, needless to say, usually of a high order. Borromeo Lou also endeavors to keep his 'follies' within the bounds of propriety. So let's all help and make vaudeville in the Philippines an institution that we can point to with pride.[149]

In 1925, on the occasion of the first anniversary of the vaudeville company the Savoy Nifties's manager Cowper promised the Nifties audience "to merit further support by submitting vaudeville that is clean and up-to-date in every respect".[150] In 1927, periodical *Graphic* reported that "vaudeville art is making headway in the

---

[146] "Dalagang Bukid se va en una misión de arte patriá", *PFP*, 19 June 1926.

[147] "Voice of The People", *Maui News*, 21 Aug. 1926. Atang de la Rama collection, Cultural Center of the Philippines.

[148] "Labour Exodus is Fought by Atang", *Philippine Herald*, n.d. Atang de la Rama collection, Cultural Center of the Philippines.

[149] "Does Simple Stupidity Characterize Local Shows?", *PFP*, 17 Nov. 1923. Director Ignacio Puig was also a vaudeville impresario.

[150] "Nifties Continue Birthday Show at The Savoy", *MT*, 3 May 1925.

Philippines" articulating what can be read as a cautious assessment of vaudeville as "popular art". At the same time the popular magazine also noticed that: "There is, however, a present tendency among a number of vaudeville performers to try to be funny by being raw and crude. [...] that they only serve to justify criticism often levelled against the legitimate stage in Manila that vaudeville numbers are not but imitations of cheap burlesque shows in other countries."[151] In spite of the efforts of Borromeo and his contemporaries to present vaudeville as classy, the artistic sophistication, legitimacy and popularity of this form of theatre began to wane quickly in the early 1930s, marking the end of a cultural eruption that had begun in the early 1920s.

---

[151] "With Our Filipino Stage Stars", *Graphic*, 31 Dec. 1927.

Chapter 6

New Directions

The year 1929 was pivotal in the development of popular culture in the Philippines. Luis Borromeo left Manila to tour the southern Philippines with his vaudeville troupe, returning briefly in 1934 to the capital without a company. It is exactly in this five-year period that significant changes in the realm of popular culture occurred. The effects of the economic depression of 1929 gradually sank in. Apart from discouraging consumerism and investment in the culture industry, the crisis also fuelled American economic protectionism, restrictions on migration and even violence against Filipino migrants in the US. These events, in turn, invigorated a new wave of Philippine nationalism that coincided with the introduction of the new audio technology of the sound movie in 1929. Between 1929 and 1934, existing connections between the arts weakened, if not severed, and vernacular theatre declined.

The first section of this chapter highlights the case of a commercial phonographic recording "expedition" launched in the islands by Columbia Records in late 1929. This recording project can be considered the last convulsion of the popular art that had characterised the 1920s. The interest of foreign recording corporations in Filipino popular music and artists ended abruptly in 1932, possibly as a result of the global economic crisis.

A new media technology, the sound movie, or "talkie" was also introduced in Southeast Asia in 1929. Sound movies instantly offered competition to vernacular zarzuela and vaudeville, drawing away their audiences. But this competition, as I will elucidate in the final section on "The Old Vaudeville Director", worked in tandem with other forces, like nationalism and the economic depression, leading to the demise of a once dynamic and exciting vernacular theatre.

Jazz, *Kundiman* and the Phonograph

In August 1927, Governor General Leonard Wood passed away, opening up fervent discussions about his successor and his stance on Philippine freedom. Wood's successor was the outspoken retentionist Henry L. Stimson. By 1929 his anti-independence attitude had reinvigorated the independence issue among Filipino nationalists.[1] In the mid-1910s, the Nacionalista leadership was caught in the paradox of, on the one hand, paying lip service to the motto of immediate, absolute and complete independence, while on the other, fearing the loss of economic and US military protection if independence was granted unconditionally. Meanwhile, the American sugar beet, dairy and vegetable oil industry, protecting their own economic interests, lobbied for independence. For these industries, independence would end American trade preferences for Philippine agricultural commodities. In turn, Quezon sought a compromise and manoeuvred behind the American political scenes, promoting independence with a transition period of 10 to 20 years during which trade preferences would be gradually lifted. This transition period would allow the Philippine economy to adjust to new economic conditions. In late 1929, under the guise of demanding unconditional independence, a new Independence Mission departed for Washington to further the Philippine's economic and political interests.[2] In its wake, a new wave of nationalism swept the islands. In late February 1930, the first Philippine Independence Congress was held in Manila's Grand Opera House, bringing together 2,000 delegates from all over the islands and from "all walks of life", with the aim to petition for "complete, absolute and immediate independence".[3]

It is against the background of a resurgent nationalism and also a commercial rivalry between foreign phonographic corporations that, in late 1929, a music recording session was undertaken in the Philippines: the Beck-Columbia recording expedition. This recording project is noteworthy for three reasons. Never before were so many Filipino artists and Filipino musical genres recorded within such a short time span. Secondly, and of social-cultural significance, this was the first concerted effort by local composers, performing artists and the Filipino political elite to define and promote a Filipino music and culture with the aid of the commercial recording industry. Finally, the Columbia recordings represented the local hybrid genres in music, theatre and oral literature, typical of the new in-between culture that had developed in the late 1910s and 1920s.

In late 1929, Isaac Beck, an American, Manila-based department store owner and local representative of Columbia Records organised a recording session in Manila with around 40 prominent Filipino artists. He recruited them from the zarzuela and vaudeville stage as well as from classical musical corners.

---

[1] Golay (1998: 272–4). Stimson was in office from December 1927 to February 1929, and was succeeded by Dwight F. Davis, who held office until January 1932.

[2] Golay (1998: 284–5).

[3] "The Independence Resolution. Why Filipinos Petition for Independence", *PFP*, 1 Mar. 1930. See also Golay (1998: 285).

The outcome was a musical gathering, lasting for a few weeks, and a batch of 250 phonographic recordings released officially in early 1930 by Columbia Graphophone. Beck proudly presented them bilingually, in Spanish and English, as "gravado en Manila" and "Recorded in Manila", emphasising the local flavour of the music. Columbia framed the recording session as an "expedition", as if it had been a pioneering exploration in a musical *terra incognita*. Given the history of recording of local music in the Philippines, this was exaggerated.[4] The scope of Beck's Columbia Expedition, however, was different from previous commercial recordings made in the Philippines and different from recordings made by Filipino artists in the US.

The recording expedition was a well-prepared nationalist and commercial campaign, as illustrated by the advertisement in the popular magazine *Graphic*, dated 8 January 1930:

> You will hear our pretty kundimans, folksongs, ballads, operettas, solos and duets [...] a veritable array of talent entirely Filipino, entirely native old folksongs—and new—by Filipino composers [...] this great enterprise [is] to diffuse Filipino Art in song and music throughout the Philippines as well as abroad.[5]

The endeavour was backed by "patronesses" drawn from the ranks of Manila's intellectual and political elite, distinguished ladies who acted as guardians of proper cultural taste. They included Mrs. Sergio Osmeña, wife of Nacionalista Party leader and Speaker of the House; Mrs. E. Nathorst, wife of the chief of the Philippine Constabulary; Mrs. Teodoro Kalaw, formerly known as Purita Villanueva and 1908 Manila Carnival Queen, by then wife of a Nacionalista, journalist and head of the National Library and Museum Teodoro Kalaw; Mrs. Jose Yulo, wife of the Secretary of Justice; Mrs. Isaac Barza, wife of a prominent businessman, and Mrs. Sefarino Hilado, wife of a senator.[6] In the absence of

---

[4] The artist, who, around 1926, recorded the bulk of songs for Columbia in the US, was baritone Jose Mossegeld Santiago. This included a dozen of kundiman, valses, danzas and a number of Filipino folksongs, such as "Planting Rice". Second to Santiago came soprano Naty O. de Arellano, who recorded solo and duets with Santiago. Others are: Isabel E. Llewellyn, soprano, who did a number of solo songs and duets with J.M. Santiago; the G. Espíritu y Filipino Serenaders, a band that recorded a few instrumental marches, foxtrots and tangos; violinist Ernesto Vallejo, who recorded an instrumental kundiman and a *habanera Filipina*; Fortunato Ramos Galong, a tenor singer, who did six songs, including comic songs in Tagalog, Ilocano and Visayan; and finally, from a completely different corner, Nacionalista leader Manuel Quezon, who recorded a patriotic call to the people of the Philippines in his "Mi Mensaja a Mi Pueblo a 'Discurso Patriótico". I. Beck Inc. Recording Expedition (c. 1930).

[5] "Beck-Columbia Recording Expedition Concert at the Opera House", *Graphic*, 8 Jan. 1930.

[6] Ibid.

permanent recording studios in the islands, Teodoro Kalaw was kind enough to offer his private residence as Columbia's makeshift recording studio.[7] Publicity was arranged in the form of a special illustrated catalogue; separate advertisements were placed in leading periodicals like *Graphic* and the *Philippine Free Press*; in early January 1930, the recordings session's participants gave a promotional concert in the Grand Opera House. The print press reported the concert to have been a great success.[8]

Columbia recorded no less than 40 artists covering a dozen "genres": kundiman, danzas, balitaw, potpourri, waltzes, tango, one-step, patriotic and folk songs, romanzas, ballads, cansonettas, serenades, operettas, marches, monologues, dialogues, Moro songs, couplets, meditations, solos and duets in Tagalog, Visayan, Pampango, Ilocano, Bicol, "Chino-Spanish" and English.[9] According to the record catalogue, the music recorded was "*Neither jazz, nor grand opera [....]*", hence indicating something distinctively original Filipino and in-between.

Let us take a closer look at this in-between Filipino popular art, the artists involved and what they recorded. Obviously, there was a dose of patriotic music performed by the pride of the Philippines, the Philippine Constabulary Band.[10] Among the recording artists, we find Jose Corazon de Jesus, noted in the record catalogue as "hari ng balagtasan" (the king of balagtasan), who performed two of his poems.[11] The two most prominent Filipino opera vocalists of the time, Jovita Fuentes and Jose Mossegeld Santiago, also joined the Columbia "expedition". Atang de la Rama, announced as "queen of the Kundiman" was permitted to do what she always did, to cross genres. She recorded Hispano-Filipino genres such as kundiman, *valse-kundiman* and *danza Filipina*, but also a Filipino Foxtrot entitled "Pugad Ng Pag-Ibig" (Love Nest).[12] And even the songs and sketches of a few leading vaudevillians were acceptable to the official patrons of the project. Included were soprano singer Dionisia Castro, stage

---

[7] "Grabanda la Musica Nativa. Come Hacen los Discos. Vicente Ocampo Habla de Industria— El Mejor Metodo de Dar a Conocer la Cultura Filipina es por Medio de la Musica", *PFP*, 21 July 1934.

[8] "Concert Successful. Many Attended Opera House Recitals", *MT*, 13 Jan. 1930.

[9] "Beck-Columbia Recording Expedition Concert at the Opera House", *Graphic*, 8 Jan. 1930.

[10] The PC Band performed two composition of D.M. Fajardo: "General C.E. Nathorst March", dedicated to the named Constabulary General and "Veteranos de Revolucion".

[11] These were two "declamations" according to the Columbia catalogue. One is titled "Ang Pagbabalik" (The Return); the other "Ang Pamana" (The Legacy), authored and performed by Jose Corazon de Jesus. None of these original recordings, or digital reproductions, have been found so far.

[12] I. Beck Inc. Recording Expedition (c. 1930). N.p.

name Toy Toy, former Borromeo Lou protégé working for the Savoy Nifties vaudeville company; Vicente Ocampo, a leading vaudeville comedian with the same troupe; Ray and Rick Alabama, a comic duo also working for the Nifties; and "Queen of jazz" Katy de la Cruz, also from the Nifty cast. Like de la Rama, Dionisia Castro recorded a number of kundiman. She also did a number of comic duets with Vicente Ocampo, "Huwak na Toy", a "Filipino Foxtrot" and "Ang Bibinka", categorised as a "Filipino One-Step".[13] Ocampo himself recorded a number of "Folk songs" and the comic Tagalog song "Chichirichit", which would become a huge hit. The Alabama brothers engaged in a few English-Tagalog comic dialogues, no doubt pioneering the hybrid dialect that emerged from the American-Philippine cultural encounter, a slang nowadays known as "Taglish".[14] And an artist by the name of Jose Arpal performed two monologues in what might be called a, now extinct, hybrid "dialect" of the Philippines, "Chinese-Spanish".[15] Katy de la Cruz recorded the jazzy American hit "I Can't Give You Anything But Love", whose original composer was omitted from the catalogue, possibly to evade copyright claims. Columbia released an eclectic repertoire of music, poetry and comic dialogues that was promoted as distinctly Filipino. And in spite of the patriotic "no-jazz-and-no-opera-this-time" mood, the expedition represented a fair amount of the new popular art pioneered by Luis Borromeo and his peers, including the musical jazzy hybrids categorised as Filipino foxtrots and one-steps.

Apart from cultural nationalism, there was another incentive for Columbia to launch its grand recording project: commercial rivalry between foreign recording corporations to obtain a share of the Philippine recording market. In December 1928, the German corporation Odeon, a Lindström concern, dispatched experts from its head office in Berlin to the Philippines to examine possibilities for recording local music. Impressed by the music they heard, including that of José Estella, Odeon's Berlin office decided to send an engineer to the islands to record

---

[13] Ibid. Some of the duets of Dionisia Castro and Vicente Ocampo recorded in late 1929 were released in early March 1932. This batch of records probably also included songs and duets recorded after 1929. See ad "I. Beck Inc.", *PFP*, 5 Mar. 1932. Before the Columbia expedition, Castro and Vicente had recorded two comic dialogues in Tagalog for Victor records in Manila in August 1929, see Spottswood (1990: 2417).

[14] On Taglish see Rafael (2008: 162–89).

[15] These are catalogued as "Spanish-Chino monologues": "Frescuras del Chino ty-meto" and "Por si acaso ty-meto". No details are known of Arpal's artistic or social background. See I. Beck Inc. Recording Expedition (c. 1930). N.p.

a number of Filipino artists, bands and genres in March 1929.[16] Odeon, thus, was actively recording Filipino artists and genres more than six months before rival Columbia would launch its grand project.

The German engineer sent to Southeast Asia was Max Birckhahn, who had 25 years of solid recording experience in Europe, Asia and Latin America. In 1927, he was recording a young singer-actress in Java, Miss Riboet, new star of modern Malay opera. She immortalised the German engineer in a Malay song entitled "Making Records", recorded by Birckhahn in a makeshift studio, likely in the harbour city of Semarang. On that occasion and in the Malay quatrain verse-style of *pantun*, Miss Riboet entertainingly sang the praises of him as "Recording engineer Mr. Birckhahn, bald headed yet sympathetic".[17] His recordings would make Riboet's voice and fame reach into the Straits Settlements and the Malay Peninsula.

In 1930, the *Philippine Free Press* captured Birckhahn in a picture posing with an employee of the local agency of Parlophone, also a Lindström company, in Pasay, suburban Manila. Birckhahn is quoted having said that: "[…] Philippine music is the best I have heard in the East".[18] In February 1930 and June 1931, Odeon released two separate batches of Filipino music. The 1931 batch was specifically advertised as "Philippine Records in Tagalog", promoted as a call to "Favour Your Own Artists!", and rather paternalistic, but nonetheless equally patriotically, "To Help Develop Philippine Music".[19] Among the artists recorded in Manila, Iloilo and Cebu in 1929 and 1930 were several vodavilistas and zarzuelistas. Vaudevillian Enrique Davila did a Tagalog version of the global hit "Ramona".[20] Birckhahn also recorded Luis Borromeo and his orchestra, a song separately with Luis's sister Lourdes, and Luis with three prominent zarzuelistas from Iloilo city. Included was Borromeo's original composition "Hello Mr. Carabao?", performed by Borromeo Lou's Entertainers. The song cut with Luis's younger sister Lourdes was entitled "sang Bulaklak ng 'Ang Tibay'" (Everlasting

---

[16] Odeon's exclusive distributor in Southeast Asia was German trading company Behn Meyer & Co. with offices in Manila and Cebu, "Hay Dinero en las Placas Fonograficas", *PFP*, 11 May 1929. The recording artists included: the Manila Chamber Music Society orchestra conducted by Maestro Bonifacio Abdon; Ms. Carmen Bernabe and Raymunda Guidote (duet); The Band of Pasig; the Manila Symphony Orchestra; baritone Eduardo Llamas; soprano Nieves Roco; and the bass Gerardo Ayllon.

[17] "Making Records", Miss Riboet. Beka 27828. Private collection of Jaap Erkelens.

[18] "Manila Sonora", *PFP*, 12 Apr. 1930.

[19] Ad "Lavadia & Company, Inc. Manila", *Graphic*, 3 June 1931.

[20] The flipside of "Ramona" was another Tagalog song, "Sa Duyan Ng Pagibig" (In the Cradle of Love), a duet of Enrique Davila with his wife Consuela. Ad "A. & P. Co. Inc.", *The Tribune*, 14 Feb. 1930.

Flower), and also one of Borromeo's own compositions.[21] So far, these are the only known phonographic recordings by this pioneer of Filipino vaudeville.[22]

In response to the activities of Odeon/Parlophone and Beck-Columbia in the Philippines, American record companies Gennet, Brunswick and Victor became active. In February and May 1930, Gennet advertised "Thousands of Gennet Philippine Records" that had "Just Arrived", distributed in Manila by Starr Phonograph Co. of Gonzalo Puyat & Sons. The store particularly promoted "kundimans" rendered by Filipino tenor Ramon P. Crespo recorded in the US.[23] To keep up with the commercial rivals, Brunswick recorded in Manila in March and May 1930.[24] For this occasion, Teodoro Kalaw once again offered the *sala* (guestroom) of his spacious home in Santa Mesa, Manila, to be temporarily converted into a Brunswick recording studio. Kalaw leaned back on a long history in different capacities in the Philippine government.[25] He was an open-minded intellectual and cosmopatriot, as witnessed in his "Dietario espiritual", a collection of Spanish news columns originally published in *La Vanguardia* between 1926 and 1927. His sensitivity to cosmopolitanism in relation to nationalism is, for instance, articulated explicitly in a column entitled "The Usefulness of Travel": "As cosmopolitanism and humanitarian ideals gain ground, in our thinking and observance, because of travel, the nationalist spirit becomes at the same time more profound, more perfect, more human."[26] Given his patriotism and openness to alien cultures, it is perfectly understandable that he and his wife supported commercial recordings of Philippine popular music, whether by Columbia or Brunswick. As collaborators of the recording industry, Kalaw and his wife not only actively participated in creating a Filipino pop cosmopolitanism, they also assumed roles as cultural brokers. The same can be

---

[21] Odeon 225, 132: "Hello Mr. Carabao?" (Borromeo Lou)—Borromeo Lou's Entertainers. Flip side: "Siana" (Borromeo Lou) (Sa Bisaya)—Rosa Palacios, Soprano, Boni Cenizo, Baritono Odeon 225, 135: "Sa Tabi ng Batis" (Borromeo Lou), Boni Ceniza and Juan Ledesma (barítono). Flip side: "Bulaklak ng 'Ang Tibay'" (Borromeo Lou)—Lourdes Borromeo (soprano). Ad "Lavadia & Company, Inc. Manila", *Graphic*, 3 June 1931. Rosa Palacios was one of Iloilo's most celebrated zarzuela actresses-singers. See Fernandez (1978: 152–5).

[22] I was unable to trace copies of Borromeo's Odeon recordings or digital reproductions.

[23] See ad, "Starr Phonograph Co", *The Tribune*, 19 Feb. 13 and 21 May 1930.

[24] Brunswick's representative in Manila expressed the intention "to establish branch studios in the islands for continuous year round recordings, as is done in the United States". This did not materialise. On the recording activities, see "Phonograph Firm Officials Make Records of Filipino Musicians", *The Tribune*, 28 Mar. 1930; "Filipino Records in the Making", *The Tribune*, 28 Mar. 1930; "Songs of Blind Bard of Cebu are Recorded", *The Tribune*, 30 Mar. 1930.

[25] Kalaw (2001: vii).

[26] Ibid., p. 163.

argued for composer and professor of UP's Conservatory of Music, Francisco Santiago, who also had a significant hand in the Brunswick recordings. He was in full charge of selecting the artists, selecting Filipino folk songs, and in directing the recording sessions of the Philippine Constabulary Orchestra.

In August 1930, as if alarmed by the expansion of its commercial rivals, Victor records launched a large recording project in the islands that would last until early 1931. Victor had assigned prominent composer José Estella to select "native artists" from four provinces.[27] Involved once again was Francisco Santiago, who directed several of the orchestras. In terms of the number of artists, genres and songs, Victor's musical production was as impressive as that of the Beck-Columbia Expedition. Around 120 artists, several artists who had also recorded for Columbia, including bands and poets, such as Flavio Zaragoza Cano from Iloilo, performed over 400 all-Filipino compositions.[28] Distinguished composer Nicanor Abelardo wrote several of the songs.[29] In addition to a few poems and comic duets, the full spectrum of popular musical genres current in the Philippines in the late 1920s was covered: waltz, danza, operetta song, rag, foxtrot, one-step, balitaw, kundiman, habanera and tango. The Victor recording project was likely the last grand commercial recording session of hybrid Filipino musical genres in the islands. No evidence was found of similar recording projects in the years leading up to the Second World War, the reasonable explanation being that, by 1932, the economic crisis was increasingly felt, discouraging further investment by foreign phonographic corporations. This development was preceded by the introduction of the sound movie in 1929, a media technology that contributed to the decline of the popular vernacular theatre, the latter having been intimately connected to the recording industry in Southeast Asia since the turn of the 20th century.

Death of the Stage, Rise of the Local Cinema Industry

In 1931, Eliseo Carvajal, by then veteran of the Hispano-Filipino stage who in 1915 had introduced Cebuano audiences to the novelty of the tango, looked back

---

[27] "Native Artists Picked in 4 Provinces making Victor Record", *The Tribune*, 27 Aug. 1930.

[28] For what is probably the most comprehensible overview of Victor's output of Filipino music recorded in Manila between 1929 and 1931, see Spottswood (1990: 2413–49). Spottswood's overview also includes recordings made by Filipino artists in the US.

[29] See Spottswood (1990: 2413–49). For the songs written by Abelardo, see also Discography of American Historical Recordings: http://adp.library.ucsb.edu/index.php/talent/detail/43521/ Abelardo_Nicanor_songwriter. Abelardo also co-wrote with Florentino Ballacer, including a Tagalog comic duet performed by Ballacer and Leonara Reyes: http://adp.library.ucsb.edu/ index.php/matrix/detail/800033185/BVE-63838-Sa_pugad_ng_pag-giliw.

in time, lamenting the demise of "Spanish theatre" in the Philippines. He gave a personal impression of what he recorded as a cultural crisis in local vernacular theatre. Hispano-Filipino theatrical troupes had been dissolved in tandem with the declining number of Spanish-speaking Filipinos. Carvajal's main explanation, however, for the collapse of "Spanish theatre" in Manila was the introduction of the talkie. He argued that cinema tickets were cheaper than theatre and that spectators had to sit shorter, leading to dwindling numbers of theatre spectators. Carvajal foresaw the death of "the Philippine stage" and as far as classy vaudeville and vernacular zarzuela in the Philippines was concerned, he was proved right.[30]

On 2 August 1929, the Radio Theatre, formerly known as the Majestic, introduced the Manileños to the novelty of the talkie. As 1929 was about to close, Manila had seven new talking pictures theatres.[31] The sound movie had caused instant excitement, attracting thousands of spectators accompanied by an immediate crisis in the capital's theatrical and silent movie circles. Within six months after its introduction, an almost total recast from silent movie houses-cum-theatres to sound movie theatres had occurred that proved devastating for existing forms of popular commercial entertainment, silent movies and vernacular theatre.[32] Cine musicians of the silent movies lost their jobs. The talkies also drew away audiences from vaudeville and zarzuela alike. Thus, already in 1930, only one of Manila's vaudeville troupes, the Savoy Nifties, remained. To lure audiences to vaudeville shows, a trial-and-tested format was reintroduced, to programme vaudeville with motion pictures, that is the talkies.[33] Without film screenings, theatres simply could not survive. Even the new prestigious Metropolitan Theatre, inaugurated in December 1931, seen by many as "national theater and opera" […] "in the service of the community and the nation" depended on cine screenings for its existence.[34] The editors of *Philippine Magazine* perfectly

---

[30] "The Last Act. The Decline of the Spanish Stage in the Philippines, as Recalled by Eliseo (Cheong) Carvajal", *The Sunday Tribune Magazine*, 31 May 1931.

[31] The new sound movie theatres were: The Palace The Lyric, Ideal, Columbia, Radio, Rialto and Tivoli; Ad "The Palace", *MT*, 14 Aug. 1929; "Lyric Will Show First All Talking Film Tomorrow"—'The Letter' with Joanne Eagels", *MT*, 4 Sept. 1929; "Sound Coming to the Tivoli Theatre", *MT*, 20 Dec. 1929. Of the dozen that once existed, only two silent movie theatres survived, one of them the Savoy.

[32] "Do You Want the 'Talkies'?", *The Sunday Tribune Magazine*, 5 Jan. 1930.

[33] Ad "Savoy", *The Sunday Tribune*, 11 Jan. 1933. In 1933, there were three vaudeville companies, in addition to the Nifties, one of which was named "Lou Salvador's Imperial Entertainer" at the Imperial Theatre, featuring many of the "old" stars, such as Miami, Naty Fernandez, Nena Warsaw, Vicente Ocampo, Padovani and others. See ad "Imperial", *The Sunday Tribune*, 11 Jan. 1933.

[34] "National Opera for the Philippines", *Philippine Magazine*, Sept. 1931.

expressed what was likely widely shared, namely that this high temple of art ran the risk of degenerating into a vaudeville house and "cine".[35] To save its "high-cultured" image, the Metropolitan Theatre staged operas, dance shows, classical music alongside film screenings. Vaudeville was unofficially "banned". And this situation of the Metropolitan Theatre would remain the same during the Second World War, when the Japanese military administration and the Philippine puppet government fostered Philippine cultural nationalism and anti-Americanism.

In December 1929, the *Tribune* conducted a survey to gauge how people in the Philippines received the novelty of the sound movie. Apart from the *Tribune*, advertisements were also placed in *La Vanguardia* and *Taliba*, asking readers' opinion of the talkie. These public calls produced hundreds of letters from readers who compared the talkie to the silent movie. In January 1930, the *Tribune* concluded that 60 per cent of the respondents favoured the talkie, while 40 per cent favoured the silent movie.[36] The paper gave a brief overview of some of the pros and cons expressed by prominent Filipinas and Filipinos. For example, Rafael Palma, president of the University of the Philippines wrote: "Yes, I like the talkies for they offer varied means of entertainment. The flickers that appeal to me most are the musical comedies, dramas and vaudeville sketches." Mrs Sergio Osmeña gave a similar positive comment and confessed to being a fan of musical comedies. The opponents of the talkie in general particularly focused on poor sound quality. In addition to the abovementioned call, the Lyric Film Exchange in Manila also tested audience preferences by showing two versions, silent and sound, of the movie *Alibi*, an American crime story. Seventy per cent of the viewers who had seen both versions favoured the talkie.[37]

In July 1930, the *Free Press* reported on the vodavilistas being so adrift that "local jazz babies and kundiman songbirds were hoping against hope that something would happen to keep them from looking around for another means of securing a livelihood".[38] Vaudeville, at least for the time being, survived in the provinces. By 1932, with declining patronage and profits theatre owners slashed vodavilistas's salaries.[39]

In order to survive, vodavilistas sought ways to secure an income. The dance hall was one option, but one with a downside. Not only was dance hall attendance in decline, its reputation as highway of perdition had grown. Between 1932

---

[35] "Editorial", *Philippine Magazine*, June 1931, p. 24.

[36] "Do You Want the 'Talkies'?", *The Sunday Tribune Magazine*, 5 Jan. 1930.

[37] Ibid.

[38] "Going Going?", *PFP*, 5 Apr. 1930.

[39] "Will Vaudeville Stars Shine Again? Supplanted by Talkies, Stage Shows Apparently Starting Comeback at Present—Many Difficulties to Be Overcome", *PFP*, 10 Sept. 1932.

and 1934, the effects of the economic crisis had sunk in. Dance hall patronage dwindled in tandem with wage cuts. The uncertainty about the limitation of sugar exports to the US, the threat of a tax on copra exports and the oversupply of abaca on the world market had also reduced the people's purchasing power. Cabaret entrance fees, however, remained the same as in 1929.[40] In an effort to turn the tide of declining patronage, cabaret owners introduced all kinds of novelties, including dancing and singing acts by experienced vaudevillians.[41] The economic crisis, however, also had another detrimental effect on the dancehall. A problem latent since the 1910s had become pressing and real in the early 1930s: prostitution and gangsterism. Prostitution was thriving in and outside the dance halls. According to findings of the Philippine Medical Association, prostitution had "commercialised" "on a sort of brokerage basis".[42] The picture that emerges is that of a system in which employment agencies played a key role in the traffic of women from the remotest *barrio* to the city.[43] Prostitution had also developed along class lines. Sophisticated madams ran the high-class brothels of Manila that enjoyed upper-class patronage. In contrast, the dance halls in the provinces were known for its "low-class" prostitutes and clientele. Particularly notorious were the dance halls in Rizal province surrounding Manila.[44] Moreover, gangsters had discovered the world of the popular cabarets as a safe haven for investment and extra-legal sidelines in times of economic distress. In 1934, of all cabarets, the Santa Ana was reported as the only place where "patrons and cabaret habitués are not molested by thugs and cutthroats".[45] La Loma, in north Manila, was known as "the hell-kitchen of Manila" ruled by the "unholy combination" of bailerina, local mobsters and corrupt policemen managing prostitution and extorting patrons. The criminalisation of the dance hall can tentatively be explained as a long-term effect of the banning of legal prostitution in the late 1910s combined with the economic crisis of the early 1930s. These factors forced prostitution underground and people to look for other, often illicit sources of income at a time when the prospects of the sugar and abaca cash crop industries were gloomy.

---

[40] Wage rate cuts ranging from 5 to 50 per cent are reported for business enterprise employees. "Does 'Chow' Cost?", *PFP*, 13 Aug. 1932; "Business and Finance", *Philippine Magazine*, June 1934.

[41] "Thirty-Cent Press Agents. Bailerinas Believe It Pays To Advertise So they Hire Gigolos To Help Them Strut Their Gift", *PFP*, 31 Mar. 1934.

[42] "Clandestine Vice Exposed", *PFP*, 24 Dec. 1932.

[43] "One Prosperous Business. Depression Hasn't Hurt Traffic in Women—Still Thrives in Cities and Even in Remote Barrios", *PFP*, 17 Sept. 1932.

[44] "Clandestine Vice Exposed", *PFP*, 24 Dec. 1932.

[45] "The Ruling Trio of Manila's Cabarets", *PFP*, 28 Apr. 1934; "In Cabaret's As In Jueteng. Laguna Tops 'Em All'", *PFP*, 12 May 1934.

And finally, also conducive to this situation of the dance halls, were weak law enforcement and police officers' low wage rates.

Facing the theatrical crisis, and the bad image of the dance hall, artists also pinned their hopes on the phonographic industry.[46] But it was only a dozen or so who benefitted from this, particularly from the novelty of royalties.[47] Moreover, and as indicated previously, the interest of the recording industry in recording Filipino music waned after 1932. Among the privileged recording artists was vaudevillian Vicente Ocampo, who profited from the success of his song "Chichirichit", recorded during the Beck-Columbia recording expedition of 1929. In 1932, Columbia claimed to have sold 20,000 copies of the songs and they were still selling.[48]

In 1932, the Savoy Nifties vaudeville company disbanded as the theatre focused exclusively on sound movies. Two other Manila theatres, the Imperial and the Palace, however, offered the old Nifties stars employment. The two companies were, according to the *Free Press*, "waging a brave fight for existence against increasing popularity of the talkies".[49] The same paper related that: "The old applause is still there but it does not have the old click it had when Dimples, Vitang Escobar, Katy de la Cruz, Toytoy and Atang de la Rama were at the height of their stage career." What was at stake was not simply decline of the number of vaudeville companies and loss of spectatorship, but also the nature of the theatrical art itself. The *Free Press* paper spoke of the "retrogression of vaudeville". The paper blamed vaudeville promoters for having made "no attempt [...] to discover or develop new talent and little effort has been exerted to make local vaudeville elaborate, high-class entertainment".[50] Retired vaudeville impresario

---

[46] "Manila Sonora", *PFP*, 12 Apr. 1930.

[47] Royalties appeared to have become practice in the Philippine in the late 1920s. In 1924, it was certainly not common, as illustrated by the conflict of composer Benito Trapagas with one of the recording companies over the sharing of profits between artist and company. See, "Hay Dinero en las Placas Fonograficas", *PFP*, 11 May 1929.

[48] Columbia records offered Vicente Ocampo a recording trip to Japan, where a permanent recording studio had been established by Columbia. "Manila Sonora", *PFP*, 12 Apr. 1930; "Grabanda la Musica Nativa.Come Hacen los Discos. Vicente Ocampo Habla de Industria— El Mejor Metodo de Dar a Conocer la Cultura Filipina es por Medio de la Musica", *PFP*, 21 July 1934. Others who benefitted from the phonographic industry were Dionisia Castro aka Toy Toy and Atang de la Rama. Ad "I. Beck Inc.", *PFP*, 5 Mar. 1932.

[49] "Behind The Scenes", *PFP*, 20 Aug. 1932. Actor Lou Salvador managed a vaudeville troupe at the Imperial Theatre, while Enrique Davila managed a group at the Palace. See ad "Palace", *Tribune*, 29 Nov. 1932, and ad "Imperial Theatre", *Tribune*, 29 Nov. 1932. See also "Will Vaudeville Stars Shine Again?", *PFP*, 10 Sept. 1932.

[50] "Will Vaudeville Stars Shine Again? Supplanted by Talkies, Stage Shows Apparently Starting Comeback at Present—Many Difficulties to Be Overcome", *PFP*, 10 Sept. 1932.

and former manager of the Savoy Nifties, J.C. Cowper, implicitly affirmed the *Free Press*'s conclusions. In 1932, interviewed by the paper, he, like Carvajal, also looked back acknowledging that the period between 1923 and 1928 had been vaudeville's heydays. Cowper wished to revive vaudeville and the Nifties with a mix of foreign and local artists, apparently to bring back some of the pop cosmopolitan flavour that had evaporated. Moreover he stated, "[t]he low innuendos and the coarse jokes of the comedians must be cleaned up", as he had received many complaints "from prominent Filipino women, clubs and associations".[51] These statements strongly suggest that vaudeville had lost its classy image and its middle- to upper-class patronage and had drifted in the direction of banal entertainment. It would not recover from this trend.

What veteran of the Spanish stage Eliseo Carvajal did not foresee was that the new sound movie technology would give new impetus to the local film industry that had once began in 1917. Between 1932 and 1935, a few new film companies were founded that produced sound movies that propelled new local talent.[52] These companies were Parlatono Hispano-Filipino Inc., formerly Malayan Movies and the Filipine Film Company. Both companies aimed at exporting films, especially to Hawai'i and the Pacific coast, centres of migrant Filipino communities.[53] A closer look at these two companies shows that they were linked through producer and director Jose Nepomuceno, one of the owners of Parlatono Hispano-Filipino Inc. Nepomuceno directed films for the Filipine Film Company, and the latter company used Nepomuceno's film studios. Former boxing promotor, vaudeville pioneer and Manila carnival entrepreneur Eddie Tait, was one of the co-owners of the Filipine Film Company.[54] The year 1932 was exceptional in terms of the number of local films produced; it was however between 1937 and 1942, when the economy had recovered from the global crisis, that the local industry seriously expanded in terms of the number of film companies and productions. The Second World War halted this artistic output.[55]

Like the silent cine before, the local sound movie industry offered employment opportunities to zarzuela and vaudeville stars, but also to poets, novelists,

---

[51] "To Bring Back Vaudeville J.C. Cowper Plans to Mix Foreign With Local Talent—Would Have Companies Imported for Six Weeks", *PFP*, 17 Sept. 1932.

[52] "The Silver Screen In The Philippines", *PFP*, 28 June 1930; "News of The Week", *PFP*, 12 Aug. 1935. According to Yeatter (2007: 19), Jose Nepomuceno's 1933 film *Punyal Na Ginto* (The Golden Dagger) was "the first complete sound production [...]".

[53] "Local Cinema Companies Move Ahead. Ambitious Plans for Philippine Pictures Call New Crop of Stars Into Limelight", *PFP*, 24 Aug. 1935.

[54] Yeatter (2007: 20–3).

[55] Del Mundo (1994: 59–61).

playwrights, composers and musicians.[56] In 1934, *The Philippine Herald* wrote: "Local writers, actors, and labor have benefited immensely from the impetus given the industry by the Filippine Films. Stories screened are by local writers; the actors are all natives of the Philippines; the directing and camera staffs are also made up of young people 'made' in the Philippines."[57] Filmmakers adopted stories from both the moro-moro theatre and zarzuela.[58] In addition to this, Clodualdo del Mundo, in his history of Philippine cinema, asserts that film contributed significantly to the popularisation of Tagalog and Tagalog songs and vice versa.[59] Among the local writers connecting to this nascent sound movie industry was vernacular poet Jose Corazon de Jesus. His involvement in the blossoming film industry is consistent with his interest and active participation since the mid-1920s, in modern, popular vernacular literature, theatre and music. As a playwright, he was connected to film producer and director Jose Nepomuceno. De Jesus even appeared on screen in 1932, in a leading role as hero, in the first Filipino talkie *Sa Pinto nga Langit* (At Heaven's Door), a screen adaptation of his poem *Nostalgia*. De Jesus passed away unexpectedly in May 1932.[60] Putting his activities in perspective, we can see de Jesus as a person whose literary talent and performative skills led him to contribute to Filipino pop cosmopolitism and popular art through his cross-border activities in balagtasan, theatre, music, and, eventually, sound movie. This creative mind and trendsetter was no more, as if his death marked the end of an era. And it should be noted that balagtasan, the poetic joust, a popular vehicle for social and political critique in the 1920s, was no longer part of the vaudeville repertoire in the 1930s. The two had been disconnected. And like vaudeville and zarzuela, the popularity of this literary genre was itself in decline.[61] Vernacular vaudeville, zarzuela and balagtasan did not entirely disappear; they were detached, stripped of their modern and cosmopolitan appeal and, as a result, lost its middle- and upper-class patronage. A process of cultural reassessment and transformation

---

[56] For example, in August 1930, Manileños could witness vaudevillian Naty Fernandez in "The Child of Sorrow" at the Tivoli Theatre, see ad "Tivoli", *The Tribune*, 1 Aug. 1930.

[57] "The Philippine Motion Picture Industry", *The Philippine Herald Year Book*, 29 Sept. 1934.

[58] On the connection between the zarzuela stage and the Philippine movie industry, see Yeatter (2007: 31), see also del Mundo (1994: 66–7).

[59] Del Mundo (1994: 121).

[60] According to de Jesus's wife, his death was the result of a severe cold he contracted during the production of *Sa Pinto ng Langit*, doing a prolonged scene standing in a river to save a girl. "¡A Las Puertas del Cielo!", *PFP*, 26 Mar. 1932; "The 'King' is Dead", *PFP*, 28 May 1932.

[61] See Almario (2003).

had set in, captured by one periodical in 1937 stating in its headlines that "Manila vaudeville isn't too artistic [...]".[62]

The Old Vaudeville Director

In 1929, Borromeo left Manila and settled in La Paz, Iloilo City with his family. He performed regularly in Iloilo itself and toured the other Visayan Islands and Moroland. In Iloilo, following his tried-and-tested model of integrating vernacular zarzuela with vaudeville, he was connected to prominent Ilongan playwrights, musicians and zarzuela artists. On 11 and 12 September 1931, Borromeo staged a play written by local zarzuela celebrity Rosing Palacios, "prima donna from Iloilo, Negros and Capiz". The play was entitled "Cailo si Rosing" (Poor Rosing), a moralising and didactic piece warning against the dangers of vice, particularly the dance hall and bailerinas.[63] One zarzuela playwright Borromeo collaborated with was newspaperman and trade union leader Jose Ma. Nava. He was from the same generation as Borromeo, and also came from a well-to-do Hispanicised merchant family of Chinese *mestizo* origins, who moved back and forth between the cosmopolitan port cities of the Visayan islands and Manila.[64] It is, however, difficult to place Nava within the politically conservative upper-class with which Borromeo sympathised. Nava identified with the working class and he actively laboured for their emancipation. In the early 1920s, and again in the early 1930s, Nava came to be known for his leftish political leanings and as president of trade union Federación Obrera de Filipinas (FOF). The 1929 worldwide collapse of the colonial export-oriented agriculture sector forced corporations active in the Visayan sugar industry to cut on wages and to lay off workers. In response to these measures, the Iloilo and Negros labour movement radicalised and Nava took a leading role. While Borromeo was staging his vaudeville in Iloilo, Jose Nava revived the Federación Obrera de Filipinas and organised labour strikes. Alfred McCoy suggests that, by 1930, the working class in Iloilo City had lost interest in the moralising and didactic plays of the vernacular zarzuela, written by local middle- to upper-class playwrights. He asserts that: "Working-class consciousness had outgrown the zarzuela and the vernacular theatre lost its audience."[65]

---

[62] *Fotonews*, 15 Oct. 1937.

[63] See Fernandez (1978: 153, 158). In 1930, Rosing Palacios also recorded songs with Luis Borromeo for German record company Odeon, see note 21.

[64] Fernandez (1978: 74–8, 146–7); McCoy (1981: 56–7).

[65] McCoy (1981: 61).

Though they may have differed radically on socio-political issues, Nava and Borromeo worked together on the vaudeville stage. In 1931, Borromeo staged the drama "Duha ka Gugma" (Two Loves), said to be a "Drama Patriotico en 3 actos", likely written by Nava and a play in which he probably also had an acting part.[66] Borromeo was apparently able to maintain, at least for the time being, the Iloilo public's interest in his vaudeville. In 1934, ignoring the theatrical crisis in the capital, he boldly announced to establish a chain of vaudeville theatres in the Visayan Islands. This plan brought Borromeo briefly back to Manila, where the *Free Press* spotted the "Old Vaudeville Director" that same year. He also appeared on the radio, accompanying his wife on piano rendering a kundiman song.[67] His main goal in the capital, however, was to reunite some of his former vaudeville protégées, and take them back to the Visayan Islands for the vaudeville theatre circuit he envisaged. Like his debut in Cebu City and Manila more than a decade earlier, Borromeo was out to entice the "Iloilo businessman and the sugar baron from Occidental Negros", thus continuing to pursue his ideal of attracting upper-class patronage.[68] This was quite a different audience than that targeted by Iloilo's zarzuela playwrights, such as trade union leader Jose Nava who, according to Alfred McCoy, promoted their zarzuela plays "as didactic forum to uplift the urban mass", which is to educate Iloilo's working class.[69] It should, however, be recalled that Borromeo's vaudeville had been highly didactic and moralising in the 1920s as well, for instance, through the balagtasan contests.

Borromeo's Visayan vaudeville circuit did not materialise. One reason for this failure was that the pool of artists was thin and there was little new talent on the horizon. Several artists chose to stay with the few remaining vaudeville troupes in Manila or had simply retired from the vaudeville stage.[70] Some had moved abroad, working for the American vaudeville stage, while others had sought a career in the dance halls or in the burgeoning local cinema industry. Another

---

[66] Ad "Cine Lux Theatre", *Makinaugalinon*, 13 Aug. 1931. No further details are available on the content of this patriotic play. The show was preceded by a silent movie. Fernandez (1978: 153).

[67] "Borromeo Lou 'Come Back', Old Vaudeville Director Gathers His 'Children' Together for New Circuit in Visayas—Comparative Salaries of Stars", *PFP*, 2 June 1934.

[68] Ibid.

[69] McCoy (1981: 35).

[70] In 1932, Elisabeth Cooper had moved to the US, married and worked as a waitress in a New York establishment. In the Philippines, it was assumed she had succumbed to tuberculosis during her trip to the US. In early 1934, she returned from the States and became a painter. "'Dimples', La Muerta Que Resucito", *PFP*, 10 Mar. 1934. Other female stars of the 1920s who had retired from the vaudeville stage were Vitang Escobar and Lucy Martin.

reason for the failure of a vaudeville circuit to develop in 1934 was that, from a political and economic perspective, it was rather unrealistic and untimely. The Visayan sugar barons had barely recovered from the economic downturn of the early 1930s, and as a consequence of impending Philippine independence in 1935 the sugar industry faced the uncertain prospects of trade with the US.

In Iloilo, Borromeo might have occasionally staged vaudeville after 1934, but he appears to have focused on composing and publishing sheet music, partly through a music publishing enterprise. Inferred from his compositions, published from the mid- to late 1930s, we can see that he had drawn closer to composing distinctly patriotic music. This is reflected in a number of songs dedicated to the National Economic Protection Association (NEPA). NEPA had been established in November 1934 in response to the Tydings-McDuffie Independence Act, approved by the Philippine legislature in May 1934. NEPA sympathisers feared that independence and free trade between the United States and the Philippines would prove detrimental to Philippine industry and commerce. They called for protective measures and promoted locally manufactured produce. The NEPA leadership was explicitly looking for cultural symbols and emblems to express Filipino nationalism.[71] As an experienced composer, Borromeo provided his patriotic services with compositions such as "Marching with NEPA", stylistically labelled a "NEPA-trot".[72] With vaudeville in decline, such commissioned work offered the old vaudeville director an income.[73]

By 1934, vaudeville's potential as classy popular art with social relevance was lost. This form of theatre was relegated to the realm of light entertainment, incompatible with Filipino cultural nationalism and high art. The exciting cultural developments of the 1920s that had once made vaudeville a popular

---

[71] "NEPA Needs an Emblem", *PFP*, 6 July 1935.

[72] Borromeo composed and published at least five songs in connection to NEPA, the National Economic Protective Association, roughly dated 1934–39. The following titles were found in the collection of sheet music of the National Library of the Philippines and in the *Union catalog on Philippine culture. Music*, published by the Cultural Center of the Philippines (1989): "Marching with NEPA" (lyrics by Elisio Quirino); "Noravic" (or NEPA-trot) (lyrics by Maximo G. Salvador). The latter song is dedicated to Nora and Victor Kilayco (Noravic). The song is also referred to as "blues"; "My NEPA Girl": A Nepa waltz/music lyrics by Elisio Quirino. Manila. Q.B.A. Productions; "Nepa Melody: kundiman ng Nepa", words by Elisio Quirino. Manila; "Ylonga Mia. Tango Ylongo" (Canto Nepa). Letra de Flavio Zaragoza Cano. Musica de Luis F. Borromeo. H & B Music Publishing. City of Iloilo.

[73] "Votad. A Patriotic Call of the Filipino Women", published by Borromeo Lou, Manila, P.I. c. 1935. This score contains a list with Borromeo's other compositions. His published song repertoire from the mid-1930s suggest that, stylistically, he was still very much into musical eclecticism as well as a hybridity of old: tango moderato, rumba, tango occinegrino, waltz, classic waltz, oriental foxtrot, habanera Ylonga, hymn blues, and tango lento.

Illus. 6.1   Cover of the score "NEPA Melody" by Luis Borromeo aka Borromeo Lou, c. 1939.

art quickly faded. The same happened to those who together had contributed to the new popular art. Some of Luis Borromeo's collaborators are still remembered and honoured, like Jose Corazon de Jesus for his literary achievements; but these people are rarely understood as being once closely connected forging a new innovative popular art.

Between 1925 and 1936, similar processes of the waxing and waning of popular culture occurred in colonial Indonesia, albeit under different socio-political conditions. Unlike Luis Borromeo, who was from the educated upper class, it was a young illiterate Javanese woman, Miss Riboet, who, together with her educated husband, would pioneer a new culture in colonial Indonesia.

Chapter 7

Doing the Charleston Gracefully

Luis Borromeo had established himself as a new, popular star and as an icon of a new culture in the Philippines. Meanwhile, a young Javanese woman from humble origins, Miss Riboet, was going through a similar process, albeit under different socio-political conditions in colonial Indonesia. Her artistic versatility and repertoire struck contemporaries as novel and innovative and, above all, exciting. In the chapters that follow, we will take a closer look at how Miss Riboet rose to stardom, how she assumed the role of a cultural broker, connecting arts and artists and opening up Malay opera to the masses. In Chapters 9 and 10, the case of rival Malay opera company Dardanella is used to show how a popular culture was not only fully emergent, but how modern Malay opera, and Dardanella in particular, formed a cultural node within a socially relevant new culture. In the early 1930s, this new culture was gradually being debated in the politically and socially (racially) segregated and polarised environment of colonial Indonesia. Under these conditions, a shift in Miss Riboet's audience would occur, which marked her alienation from a socially significant popular culture and the nationalist movement.

This chapter opens with two general sections dealing with the cultural and socio-political context in which Riboet and Dardanella were operating. The first section loosely addresses global and local cultural encounters, the second focuses on the struggle for emancipation and independence in the Dutch East Indies.

Riboet, as we will learn from the third section, was of humble Javanese origins. She married an educated peranakan Chinese, Tio Tek Djien Jr. The peranakan Chinese, as we will see in this and other sections, contributed significantly to a hybrid popular culture in the East Indies as well as in the Straits Settlements. Riboet and Tio modernised Malay opera, and attempted to make it a legitimate form of theatre. Like Luis Borromeo, they would build on existing arts, including an older form of Malay opera, *Komedie Stamboel*, which is central in the section "The Stamboel Mould". This is followed by a section devoted to one of Riboet's major innovations in Malay opera: topical singing. Topical singing established her status as a daring female artist as well as her popularity as a socially significant performer.

While foreigners generally held homegrown popular music and theatre from the colonies in contempt, foreign record companies were not bothered by such moral and aesthetic considerations. As will be shown in the final section, Riboet was the first female in colonial Indonesia to be recorded extensively by a German record company on 78rpm shellac disc, the modern media and consumer item of the 1920s. These records brought her name and fame beyond the Dutch East Indies, into British Malaya as well.

Cultural Encounters of the Local Kind

In 1927, the Englishman Hubert Banner published a book on his 12 years of residence on the island of Java. Reminiscing about one of his many cultural encounters on the island, he wrote:

> At a jollification on an estate in 1925 I saw several Javanese notables who were present fox-trotting with every appearance of delight. But the dance was ill-suited to the gravity of their attire and demeanour. For dull and uneventful as the Javanese dance may appear to our eyes, it possesses at least a grace and dignity completely alien to the grotesqueries to be seen in European ballrooms. But perhaps we need not wonder at that. The Javanese is a creature infinitely higher in the scale of creation than the West-African buck to whose carnal, gin-cum-ju-ju frenzies we, following America's lead, owe the inspiration of such quasi-epileptic buffooneries as, for example, the Charleston.[1]

Like Filipinos, the Javanese and other colonial subjects in the Netherlands East Indies had enthusiastically picked up modern social dances.[2] Banner, like Filipino Hispanicised elites assessing Filipino modern dance lovers, was simultaneously surprised and disgusted that the Javanese, most likely of aristocratic origins in this case, had embraced popular Afro-American dances. In the Englishman's view, a mismatch had evolved between the refined and emotionally restrained Javanese court culture with its "grace and dignity" and the "quasi-epileptic" foxtrot of the jazz age.[3] Modern American popular culture, in the form of the foxtrot and the Charleston, were at the lowest levels of Banner's imagined cultural hierarchy. In other words, the Javanese had succumbed to banal entertainment imported from the West.

---

[1] Banner (1927: 97).

[2] In spite of the popularity of modern jazz dances, a dance hall culture as in the Philippines or the Straits Settlements, did not develop in colonial Indonesia.

[3] Banner (1927: 177–8), condemned jazz dances in the popular parlance as a "neurasthenic variety". See Evans (2000: 101–2), on such widely shared negative psychological meanings attributed to jazz.

Apart from being startled by other colonials mimicking modern social dances from the West, Hubert Banner also looked down upon "natives" creating hybrid forms of travelling theatre known as Komedie Stamboel and bangsawan. The two theatrical genres initially developed independently in the late 19th century to converge into "Malay opera", through the exchange of play repertoire, songs and casts. Surabaya was the birthplace of Komedie Stamboel, "Indonesia's first translocal cultural form".[4] Bangsawan had originated slightly earlier in the Straits Settlements.[5] The central piece of a Malay opera show was a play, in the form of a musical or comedy, or a combination of the two, alternated with intermissions featuring dancing, singing, or acrobatic acts. The sources for the plays were often adapted versions from the stock of Arabian nights stories, European popular novels, Sino-Malay literature, Javanese theatre (*wayang wong*), Chinese opera and, from the 1920s, also from American (silent) movies.[6]

Banner characterised these vernacular theatrical forms as "the grotesque travesty of opera" and his derogatory view was widely shared by Dutchmen in the colony.[7] But it was precisely these travesties that underwent transformation in the mid-1920s. They would fuse into what came to be known as modern Malay opera, which formed a node of a new, popular culture in colonial Indonesia. Moreover, like the popular reception of classy vaudeville promoted by Luis Borromeo in the Philippines, this modernised theatre was surrounded by a renewed cultural dynamism and exhilaration, embodied by Miss Riboet. Across the main cities and towns of the Netherlands Indies, this excitement was shared by a multi-ethnic spectatorship, cutting across the working and middle classes. This spectatorship would eventually include Dutchmen and Eurasians who had initially ignored and dismissed Miss Riboet's Malay opera as second-rate theatre of the native working classes.

In 1926, like a wild fire, this Javanese Malay opera actress and singer caught the public attention of the Sino-Malay and Dutch print press across Java's urban north coast. Banner, in his work on Java, however, made no mention of her. Given his cultural biases, and possibly because his command of Dutch and Malay was insufficient, he apparently failed to see the cultural and social significance of this young Javanese woman. In contrast, local audiences were amazed by her daring stage appearance and the modern outlook of her theatre. According to non-European contemporaries, she danced the Charleston gracefully and brought a new fashion into the "native world", namely dancing the tango, waltz and foxtrot

---

[4] Cohen (2006: 84).

[5] Tan (1993); Cohen (2002).

[6] Jedamski (2008: 489, 492).

[7] Banner (1927: 86).

to the local hybrid musical style of *kroncong*.[8] The latter was also the name for a ukulele-type instrument, of which Banner wrote: "The kronchong, a species of guitar, is exceedingly popular among Eurasians and young native bucks, many of whom play very skilfully. The airs they play, such as the famous 'Star of Surabaya', are characterised by an eerie, haunting sadness."[9] Miss Riboet not only performed kroncong, she was also among the first in Malay opera to employ explicitly a "jazz band". In 1926, she was the undisputed star of Surabaya, a harbour city in East Java, where she debuted in late 1925 with her Malay opera company Orion, co-owned and managed by her husband. Until the economic collapse of early 1930s, the 1920s proved the plantation economy's heydays. Within the colonial cash-crop economy, Surabaya formed an important commercial node creating the conditions for a wealthy multi-ethnic middle class to develop and for Riboet to become a star of a new popular culture.[10] By the early 1930s, when the great depression had sunk in, she had grown into the first supra-local popular culture star, whose fame reached beyond the cities of Java's north coast (*pasisir*) into the so-called Outer islands of Indonesia and British Malaya.

Between 1930 and 1934, and again in 1938, Miss Riboet toured British Malaya. In 1932, she was taken by boat to Sandakan, British Borneo, with a Malay opera cast of around 100 individuals, including a large orchestra and a soccer team. At Sandakan, the local press recorded a successful performance.[11] From there, the journey continued north through the southern Philippines up to Manila. In February 1933, Riboet appeared in the Philippine capital, possibly at the Manila Carnival.[12] Reminiscing about her visit to the Philippines on the radio in 1934, she related how she was awestruck by the fact that Filipinos walked down the streets with shoes. She was also impressed by the fact Manila was awash with female dance experts. Riboet may have had the bailerinas in mind, many of whom she jokingly told a reporter, look like "dried fish". Her journey to the Philippines enriched her song repertoire with a few Hispano-Filipino airs, and Filipino and Filipina vaudevillians became members of her cast.[13] From the Philippines and passing through Saigon, the journey continued to British Malaya, where she arrived in 1933. Before moving back to the Netherlands East Indies in 1934, the harbour town of Kelang, close to Kuala Lumpur, was chosen as the

---

[8] On the musical genre of kroncong and its stylistical transformation, see Yampolsky (2010).

[9] Banner (1927: 290).

[10] Dick (2002: 64–72, 120–2, 429).

[11] "Sandakan notes", *British North Borneo Herald*, 3 Jan. 1933.

[12] Unfortunately, I was unable to find any reference to Miss Riboet in contemporary Philippine periodicals.

[13] "Boeal. Omong omong dengan Miss Riboet", *Sinar Deli*, 31 Oct. 1934.

temporary residence and base of operations for touring the Straits Settlements of Singapore, Penang and Melaka and the Federated Malay States (FMS).

In many respects, 1926 was pivotal in the history of Indonesia. Riboet's rise as the first trans-local star of a nascent modern theatre coincided with increased social unrest and political turmoil. Industrial strikes in the harbour cities Semarang and Surabaya in 1925, were followed in 1926 by a communist uprising in Java and Sumatra that lasted into 1927. While Hubert Banner may have been ignorant of Riboet's ascendency as a popular star, the political upheaval of 1926 did not escape his attention. In his book on Java, two chapters are dedicated to the turbulence. One chapter was entitled "The Native as a Nationalist" and the other, rather euphemistically, "Some Present Day Problems of the Dutch Colonists". It was exactly in this climate of social discontent and political confusion that Riboet came to the fore as a new, popular star.

Emancipation

Since the 1910s, a new generation of Indonesians, local Chinese, Indo-Arabs and Eurasians emerged. They had enjoyed a Western-style education, had become political conscious, aspired social mobility, which was frustrated by a Dutch colonial policy of racial discrimination, and were interested, if not intrigued, by modernity and cosmopolitanism.[14] These people were at the inception of voluntary associations like Tiong Hoa Hwee Koan (The Federation of Chinese Associations, est. Batavia, 1900), Al-Irshad (est. Batavia, 1914) and the modernist Islamic organisation Moehammadijah (est. Yogyakarta, 1912). They were also the driving force behind vernacular newspapers, schools, hospitals and orphanages. In 1900, with the rise of Chinese nationalism and the colonial government's failure to provide education for Chinese, local Chinese founded the Tiong Hoa Hwee Koan (THHK). The federation offered a modern Chinese-language education based on Confucianism.[15] In 1926, THHK ran around 100 schools in Java, 10 of which were in Surabaya.[16] THHK's success inspired Indonesian-Arabs in 1914 to found the Indo-Arab organisation Al-Irshad (Guidance).[17] In 1925, Moehammadijah operated 55 schools, 2 hospitals and an orphanage.[18] In spite of the common aim of emancipation, these organisations remained divided (also internally) over issues of race, class, citizenship, religion, education and

---

[14] Shiraishi (1990: 30); Mobini-Kesheh (1999).

[15] Govaars (2005: 45, 47, 58–9).

[16] "Sekolah-sekolah Tionghoa di Indonesia", *WW*, 30 Nov. 1926.

[17] Mobini-Kesheh (1999: 35–8).

[18] Poeze (1982: xxxi).

cultural identity. Many locally rooted "Europeans" or "Dutchmen", including many Eurasians, perceived the ethical policy of uplifting native Indonesians and those sympathising with the emancipatory movement (pergerakan) as a threat. In 1917, the colonial government opened up the lower to middle bureaucratic ranks to native Indonesians. In 1919, in response to this policy, Eurasian white-collar workers organised and founded the Indisch Europees Verbond (IEV, Eurasian League). IEV developed into a social organisation to protect the economic interests and privileges of middle-class Eurasians who were rooted in the Indies. The organisation followed much the same trajectory as the other emancipatory organisations, establishing an educational fund and a teaching school in the early 1920s.[19] By this time, many of the emancipatory organisations faced financial troubles, possibly caused by the economic crisis at that time.[20] During 1921–22, exports dropped and an economic recession ensued. Even after 1925, when the export economy rapidly recovered, the financial conditions of most organisations remained precarious.[21] As I will show in Chapter 9, as the colonial government rarely endorsed social welfare activities and with the economic setbacks of the early and particularly late 1920s, popular culture would gain new social significance.

The social and political climate of the 1910s induced discussions about the impact of modern Western influences on Javanese culture. This concern was part of a growing Javanese elitist nationalism that had gained momentum in the 1910s in response to new social movements like Sarekat Islam.[22] As in the Philippines, anxieties about modernity evoked renewed interest in "tradition", in this case in ancient, pre-Islamic Hindu-Javanese cultural heritage, from architecture to music.[23] In June 1921, a meeting was held by the Java-Instituut, a private organisation that aimed at developing and disseminating the native cultures of Java, Madura and Bali. The meeting's theme was how to protect and preserve Javanese music. Present were Dutch and Javanese members of the institute, the latter without exception *priyayi* (Javanese bureaucratic elite), and a number of guests, including economist Julius Boeke and founder of modern ethnomusicology Jaap

---

[19] In 1926, IEV membership amounted to around 12,000, spread over 84 branches, see Meijer (2004: 85–9).

[20] Govaars (2005: 57–8) notes the financial troubles that THHK faced running schools between 1917 and 1922. Mobini-Kesheh (1999: 59–60) relates that Al-Irshad's "finances was a constant concern [...]", and "[...] the state of al-Irshad finances compares favorably with the often parlous financial situation of its contemporary, Sarekat Islam".

[21] The Indonesian colonial economy, according to Touwen (2001: 47), in the 1922–29 period was one of "increasing prosperity and rising export volumes".

[22] Shiraishi (1990: 41–90).

[23] On this revival of Javanese culture, see also Cohen (2010: 81–3).

Kunst. All present at the 1921 meeting shared similar assumptions about the decline of Javanese arts and perceived Western music, particularly non-classical music, as a threat to Javanese music that deserved to be banned. Boeke's ideas on a weak native economy endangered by Western capitalism proved perfectly compatible with those on the state of Javanese arts. Both the economy and arts needed protection from outside influences.[24] The meeting concluded that to turn the tide of "the cinema music, violin orchestras, the gramophone and the vulgar American dances", it was imperative that government-sponsored music schools be established to expose Javanese society to Western-style musical education and to save the *gamelan* (gong ensembles) from perishing.[25] Kunst's advent in Java in this period coincided with a growing concern among the priyayi that Javanese performing arts were on the decline. He found it difficult to accept that cultural transformations had occurred in Indonesia (for centuries, in fact) and assumed that indigenous musical traditions were under threat due to "the hybridizing influence of alien musical influences".[26] Kunst was also averse to theatre or music as vehicles for social or political critique. Similar to his contemporary Raymundo Bañas in the Philippines, Kunst took an ambiguous yet basically anti-modernity position; a response to accelerated cultural transformations in the jazz age. His answer to this state of affairs took the form of documenting, conserving and reviving what this Dutchman perceived as authentic and traditional Indonesian music, particularly Javanese court music. The other side of the coin of his anti-modern reflex was that he downplayed and ignored modern, hybrid forms of popular culture as a subject of ethnomusicological research. This blind spot would include Miss Riboet and her artistic endeavours and many Malay opera troupes that flourished while Kunst was in Java.

Unlike Kunst and the Javanese bureaucratic elite, Riboet's husband Tio Tek Djien Jr. did not see a demise of cultural traditions, rather the reverse. Without

---

[24] As early as the 1910s, Julius Boeke propagated his thesis of the dual economy based on his experience in colonial Indonesia and India. Boeke saw a fundamental and unbridgeable difference between two co-existing Western and Eastern economic systems; one capital intensive and high tech, the other labour intensive and technologically underdeveloped. In his view, the penetration of capitalism in rural Java, for instance in the form of a money economy, was detrimental to the Javanese subsistence economy. It drove peasant into the hands of moneylenders who through credit controlled labour and land. Boeke promoted actual measures such as cooperative societies to protect Javanese peasants from these alleged evils of capitalism. This "ideology of protecting the peasant", as it has been coined by Jennifer and Paul Alexander (1991), had the effect that non-farm activities, such as trade and manufacturing by Javanese, were ignored and regarded by colonial officials and intellectuals as insignificant.

[25] *Djåwå*, no. 1 (1921).

[26] Kunst cited in Heins (1994: 20–1).

being specific about traditional customs or practices, Tio believed that tradition hampered progress. In 1927, he explicitly propagated the movement and transformation of "tradition", at least when it concerned Malay opera. He and his wife consciously aimed to create a modern form of Malay opera to break away from the conventional Stamboel theatre. This became their mission and they would be very successful.[27] At the same time, the couple remained wary about the influence of modern Western culture on, especially, Indonesian youngsters and, in particular, young women. This tension between tradition and modernity was reflected in the plays staged by the company, a topic that will be discussed in detail in Chapter 8.

A Bit Stiff

In 1927, a reporter of the Sino-Malay newspaper *Warna Warta* from the city of Semarang, Java, reviewed Riboet's dancing skills. He scrutinised her Javanese dance as "a bit stiff" (*sedikit kakoe*); her performance of the Charleston, however, was judged as skilful (*pande*).[28] In 1930, the Penang-based Anglo-Chinese newspaper, the *Straits Echo*, wrote about Riboet in similar terms, namely that "[a]s a dancer from the Indies she has no equal. She […] even [does] the Charleston gracefully […]."[29] She was not entirely self-taught, at least when it concerned dancing. Between 1926 and 1928, Riboet took dance instructions from a Javanese court dancer. In 1928, she was under the wings of American professor C. Thereses, who attempted to polish her modern jazz dances skills, like that of the Charleston.[30] This modern dance instructor toured with Miss Riboet and, a year later, in 1929, he was at the heart of a moral controversy about modern dances within the Singapore Anglicised Chinese community.[31] It was a controversy reminiscent of the moral discussions on modern social dance in the Philippines of the late 1910s and early 1920s.

---

[27] "Het een en ander over den Stamboel", *De Locomotief*, 18 June 1927.

[28] "Gagak Solo", *WW*, 25 June 1927.

[29] "Miss Riboet's 'Orion' in Penang. A Capital Show. Drury Lane Crowded Every Night", *The Straits Echo*, 13 Jan. 1930.

[30] Ad "Miss Riboet", *WW*, 12 Apr. 1928; "Miss Riboet", *WW*, 3 May 1928.

[31] Some prominent people within Anglo Chinese community depicted foxtrots as evil dances and the professor and his female students became the subject of debate in the print press. On the controversy see "A Dancing Lesson. III. The Backward Chassee. By Prof. Thereses", *The Malaya Tribune*, 23 Oct. 1929; "Is Dancing An Evil", 24 Oct. 1929; "Is Dancing an Evil?", *The Malaya Tribune*, 28 Oct. 1929; "To Dance or Not to Dance?", *The Malaya Tribune*, 28 Oct. 1929; "Is Dancing An Evil?", *The Malaya Tribune*, 30 Oct. 1929; "Is Dancing An Evil?", *The Malaya Tribune*, 7 Nov. 1929.

The assessment of Riboet's Javanese dance by a peranakan Chinese from Semarang is evidence of the aesthetical intimacy of locally-rooted Chinese with Javanese performing arts, a familiarity that dates back to the early 19th century.[32] The peranakan Chinese reporter understood the high artistic standards required for Javanese court dancing; the refined, prescribed bodily movements learned through protracted training. For the reviewer and the newspaper reader, Riboet clearly did not meet these artistic standards. This critical review suggested that she was not, or insufficiently, initiated in the arts of the Javanese court, let alone of Javanese aristocratic origin. In spite of this critique, her performance was nonetheless appreciated.

As the foregoing suggests, Riboet was indeed raised outside the environment of Javanese court culture. She was born in 1900 to a humble Javanese family and her social origins were no secret to her adoring audience. Raised in the social environment of the *tangsi* (military barracks) of the Royal Netherlands East Indies Army (Koninklijk Nederlandsch-Indisch Leger, KNIL), Riboet's very first performing experience as a child was entertaining the multi-ethnic group of native soldiers with her singing.[33] The colonial army formed an outlet for the vast labour reservoir of illiterate and poorly educated natives, particularly from rural areas in Java where unemployment was high.[34] Among the recruits was Riboet's father, who at the turn of the century, was stationed in Aceh, North Sumatra. The late 19th century was an era of imperialist expansion. The Dutch launched several military campaigns in various parts of the archipelago, including Aceh, to subdue "independent" native rulers and to expand and consolidate its territory from claims by other colonial powers. By the turn of the 20th century, the Dutch broke Acehnese resistance in a series of military campaigns, involving Riboet's father.[35] Inspired by the military and social turmoil of his time, and according to Javanese name-giving custom, the girl was given the name of Riboet. In both Malay and Javanese, the word *riboet* (*ribut* in modern Indonesian) is used to indicate a "storm", "turmoil", or "excitement". Her parents could not have foreseen the appropriateness of the name. During the second half of the 1920s, exactly when Miss Riboet rose to fame, the colony witnessed another period of political turmoil. In addition, her Malay opera performances excited audiences to

---

[32] Kartomi (2000: 282–6). See also Rustopo (2007).

[33] This biographical data on Miss Riboet was obtained from a rare 1935 NIROM radio broadcast relayed from Bandung to the Netherlands on 18 Aug. 1935. HA-000016, NIROM 31-08-1935. Collection Nederlands Instituut voor Beeld en Geluid.

[34] Teitler (2006: 155–9).

[35] According to Miss Riboet, her father was awarded medals by the colonial government for his military services in Aceh, see "Miss Riboet", *Algemeen Dagblad de Preangerbode* (*Preangerbode*), 22 May 1931.

the extent that the catchy phrase "Riboet bikin riboet" (Riboet causes upheaval) was repeated in the print press wherever she staged her shows.[36]

In 1922, when she started performing professionally in Malay opera, Riboet was still an inexperienced and mediocre singer-actress. She worked for a Stamboel troupe managed by Tio Tek Djien Jr. in the city of Pekalongan, north central Java. Tio, born in 1895 in Nganjuk, East Java, was from a wealthy peranakan Chinese family. In the early 1920s, his family had moved to the city of Pekalongan. The Dutch-educated Tio was a well-known figure in town.[37] He managed a family-owned amusement park that included a cinema theatre and a Stamboel troupe and also worked as editor-in-chief for a local Sino-Malay weekly published in Pekalongan.[38] The park, or at least its cinema, closed down in September 1925, possibly due to the aftermath of the economic downturn of the early twenties.[39] The amusement park's demise apparently stimulated, rather than discouraged, Tio and Riboet to embark on a new venture. In 1925, they married and founded the itinerant Malay opera company with the Dutch name of Maleisch Operette Gezelschap Orion.

As Hubert Banner had already emphasised unambiguously, Europeans tended to rank Malay opera and its predecessors (Komedie Stamboel and bangsawan) as inferior to European theatre. In European eyes, Malay opera represented diluted Euro-American plays and songs. In short, Malay opera, and this was shared by many intellectual Indonesians, was considered unsophisticated entertainment for the native and Eurasian lower classes.[40] As we will learn in the following chapters, the innovations Riboet and her husband brought to Malay opera would change such derogatory views, particularly among the "European" middle class, and even some upper-class Indonesians.

---

[36] "Apa jang kita soeda liat", *Soeara Publiek* (*SP*), 19 Aug. 1927; "Miss Riboet bikin riboet", *SP*, 29 Aug. 1927; "Miss Riboet di Malang", *SP*, 1 Oct. 1927, Modjokerto; "Miss Riboet bikin 'riboet'", *WW*, 3 Apr. 1928; "Miss Riboet bikin riboet kota", *Pewarta Soerabaja*, 18 Apr. 1940.

[37] "Saben Saptoe", *Sindoro-Bode*, 9 Sept. 1922. "Miss Riboet", *Nieuwe Soerabaja Courant*, 20 Aug. 1927.

[38] Whether Tio Tek Djien Jr. combined his editorial job with managing the amusement park is not clear. *Sindoro-Bode* was in circulation between May and September 1922. The weekly aimed at a readership of all races (*boeat segala bangsa*). Tio was temporary editor-in-chief. Editors were: M.H. Sastroamidjojo; Kwee Hoo Tjien; P. Johannes, Cirebon-agent; Bratanata, Cirebon-agent and Souw I Hok, Indramayu-agent.

[39] The Court of Justice in Semarang publicly declared the cinema bankrupt on 1 September 1925. The owner was mentioned as Tik Djien Tio, cinema entrepreneur and merchant in Pekalongan ("bioscoopondernemer dan soedagar di Pekalongan"). This was probably Jr.'s father. "FAILLISEMENT2", *WW*, 7 Sept. 1925; "Faillisementen", *WW*, 16 Feb. 1926.

[40] Jedamski (2008: 482).

Rowdy and undisciplined audiences were a reality, compounding the image of Malay opera as unsophisticated, working-class entertainment.[41] Interaction between actors-singers on stage and the audience was common, if not central to the Malay opera spectacle, and did not fade with the ascendency of Miss Riboet. Audiences identified with stage characters and this would sometimes evoke their emotions publicly. For example, in 1930, during a drama staged by another leading Malay opera company, Dardanella, which featured feuding members of competing royal families, spectators exclaimed "Boenoeh sama dia" (Kill him/her!) or "Boesoek Dia!" (Damn Him/Her!).[42] If audiences behaved improperly during performances, artists would sometimes mock them. This could be straightforward verbal attacks. For example, in 1929, Riboet delivered pantun, a Malay-Javanese tradition of four-lined verse, in the musical style of kroncong to a number of intoxicated Dutch spectators, singing: "Gentlemen if you drink so much you will not be able to work tomorrow."[43] Verbal quarrels between artists and spectators were also frequent. In some instances, the excitement turned into scolding, often of a racialist nature, which would disrupt shows and call for police intervention.[44] For example, in 1927, when a group of Chinese spectators disturbed one of Riboet's shows at the Stadstuin Theatre in Surabaya, her director husband Tio called in the police to restore order. The Chinese violators, however, did not appreciate this decision. They opined that Chinese community leaders, instead of colonial authorities, should have handled what they considered an internal Chinese affair. The culprits retaliated with a tar attack on the white plastered theatre walls, the ticketing booth, the temporary Surabaya residence of Riboet and Tio and, to complete the list, the residence of one of Riboet's staunchest fans, a wealthy Chinese merchant. The police apprehended the violators. This fuelled rather than dampened the latter's discontent. In response, these Malay opera lovers now called for a total boycott of the troupe. Boycotts were a common Malay opera fan strategy to

---

[41] Cohen (2006: 68–9, 128).

[42] "De Dardanella Opera", *De Sumatra Post*, 2 Dec. 1930.

[43] "Miss Riboet. Hamlet, rumoer en watersnood", *Deli Courant*, 9 Sept. 1929.

[44] "Penonton contra eigenares Opera Kim Ban Lian", *WW*, 19 Oct. 1926; "Mabok, masoek tooneel", *Bintang Timoer*, 1 Nov. 1926; "Tida sopan", *WW*, 4 Oct. 1926; "Riboet", *Sin Jit Po*, 25 Aug. 1927; "Kliwat sopan …?", *WW*, 5 Dec. 1928; "Pertoendjoekan amal", *WW*, 4 Feb. 1929.

demonstrate publicly discontent with certain actors or troupes.[45] In the case of Orion, the boycott seemed not to have found resonance and the troupes popularity continued to grow undisturbed.

The image of unsophisticated theatre also developed as the *anak wayang*, the cast, generally had little or no education at all, placing them low on the social ladder. Riboet herself was illiterate. Females formed a specific category. As with bailerinas in Manila's dance halls, moralists among sections of the European and peranakan Chinese middle classes associated female actresses-singers with low moral standards, who entertained lax sexual relations. For example, the fact that (unmarried) female actresses appeared on the stage before male audiences evoked debates among peranakan Chinese in Bandung and in other places.[46] Some reporters perceived female actors-singers as prostitutes.[47]

The Stamboel Mould

On 10 November 1925, Tio and Riboet premiered with their Maleisch Operette Gezelschap Orion at the Stadstuin Theatre, Surabaya. Surabaya was the commercial node within Java's plantation sector and it would be the place where Miss Riboet's breakthrough as star of a novel Malay opera would occur. Orion's Surabaya season lasted six months, from early November 1925 to late May 1926. In a city as big as Surabaya, it was common to have two or even three Malay companies simultaneously staging their shows for weeks or even months and to have other types of entertainments. For example, Orion's Surabaya debut overlapped with the presence of two other Malay opera companies in the city, the Malay Opera Constantinopel and Union Dalia Opera.

Moreover, in early November 1925, a Javanese theatre (*wayang*) troupe, Saritomo, stayed in town briefly; a night fair was held in November featuring kroncong competitions and gamelan (Javanese gong ensemble) performances, not to mention Hollywood film productions screened in two silent film theatres,

---

[45] "Miss Riboet en de Chineezen", *Soearabaiasch Handelsblad*, 13 Sept. 1927. Another example is Malay opera company Komidi Amoenaris, which was effectively boycotted by Chinese in Tulungagung, East Java for its alleged racial discrimination of Chinese. "Amoenaris di boycot", *WW*, 16 Aug. 1926. A similar case of alleged racism and boycott occurred with Miss Inten's Malay Opera Company in Juana, Central Java, see "Miss Inten's Indisch Operette Gezelschap diboycot?", *WW*, 30 Nov. 1928.

[46] "Hal prampoean Tionghoa naek di atas tooneel toeroet tjampoer maenken lelakon sama orang lelaki", *Sin Po*, 11 Aug. 1922. "Dari Anak Hartawan Mendjadi Actrice Bangsawan", *Pewarta Deli*, 30 Aug. 1929.

[47] "Gara-garanja Krontjong Bandoeng", *WW*, 17 Sept. 1927; "Gamboes padang prampoean", *WW*, 25 June 1928.

Rialto and Sirene Bioscope.[48] This list of very local and global entertainments is obviously proof of the urbanites' appetite for popular culture. Popular entertainments formed a considerable source of municipal revenue. City authorities, for instance, taxed Malay opera by imposing a levy on tickets.[49] In 1931, during the annual Pasar Gambir fair in Batavia, Miss Riboet was reported to have been a significant source of municipal income due to the great number of spectators she drew.[50]

Illus. 7.1 Union Dalia Opera company, one of the modern Malay opera companies of the 1920s, its cast, some with their offspring, and a jazz band inspired orchestra during its Surabaya season, Kranggan theatre, 1927. Among the popular actresses-singers of this troupe was Miss Inten, one of the ladies pictured centre stage. From *D'Oriënt*, 20 August 1927.

---

[48] Opera Constantinopel performed from late November 1925 to 13 January 1926. Union Dalia Surabaya season lasted from late April to mid-July 1926. See ad, "Opera Constantinopel", *Pewarta Soerabaia*, 5 and 13 Jan. 1926. In March 1926, Rialto cinema screened *The Thief of Bagdad*, featuring Douglas Fairbanks, ad "Rialto", *Pewarta Soerabaia*, 5 and 13 Jan. 1926.

[49] From January to May 1926, the municipality of Surabaya received f 64.311 (f = guilders) on entertainment revenue. In this five-month period, the urbanites had spent no less than f 385.871 on Malay opera, cinema and so forth. The total entertainment revenue in 1926 was estimated at f 175.000, based on an average of f 15.000 a month. "Belasting tontonan", *SP*, 14 June 1926. Entertainment revenue returns in the city of Semarang were also significant, see "Oeang jang masoek pada gemeente", *WW*, 29 Oct. 1926.

[50] "De Tent van Miss Riboet", *Het nieuws van den dag voor Nederlandsch-Indië*, 5 Sept. 1931.

Right from the first public appearance in Surabaya, the company announced that it offered a modern form of Malay opera or Stamboel.[51] Riboet's and Tio's attempt to modernise the existing Stamboel and bangsawan theatrical genre did not, however, come overnight. [52] As witnessed in the stock of plays, playwrights involved and the company's cast, at this stage of their career they relied heavily on the existing Stamboel format and on peranakan Chinese opera. The 1925 Surabaya cast links Riboet and Tio to people surrounding the original Komedie Stamboel of 1891 and to a famous peranakan Chinese opera troupe from Batavia. It is with these significant assets of experience and fame that Orion took off in Surabaya, and very much in the conventional Stamboel mould.

Although Riboet was announced in advertisements as *sri panggoeng* (heroine or leading actress), she actually shared leading roles and the stage with renowned Stamboel and peranakan Chinese opera performers. She was not yet the star she would become within a year or so. One of these renowned artists was Pieter Willem Cramer, an Eurasian from Batavia. By 1926, he was a veteran Stamboel actor, director and playwright, who, around the turn of the century, had worked together with one of the originators of the Stamboel theatre, Auguste Mahieu. Cramer was also a kroncong singer and recording artist who had collaborated with Indonesia's first phonographic recording entrepreneur, shop owner Tio Tek Hong from Batavia.[53] Cramer offered Malay opera company Orion his services as leading actor, singer, director and playwright and this led to full houses and a brief revival of his fame during Orion's Surabaya debut.[54] His reappearance on the stage was a stimulus for local music and gramophone store Lyra in Surabaya to reissue and advertise his recorded songs, like "Lagoe Nasib Cramer" (Cramer's Fate).[55] This song was composed and sung by Cramer himself and had been recorded 20 years earlier, in or around 1906, by Tio Tek Hong. With his long

---

[51] "Komedi Stambul Orion pada pers", *Sin Jit Po*, 9 Nov. 1925.

[52] For example, Cohen (2006: 338, 366), insists that Riboet claimed they presented *toneel* (*tonil*) that came closer to European drama, to distinguish themselves from Komedie Stamboel and bangsawan. Such claims came later and were often made by others. It is safe to say that throughout their career, Riboet and Tio remained ambiguous about how to label their form of theatre.

[53] On Cramer, see Cohen (2006: 242–56). On Tio Tek Hong, see Keppy (2008: 148–9).

[54] Cramer directed several plays such as "Pembalesan Heibat" (The terrible revenge). Ad, *SP*, 25 Dec. 1925. He took the leading role in the play "Eleonora", ad, *SP*, 9 Jan. 1926. Cramer's "new" drama Haroon-Sjah & Siti Wania was staged on 13 Jan. 1926. Ad, *SP*, 13 Jan. 1926. He took a co-leading role with Miss Riboet in the play "Kedjahatan2 di Astana Koerdistan" (Crimes in a Kurdistan Palace) that he also wrote himself, see ad, *SP*, 16 Jan. 1926.

[55] Ad "Muziekhandel Lyra", *SP*, 9 Dec. 1925. *Daftar dari namanja plaat Odéon Malajoe dan Tjina* (c. 1912), pp. 84–5.

Illus. 7.2 Pioneer Malay opera actor and director, singer and recording artist Pieter W. Cramer and a leading lady (*sri panggung*) from the Malay opera stage in Batavia, promoting Odeon records and equipment, c. 1912. The Malay texts reads: "Stamboel Batavia, presenting selected songs from the cast of Mr. Mahieu's theatre", the originator of Komedi Stambul. Courtesy of Jaap Erkelens.

standing in Komedie Stamboel, spanning around 30 years, it is very likely that
Cramer was instrumental (and crucial) in teaching Tio and Riboet some of the
theatrical ins-and-outs. From December 1926 onwards, Cramer is no longer
mentioned in relation to Orion or any other Malay opera company.[56] By then,
Riboet was in the process of becoming the company's leading lady.

In the early stage of Riboet's career, we also find two peranakan Chinese opera
actors on Orion's bills: Hwan Lee Hwa and Sim Tek Bie. They were from the
well-known peranakan Chinese opera company Komedie Swie Ban Lian from
Batavia.[57] These peranakan Chinese actors showed close connections and affinity
with the Stamboel stage, local hybrid music, the early commercial recording
industry and Sino-Malay literature. In sum, peranakan Chinese actively
participated in and represented a proto-popular culture of Java's urbanised North
coast.[58] Sim Tek Bie directed plays and also took leading roles, as in the play Sie
Lay Kon atawa Aboenawas Tionghoa (Sie Lay Kon or the Chinese Abuwanas).[59]
In contrast to Stamboel icon Cramer, the Chinese opera veterans of Swie Ban
Lian continued to work with Orion during the company's Batavia debut in
December 1926.

Riboet and Tio relied heavily on Sino-Malay stories. One example is the
very popular story "Nyai Dasima", about the ill fate of a *nyai*, a "housekeeper",
a "kept woman", basically meaning a concubine, often of wealthy Europeans
and Chinese.[60] Dasima is lured away from her European master-cum-lover by a
man greedy for her wealth, and eventually murdered on his orders.[61] Up to the
Japanese invasion of Southeast Asia in late 1941, Sino-Malay classics like "Nyai

---

[56] In contrast to the Surabaya season six months earlier, advertisements in *Bintang Timoer* and *Sin Po* show Cramers striking absence from the Malay opera stage.

[57] Ad "Orion", *SP*, 22 Feb 1926. Different romanised spellings were used for the Hokkien name of this company, including Soei Ban Lie and Swi Ban Li. On Soei Ban Lie, see Salmon (1981: 40) and Sumardjo (1992: 112).

[58] Around 1906, with the help of Cramer, Sim Tek Bie and many others of her company, recorded over 60 songs, including kroncong and Stamboel music as well as Chinese (Hokkien) opera songs. An Odeon gramophone record catalogue (c. 1912) lists many *lagoe* (songs), for example: "Lagoe Stamboel Satoe", "Bintang Sourabaya" and "Krontjong". Among the latter category was Dji Hong, a song that Miss Riboet herself interpreted and recorded in 1927. Swie Ban Lian's cast also performed and recorded on gramophone popular Sino-Malay stories that became Stamboel classics, such as the romance of "Sam Pek Eng Tay" and "Nyai Dasima". The plays were sold in series of five separate 78rpm records. *Daftar dari namanja plaat Odéon*, c. 1912, p. 88.

[59] Ad "Maleisch Operette Gezelschap 'Orion'", *Pewarta Soerabaia*, 18 Mar. 1926.

[60] See Siegel (1997: 54).

[61] Nyai Dasima was authored by an European G. Francis and published in 1896 as *Hikajat Njai Dasima* and adapted into verse and a short story series by local Chinese around the turn of the century. See Salmon (1981: 26, 32).

Dasima", would remain essential in Orion's play repertoire. These dramatic plays appealed to Surabaya's peranakan Chinese and beyond. In advertisements placed in the Sino-Malay press in late 1925, Orion's management politely addressed this audience as *tongpauw* (a Hokkien term for "fellow countrymen").[62]

Musical eclecticism was not novel to Orion Malay opera; from the outset it had been central in bangsawan and Komedie Stamboel.[63] What was new was that a single individual, Riboet, covered different musical genres and sang a variety of popular foreign tunes. Audiences loved both her flexibility in dancing styles and her versatility in musical genres and song repertoire.[64] Although she performed kroncong songs, unlike many other Malay opera singers, Riboet, for reasons unknown, refrained from engaging in the very popular kroncong contests that were held across Java in the 1920s.[65] Some journalists-cum-fans wished that she would challenge some of her prominent contemporaries from the kroncong stage in these exciting singing competitions. Backed by her Malay opera orchestra, Riboet thus rendered an eclectic musical repertoire, including some genres that, in spite of their labels, are difficult to pinpoint stylistically. For example, in spite of its title, the song "Orion Jazz", recorded by German company Beka, showed little or no relation to Afro-American syncopated music. The use of a wood bloc and occasional snare drum, both associated with a drum set that also went by the name "jazz", was probably sufficient to label the song as jazz.[66] Jazzy, or to be more precise syncopated dance music is a good description of Riboet's rendition of the American global dance hit "Yes! We Have No Bananas", released by Beka in 1927. Like vodavilista Natalia Morales in Manila, who had transformed the song into a Tagalog-English gag, Riboet also retained the melody, and turned the English lyrics into Malay, ridiculing the poor cooking skills of a female servant (*babu*), a domestic worker found in better-off families.[67] At the other extreme of Riboet's musical spectrum were

---

[62] Ad "Komedie Stamboel Maleisch Operette gezelschap 'Orion'", *Sin Jit Po*, 25 Nov. 1925.

[63] See Tan (1993: 37–9, 132–41) for the incorporation of foreign or "exotic" songs, such as the cake walk, Hungarian dances, waltzes, marches, tango and ragtime into the turn-of-the-century bangsawan musical repertoire.

[64] "Miss Riboet's 'Orion' in Penang. A Capital Show. Drury Lane Crowded Every Night", *The Straits Echo*, 15 Jan. 1930; "De Tent van Miss Riboet", *Het nieuws van den dag voor Nederlandsch-Indië*, 5 Sept. 1931.

[65] On kroncong contests, see Keppy (2008).

[66] Orion Jazz. Beka B 15103 – II; Ah, Ah, Ah (Lagoe Turki), Beka 27788.

[67] Riboet's rendition was entitled "Baboe ndie Lombok-se (Bananas Leloetjon)", Beka 27820. In Indonesia, the American song "Yes! We Have No Bananas" was available on 78rpm disc performed by a number of American bands with and without vocals and also available as published piano score, see ad, "W. Naessens", *Bataviaasch Nieuwsblad*, 2 Jan. 1924; ad, "K.K. Knies", *Bataviaasch Nieuwsblad*, 26 Jan. 1924.

Javanese folk songs accompanied by a gong ensemble, such as the song "Bapak Poetjoeng", also recorded by Beka.[68] She also replaced original lyrics of foreign hits songs with her own in the hybrid vernacular Malay or Javanese. Her sources of musical and linguistic learning were phonographic records and, later, also, the talkies.[69]

Modernisation of Riboet's Malay opera came through different people and ways. One key figure was peranakan Chinese journalist, poet and fiction writer Njoo Cheong Seng, who joined the troupe somewhere in early 1926 and who remained with the company until early 1933. He traded Orion for the Moonlight Crystal Follies in Penang, to Diamond Star in Sumatra, and eventually to rival Malay opera troupe Dardanella in 1934.[70] Similar to contemporary Jose Corazon de Jesus in the Philippines, Njoo would contribute to cultural innovation and to a vibrant localised popular culture, by linking vernacular literature to theatre and eventually also to film. Evidence of Njoo's early interest in popular culture dates from 1922. He published a book of over 100 verses in the Malay-Javanese poetic idiom of the pantun or *syair* dedicated to the popular kroncong musical contest. Written in a hybrid Malay, spiced-up with Dutch curses and sexual innuendo, a warning was printed on the book's cover in bold letters: "NOT FOR CHILDREN!"[71] Njoo wrote and also directed an unknown number of original plays for Malay opera company Orion.[72]

Like many Sino-Malay stories of the 1910s and 1920s, Njoo's stories centre on what Elizabeth Chandra has analysed as the "critical attitude of Indies Chinese authors towards the idea of modernity, which was seen as the progenitor of women's increasing autonomy and young people's diminishing morality in

---

[68] "Bapak Poetjoeng (extra)", Beka B 15802 – I.

[69] "Een onderhoud met Miss Riboet. Wat we zagen en hoorden", *Sumatra Bode*, 13 Aug. 1934.

[70] Between 1918 and 1962, Njoo published over 200 novels, short stories, poetry, translations, stage plays and film scripts under several aliases, Monsieur d' Amour, Monsieur Amor, Munzil Anwar, Mung Mei and M. Novel. In 1925, he was in charge of the monthly Sino-Malay magazine *Hoakiau* and was board member of a multi-ethnic association of journalists; "Pembitjara'an boekoe", *WW*, 18 July 1925; during his affiliation with Malay opera Orion as playwright, Nyoo Cheong Seng continued to work for magazines like *Penghidoepan* and *Tjerita Roman*. "Miss Riboet", *WW*, 13 June 1927. On biographical details and Njoo's literary production, see Sidharta (1995) and Maier (2002).

[71] This publication appeared under Njoo Cheong Seng, spelled Njoo Tjiong Sing Jr., under the title *Sair dan Pantoen. Krontjong trang boelan. Sair sindir menjindir nona manis* (1922).

[72] "Miss Riboet", *WW*, 13 June 1927. Njoo Cheong Seng's contribution to Orion's popularity through his stock of plays and standard was likely substantial, but remains unexplored. Claims of authorship by Tio Tek Djien Jr. complicate an assessment of Njoo's contribution to Orion stock of plays.

general".[73] Henk Maier's analysis of two of Njoo's novels point to Njoo's emphasis of misfortune, particularly as witnessed in the failure of inter-racial marriages, a recurring topic in his work. In Njoo's eyes, misadventure was the outcome of the great difficulties people experienced in attempting to reconcile social differences in a society sharply divided by colonialism, nationalism, feudalism and race.[74]

Njoo Cheong Seng's critical concern with modernity contributed to one of the innovations of Malay opera, the introduction of dramatic realism. The new realism in Malay opera operated at different levels: in the play and song repertoire, acting style and props. I will focus on the first three of these. The realism in the play repertoire was reflected in the daily realities addressed, particularly moral corruption and the anxieties of modern life; in short, the misfortune pointed out by Maier. Realism also found its way into music, and Riboet did so in a highly original and innovative way. She set storytelling known as *dongengan* to modern music, turning it into topical singing.

Dongengan

Riboet gave Malay opera intermissions, or extras, a different twist, addressing social issues in songs. This innovation leaned on older forms of vernacular oral literature; pantun and syair, and a performing style adopted from *sindiran,* a verbal battle, current in kroncong singing contests.[75] Whether Riboet was the first to introduce topical singing (dongengan) into Malay opera we will probably never know.[76] Certain is that this new way of performance set her apart from previous and contemporary Malay opera artists and popular singers as innovative, modern, witty and a socially relevant singer. In the premier show in Surabaya, Riboet featured two *dongeng* (tales) she had "written" herself and that addressed topical issues *(hal).*[77] Improvising in pantun and syair, Riboet sardonically commented on daily affairs, instead of universalistic themes such as romance. In one dongeng she raised the issue of the River Brantas's foul stench, caused by the pollution of upstream industries. Riboet indicted the municipality authorities for taxing the urbanites (read: Malay opera spectators) for the use of this contaminated water.

---

[73] Chandra (2011: 20).

[74] Maier (2002: 7–8).

[75] On sindiran in kroncong contests, see Keppy (2008: 143–4).

[76] In Myanmar (Burma), actor-singer-dancer Po Sein is credited with having introduced topical singing somewhere between the 1910s and early 1930s: "While dancing, he would talk to an audience about the story of a zat [PK: a drama based on history or legend], about the religious precepts, or about incidents in his own life, and then, ending the dance, would turn his narration into song" (Maung and Whitney 1998: 79).

[77] Ad "Orion", *Sin Jit Po*, 9 Nov. 1925.

In another tale, Riboet addressed her Surabaya audience singing about the city's industrial labour force and the recent walkouts that occurred during her presence in the city. These topics hit a chord with illiterate, lower-class Indonesians who were informed orally and visually, and even more so with the inter-ethnic newspaper-reading middle-class audience. The latter group read, were concerned about or had opinions on urban revenue rates, hygiene, labour unrest, ethnic strife, indebtedness, poverty, prostitution and so on, as reported daily in the Dutch and Sino-Malay newspapers. Her novelty of hilariously raising social issues caused a stir among and left a deep impression on the Surabaya spectators, including peranakan Chinese journalist Kwee Thiam Tjing, who would become her first outspoken devotee.

A recurring topic in songs as well in the dramas was a critique of immoral behaviour. For example, Riboet would sing about the temptations of gambling and the ill fate of those who lost everything due to this popular pastime. Another favourite was to warn both sexes against extra-marital escapades.[78] The audience turned into a group of curious and careful listeners who did not want to miss a song or a joke and the underlying moral message. According to one reviewer, "one could hear a needle drop to the floor" during Riboet's performance.[79] Surabaya Sino-Malay newspaper *Sin Jit Po* referred to the sung tales as *pantun-nasehat* (*nasehat* meaning "advice" in Malay), indicating the act's moralising and didactic character. Hence, the public's praise for an entertaining performance implied the audience's appreciation of Riboet's moral guidance, given in a recognisable vernacular and literary form.[80] Such morality-soaked verse was popular and also circulated in print, for example in *Doenia Istri*, a women's magazine published by peranakan Chinese women Surabaya. In 1928 and 1929, the magazine published a series of *syair nasehat* addressing the issue of gambling.[81]

In 1927, Riboet's reputation as entertaining moral compass and social critic on stage led Sino-Malay newspaper *Warna Warta* to dub her "a walking newspaper", more appropriately translated as "living newspaper". One paper spoke of Riboet's sung social critique on stage as serving "the public interest". In a similar fashion, some people imagined that "journalistic blood ran through her veins", all indicating the social relevance of her popular act.[82] Encouraged by her

---

[78] "Miss Riboet", *Nieuwe Soerabaische Courant*, 25 Nov. 1925; "Miss Riboet", *Kemadjoean* IV, no. 37, July 1927; "Miss Riboet", *Midden Java*, 30 Sept. 1930.

[79] "Miss Riboet's—Melatie v. Agam", *Bintang Timoer*, 6 Dec. 1926.

[80] "Maleisch Operette 'Orion'", *Sin Jit Po*, 11 Nov. 1925.

[81] See for example "Sair Nasehat. Oleh Miss Pek Hiang Nio", *Doenia Istri*, Oct. 1928.

[82] "Miss Riboet", *WW*, 13 June 1927; "Dongenan Miss Riboet … Djoega boeat kepentingan publiek", *Pewarta Deli*, 15 Nov. 1929.

appetite for articulating social criticism in public, one newspaper offered a list of social issues she could address.[83] Her daring sung poetry also inspired the print press to reproduce Riboet's dongeng in print.[84] Moreover, it proved infectious, inspiring journalists to create their own verses to capture a similar excitement.[85]

According to one newspaper, Miss Riboet's reproaches did not strike the people, but the authorities.[86] Given the repressive political conditions, people tended to associate Riboet's performances with a certain unrestrained straightforwardness, as well as a courage to speak out on social issues in public. During a show, a reporter caught one spectator, his voice low, asking another viewer whether Miss Riboet "was not afraid of being hit by the sedition law (*spreekdelict*)".[87] Riboet, however, was careful to avoid addressing politics and nationalism openly. In 1931, in one of the few interviews she gave throughout her career, she reiterated that "she had never spoken about politics".[88] In fact, this silence on political issues appeared to have been the policy of most, if not all, Malay opera companies.

While she may have been a social critic, Riboet was still a long way from being subversive. As will be demonstrated more extensively in the next chapters, Malay opera would briefly develop into a socially significant theatre; it was, however, never associated with resistance and subversion as, for instance, Hispano-Filipino zarzuela theatre in the American-occupied Philippines. If there was a candidate for such subversive theatre in colonial Indonesia it was the Javanese theatrical art of *ketoprak*. We first hear of it in 1926, when newspapers, amazed by the popular appeal, report of a novel and innovative form of theatre drawing thousands of Javanese villagers in the Yogyakarta and Solo areas of Central Java. At this early stage, most of the spectators were reported as being of working-class origins.[89] The theatre's name was interchangeably referred to as "wajang orang ketoprak", "wajang ketoprak", "komidi ketoprak", "toneel Djawa ketoprak" or just simply "ketoprak". The term was said to have been either derived from the sound produced by a case used by peasants to carry machetes, and a so-called *arit*, a

---

[83] "Miss Riboet Review", *Pewarta Soerabaja*, 18 Aug. 1927.

[84] "Miss Riboet", *Kemadjoean* IV, no. 37 (July 1927). The dongeng concerned was a syair in Javanese, in which Riboet amongst others warned against the evils of gambling and adultery.

[85] "Ada ada sadja. Dongeng diserahken pada Miss Riboet", *Bintang Timoer*, 30 Oct 1926; "Mas Chauffeur ngantoek?", *WW*, 13 June 1927; "Miss Riboet dan Journalistiek", *Pewarta Deli*, 2 July 1929; "Boeal. Omong-omong dengan Miss Riboet", *Sinar Deli*, 31 Oct. 1934.

[86] "Pengisi Soedoet", *Bintang Borneo*, 6 June 1932.

[87] "Miss Riboet", *WW*, 13 June 1927.

[88] "Miss Riboet", *Preangerbode*, 22 May 1931.

[89] "Indonesia. Jogjakarta", *WW*, 25 Oct. 1926; "Binnenland. Een zonderlinge opera", *De Indische Courant*, 1 Nov. 1926.

sickle, or from a wooden utensil used to pound paddy. Both readings, true or not, hint at the theatre's rural origins.[90] In contrast to modern Malay opera, and right from its inception, ketoprak was associated with vulgarity, immorality and soon also political resistance. Within a year, in 1927, and in spite of its dubious artistic and subversive nature, it moved from a form of rural entertainment for Javanese peasants into one equally patronised by urban middle- to upper-class Javanese, including priyayi, Javanese aristocrats working for the colonial bureaucracy. For instance, in May 1927, a certain Djojodipoero, a former *bupati* (regent), sponsored a ketoprak benefit show in the city of Yogyakarta and was even reported to own a troupe in 1928.[91] Prince Pakoe Alam from Yogyakarta, who normally patronised *wayang orang* plays, the Hindu-Javanese versions of the Ramayana and Mahabharata stories, also started to take an interest in the novelty.[92] In June 1927, we hear of the first ketoprak troupes in the city of Yogyakarta, owned and managed by peranakan Chinese.[93] By then, the genre was so popular that the Semarang-based Sino-Malay newspaper *Warta Warna* spoke of ketoprak troupes mushrooming in the so-called principalities of Yogyakarta and Solo.[94] By 1928, ketoprak companies were found across the island of Java. Given the fact that Javanese was ketoprak's medium of communication, it was only Javanese-speaking people who had access to this form of theatre.[95] The popularity of the genre and its musical repertoire had grown to such heights in 1928 that it had come into the orbit of the commercial recording industry. German phonographic corporation Beka started recording ketoprak songs performed by Javanese kroncong divas, such as Herlaut.[96]

Like Filipino vaudeville and modern Malay opera, ketoprak went through a process of cultural borrowing and experimentation. Early observers of this form of theatre found it difficult to grasp its meaning and felt insecure about where or

---

[90] "Oude en nieuwe kunst op de Djokjasche jaarmarkt-tentoonstelling", *Het nieuws van den dag van Nederlandsch-Indië*, 19 July 1927; "Ketoprak in de praktijk", *Soerabaijasch handelsblad*, 26 June 1929.

[91] Djojodipoero was most likely Raden Mas Toemenggoeng Djojodipoero, musician at the court of Yogyakarta, who, according to contemporary and ethnomusicologist Jaap Kunst, was the "greatest musician and expert of Javanese gamelan music". Letter dated 12 Mar. 1928 from Jaap Kunst to German record company Odeon. Jaap Kunst collection, University of Amsterdam special collections. Box no. 877.

[92] "Ketoprak", *WW*, 20 May 1927; "Djokja", *De Indische Courant*, 14 July 1928.

[93] "Ketoprak", *WW*, 27 June 1927. The Chinese troupe concerned was named "Pakoempoelan Ketoprak 'Tionghoa- Toegoe Djogja'".

[94] "Oedjan ketoprak", *WW*, 19 May 1927.

[95] "Gemengd Indisch nieuws", *Het nieuws van den dag van Nederlandsch-Indië*, 28 July 1928.

[96] "Opname plaat Beka", *WW*, 8 Mar. 1928.

how to place it. Similarly, as the hybrid theatre of Komedie Stamboel had been assessed, journalists tended to emphasise that ketoprak was simply an artistically poor form of theatre. It had an eclectic and, for outsiders, rather confusing, musical and play repertoire of kroncong songs, Chinese plays and wayang stories mixed with scenes from *One Thousand and One Nights* stories accompanied with and without a gamelan or with banjos or European violins. Some even doubted whether such hybrid experimental theatre would survive as a separate theatrical genre at all.[97] Reports also note the "democratic" character of ketoprak being open to and performed by people from all walks of life, without prior education in Javanese arts: high school students, *sado* (carriage) drivers, laundry bosses and coolies.[98] In 1927, according to locals themselves, the genre had already been around for years and therefore could not be named a modern achievement (*pendapatan modern*) at all.[99] In fact, and based on preliminary research by ethnomusicologist Philip Yampolsky, ketoprak was a musical genre that had existed at least since the beginning of the 20th century, which transformed into a theatrical genre in the 1920s.[100] As said, ketoprak theatre was associated with vulgarity and immorality due to its working-class audience, the simple and often filthy rural venues where plays were staged, and also because of rough dialogues and cursing on stage. According to some newspapers, it was better for youngsters' education that they avoid ketoprak, as it would promote prostitution, divorce and theft.[101] According to a Dutch observer in 1929, ketoprak served primarily to ridicule the Dutch and native officials working for the colonial government, secondly, to mock the industrialists (presumably Dutch and Chinese), and thirdly, the Europeans. Ketoprak troupes staged scenes of village heads implicated in exploitative Dutch-imposed tax revenue and land owning systems, of political exile camp Boven Digoel, and of life at the Javanese royal palaces (*kraton*). This not only demonstrates that realism had entered ketoprak, it also shows that this theatre, unlike modern Malay opera propagated by Miss Riboet, offered a straightforward critique of Dutch colonialism and its native collaborators who

---

[97] "Indonesia. Jogjakarta", *WW*, 25 Oct. 1926; "Binnenland. Een zonderlinge opera", *De Indische Courant*, 1 Nov. 1926; "Oude en nieuwe kunst op de Djokjasche jaarmarkt-tentoonstelling", *Het nieuws van den dag van Nederlandsch-Indië*, 19 July 1927; "Ketoprak in de praktijk", *Soerabaijasch Handelsblad*, 26 June 1929. It should be noted that, unlike Malay opera, ketoprak has survived until today.

[98] "Ketoprak in de praktijk", *Soerabaijasch Handelsblad*, 26 June 1929.

[99] "Ketoprak tersiar", *WW*, 1 Oct. 1927.

[100] Email communication with Philip Yampolsky, 23 and 26 Oct. 2011.

[101] "Ketoprak", *WW*, 8 July 1927; "Gemengd Indisch nieuws", *Het nieuws van den dag van Nederlandsch-Indië*, 28 July 1928.

were depicted squeezing the Javanese common people.[102] According to one reading of the origins of ketoprak, it was born exactly in the wake of and in response to Dutch regulations to curb political meetings in the early 1920s.[103] Hence, the theatre became a popular Javanese vehicle for articulating social and political critique and for promoting Indonesian nationalism. This is exactly why, already in its early stage, this Javanese theatre started to draw the interest of the Dutch authorities who linked ketoprak to communist and nationalist propaganda and agitation. The police started policing and prohibiting shows. For example, in one case, the local authorities banned a ketoprak play representing the 19th-century Java war, the struggle of the Javanese prince Diponegoro against the Dutch, because it was regarded as being veiled Indonesian nationalist propaganda.[104] The police monitored travelling ketoprak troupes that toured estates in central Java and Sumatra believed to disseminate communist propaganda among Javanese plantation workers.[105] Because of its subversive content, somewhere in 1928 or 1929, the Dutch governor of central Java prohibited by decree ketoprak shows for the whole of his administrative region, a measure that proved impossible to implement and that was therefore lifted shortly after.[106]

Its highly Javanese and radical character probably prevented ketoprak from turning into a form of theatre with "national potency" acceptable to political moderate non-Javanese Indonesians. After 1929, reports about its subversive nature dried up. By 1934, ketoprak was an accepted and largely depoliticised genre; the Indies radio aired its songs and scenes and the genre had been adopted by the Javanese royalty it had once ridiculed. This historical trajectory of ketoprak would, in many ways, be similar to Miss Riboet's modern Malay opera and the development of Malay opera in general.

Reigning Supreme

Between 1927 and 1932, Riboet recorded around 180 songs for German phonographic recording company, Beka. These songs covered a variety of genres, including some of her dongeng, released as the special Miss Riboet Records series. This audio output probably makes her the biggest recording artist in the

---

[102] "Ketoprak in de praktijk", *Soerabaijasch Handelsblad*, 26 June 1929.

[103] "Inheemse Volksvermaken. De Ketoprak", *Het nieuws van den dag van Nederlandsch-Indië*, 26 Aug. 1930.

[104] "Een verbod", *De Indische Courant*, 26 Apr. 1927.

[105] "Cultures. De Vorstenlandsche Landbouwvereeniging in 1927", *De Indische Courant*, 9 Mar. 1928; "Deli. Klachten zonder grond", *Bataviaasch Nieuwsblad*, 24 Oct. 1929.

[106] "Ketoprak in de praktijk", *Soerabaijasch Handelsblad*, 26 June 1929; "Ketoprak-opvoering", *Soerabaijasch Handelsblad*, 4 Sept. 1929.

pre-Second World War Malay world, and possibly Southeast Asia.[107] German engineer Max Birckhahn, who was also active in the Philippines, recorded the bulk of these songs during Riboet's 1927 season in the city of Semarang, Java.[108] It was common for the phonographic corporations to dispatch their engineers overseas with mobile recording equipment. The engineers relied on brokers, as we witnessed in the case of the prominent Filipino Teodoro Kalaw in Manila. These were locals who assisted and led these engineers to artists, and who directed them to sites suitable for audio recordings where makeshift studios were created. This was the way Birckhahn worked in the Philippines in 1929, and with Riboet two years earlier. The newborn diva had caught the attention of Beka, through people working for Beka's local agent in Indonesia, Behn Meyer and Co.[109] As the recording artist herself related, the recording sessions with Birckhahn proved exhausting, even for a young woman with her stamina. Recordings were made during daytime, a period when Riboet would normally take a rest to recover from the previous night show, or when she usually rehearsed with the opera company. Within a time span of nine days, Birckhahn recorded 100 songs in between Riboet's Malay opera performances and rehearsals.[110]

The shellac discs found their way to the consumer through Behn Meyer & Co., who sold the Riboet series at the popular night fairs, and who supplied many retail shops across Java. In Singapore, Mong Huat & Co. and Lohman & Co. Ltd. acted as Beka's sole representative.[111] Orion's management also sold records at shows. From different sources, we can infer that Miss Riboet's records were in demand, even during the economic depression of the early 1930s. And in 1931, according to her own testimony, in the face of the global economic crisis, from a

---

[107] Even a popular kroncong singer like Siti Amsah, who recorded a respectable number of at least 40 songs for Odeon in or around 1930, failed to approach the number of 180 songs recorded by Miss Riboet. Information on Siti Amsah's phonographic production courtesy by Jaap Erkelens.

[108] The other recording German engineer active for the Lindström concern in Asia was Heinrich Lampe, who also recorded Miss Riboet in Java. According to information gathered by Jaap Erkelens from a Beka catalogue, Riboet was recorded in Batavia in 1926–27, 1928 and 1930; in Surabaya in 1926–27; in Bandung in 1928; in Cilacap in 1929 and 1930. No mention is made of Semarang, indicated by Riboet herself as recording site. Email communication with Jaap Erkelens, 26 Jan. 2018.

[109] "Miss Riboet", *Preangerbode*, 22 May 1931.

[110] "Het een en ander over den stamboel", *De Locomotief*, 18 June 1927.

[111] "Behn Meyer & Co", *De Indische Courant*, 8 Oct. 1927; ad "Toko Tan Tjin Diok, Soerabaja: Inget! Miss Riboet Platen, 1 September", *Sin Jit Po*, 23 July 1927; ad "Toko Willem Odeon Platen", *WW*, 26 Oct. 1927; ad "S.H. Dhoebijan, Semarang", *Boemi Melajoe*, 29 Sept. 1927; ad "Mong Huat for Beka", *The Straits Times*, 15 Jan. 1928; ad "Beka", *The Malaya Tribune*, 4 Oct. 1930; ad "Beka", *Sin Po*, 28 Oct. 1930; ad "Beka", *Sin Po*, 29 Oct. 1931.

much larger group of artists previously recorded in Indonesia, Beka continued to record Miss Riboet only.[112] In that same year, even Jaap Kunst, founding father of modern musicology and hostile to modern hybrid popular musical genres, to his great regret had to admit that "Miss Riboet and her Stamboel repertory are reigning supreme in [...], kampungs via the gramophone".[113] In 1934, the colonial authorities in Singapore enhanced Riboet's reputation as "Miss Noise" with a regulation regarding "post-midnight noises in the Colony". The regulation was introduced to reduce the disturbing sounds of gramophones played in private and public, amongst others during Muslim praying hours. Based on a 1934 report from *The Straits Times*, ethnomusicologist Tan Sooi Beng relates that "an outraged house-holder, unable to listen any longer to Miss Riboet's ditties in the neighbouring servants' quarter could 'invoke the aid of the law'".[114] Similar reports about phonographic noise are found in the print press in colonial Indonesia. Also in 1934, an European lady complained about a Chinese family residing next to her: "if the radio is not playing, the gramophone is—the Chinese adolescents in the house under consideration have one single Miss Riboet record, and they get never tired listing [sic] to the piercing voice of this celebrated vaudevillian".[115] Popular culture had produced a novel urban "sound scape", or maybe "noise scape" for those not in favour of Miss Riboet's vocal qualities.

It is difficult to tell to what extent the gramophone, a relative expensive luxury, had become affordable for the new inter-ethnic middle class. We have to rely on impressionistic notes referring to consumption of phonographic players and records. For example, in 1932, the Dutch paper *Sumatra Post* reported on what was regarded the usual furniture of a native Post Office official. The official's movables included "a complete modern outfit, including a mirror-faced wardrobe, a dressing table, a gramophone player panelled and complemented with a small sprung seat". The same source claimed that hundreds of such Post Office employees were said to exist, thus suggesting they had a similar consumer taste.[116]

Another example on consumer taste from 1937 is related by another Dutch newspaper. Rubber production by native smallholders in Sumatra witnessed an upsurge around 1937, bringing these rubber producers new and unprecedented wealth. On the consumer-oriented lifestyle of these smallholders, the newspaper

---

[112] "Miss Riboet", *Preangerbode*, 22 May 1931. This policy of restricted recordings, however, changed after 1931, when Beka recorded several members of Malay opera troupe Dardanella.
[113] Kunst cited in Frijn (1994: 53).
[114] Tan (1996/97: 15).
[115] "Burenruzie en nog wat", *De Indische Courant*, 19 June 1934.
[116] "De overgeplaatste postcommies", *De Sumatra Post*, 1 June 1932.

reported: "A rubber tapper would hang his machete to the highest nails pinned to the wall, put aside the coconut cups [PK: for collecting latex from the trees], and he will purchase the biggest gramophone player and 'schlagers' [PK: hit songs] by Miss Riboet."[117]

Illus. 7.3 A 78rpm shellac disc of the song "Nasibnja Kambing Hitam" (The black sheep's fate), performed by Miss Riboet and her jazz orchestra and recorded by Beka around 1929–30 in the town of Cilacap. The track was taken from a larger set of songs from the musical drama "Kambing Hitam" (Black Sheep). Courtesy of Jaap Erkelens.

What attracted a multi-ethnic urban spectatorship in musical dramas such as "Black Sheep"? The next chapter will delve deeper into Malay opera-drama, focusing on the aspects of realism and morality in relation to modernity. We will also move closer into the world of the often neglected "audiences" or consumers of popular culture, with special attention for a Miss Riboet fan, the provocative peranakan Chinese journalist, Kwee Thiam Tjing.

---

[117] "Makan pensioen karet", *Het Nieuws van den Dag voor Nederlandsch Indië*, 24 Mar. 1937. "Schlager" is a German term for a very popular song that found its way into Dutch colloquial language.

Chapter 8

Constructing Meaning, Electrifying Audiences

Realism in modern Malay opera represented more than simply a departure from the tales of genies and royalty of the Komedie Stamboel repertoire. As I will demonstrate in the first section, in tandem with developments in vernacular Malay literature, particularly as produced by peranakan Chinese, realism on stage was a way to address the problems of modern life, especially ethical issues. This was a major innovation in both vernacular literature and theatre and one that proved successful in drawing mass audiences to Malay opera. In the remainder of the chapter, I will pay attention to this mass audience, the often neglected consumers of popular culture, Malay opera spectators. Miss Riboet's audience was not socially homogenous and not static in terms of social composition; a shift would occur. The final three sections of this chapter are dedicated to a specific category of Malay opera lover, the fan. I will follow the case of the fan–star relationship between the provocative peranakan Chinese journalist Kwee Thiam Tjing and Miss Riboet. Correspondence developed between the two, mutually reinforcing their stardom status: one as a sardonic columnist struggling for legal and political emancipation for the colonised in Indonesia; the other as a female star of a modernised Malay opera with a similar sense for satire, but on the safe side of politics.

Modernising Malay Opera

Malay opera play scripts have not survived, making it difficult to judge content and authorship. We must rely on titles, synopses in advertisements or, sometimes, reviews. Thus, for example, although it was announced that Orion staged two plays written by Njoo Cheong Seng, "Prampoean dan Wet" (The Lady and the Law) and "Ketawa dan Menangis" (Laughing and Weeping) in March 1926, we are largely left in the dark about the contents.[1] There is, however, no need

---

[1] Ad, *SP*, 26 Mar. 1926; ad, *Pewarta Soerabaia*, 30 Mar. 1926.

to be discouraged. We can rely on Claudine Salmon's seminal work on Sino-Malay literature in Indonesia, and the more recent work of Elizabeth Chandra; moreover, we have access to previously untapped information on Orion's play repertoire from original advertisements and reviews. These sources combined offer sufficient clues that Njoo and his contemporaries and colleagues were preoccupied with the ambiguities of modernity. From the analysis, undertaken below, of some of the most popular plays emerges the notion that it was Njoo, Tio and Riboet who firmly rooted realism in Malay opera drama repertoire, hence successfully modernising this form of theatre.

A great number of plays staged dealt with the kind of misfortune outlined by Maier. The play "Saidjah", for example, follows a rural Javanese family who have won a lottery. Unable to cope with the newly-acquired wealth, the family's happiness and harmony is eventually destroyed.[2] Disaster might have been central to the story, nevertheless, Riboet staged scenes light-heartedly and humorously. And while many comedians of the Malay opera stage were criticised for not being able to dose their jokes, Riboet's gags and witty scenes were judged as well balanced.[3]

Another recurring theme closely related to the tensions evoked by modernity was the opposition of young women to the traditional customs observed by Javanese and peranakan Chinese and, in turn, opposition of parents to modern educated and autonomous daughters. This latter issue is, for example, central in the drama "Raden Adjeng Soemiatie", written and directed by Tio, a drama genuinely popular with audiences. In 1934, it was reported that Riboet had staged "Raden Adjeng Soemiatie" over 200 times, indicating the popularity of this particular drama.[4] The story is about the troublesome relationship of a crooked Javanese aristocrat-cum-bureaucrat with his Western-style educated daughter, Soemiatie, who is "too modern" in the eyes of her conservative father. Eventually, the relationship becomes strained to the point that the daughter, played by Riboet, kills her father who is involved in dark affairs.[5]

Another example dealing with the ambiguity of modernity are stories about resistance to arranged marriages, as in, for instance, "Melati van Agam", originally published in 1923 by an obscure peranakan Chinese writer, Swan Pen, and staged

---

[2] "Saidjah", *Preangerbode*, 22 Sept. 1928.

[3] "Miss Riboet. Memang moesti dipoedjo kepandeannja", *Perniagaan*, 20 Oct. 1926.

[4] "Miss Riboet's Orion. Raden Adjeng Soemiatie", *Radio*, 15 Aug. 1934.

[5] "Javanese Drama. Miss Riboet's Company at Victoria Theatre", *The Singapore Free Press and Mercantile Advertiser*, 23 Feb. 1933; "Miss Riboet's Orion. 'R.A. Soemiatie'", *Sinar Deli*, 5 Jan. 1938.

by Orion in 1926.[6] We are fortunate to have a review of the play that allows us to gauge audience reception to this story and thus the intended meaning. The story relates an arranged marriage, or, according to a review, the struggle between youth and the older generation. A girl, Norma, impersonated by Riboet, falls in love with a young man, Idrus, who works for a mining company. They plan to marry, but meanwhile and without knowing, Norma's parents have married her off to an elder educated man, Nazzarudin. Norma complies and accepts her fate. The marriage, however, falls apart due to Nazzarudin's jealousy about Idrus. Feeling trapped in an unhappy marriage, but not wishing to resist her parent's wishes, Norma commits suicide.[7] An anonymous reviewer summed up the story as staged by Orion: "This story has been accurately written according to real conditions and events that happened recently; as such all is in accordance with the conditions as observed by the spectators in Indonesian households, [namely] disastrous arranged marriages."[8] The reviewer was referring to a recent real event, the anecdote of a 14-year-old girl from a minor aristocratic family in Bandung. The girl's parents decided to marry her off to an aged and retired district head (*wedana*). Upon hearing of the story of "Melati van Agam", the girl asked her parents to postpone the final decision for two weeks. Meanwhile, the girl bought Swan Pen's book, read it, handed it to her parents and asked them to examine its content. Three days later, the parents rejected their marriage candidate and the girl married a young man working for the State Railroad Company. Tragedy had been averted.

A similar story, in which another disastrous arranged marriage is effectively prevented, is that of "Kambing Itam" (Black Sheep), a musical drama reported to have been "written" by Miss Riboet herself. The story tells of a Javanese middle-class family troubled by the immoral and irresponsible behaviour of a father and one of his sons. The father frequents brothels, builds up huge debts and has little concern for one of his sons who is seriously ill. In order to survive financially, the parents decide to marry off their daughter Hartini to a wealthy usurer. Hartini,

---

[6] Swan Pen is very likely the same person as Noerhati Swan Pen, mentioned by Claudine Salmon (1981: 70). In spite of claims by Biran (1993: 99, 108, 111), "Melati van Agam" was thus not written by Parada Harahap. In 1931, the novel was turned into a movie by director Lie Tek Swie, the script written by Parada Harahap. See Biran (1993: 108–11). Swan Pen had also authored a book of verse (syair) under a Dutch title *Moderne meisjes* (Modern girls) in 1925, dealing with modernity and girls in urban colonial Indonesia. The title of another book *Roos van Batavia. Atau gadis terpeladjar jang bebas merdeka* (Rose of Batavia. Or the Educated Girl Who is Free) published around 1925, suggests that the issue of young women's autonomy was again central.

[7] "Kunst en Tooneel. Miss Riboet's—Melati v. Agam", *Bintang Timoer*, 6 Dec. 1926.

[8] Ibid.

played by Riboet, however, is an aspiring kroncong singer. The prospect of carving out a professional career in popular culture—she had been offered the opportunity to perform on the radio and to make phonographic recordings—is suddenly jeopardised by the marriage. Setting her individual career and ambition aside, she takes on the responsibility of nursing her elderly brother. Hartini resists her parent's decision to be married off, or, in her words, to be "sold" to the usurer; she confronts the usurer for his lack of compassion for the disabled and the destitute; she accuses her father for immoral behaviour. In the end, Hartini comes to the family's moral rescue.[9]

Audiences viewed the story of "Kambing Hitam" as a moral lesson. A reviewer of the show staged in the central Javanese town of Cepu in 1936, explained that Riboet's words "presented reality with an educational value for the spectator [brought] in a popular manner, easy to understand".[10] When, during this show, Hartini addressed the usurer about his immoral behaviour, the audience applauded, identifying and sympathising strongly with the character of Hartini. The show's reviewer went as far as to suggest that the play was socially significant, as it mirrored the social conditions of immorality prevalent in Cepu.[11]

The story "Kambing Hitam" can be read as a plea for women's autonomy, but, as previously explained, Tio, Riboet and their audiences had second thoughts about modernity, including individualism and women's autonomy. For example, in 1938, a newspaper praised the aforementioned play "Raden Adjeng Soemiatie", the modern Javanese girl with aristocratic roots, for its educative character. The paper recognised Soemiatie as having a moral compass, correcting the youth "intoxicated with modernity imported from the West and America" and who "just pick up modern elements without being selective". According to to the paper, Soemiatie did not spare parents either, who "later criticise their children's modern attitudes, while they themselves did not draw a line and took no measures to repress their children from 'indulging' in that modernism".[12] What is striking about this review, and other similar ones, is that no distinction was made between Miss Riboet as a person and the character staged. In other words, Miss Riboet was seen being synonymous with Raden Adjeng Soemiatie.

---

[9] "Kambing Hitam memboeka rahasia Tjepoe (I)", *Darmokondo*, 22 Aug. 1936; "Kambing Hitam memboeka rahasia Tjepoe (II)", *Darmokondo*, 24 Aug. 1936.

[10] Ibid.

[11] "Kambing Hitam memboeka rahasia Tjepoe (III)", *Darmokondo*, 25 Aug 1936.

[12] "[…] jang sedang dimaboek aliran modern jang diimport dari Barat dan Amerika". "[…] jang menerima sadja modern elements itoe zonder bikin selection dahoeloe". "[…] tetapi kemoedian mentjela kemodernan anaknja, sedang ia sendiri tidak watasi dan tidak adakan breidel soepaja anaknja itoe tidak 'menggeboe' dalam modernisme itoe". "Miss Riboet's Orion. 'R.A. Soemiatie'", *Pewarta Deli*, 5 Jan. 1938.

Let me end this discussion about the tension between tradition and modernity with another recurring theme, which surfaces in at least nine plays in the Orion's repertoire: concubinage. Orion often staged stories about the fate of the native mistress or concubine (*nyai*), like the classic "Njai Dasimah".[13] Let us briefly consider the play "De Smarten van Amor" (Amor's Heartaches), about a wealthy Chinese coffee estate owner who dumps his concubine in favour of an official marriage with a Chinese lady. Twenty years after having left his nyai, the businessman meets an attractive village girl whom he wishes to take as his concubine. The girl however refuses. Outraged by the refusal, the man kills the girl, to discover shortly after that he has murdered his own daughter, a child conceived with his former concubine.[14]

These dramatic plays, in which Riboet indulged in the role of a despairing daughter being married off, or featuring the ill-fated concubine, did not necessarily advocate for the abolition of the institution of the nyai, nor did they deliberately go against Javanese or peranakan Chinese practices of arranged marriages. As James Siegel has pointed out in his discussion of "Melayu" literature, it is not modernity that is propagated by the authors, or *adat*, customary law, that is denounced. The authors and playwrights of these stories sought to show that adat needed to keep up with modern times.[15] That was exactly the position taken by Tio and his wife, and this is reflected in the plays staged and interviews given.

A significant element in these dramatic realistic plays was Riboet's "natural acting". This was another of the major innovations introduced by Tio and Riboet in their efforts to modernise Malay opera. In many of the dramas, Riboet took the leading role of a struggling mother or daughter, the heroine who, against the odds, attempts to keep the family or a relationship afloat, takes revenge to undo injustices or who commits suicide. By her own account, such dramatic roles were said to be her favourites.[16] The public adored Riboet for her histrionic acting. As no-one had done before on the Malay opera stage, Riboet expressed emotions such as grief and anger. According to one review, spectators identified with her

---

[13] The concubine theme featured in the following of Orion's plays: "Hajati" (this was Orion's adaptation of Nyai Dasimah); "Njai Aisah"; "Njai Saminah atau Roesia Padang" (Nyai Saminah or The Secret of Padang); "Njai Mohani/Roesia Tandjoeng Priok" (Nyai Mohani/ The Secret of Tanjung Priuk); "Nancy, de dochter van Njai Dasimah" (Nancy, Nyai Dasimah's daughter); "De Concubine, tjoema satoe Njai Sadjah" (The concubine, It is Just a Nyai); "De Smarten van Amor" (Amor's Heartaches). Tio Tek Djien Jr. claimed to have written a sequel to "Nyai Dasima", see "Het een en ander over den stamboel", *De Locomotief*, 18 June 1927. This sequel was no doubt "Nancy de dochter van Nyai Dasima".

[14] "De Smarten van Amor", *SP*, 29 Nov. 1928.

[15] Siegel (1997: 135–6).

[16] "Het een en ander over den Stamboel", *De Locomotief*,18 June 1927.

"feeling themselves the sadness, rage and joy".[17] As a self-confessed film fan and autodidact, Riboet revealed that she had modelled her dramatic acting after her contemporaries and favourite American silent motion film actresses: Pola Negri, Norma Talmadge and European film diva Asta Nielsen.[18] Riboet's dramatic acting could literally move spectators to tears, as a journalist of the paper *Bintang Timoer* observed in 1926 during a performance of the play "Melati van Agam".[19]

A rare visual testimony of Miss Riboet's histrionic acting is a picture published in *Bintang Hindia*, 21 July 1928. It is a scene from the play "Kesedihan dalam pertjintaan" (De Smarten van Amor, or Amor's Heartaches), a story about a doomed love affair between a wealthy Chinese and his native concubine.

Illus. 8.1 The play "Kesedihan dalam pertjintaan": Miss Riboet performing her signature melodramatic acting in the role of a Javanese concubine dumped by her wealthy middle-class patron, 1928.

---

17 "Kabar Kota. De Smarten van Amor", *SP*, 29 Nov. 1928.

18 "Het een en ander over den Stamboel", *De Locomotief*, 18 June 1927.

19 "Kunst en Tooneel. Miss Riboet's—Melati v. Agam", *Bintang Timoer*, 6 Dec. 1926.

Decent Public

After the Surabaya debut, Miss Riboet's name as innovative performer of modern Malay opera quickly spread to other cities on Java's north coast. Her public grew in numbers, and from a social perspective this audience was also one in motion in terms of ethnicity, gender and class. A significant shift in audience composition was already underway in 1926, and this would eventually manifest itself more clearly in 1929.

In the first two years of her career, the peranakan Chinese and the native lower and middle classes claimed Riboet as their darling. Native lower-class interest is revealed in 1926, when the editors of the weekly *Bintang Timoer* praised Orion's director Tio for making the story "Amor's Heartaches" accessible to domestic workers, female and male servants, who were present during a performance in Batavia. According to the weekly, these domestic workers were "hardly acquainted with reading books" ("tjoema sedikit dalam boekoe"): a polite euphemism for being illiterate.[20] In other words, according to the paper, Tio was reaching out to the lower classes, offering them a moral education. Newspaper *Bintang Timoer* thus recognised Tio as a cultural broker who bridged the separate worlds of those with access to intellectual literature and those without, the ill-educated colonial underclass. Tio himself saw his role slightly differently and modestly, stating that he was attempting to bring Malay opera to a larger audience with his adaptations of Western literature.[21] In sum, Tio literally engaged in, to use Kahn's terminology, "constructing meaning for the masses".[22]

Peranakan Chinese interest in Miss Riboet existed right from her debut show in Surabaya in 1926. In 1928, for example, a theatre critic of the Surabaya Sino-Malay newspaper *Sin Jit Po*, using a hybrid of Malay, outlined Riboet's Surabaya audience in more detail: "This prima donna is the favorite of *empe-empe* [PK: Hokkien for elderly men), *entjim-entjim* [PK: Hokkien for elderly women] and women of all races […]."[23] Between 1926 and 1929, a transformation took place, away from a predominant peranakan middle-class and native working-class audience to a European and native middle-class spectatorship. Initially, the Dutch press in the colony acknowledged Miss Riboet's performances as entertaining but stated that they were not up to Western theatrical standards.[24] Such denigrating assessments of Malay opera, widely shared by Dutchmen and British subjects like Hubert Banner, began to alter during Orion's season in Semarang in 1927. In

---

[20] Ibid.

[21] "Het een en ander over den stamboel", *De Locomotief,* 18 June 1927.

[22] Kahn (2001: 18–9).

[23] "Opera Gezelschap Orion", *Sin Jit Po,* 26 Nov. 1928.

[24] "Prinses Hamlet. De schoone miss Riboet", *De Sumatra Post,* 28 Sept. 1926.

contrast to earlier doubts about the artistic level of Malay opera and its future, a reporter of Semarang newspaper *De Locomotief* concluded that:

> a separate Indisch theatre will develop, different from Western theatre, and different from the old, native wayang theatre, with its own standard of literary beauty and stage techniques. All efforts in this direction need to be noted and deserve encouragement.[25]

The Dutch press in the colony had begun to appreciate Riboet as an exceptional actress and singer, one that could compare to professional European artists.[26] And this appreciation was also reflected in her spectatorship. After the successful debut season in Surabaya, Orion reached Batavia, the colonial capital, in October 1926 to embark on another six-month season. Compared to the spectatorship in Surabaya, the audience in Batavia turned out to be far more ethnically mixed and it had a different socio-economic quality, as reported by Malay newspaper *Bintang Timoer*: "Many educated (kaoem terpeladjar) natives (Boemipoetra), together with their wives have already witnessed this play, the same for many from the Chinese quarters who paid a visit […]."[27] Two years later, this shift in the class and ethnic composition of her audience had persevered. In 1928, another significant change took place. By then, "Europeans", including high-ranking Dutch officials and native colonial officials had started to take an interest in Riboet's shows. One of the earliest reported examples of Dutch spectatorship is reported for February 1928, when resident Willem Hardeman, the highest authority of Surabaya district, patronised a show. The newspapers reported: "This visit […] is the telling example of the growing popularity of Miss Riboet", which, according to weekly *Bintang Timoer* and echoed by Dutch newspaper *De Indisch Courant*, was the best form of advertisement anyone could wish.[28] A couple months later, the *Java-Bode* reported from Batavia's Chinese quarter Glodok:

> No less than 1,200 people occupied the not very appealing theater, while 200 were unable to secure seats. Even two native members of the People's Council (Volksraad), without having the chance to witness Miss Riboet, had to return home. Pancoran road was jammed with automobiles, proof of the standing of yesterday's evening patrons. The press was as well fully represented.[29]

---

[25] "Het een en ander over den stamboel", *De Locomotief*, 18 June 1927.

[26] "MISS RIBOET IS ER WEER. 200 Menschen teruggestuurd", *Java-Bode*, 30 June 1928.

[27] "Kunst en Tooneel", *Bintang Timoer*, 20 Dec. 1926.

[28] "Miss Riboet", *De Indische Courant*, 20 Feb. 1928.

[29] "Miss Riboet Is Er Weer. 200 Menschen teruggestuurd", *Java-Bode*, 30 June 1928.

Reporters were struck by the fact that Riboet drew members of both the European and the native middle to upper classes to her shows. In other words, this middle- to upper-class patronage suggested her Malay opera was different, if not better, than any other: it had surpassed the days of the Komedie Stamboel. Another Dutch language paper noted that a "decent public" (poeblik jang sopan) was making it to Thalia Theatre, a venue normally patronised by working-class peranakan Chinese, Indonesian Arabs and native Indonesians and, for that reason, a virtual no-go zone for the middle to upper classes, especially those who considered themselves Europeans.[30] In 1928, given Riboet's growing Dutch patronage, Sino-Malay newspaper *Sin Po* went as far to suggest that Tio even privileged white people (bangsa koelit poetih) over Chinese patrons during shows, implicitly blaming him of racial discrimination.[31]

In 1929, the trend of Dutchmen discovering Riboet and patronising her shows continued; this was also observed in the city of Malang, East Java and in Medan, on the East Coast of Sumatra. Slightly bewildered by this development, a Malang-based Dutch language newspaper wrote:

> The performances staged by Malay Opera Company "Orion" […] are a curious affair. It is not just that throngs of spectators turn up (yesterday evening the show was practically sold out!); what is striking is that public attention from the European public is starkly increasing. One observes, […] more European than native spectators, which must be evidence of the standard offered.[32]

Regarding the interest of an "European" (read: Dutch) spectatorship in Medan for Miss Riboet, the newspaper *Oetoesan Sumatra* stated that: "Europeans and their wives who had little sympathy for our Malay opera, do not stay behind in hasting to find a seat every night for this opera company."[33] And, as if the colonial order and racial hierarchy had been reversed, the same newspaper also noted that when first-class seats were sold out, Dutch spectators took the lower-ranked seats that were normally occupied by the native working class. And among the first-

---

[30] "Chinese Opera", *Het Nieuws van den Dag van Nederlandsch-Indië*, 25 Feb. 1926. Thalia Komediegebouw, Prinsenlaan, Mangga Besar, was a theatre close to downtown Batavia, and a centre of Malay and Chinese opera since 1908. It was owned by Tio Tek Kang, a wealthy peranakan Chinese businessman and former landowner. Until 1928, Tio was the owner of the private estate by the name of Pesing Kalimat, Cengkarang, just outside Batavia, before he was compensated by the Dutch colonial government under the private estate abolition regulations.

[31] "Kabar Kota", *Keng Po*, 30 June 1928.

[32] "Het Gezelschap van Miss Riboet", *De Malanger*, 9 Feb. 1929.

[33] "Miss Riboet dan penonton", *Oetoesan Sumatra*, 5 Sept. 1929.

class seats occupied, the same newspaper spotted the Dutch governor of the East Coast of Sumatra, L.H.W. Van Sandick.[34]

In particular, plays that addressed the clash between "native tradition" and Western modernity appeared to appeal to "Europeans". Or, to use Tio's words when he announced the play "Raden Adjeng Soemiati": "A piece that offers Miss Riboet the full opportunity to display her theatrical talents, a sketch of life, that will appeal especially to the European, as it represent in a realistic manner the Old and New!"[35] Miss Riboet's dramatic plays unveiled aspects of daily rural Javanese life that otherwise remained distant and hidden for the majority of her European middle- to upper-class audience.[36] For instance, in the play "Saidjah", which was about the ill fate of a Javanese peasant family after winning a lottery, the audience followed Miss Riboet impersonating a Javanese villager who was confronted with modern city life. Tio could not stop emphasising that particularly the Dutch spectatorship was thrilled by this story "drawn from real village life".[37] Within the secure confines of the theatre walls and through the medium of Miss Riboet's Malay opera, "Europeans" were offered the opportunity to peep at the "native".[38]

In 1928, in spite of growing acceptance by an European middle-class audience, the Dutch ruling elite remained wary of Malay opera and Miss Riboet. Encouraged by the company's popularity and increasing Dutch patronage, Tio requested the Batavia Municipal Council to play the Bataviasche Schouwburg, the temple of high art in the colony. The council turned down the request, arguing that the theatre was not the place for "native theatrical companies" and that admittance of these sort of troupes would lead to "pollution" of the venue.[39] It is not difficult to read this in a literal as well as a proverbial sense. The idea that undisciplined Malay opera spectators would litter the site also refers to "contamination" or the downgrading of highbrow European and native

---

[34] "Toneelgezelschap Miss Riboet", *Pewarta Deli*, 30 Aug. 1929.

[35] Ad "Miss Riboet", *De Sumatra Post*, 30 Aug. 1929.

[36] "Onder vier oogen. 'Naast Elkander'", *De Indische Courant*, 12 Dec. 1933.

[37] The Malay advertisement for the play "Saidjah" read: "Satoe lelakon dalem satoe penghidoepan desa jang aseli"; ad "Saidjah", *Perniagaan*, 6 Oct. 1928. In a similar vein in Dutch, see ad, *Bataviaasch Nieuwsblad*, 6 Oct. 1928; ad, *Java-Bode*, 6 Oct. 1928.

[38] Miss Riboet's appeal to a "white" audience is reminiscent of American "Queen of Jazz" Sophie Tucker who, although not African-American, appealed to white American audiences. According to Evans (2000: 129–30), Tucker owed much of her popularity due to her "[...] ability to grant white audience access to the cultural 'blackness' that they desired as a form of primitive therapy". "The contact was possible as her 'whiteness' protected them [the white audience] from direct, miscegenatory exposure to African Americans."

[39] "Miss Riboet in den Schouwburg. Groote Belangstelling verwacht", *Het nieuws van den dag voor Nederlandsch-Indië*, 29 July 1935; "Miss Riboet in den Schouwburg. Groot Success", *Nieuws dan den Dag voor Nederlandsch-Indie*, 2 Aug. 1935.

theatrical standards by the Malay opera hybrids. In 1928, when Tio Tek Djien Jr. asked for permission to play the Schouwburg, the situation was the same as it had been since Stamboel originator Mahieu's request in October 1900. Mahieu's request to present his newly-created hybrid form of theatre was also turned down by the municipal board-controlled directorship.[40] In the case of Riboet, the Schouwburg manager had branded Malay opera companies as "second rate" (*tingeltangel*) theatres of the "coffee shop dancer type", indicating Malay opera's inferior artistry. In response to this "insult", Riboet stated that she had performed before the Mangkunegoro, one of the two royal houses of Solo, one of the cradles of Javanese court culture, and that she had entertained its highest Dutch district official, the Resident.[41] As we will see in Chapter 10, Tio and Riboet had to wait another six years before their hope of playing the Schouwburg was fulfilled, and they would be the only Malay opera company ever to achieve this. But, as we will see, this came at a price.

In contrast to Riboet's ambivalent Dutch audience, peranakan Chinese were generally in closer cultural proximity to Malay opera, due to their sensitivity to Malay and Javanese culture, and due to their closer interactions with native Indonesians. It should be emphasised that peranakan Chinese, as embodied in Njoo Cheong Seng, Tio Tek Djien Jr. and, as we will see in the next sections, Riboet-fan Kwee Thiam Tjing, participated actively in the hybrid popular culture of the 1920s as consumers *and* as producers. Compared to Dutch newspapers, the Malay and Sino-Malay press also stressed different aesthetic and social qualities of the company and Riboet as an artist. For instance, in 1928, the editor of *Bintang Hindia* (Batavia) Parada Harahap, labelled Riboet "The first Indonesian woman to advance in theatre."[42] The use of the word "Indonesian" should not be underrated. The editor could have chosen to say nothing about her ethnic background, presented her as a "native actress" or could have used the common term "Indisch", indicating something rooted in the colony. The use of the term "Indonesian" expressed the editors' self-confidence and a vision of a new national identity or society to which Riboet, in his view, contributed. The same paper wrote in veiled political language: "We take off our hat to the strong desire and capability of the leader of Miss Riboet's Opera, who, in a short period, achieved such a good result, not just as a gift to the world, but as food for thought for spectators in accordance with today's world movement (*pergerakan doenia*)." The "world movement" referred to by the editors can be read as emancipatory or

---

[40] See Cohen (2006: 304–5).

[41] "Miss Riboet mengadoe pada publiek", *Keng Po*, 3 July 1928.

[42] "DARI GEDONG OPERA. Satoe perempoean Indonesia jang pertama madjoe dalem Tooneel", *Bintang Hindia*, 21 July 1928.

anti-colonial movements occurring worldwide; in this case, it was a reference to the Indonesian nationalist movement that *Bintang Hindia*'s editors endorsed. Underlining the cultural in-betweenness of Malay company Orion, another Malay newspaper from Batavia, *Bintang Timoer*, publishing under its column "Art World" (Doenia Seni), classified the company as "more than half way the road of developing Indonesian theatre *(toneel Indonesia)*".[43] Miss Riboet was thus regarded as someone who had the ability to set things into motion, someone who moved within the realm of popular culture, but who was heading towards "art".

Of all the people who, at an early stage of her career, registered and promoted the social significance of Riboet and her modernised Malay opera, one stood out for his original ways: peranakan Chinese journalist Kwee Thiam Tjing from Surabaya. He was Riboet's first articulate fan.

'Mr. In-between'

In March 1925, the renowned peranakan Chinese journalist Liem Koen Hian invited 25-year-old Kwee Thiam Tjing to join the new editorial staff of the Surabaya-based *Soeara Publiek* (Voice of the Public).[44] Kwee would become Riboet's first publicly self-confessed fan. He would assert his own local fame under the alias of Tjamboek Berdoeri (Spiked Whip), as the author of a provocative column in *Soeara Publiek* titled "Saturday's Speech" *(Pridato hari Saptoe)*.

Surabaya had a well-established print media industry. In 1925, six newspapers catered for the demand for "news" by the multi-ethnic middle to upper classes of urban professionals and colonial government officials in Surabaya and East Java's rural hinterland of sugar and tobacco estates: three Dutch-language, three Sino-Malay and at least one bilingual Indo-Arab newspaper.[45] It is exactly in this city, during a period of economic upsurge from 1925 onwards, that Riboet rose to stardom as the prima donna of Orion Malay Opera Company. The majority of the Surabaya newspapers would contribute to Riboet's name and fame, spearheaded by the Sino-Malay print media and followed by the Dutch.

---

[43] "Doenia Seni", *Bintang Timoer*, 7 Dec. 1928.

[44] "Chineesch-Maleische Journalistiek", *De Indische Courant*, 26 Mar. 1925. According to Kwee's memoir, he was assigned editor by Liem Koen Hian in 1924. Kwee (2010: 64, 67).

[45] The Sino-Malay dailies included *Sin Jit Po, Pewarta Soerabaja* and *Soeara Publiek*. The Dutch dailies were *Nieuwe Soerabaja Courant, Soerabaiasch Handelsblad* and *Indische Courant*. *Soerabaiasch Nieuwsblad* had a smaller distribution and a short existence as it was terminated in 1926. See Termorshuizen (2011: 314–77). Indo-Arab association Al-Irshad published two newspapers in Surabaya, *Al-Salām* and weekly *Al-Irshād*, see Mobini-Kesheh (1993: 62–3). It is not clear which one of the two was in circulation in 1926.

The papers reviewed her shows, almost without exception favourably, and they cashed in on the proceeds from advertisements of this Malay opera company.

Kwee Thiam Tjing was born in the town of Pasuruan, about 60 kilometres southeast of Surabaya. He had moved to the East Javanese city of Malang in 1907, enjoyed Dutch-language primary education and in 1924 started as correspondent at the Sino-Malay newspaper *Pewarta Soerabaia* in this town.[46] Apparently, Kwee's work for this newspaper impressed Liem Koen Hian and resulted in the latter inviting the young journalist to join *Soeara Publiek*.

In 1924, Surabaya had a population of approximately 200,000, making it the second-largest city in the Netherlands East Indies after Batavia. According to colonial racial legal classification and the ethnic composition of most cities in the Indies, the majority of the urbanites were "native" Indonesians (c. 150,000), together with three other significant minorities: Europeans, Chinese and Arabs.[47] In reality, these groups were highly differentiated in terms of socio-economic position, and political and cultural orientation. For example, the legal category of Europeans comprised both people born in the Netherlands as well as local-born Dutch, the latter included many mixed-ethnic Dutch-Indonesian offspring, Eurasians. "Europeans" and Chinese dominated the economic life as owners and managers of business enterprises connected to the sugar and tobacco companies in Surabaya's fertile hinterland. Chinese millionaires (*hartawan*) who had made their fortunes in the sugar industry, and other well-to-do citizens, emerge in newspaper reports as consumers and fans of theatre, music, cinema, prostitution and gambling.[48] Sino-Malay novelists and Malay opera playwrights, who claimed their stories to be based on real events, often took such people as central characters. They tell how well-to-do people with moral standing lose their wealth, dignity and respect through gambling, mistresses and other hard luck.[49] Through literature and Malay opera, readers and opera spectators were thus confronted with the downside of making money (read: capitalism) and individualism, and educated to praise modesty and compassion instead.

---

[46] Suryadinata (1995: 72); Kwee (2010: 4, 54). Little is known of the social background of Kwee's parents. According to Ben Anderson, Kwee's father was an official working on a, possibly Dutch-owned, sugar plantation in the vicinity of Malang. See Tjamboek Berdoeri (2004: 5).

[47] According to statistics published in *Soeara Publiek* in 2 Nov. 1925, Surabaya's population was: Europeans 20,855; Chinese 30,653; Arabs 3,639; Foreigners 644; Indonesians 149,000. As no official birth and death registers were kept on native Indonesians, the municipal authorities estimated the size of this latter group.

[48] See for instance "Dari satoe plosok 'Recept' boeat millionair Tionghoa", *SP*, 17 Aug. 1926.

[49] For example, Miss Riboet's play Hajati is about an Indonesian woman who descends into hell after she was involved in *tjeki* (ceki), a card game. See ad "Orion", *Pewarta Deli*, 9 Sept. 1929.

Kwee Thiam Tjing and his superior and comrade Liem Koen Hian identified with and were part of the Indonesian emancipatory movement. Chinese nationalism, the Dutch ethical colonial policy of "uplifting" native Indonesians, and increasing discontent about the racialist legal classification and institutionalised discrimination imposed by the Dutch triggered this social and political awakening movement. In 1899, citizenship became an issue within the Chinese community after the Dutch, for political-economic reasons, had decided to grant local Japanese the status of Europeans. In 1925, this legal inequality evoked bitter sentiments among the local-born Chinese, including the editorial staff of *Soeara Publiek*. It would lead to Kwee's first legal encounter with the colonial authorities, and subsequently his imprisonment. The Federation of Chinese Associations (THHK) added to the complexity of the citizenship issue propagating resinification, that is political and cultural reorientation on China. Resinification was disputed within Chinese circles and Kwee's position is instructive. He and Liem were Indonesia rather than China oriented. *Soeara Publiek*'s editors openly questioned Chinese "traditions", engaging themselves in debates about Westernisation, religious beliefs, gender role models and modernity and what this meant for the local Chinese. They also questioned THHK's educational system that was geared to Chinese only.[50] Liem and Kwee advocated an educational system that was open to all racial groups. In fact, they propagated the lifting of racial division in all fields. As James Siegel outlined in the introduction of Kwee Thiam Tjing's memoir, *Soeara Publiek*'s editors sympathised with an inclusive Indonesian cosmopolitan-nationalism, instead of a Chinese or an exclusive Indonesian nationalism.[51]

Kwee Thiam Tjing's cultural orientation towards Indonesia was of a highly complex, hybrid cultural nature. As he evidenced in his columns, he was familiar with Chinese, particularly Hokkien, language and cultural practices, but equally intimate with Javanese culture. Kwee's columns appeared irregularly. The content varied from one to four separate sections, each dealing with distinct topics and stylistic formats, from difficult to decode metaphorical ponderings to venomous syair (Malay-Javanese poetry) covering about half a page. The separate sections could be a dialogue between two characters, a polite response to someone who had written him a letter, or a piece on a simply daily affair, such as a funny telephone conversation. He used a hybrid Malay, common in urban Java, heavily

---

[50] Govaars (2005: 71–85); Liem Koen Hian and Kwee Thiam Tjing also did not support the Dutch-Chinese Schools, established by the colonial government since 1908 in a bid to undermine the THHK-sponsored schools. According to Liem Koen Hian, this type of school was part of a colonial policy of divide and rule, see "Debatclub dari Chung Hsiok", *SP*, 8 Feb. 1926.

[51] Siegel in Kwee (2010: pp. xix, xxi, xxiii).

garnished with Hokkien, local Javanese and Dutch colloquial.[52] This was very much the language spoken and understood by Miss Riboet and her Malay opera audience in the north coast area of Java, the *pasisir*. In 1927, Kwee articulated his ambiguous position towards Chinese identity in relation to modernity in a piece on changing Chinese gender roles as follows: "I do not belong to the modern and also not to the old-fashioned group. [...] In short, I am in-between."[53] As a Javanised peranakan Chinese fluent in low Javanese (*ngoko*), Kwee's self-confessed "in-betweenness" should also be understood in relation to Javanese culture. He showed an interest in Javanese mysticism, witnessed in two of his columns in which he referred to the Javanese tale of Joyoboyo that predicted the coming of a rightful ruler and the demise of white rule in the archipelago. But according to Ben Anderson, Kwee clearly had affinity with Dutch culture as well.[54]

Tjamboek Berdoeri's columns varied from dealing with very local issues to those bearing broader social significance: how to deal with wealth and social status; the position of the modern Chinese girl; intimate relationships such as friendship and marriage; or the journalistic trade as a profession of calling.[55] The tone of Kwee's columns varied from a young and rebellious journalist out to shock his readership and confront the colonial authorities, to a surprisingly polite, witty, warm and sometimes philosophically minded journalist. Some of his columns and also poetry read as if to make the readership aware of the injustices of Dutch colonialism. Kwee explored the boundaries of what the colonial authorities considered permissible to be published. Although many of his columns contained a moral message, Kwee's humorous, self-mockery style kept him from becoming a patronising moralist. For instance, he frequently ridiculed himself for being a married man tied to the whims of his wife, who was consequently anonymously staged as "hoedjin Tjamboek Berdoeri" (*hoedjin*, meaning wife in Hokkien). He also wrote emphatically about people, especially when expressing his concerns about close friends.[56]

---

[52] James Siegel noted this as Kwee's "linguistic cosmopolitanism" in Kwee (2010: xvii–xviii). The colonial government attempted to standardise Malay. See Maier (1993).

[53] Kwee's original Malay text reads: Saja boekan masoek golongan orang jang modern, tapi djoega boekan masoek golongan orang jang kolot. [...] Pendek sedeng sedeng saja. "Pridato hari Saptoe", *SP*, 16 July 1927.

[54] Tjamboek Berdoeri (2004: 5).

[55] See for example "Pridato Hari Saptoe", *SP*, 15 May 1926, 12 June 1926, 31 July 1926, 14 Aug. 1926, 9 July 1927.

[56] In the course of 1926, a dialogue evolved between Kwee and one of his admirers, a young female by the name of Nona Mathilde. It cannot be ruled out that Nona Mathilde was a pseudonym of Kwee's wife and that he addressed his writings to her and vice versa to keep her informed about his condition in prison. See "Pridato hari Saptoe", *SP*, 31 Oct. 1926.

When in the late 1910s and early 1920s trade unions and political parties such as the Indische Partij and the Partij Komunist Indonesia emerged from the pergerakan, policing of colonial society by the authorities expanded and intensified. Social upheaval erupted in 1925, witnessed by industrial labour strikes in Semarang and Surabaya, followed by trials against the trade union leaders, terrorist bombings in late 1926, soon followed by a communist party-led uprising in Java and Sumatra that lasted into 1927. In response, the colonial government stepped up intelligence activities and established a political prison in Boven Digoel, in the easternmost part of the archipelago.[57] The Dutch authorities watched the awakening movement with concern and vigilance. The legal device of the "press offence", for instance, was one of the measures the colonial government designed to counter a variety of what the authorities considered press offences, from subversion to inciting of racial hatred.[58] Kwee Thiam Tjing would be charged no less than nine times, on the basis of penal code provisions for various press offences.[59]

In this context of increased political polarisation and social confusion, a young female who took the Malay opera stage in Surabaya in late 1925 electrified the socially engaged Kwee Thiam Tjing. She confronted the young aspiring journalist with a novel style of articulating social criticism through popular entertainment. Mutual understanding and actual recognition developed into a fan–artist relationship.

The Making of a Fan

Claiming Kwee Thiam Tjing as the first self-confessed devotee of Malay opera does not mean that "fans" of Malay opera were absent prior to the rise of Miss Riboet. Matthew Cohen's fascinating study of the early history of Komedie Stamboel offers sufficient evidence of an emerging fandom for this form of theatre and its artists.[60] Yet, as I will sketch in this and the next section, journalist Kwee Thiam Tjing, alias Tjamboek Berdoeri, was the first to articulate fandom for a star of modern popular entertainment in colonial Indonesia. Moreover, he would do so in a highly original manner in print and under unusual conditions.

---

[57] Poeze (1982: lxvii); Shiraishi (1996: 93–118).

[58] Yamamoto (2011: 101–3); Maters (1998: 97–9, 109–18, 163–5).

[59] Kwee (2010: 68).

[60] One striking feature of this early fandom was the male adoration of Eurasian actresses. Other evidence is that, inspired by Komedie Stamboel, fans established their own (amateur) theatre groups. Cohen (2006: 105, 110, 112, 128, 152, 157).

In the 1920s, mutual commercial interests between Malay opera and the local press developed into a symbiotic relationship. To ensure favourable press coverage, that, in turn, would help to draw audiences, Malay opera managers offered newspaper editors and reporters free seats. So, for example, the first thing Tio did when arriving in a new town was to frequent the major newspaper offices, socialise with the editors and invite them to the shows. Publicity generated publicity. Cajoling the print press turned into a regular practice.[61] In turn, newspapers benefitted from the earnings from advertisements placed by the many visiting Malay opera companies, or others, similar to the Filipino papers making money from the burgeoning vaudeville industry.[62] Tio also hired newspaper boys to distribute leaflets, printed by the newspapers, featuring the evening's playbill.[63] For printing matters, Tio often relied on credit arrangements with the newspapers.[64] With the commercial success of Orion, we would easily forget that credit was essential for the company's survival, not only to cover publicity, but also to bear the expenses of travel, accommodation, wages and the rent of theatres and tents.[65] Debt was likely one of the main causes for many a Malay opera company to perish. It explains the high turnover of troupes and the frequent shifts of actors from one company to another.

---

[61] Tio Tek Djien Jr. meticulously kept track of individual reviews of his company in the Dutch, Sino-Malay and later, having toured British Malaya, Anglo-Chinese newspapers. To stress the legitimacy and the Java-wide success of the company, Tio borrowed, recycled might even be a better word, the favourable reviews from leading newspapers and used them as new content for advertisements in other newspapers. One announcement for the season in Padang, West Sumatra, published in *Radio*, 8 Aug. 1934, lists a total of 100 periodicals from Java, Sumatra, Sulawesi, Singapore, Penang, Kuala Lumpur and Ipoh. Each of these newspapers was said to have given Miss Riboet full praise (poedjian-poedjian jang sepenoehnja).

[62] In 1926, Sino-Malay newspaper *Pantjadjania* from Solo was very explicit about the significance of advertisements for the paper's survival. The editors acknowledged that many well-to-do readers supported the paper, but simultaneously affirmed that advertisements were indispensable for the paper's futures existence. See "Pendahoclocan", *Pantjadjania*, 17 Feb. 1926.

[63] "Opera Orion", *Pewarta Soerabaia*, 24 Mar. 1926.

[64] "Tooneelgezelschap 'Miss Riboet' dibeslag di Cheribon", *Pewarta Deli*, 23 Dec. 1935. In 1935, a bailiff summoned Tio to pay outstanding debts with a local newspaper in Cirebon that had printed publicity materials for Orion four years earlier. Tio settled the matter with the newspaper.

[65] "Miss Riboet. Diriboetkan", *Bintang Timoer*, 13 Apr. 1929. This newspaper article reports payment arrears by Orion. Tio owed substantial debts to two creditors: Oei Tiong Ham bank (f. 12.500) and to an anonymous "wealthy Chinese from Batavia" (f. 25.000). Apparently, these debts were settled as Orion continued to stage shows. Oei Tiong Ham was known as "the sugar king of Java", but he was also active in banking, shipping and wholesale trade. See Post (2011).

Kwee's fandom took a couple of months to develop. He witnessed Riboet's stage performances on more than one occasion. He was certainly present on 4 December 1925, when Orion staged a kroncong competition. Acting as an occasional Malay opera critic, Kwee reported on the event the next day in his column "Saturday's Speech" under his pen name Tjamboek Berdoeri. The event was of special significance to *Soeara Publiek*. Orion's management had given the paper's bookkeeper and Kwee's personal friend, Jan Hie, who had a professional background in Malay opera, the opportunity to take a minor role in a play and to perform a kroncong song.[66] To Kwee's great pleasure, Tjoa, "[…] his highness the champion of kroncong" (Sang djago krontjong Jan Hie) brought the house down singing a standard kroncong song entitled "Stamboel Dua".[67] Orion awarded the singer a golden medal for his successful appearance. Relations between Orion's management and *Soeara Publiek*'s editors were thus cordial. Although he expressed joy about the performance of his colleague Tjoa, there was little sign yet of an affective relationship between Kwee, or to be precise his alter ego Tjamboek Berdoeri, and the singer-actress Miss Riboet.

During Riboet's debut in early November 1925, Kwee was working in freedom, but this would soon change. Drawing on information from his memoir and publications in *Soeara Publiek*, Kwee was imprisoned for most of 1926, around ten months in total.[68] From roughly January to May 1926, he was in Kalisosok prison, Surabaya; and from mid-July to the end of October he was in Cipinang prison, Batavia. It was precisely in this period of restricted freedom that Kwee developed his fandom for Miss Riboet.

Kwee, under his pen name Tjamboek Berdoeri (Spiked Whip), was out to criticise if not castigate colonial institutions and individuals in the print press.[69] He engaged in the provocative style of scolding (*caci*) and insulting (*maki*), a common journalistic practice in the Indies, popular with both Dutch and peranakan Chinese journalists. Many decades later, Kwee described this as "wild

---

[66] "Siapa lagi jang toeroet maen", *SP*, 3 Dec. 1925; ad "Orion", *SP*, 4 Dec. 1925; "Pridato hari saptoe", *SP*, 5 Dec. 1925.

[67] "Pridato hari Saptoe", *SP*, 5 Dec. 1925. On the history of the song "Stamboel Dua" and the special relationship between the musical style of kroncong and Komedie Stamboel, see Cohen (2006: 59–60).

[68] "Pridato hari Saptoe", *SP*, 18 Dec. 1926. This is Kwee's first "Pridato hari Saptoe" after his release from prison, and the only one published under his real name, albeit under his initials: K.T.T. Kwee (2010: 45, 47) writes that he was released from Cipinang prison in Batavia on 1 Nov. 1926.

[69] He had already used this pen name when still working for *Pewarta Soerabaia* in 1924, publishing a column "Tjorat-tjoret", see Kwee (2010: 67).

west journalism".[70] What this journalistic style implied can be read from several court cases in which Kwee was involved.

On 5 January 1926, the Dutch chairman of the Landraad (Court of Justice for Indonesians and peranakan Chinese under the pluriform judicial system of colonial Indonesia) summoned Kwee's arrest, for having incited violence in *Soeara Publiek* on 19 September 1925. Because the authorities feared he would disappear without a trace, he was handcuffed and taken to prison.[71] Kwee had addressed the issue of the notorious private moneylending trade and the rude ways debts were collected. In his view, it was legitimate for debtors to use violence against creditors. In another column, he commented on the murder of a policeman committed by a *tukang sate* (a street vendor selling skewers). According to Kwee, the public generally held the police in contempt for their unjust behaviour, hence the killing of a policeman was perfectly understandable. A trial followed on 12 January 1926 and he was sentenced to six months imprisonment for sowing hate against the "propertied class" (moneylenders) and for giving public consent to the killing of a police officer.[72] Kwee appealed.

On 26 January, awaiting his appeal in prison, the young journalist was charged with two additional press offences, committed in two separate articles published six months earlier in *Soeara Publiek* on 14 and 15 August 1925. This time, Kwee was accused of having insulted the Dutch race and Dutch officials. One article had appeared anonymously, the other under the name of Tjamboek Berdoeri, which the authorities suspected, but eventually could not prove, to be the product of Kwee's pen.[73] Consistent with his objections against institutionalised racial discrimination of Chinese in the Netherlands East Indies, Kwee had sardonically commented on the visit of a prominent Japanese representative of the Department of Trade and parliament member, Fukiyama, in Surabaya. He maliciously accused the Dutch of hypocrisy, permitting a Japanese privileges denied to the local Chinese. Dutch officials felt insulted, spurring them to legal action.[74] Kwee flatly denied all accusations. On the basis of witness accounts, the court sentenced him to one month in prison for his seditious writing of 14 August 1925. The prosecutor, however, was unable

---

[70] Ibid., pp. 61–2.

[71] "Persdelict Ang Kian Hie", *SP*, 5 Jan. 1926; "Een journalist gearresteerd", *De Indische Courant*, 5 Jan. 1926; "Pridato hari Saptoe", *SP*, 30 Jan. 1926.

[72] "Persdelict Kwee Thiam Tjing", *SP*, 12 Jan. 1926; "Persdelict", *De Indische Courant*, 12 Jan. 1926.

[73] "Pridato hari Saptoe", *SP*, 15 Aug. 1925.

[74] "Kalo sobat Japan …!!!", *SP*, 14 Aug. 1925; "Beleediging", *Bataviaasch Nieuwsblad*, 28 Jan. 1926.

to reveal the identity of Tjamboek Berdoeri, and therefore acquitted Kwee from the second charge.[75]

Undeterred by his sentence and prison confinement in Surabaya, Kwee continued his column, smuggling copy out of prison via his *Soeara Publiek* colleagues.[76] In his role as Tjamboek Berdoeri, he purposely led his readership astray, in particular the police and rival journalists, pretending to engage in a dialogue with his colleague "toean Kwee Thiam Tjing" in prison.[77] The most fascinating aspect from the perspective of fandom and popular culture, however, is that Kwee's time in jail largely coincided with Orion's debut season in the city. In this period, his fandom for Riboet started to blossom. He was able to follow her career indirectly through a two-month backlog of advertisements and reviews of her shows from local newspapers that were given to him by the prison guards.[78] Released from prison in May 1926, Kwee was able to witness Riboet during her farewell performance in Surabaya later that month.[79] It turned into an exceptional performance that he recalled vividly in a column.

Sweet Miss Riboet

It is intriguing to see that while being persecuted, going in and out of prison, being separated from his wife and from family and friends, and keeping up with his work in 1926, Kwee was capable of sensing and registering the excitement surrounding the unprecedented potential of Miss Riboet as a popular star. By April 1926, she had won his sympathy, which turned into fandom.

Behind bars, Kwee continued his column "Pridato hari Saptoe". The earliest column to date was published on 9 January 1926, only four days after he had been detained on the issue of press censorship.[80] And while unable to attend Riboet's performances and witness her growing popularity among the urbanites of Surabaya, Kwee moved from an occasional Malay opera critic to a fan. While he had reported on Miss Riboet in early December 1925 in a rather detached manner, this had changed completely by April 1926 and would continue to develop into genuine affection. On 26 April, his column reappeared after weeks

---

[75] "Persdelict Kwee Thiam Tjing", *SP*, 26 Jan. 1926.

[76] Kwee (2010: 25–6).

[77] See for example "Pridato hari Saptoe", *SP*, 30 Jan. 1926.

[78] Kwee (2010: 25). *Sin Jit Po* was the first paper to pick up on Miss Riboet in early November 1925, followed by *Soeara Publiek* and *Nieuwe Soerabaja Courant*, see "Komedie Stamboel Orion kepada Pers", *Sin Jit Po*, 9 Nov. 1925; "Miss Riboet", *Nieuwe Soerabaja Courant*, 25 Nov. 1925.

[79] Kwee refers to his release in Kwee (2010: 1–2, 52).

[80] "Pridato hari Saptoe", *SP*, 9 Jan. 1926.

of silence. The column contained a Javanese poem with a Dutch title: "Als ik eens 'Miss Riboet' was….!!!" (If I Were Miss Riboet ….!!!).[81] A similar column followed in May. Taken together, these two separate columns should be read as Kwee's public fandom confession.

The Dutch title of "If I Were Miss Riboet….!!!" reveals one of Kwee's sources of inspiration: the seditious pamphlet written by the Javanese journalist and pergerakan pioneer Soewardi Soerjaningrat entitled "If I Were a Dutchman", published originally in Dutch in 1913 and later translated into Malay. Soerwardi's publication is an early form of subtle critique of Dutch colonialism in print. It shocked the colonial authorities and was one of the reasons for Soewardi being exiled in 1914.[82] In 1914, in response to Soewardi and other seditious writers, the Dutch authorities introduced a number of legal articles to curb those "inciting hatred, contempt or enmity by way of words, signs, performances or otherwise against the lawful authorities".[83] These legal articles proved an instrument for the Dutch colonial government to curb the emancipatory movement and its most vocal advocates in the print press.[84]

Kwee Thiam Tjing was not impressed or discouraged by the legal measures. His appeal to Soewardi's subversive writing is evidenced by the fact that he experimented with Soewardi's title on a few occasions.[85] Miss Riboet herself was also a source of inspiration, as Kwee recollected in his memoir: "Riboet was very well known in Surabaya and other places." He confessed to have "borrowed" one of her songs that was very popular at the time, suggesting that his poem could actually be sang to an existing tune.[86] This Javanese song was transformed into a subversive political pamphlet, "If I Were Miss Riboet….!!!", in which Tjamboek

---

[81] Ibid., 24 Apr. 1926.

[82] James Siegel (1997: 37) has pointed out that, in this piece, Soewardi did not seek confrontation with the colonial authorities, let alone call for independence. Soewardi presented the unconceivable "idea that a Javanese could think of himself as a Dutchman". This reversal of roles, which blurred the racial hierarchy, was sufficient to arouse concerns with the Dutch authorities and this made Soewardi's piece of political significance. For similar seditious writings by others such as Tjipto Mangoenkoesoemo and Mas Marco Kartodikromo, and Dutch counter-measures, see Shiraishi (1990: 87, 119–20, 214).

[83] Maters (1998: 99). The act was amended in 1918 and again in 1926, see Maters, pp. 110–11, 165.

[84] Yamamoto (2011: 101) takes issue with the general assumption that the persdelict penal code articles applied to political writings only. He shows that it was actually applied to various forms of offences.

[85] A column titled "Kalo saia mendjadi seorang Atjeh …!" (If I were an Achenese…!") was published in *Soeara Publiek* on 29 Oct. 1925. A pantun titled "Als ik eens Volksraadlid was" (If I were a member of the People's Council) appeared in "Pridato hari Saptoe", *SP*, 13 Aug. 1927.

[86] Kwee (2010: 25).

Berdoeri bemoans the social injustices of Dutch colonial rule. The tale consists of seven verses, of which the following three reveal its essence.

Who wishes to hear my tale
The tale of a journalist who served prison
Death nor alive
Just locked up behind iron bars
Imprisoned day and night
Because of the courage to challenge the Lord. [87]

Verse two tells the story of oppression and suffering of the Javanese majority under colonial rule that was foreseen in the Javanese Joyoboyo prophecy.

This era is a heartless time
As predicted by Joyoboyo
The iron hand of Dutch rule
afraid of losing a grain of rice
Although Java is very fertile
The common people, however, have nothing!

The closing verse relates:

At this point I stop
Twitching eyes, feeling moved
I will not again enter
that danger that is the provocative press
I also only reiterate the above tale
If I were sweet Miss Riboet.

Tjamboek sensed Riboet's potency as a spokeswoman for the Javanese underclass, and wanted her to articulate colonial social injustices in public. In a syair that followed on 8 May 1926, Kwee expressed his respect and affection for Riboet more explicitly and directly. This latter poem was actually Kwee's farewell to Miss

---

[87] The second line of the verse as given by Kwee in his memoir, p. 25, slightly deviates from the original as published in *Soeara Publiek*, 24 Apr. 1926. His memoir reads: "Dongenganne djurnalis sing *sih* dibuwi" [My italics] (The Tale of a Journalist Who *Is* in Prison), *Soeara Publiek* reads: "Dongenganee djoernalis sing *tas* di boewi" [my italics] (The Tale of a Journalist Who *Has Served* in Prison).

Riboet and company, as the troupe moved on to tour other parts of East Java.[88] The poem suggests a correspondence between him and the diva, revealed in the first two opening verses:

The purpose of my poem this time,
is to answer Miss Riboet currently present,
the sweetheart of the spectators who love to watch Malay opera
who has been singing her tales last Wednesday night
and unexpectedly lashing out at Soeara Publiek
yet without causing resentment.

This poem, I need to clarify firmly
is not me going out for destruction
This messy poetry
is not aimed at competing with Miss Riboet
who while smiling makes people flinch
if not to give them a stomach ache.[89]

These two verses underline Miss Riboet's enormous popularity among Surabaya's urbanites, who took her sardonic topical singing with a mix of awe and hilarity. Journalists, Kwee in the first place, appreciated if not envied this daring style of critique that was very similar to the one he used in print. And although Riboet surprised him by striking out against the newspaper he was working for (Kwee was apparently present during the performance), she still evoked his respect and admiration as the final verse illustrates:

What remains is that we wish
that in other places in Indonesia
Miss Riboet will achieve much success and glory,
will have a long healthy life and amass a lot of wealth
to provide for her old age
and that she will not forget ... about me.

---

[88] *Soeara Publiek* reported that, on 22 May, Orion performed in the East Javanese city of Gresik. "Kabar Kota", *SP*, 22 May 1926. In July, the company was playing the city of Solo, central Java. By September 1926, the company appeared in Bandung in West Java ("Prinses Hamlet. De schoone miss Riboet", *De Sumatra Post*, 28 Sept. 1926). In early October, the company had reached Batavia, opening its first season in the capital.

[89] "Pridato hari Saptoe", *SP*, 8 May 1926.

Kwee's fascination with Riboet can be contrasted with the relative disinterest that he took in other Malay opera companies and their leading ladies performing in Surabaya in the same period as Orion. For example, the Union Dalia Opera from Medan that played the city from late April to mid-July 1926.[90] In spite of the popularity of this company in Batavia and Surabaya, Kwee did not mention Union Dalia Opera once in 1926. Only during its second season in the city, more than a year later in August 1927, did Kwee praise the beauty and sweet voices of two of Union Dalia's leading actresses, Miss Inten and Miss Mama, in a syair.[91] In spite of this acclaim, Union Dalia and its leading ladies failed to evoke the same thrill with Kwee as Riboet did.[92] It is also striking that in 1927 and thereafter, Kwee completely ignored, at least in print, another Malay opera company that would become as popular and as much the talk of the town as Miss Riboet's Orion: Dardanella.

In a separate and additional comment that followed the 8 May 1926 poem, Tjamboek Berdoeri once again subtly stressed the risks and limitations involved in the journalistic trade under a repressive and authoritarian colonial regime.[93] In the same comment, he once more suggested a correspondence between Riboet and himself, aka the columnist Tjamboek Berdoeri: "[...] Miss Riboet has often sung about me, offending [me], just as she did to brother Kiem Tiong, screaming out loud last Thursday: 'Tjan Kiem Tiong, the millionaire!'".[94] Indirect communication between Tjamboek and Riboet continued during the second season of Orion in Surabaya, from July to August 1927. It started out with Kwee's column, in which he ridiculed a group of prominent Chinese in the city who held a debating club. He compared this group with the People's Council (Volksraad) and Surabaya's municipal council, two bodies that, in his view, consisted of people who made easy money merely attending debating sessions, rather than representing and defending the interests of the people.[95]

---

[90] "Satoe stamboel baroe", *SP*, 27 Apr. 1926.

[91] "Pridato hari Saptoe", *SP*, 20 Aug. 1927.

[92] "Miss Inten moentjoel lagi", *Sin Jit Po*, 15 Aug. 1927; "Dalia Opera", *Sin Jit Po*, 16 Aug. 1927.

[93] Tjamboek Berdoeri told his readers: "This occasion of devoting a poem to his highness Miss Riboet who keeps Orion's throne, makes this [journalistic] trade not as dangerous as when I am devoting a poem to other highnesses in charge of thrones in other places" (Kalo ini kali saja berpantoen boeat kandjeng miss Riboet, jang bersemajam di 'Orion', adalah dari sebab ini pakerdjaan tida begitoe berbahaja seperti berpantoen boeat kandjeng jang laen, jang bersemajam di laen tempat). "Pridato hari Saptoe", *SP*, 6 May 1926.

[94] "Pridato hari Saptoe", *SP*, 6 May 1926.

[95] Ibid. "Oh, als ik een's volksraadlid was, Pridato hari Saptoe", *SP*, 13 Aug. 1927.

In response, Miss Riboet picked up this item in a dongeng during her farewell performance.[96]

Kwee's wish that Riboet would rise to stardom swiftly materialised, as can be inferred from a play staged by a competing Malay opera company in early 1927. Trying to come to terms with Riboet's rocketing popularity, Malay opera company Dalia Opera launched a play entitled "Riboet, The Secret of a Successful Actress in Java". A reaction from Miss Riboet was inevitable. In response, Orion offered its own version of the play, with the title: "Riboet, The Secret of a Successful Actress in *Indonesia*" [PK: my emphasis].[97] Brashly underscoring Riboet's celebrity status, her fame had travelled beyond the island of Java into "Indonesia", rather than the Netherlands East Indies (Hindia-Belanda in Malay or Nederlandsch-Indië in Dutch), making her the first translocal popular culture star in the Malay world.

Kwee Thiam Tjing's fandom for Miss Riboet suggests more than just admiration for a daring woman, and suggests that he recognised the social potential in stars of the popular stage. This social potential is explored more thoroughly in the following chapter through a discussion of the ideas circulating in colonial society about stardom, compassion and progress, associated with or attributed to Miss Riboet and a new prominent and rival Malay opera troupe on the popular culture horizon: Dardanella.

---

[96] "Satoe pertoendjoekan loear biasa", *SP*, 13 Sept. 1927. The song was announced as "Special dongeng; Bongkaran's People Council" (Dongeng speciaal: Volksraad Bongkaran). Ad "Miss Riboet", *Sin Jit Po*, 14 Sept. 1927. Riboet's closing night of the Surabaya season on 21 September was, unfortunately, not reviewed by the Sino-Malay newspapers because of a Chinese public holiday the following day. "Malem pengabisan", *SP*, 21 Sept. 1927.

[97] "Si Riboet, Resia Actrice jang djempolan di tanah Djawa", *Sin Po*, 22 and 26 Feb. 1927.

Chapter 9

Stardom, Compassion and Progress

In the mid-1920s and early 1930s, popular culture in Indonesia acquired a social meaning that is worthy of further exploration. One striking social phenomenon in this regard is philanthropism, another the notion of progress. In the 1920s, it was in the field of a burgeoning secular popular culture, and not within the religious realm, where compassion was most clearly articulated and practised in the form of philanthropy.

Before exploring the meaning of popular entertainment in relation to compassion, the first section takes a little detour to stardom, which will help us understand this particular relationship better. Here, we will learn how Riboet's stardom could never have happened without the contribution or role of the print press, commerce and her fans.

As I will demonstrate in the ensuing sections, stardom stands in sharp contrast to philanthropy, the ideas and practices of promoting the well-being of fellow humans. Stardom was, and still is, associated with individualism, wealth, commerce and consumerism. Miss Riboet attempted to reconcile the two. She was not the only person involved in altruistic practices, however. Indeed, they occurred on a broader scale in the context of a colonial state failing to deliver basic social services. I have chosen to call this social phenomenon of the close relationship between compassion and entertainment "dermatainment", a combination of the Malay-Javanese term for alms (*derma*) and entertainment. This situation was remarkably different from the one in the Philippines during the jazz age, where charity was never intimately linked to secular popular entertainment.

Compassion found fertile ground in popular culture, transforming what was previously regarded as light entertainment into something socially meaningful. The same can be said for ideas about progress, which is the subject of the two final sections of this chapter. Intellectuals of the emancipatory and nationalist movement perceived the modernised form of Malay opera, as developed by Miss Riboet, but especially by a new Malay opera company Dardanella, not only as proof *of* progress, but a contribution *to* it. Moreover, these intellectuals regarded Dardanella as breathing the spirit of a new modern and cosmopolitan culture compatible with cultural nationalism—an Indonesian-style pop cosmopolitanism.

Female Stars

Unlike the Philippines in the same period, the phenomenon of trans-local, secular popular culture stars was unknown in colonial Indonesia. Prior to the ascendency of Miss Riboet, popular female artists did exist, like Stamboel actresses and female kroncong singers, but their popularity remained very much a local affair, even when they recorded on shellac discs.[1] One person, however, possibly came close to the status of supra-local star, the Eurasian Stamboel actor and recording artist Pieter Willem Cramer (discussed in Chapter 7), already a veteran in 1926, who helped Tio and Riboet to modernise their Malay opera. From the early 20th century into the 1910s, Cramer was most certainly a name in Batavia and possibly also in other main cities of the pasisir.

It is striking that early recording artists and the leading actresses of the early bangsawan and Komedie Stamboel did not yet carry the Anglo-Saxon honorific title of "Miss", as would become a common practice in the 1920s. Artists were simply referred to by their surnames, or, in the case of leading Malay opera actresses, they used the title of sri panggoeng (literally, goddess of the stage). The new female stars of the 1920s could have chosen a Malay, Javanese or even Dutch title. Riboet, instead, adopted the title "Miss" right from the start and her Surabaya debut in late 1925. According to Tan Sooi Beng, the title "Miss" indicated the status of a celebrity.[2] But the Anglo-Saxon term initially seemed to have specified the artist's modern and cosmopolitan orientation, rather than celebrity status. Soon after Miss Riboet's ascendency in 1926, Malay opera casts were awash with "Misses", suggesting that Riboet set the trend. It prompted Riboet-fan Tjamboek Berdoeri to exclaim in a verse: "Miss, Miss, nowadays there are all kinds of Misses!" (Miss, miss, sekarang banjak segala miss!).[3]

In her analysis of Miss Riboet's stardom, Doris Jedamski notes that her fame "was a progression that required the gradual sanctioning of Western-style individualism. To gain a place in the history of the modern (Indonesian) world,

---

[1] For example, a rare Odeon record catalogue portrays two female singers, *zangeres* (singer) Arnesah and zangeres Edjod, both from Garut, West Java, and their songs recorded. The song titles give the impression that the songs were delivered in local genres and the local vernacular, that is Sundanese, the dialect spoken in West Java. *Daftar dari namanja plaat Odéon*, c. 1912, pp. 52–3.

[2] Tan (1996–97: 7).

[3] "Pridato hari Saptoe", *SP*, 20 Aug. 1927.

a person had to prove his or her individuality [...]."[4] How Riboet developed her individualism has been detailed in the preceding chapters: versatility in singing and dancing, melodramatic acting and introducing plays and songs with a distinct moral and social message. The important role of audiences (there is no star without fans) has partly been discussed. Here, we will focus on the role of the print press and commerce in forging her stardom.

After Kwee Thiam Tjing in Surabaya, other newspapers in other cities started to publish on the new sensation of Miss Riboet, spreading her fame across and, soon, beyond Java. Sensational stories started to appear. It was not always clear why such stories were published. Did they serve the purpose of attracting a bigger newspaper readership eager for excitement or to lure audiences to see Malay opera performances? In July 1926, for example, the story circulated that a "white man who had fallen madly in love with her" had shot the Malay opera diva. Surabaya newspaper *Sin Jit Po* was happy to announce that: "Riboet is still alive."[5] That the "truth" behind such stories is not always easily established becomes clear from another anecdote with a distinct political undertone that affirmed Riboet's recently acquired cult status as a socially engaged performer. During a tour in central Java in 1927, according to a number of newspapers, the local authorities of the city of Yogyakarta had taken one of Riboet's dongeng as an insult, as she had addressed the bad condition of the local roads.[6] A judge of the native court (Landraad) in Yogyakarta was reported to have fined the diva 50 guilders for having criticised the authorities. Some of the newspapers were eager to give the story a political twist. In the wake of the 1926 communist rebellion, and widespread Dutch fears for renewed political agitation, one Dutch newspaper suggested that Riboet had been sentenced for spreading "communist propaganda".[7] Playwright and, by then, Orion co-manager, Njoo Cheong Seng, publicly refuted this and many other stories, that she was seriously ill, hospitalised, shot, dead and so forth, as being fabricated by "rivals", possibly other Malay opera companies. He emphasised that Riboet had not been fined for sedition, suggesting she had not appeared before any court, and he made no reference whatsoever to political motives.[8] To add to the confusion, Dutch newspaper *Nieuws van den Dag voor Nederlandsch-Indië* insisted that Riboet had been in court, reporting that the diva had been acquitted of all charges, that is

---

[4] Jedamski (2008: 495).

[5] "Riboet masi idoep!", *Sin Jit Po*, 15 July 1926.

[6] "Solo", *Pewarta Soerabaia*, 5 Aug. 1927.

[7] "Miss Riboet 'geknipt'", *Nieuws van den Dag voor Nederlandsch-Indië*, 1 Aug. 1927.

[8] "Miss Riboet dan delict", *Pantjadjania*, 10 Aug. 1927.

from insulting the authorities and communist agitation.[9] Riboet herself took the opportunity to strike back during a show in Solo, Central Java. Performing her infamous dongeng, she attacked the newspapers that had spread the false stories, joking about the possible prospect of imprisonment that would prevent her from performing.[10] One newspaper posited that the rumours were a publicity stunt cleverly designed by Riboet.[11]

Commerce, and particularly the novelty of new popular stars promoting brand names, was also of significance in augmenting stardom. In 1927, Miss Riboet was the first popular star to lend her name to commerce with her "Miss Riboet record series" for German phonographic corporation Beka. Very quickly the story circulated that she was a billionaire due to her earnings from an allegedly lucrative recording contract with this foreign recording company.[12] Although certainly not without means, Riboet's record contract was not as rewarding as was portrayed in the newspapers. Similar unsubstantiated news circulated about a recording career of contemporary female kroncong singer Herlaut (Aer Laoet).[13]

In 1928, commerce had discovered Riboet as a potential asset for promoting consumer items. That particular year, the Malay opera diva lent her name to a number of consumer brands and gave different corporations the exclusive right to use her name in advertisements. The consumer items included a local manufactured face powder (*bedak*), a wristwatch, a tonic wine and her name was used in connection with a local retailer selling international automobile brands. During performances, audiences received *bedak* samples and with the "Miss Riboet watch" came a photographic portrait of the prima donna.[14] The tonic wine company advertising text read: "Miss Riboet, that actor famous across all of the Netherlands East Indies, has long been using this drug (*obat*). Although Miss Riboet works day and night and must perform one week here and one

[9] "Miss Riboet", *Nieuws van den Dag voor Nederlandsch-Indië*, 10 Aug. 1927.

[10] "Miss Riboet", *De Nieuwe Vorstenlanden*, 3 Aug. 1927.

[11] "Miss Riboet", *De Java-bode*, 8 Aug. 1927.

[12] "Miss Riboet. Djadi aandeelhoudster dari soeatoe firma", *Djawa Tengah*, 29 July 1927; "Madjoe satoe tindak", *SP*, 29 July 1927; "Miss Riboet djadi tonnair", *WW*, 3 Aug. 1927; "Miss Riboet. 100,000", *Nieuws van den Dag voor Nederlandsch-Indië*, 6 Aug. 1927.

[13] Herlaut also recorded for Beka, but there is no evidence she achieved a comparable number of recorded songs as Riboet. Herlaut did win substantial amounts of prize money from kroncong competitions held across Java. Prize money ranged from 100 guilders for first prize to 25 guilders for third place. See "Itoe krontjongconcours prampoean", *SP*, 11 Aug. 1926; see also "Krontjong Concours dalem Pasar Malem", *WW*, 2 Sept. 1925; "Krontjongconcours", *SP*, 10 Aug. 1926; "Het Krontjong-concours. De Eind-uitslag", *Het Nieuws van den dag voor Nederlandsch-Indië*, 9 June 1931.

[14] Ad "Miss Riboet Bedak", *Bataviaasch Nieuwsblad*, 30 Oct.1931; ad "Miss Riboet Bedak", *Sin Po*, 28 Oct. 1931; ad "Horloge merk Miss Riboet", *Medan Doenia*, 30 May 1928.

week there, she feels her body is strong, fit and healthy, that's the reason why Miss Riboet frequently uses 'Miss Riboet tonic wine'."[15] In reality, she never took medicinal wines or even coffee, and did not smoke as many modern women did, as she confessed in an interview.[16] Other female kroncong singers and Malay opera actresses followed suit, their names being attached to similar consumer products.[17] In 1928, Riboet was seen being privately chauffeured in an American automobile that took her from one performance to another in Java. As the proud owner, she offered her "in good running condition" Dodge Sport five-seat sedan for sale and acquired a luxurious sedan Studebaker instead.[18] Studebaker's dealer in Semarang reminded the readers in its advertisement: "Obviously Miss Riboet's choice fell on a Studebaker President Limousine. Follow her example."[19] In 1932, Riboet's list of "Modern Girl commodities" had expanded to Pond's Vanishing Cream (a skin oil), "Dieng" cigarettes and "Java" beer.[20] Between 1927 and 1932, popular culture had met with a new consumer culture in colonial Indonesia, a process embodied in Miss Riboet who alternated her roles as cultural producer and consumer.

A modern, daring and outspoken woman on stage, a pioneering cultural producer and, at least in advertisements, consumer of modern girl commodities, offstage Riboet was modest and kept a low profile. She only gave a handful of interviews during the span of her active career and never bragged about her wealth. For a star of her stature, pictures in the press are also relatively rare. Such modesty was common among popular stars of the late 1920s, and would only start to change in the 1930s. In the few interviews that Riboet gave, reporters presented her as an amusing, but slightly naïve and even shy woman who confessed to refusing character roles that she morally condemned. In a 1931 interview, Riboet revealingly confessed that she would rather not perform, as the years of touring and pleasing socially mixed audiences was wearing her out. In this interview she stressed her humble origins, and the fact that she felt she was generally regarded as "just a Stamboel" actress, indicating the low status afforded to the profession. She believed that the public only took an interest in her success

---

[15] Ad "Miss Riboet medicinale wijn Anggoer Darah", *Sin Po*, 30 Jan. 1932.

[16] "Miss Riboet", *Preangerbode*, 22 May 1931.

[17] Actresses of Malay opera company Dardanella advertised for "Bedak Muguet", ad, *Sin Po*, 30 June 1934. Kroncong singer and recording artist Siti Amsah promoted "bedak Siti Amsah", ad, *Sin Po*, 26 Dec. 1934.

[18] Announcement in *De Indische Courant*, 31 Dec. 1928.

[19] Ad "Verwey en Lugard", *De Locomotief*, 26 Nov. 1928.

[20] "Tooneelgezelschap Miss Riboet. Ars longa, vita brevis", *Bintang Borneo*, 6 June 1932. In 1934, every hundredth visitor of an Orion show in the city of Padang, West Sumatra, received a pack of Dieng cigarettes, see ad "Miss Riboet's Co", *Radio*, 15 Aug. 1934.

on stage; they took no interest in her personality. Riboet also admitted that she feared attacks from the print press.[21] Ironically, she avoided interviews with the print press, a medium that was instrumental in propelling her to stardom. It is obvious that she felt insecure about her low social status and equally vulnerable to being attacked publicly in the print press. During these interviews, her husband Tio was always present, shielding his wife from difficult questions and guarding her from potential public embarrassment.[22]

With all the praise heaped on her by prominent native and peranakan Chinese journalists regarding her moral guidance, social critique, and for being a hardworking woman, one would expect that Riboet may have served as a role model for the Indonesian women's emancipation movement. As in the Philippines, Indonesian and peranakan Chinese women searched for new models of the modern Indonesian woman and, similarly, wanted to make the ideal of an educated woman compatible with that of women as mothers and caretakers. Apparently, Riboet remained too controversial to serve as an example, possibly due to her illiteracy and association with popular entertainment. She had no children of her own and this might have also worked against her in a society where offspring were highly regarded.[23] Female editors of women's emancipatory periodicals, such as *Doenia Istri*, completely ignored her. This ignorance is all the more striking as Riboet engaged conspicuously in one type of social activity that these same editors also took great interest in: charity.

Striking a Balance: Dermatainment

Riboet's philanthropy stood in sharp contrast to the individualism of stardom, personal wealth and promotion of consumerism. Compassion, or the unselfish sense or drive to alleviate other's suffering, or to gain merit as in Buddhism, is propagated and institutionalised in the form of philanthropic behaviour in world religions like Christianity, Islam, Hinduism, as well as in world views such as Buddhism. Newspapers in 1920s- and early 1930s-colonial Indonesia

---

[21] "Miss Riboet", *Preangerbode*, 22 May 1931.

[22] "Het een en ander over den stamboel", *De Locomotief*, 18 June 1927; "AFSCHEID VAN MISS RIBOET. Haar Voortdurend Succes", *Java-Bode*, 16 July 1928; "Een onderhoud met Miss Riboet. Wat we zagen en hoorden", *Sumatra Bode*, 13 Aug. 1934.

[23] Tio and Riboet adopted a girl by the name of Mia, as we learned from two interviews given in 1934 and 1935. "EEN ONDERHOUD MET MISS RIBOET. 'Wat we zagen en hoorden'", *Sumatra Bode*, 13 Aug. 1934; "Tien-Jarig Jubileum Miss Riboet-Tooneelgezelschap", *De Volksstem*, 18 Aug. 1935. In 1934, Mia was five years old and trained by her parents as a future Malay opera actress. I was unable to learn anything of Mia's whereabouts after 1935.

strongly suggested an upsurge in charitable activities.[24] The philanthropic activity, however, was not a sign of religious fervour or revival; charity was closely connected to the secular realm of popular culture. Let me put this altruistic behaviour in perspective by looking, first and very briefly, at similar practices in the Philippines and British Malaya. In the Philippines, the Catholic Church, elitist women's organisations, social associations (clubs) and private benefactors and, without exception, wealthy businessmen, provided for poverty relief and health care. Such initiatives by voluntary organisations and private individuals gained greater significance after the implementation of the 1916 Jones Law, when American Congress withdrew social welfare subsidies.[25] Hispano-Filipino theatre companies occasionally held benefit performances.[26]

A situation resembling the East Indies was found in the Straits Settlements, and particularly so after 1930, when several peranakan Chinese amateur musical and theatrical associations engaged in charity after the collapse of the plantation sector following the 1929 Wall Street Crash.[27] To raise money for the poor and unemployed, the associations performed at social occasions: anniversaries, weddings and Chinese religious festivals. They staged Chinese classical plays,

---

[24] Surprisingly little has been published on the social institution of philanthropy, underlying ideologies and fundraising practices and their economic, social and cultural significance in Southeast Asia. A notable exception is Nguyen-Marshall (2005) on poverty, poor relief and charity in French-colonial Vietnam (2005). See also Lewis (2016: 111–2) on the philanthropic activity of local elites in Bangkok, Rangoon and Penang.

[25] See for example "Filipino Women To Do Their Part", *PFP*, 30 Oct. 1915; "What the Women of the Philippines Can Do", *PFP*, 13 Nov. 1915; "Funciones Benéficas en el Zorilla", *PFP*, 20 Nov. 1915; "Grand Benefit at the Cines", *PFP*, 21 Apr. 1917; "La Sociedad Talia Por los Pobres de la Localidad", *PFP*, 16 June 1917; "Olympic Club Benefit", *PFP*, 14 July 1917; "The Orphan's Needs", *PFP*, 18 Aug. 1917; "Netted Over P5,000", *PFP*, 10 Jan. 1920; "Fiesta en el Bohemian Club", *PFP*, 10 Jan. 1920; "Pleasure and Charity", *PFP*, 7 Feb. 1920; "Filipinos Taking Hold", *PFP*, 24 Apr. 1920; "Funds for Tondo Babies", *PFP,* 24 Apr. 1920; "Nets P1300 for Charities", *PFP*, 22 May 1920.

[26] For example, in 1917, the Carvajal family staged a series of benefit shows for private hospitals in Sampaloc and Tondo districts, Manila. As a consequence of the Jones bill, the American government no longer supported these institutions that, as a result, ran short of funds. "Grand Benefit at the Cines", *PFP*, 21 Apr. 1917. At the Lux—audeville by Tagaroma-Carvajal Co, *MT*, 18 July 1918.

[27] The first of these associations was established in Singapore in 1903 and 1904. See "Minstrels", *Bintang Pranakan*, 11 Oct. 1930. "UCMA", *Bintang Pranakan*, 11 Oct. 1930, and also "Wales Minstrels", *Bintang Pranakan*, 11 Oct. 1930. These associations had names such as: "United Chinese Musical Association (UCMA)", "Moonlight Minstrels", "Merrilads", "Straits Chinese Amateur Dramatic & Musical Association", "Gaylads", "Mayflower", "Springdale", "Blue Star", "Silver Star Minstrels", "Wales Minstrels". On the Penang Chinese Jazz Lads, see "The Penang Chinese Jazz Lads", *Malayan Saturday Post*, 6 June 1931.

Malay opera pieces and modern popular music for social dancing, kroncong and jazz.[28] Proceeds from these shows were reserved for charity (*Cho-ho-sim*, likely a Hokkien term), to help victims of natural disasters in China, for local poverty relief and to support Chinese religious associations.[29] The associations' official patrons were *towkays* (wealthy businessmen) who displayed their wealth, social status and altruism by sponsoring the associations and benefit performances.[30] In 1933, the demand for and the number of these theatrical and musical groups in the Straits had grown to the extent that Singaporean newspaper *The Malaya Tribune* published a weekly "club diary" of performances.[31] It is interesting to see how naturally Miss Riboet fitted into this scheme of things during her first Singapore season in 1930. She divided the proceeds of her show in Singapore's Victoria Theatre between European and non-European unemployed funds.[32] Upon her return in 1933, at the New World Amusement Park in the Lion's City, the gross proceeds from the play "Black Sheep" (Kambing Hitam), were publicly announced to go to the Child Welfare Society Fund for the benefit of Singapore's Muslim community.[33] Riboet, thus, was not only stimulating compassion through her highly moralising Malay opera drama, she was actually practising it. And she was far from unique.

In the early days of Komedie Stamboel, benefit performances were not uncommon, but they were certainly not as frequent as in the late 1920s, and had a different social meaning. In the early period of Malay opera, Stamboel suffered from a public image as a second rate and vulgar form of theatre drawing

---

[28] "Oleh pranakan", *Bintang Pranakan*, 7 Feb. 1931. "Sport, Music and Drama. Among the Straits Chinese", *The Malaya Tribune*, 28 Feb. 1930; "UCMA", *Bintang Pranakan*, 18 Oct. 1930; "'Birthday di Malacca", *Bintang Pranakan*, 14 Feb. 1931. Some of these amateur groups recorded on shellac. For example, The Straits Chinese Amateur Dramatic and Musical Society recorded for Messrs. Mong Huat, sole agents for the "Pagoda" brand. The songs were taken from the plays "Ginufifah" (Genoveva), a Malay opera favourite also staged by Miss Riboet, "Ah Fatt, The Pork-Seller" and "The Exile Prince", with extra turns and comic dialogue. "The Straits Chinese Dramatists. Voice Recordings Taken", *The Malaya Tribune*, 25 Mar. 1930.

[29] For example, in November 1930, the Wales Minstrels gave a benefit performance at the annual Chinese temple festival on Kusu Island, just off the coast of Singapore, to entertain the pilgrims. "Untitled", *The Straits Times*, 19 Aug. 1930; "Wales Minstrels ka 'Kusu'", *Bintang Pranakan*, 15 Nov. 1930.

[30] The 1929 office bearers of the United Chinese Musical Association in Singapore included Aw Boon Haw, aka the "Tiger Balm King" and Ong Peng Hock, owner of the New World Amusement Park. "Untitled", *The Straits Times*, 18 Oct. 1929.

[31] "Club Diary", *The Malaya Tribune*, 3 Feb. 1933.

[32] Ad "Miss Riboet", *The Malaya Tribune*, 20 Feb. 1933.

[33] Ibid.; "Javanese Artistes. Miss Riboet's Efforts for Charity", *Pinang Gazette and Straits Chronicle*, 23 Feb. 1933.

disorderly working-class audiences.[34] Benefit performances were a means to correct this image and attract a more decent middle-class public. The high rate of benefit events in the mid-1920s, however, strongly suggests that different social dynamics were at play. Going through the vernacular print press, one is struck by the frequent occurrence of benefit performances (*pertoendjoekan derma*, *pertoendjoekan amal*) of Malay opera troupes (*opera derma*), Javanese *wayang* troupes (*wajang derma*) and voluntary organisations holding soccer games, cinema shows and charity night fairs (*pasar derma*). In Malay as well as Javanese, *dharma* or *derma* means "duty", "donation", or "alms".[35] Another term for charity is *amal*, of Arabic origin, and related to Islamic almsgiving practices, but less frequently used in connection to popular entertainment.[36]

Of the numerous instances of *dermatainment* mentioned in the print press, a few will suffice here. In July 1925, Komedie "Opera Setia of Singapore" announced a benefit performance in Semarang. Eighty per cent of the proceeds were earmarked for the local peranakan Chinese association Indo Tionghoa. The remaining 20 per cent were channelled to a poverty relief organisation from Bungangan in Semarang.[37] In September 1925, the Javanese association Langen Darmo in Semarang announced a "charity wayang" (*wajang orang derma*). This Javanese theatre allocated 30 per cent of the proceeds to the relief of poverty stricken native Indonesian children; 30 per cent for the benefit of school association "Kartoso"; 30 per cent for the painters association "Tjiotowinarso"; and the remaining 10 per cent flowed to the association itself.[38]

By the 1920s, the Dutch colonial state had fallen short of meeting the aims of its so-called ethical (benevolent) policy to uplift the natives. Grassroots voluntary organisations from the emancipatory and national movement moved into what, by then, had become a social vacuum. Across Java, wealthy peranakan Chinese businessmen and voluntary associations used public entertainments to raise funds for three main services that the colonial government failed to deliver and that were central to the emancipatory and nationalist movement:

---

[34] Cohen (2006: 208–11).

[35] Derma is derived from *dharma*, suggesting Hindu-Javanese ancestry, see Jones (2007: 54).

[36] Almsgiving is institutionalised in Islam in the form of contributions to the Islamic community (*ummat*), in the form of *zakat* (obligatory donation by the wealthy to the poor), *sadaqah* ("spontaneous" donation at the end of the fasting month, Ramadan) and *waqaf* (endowments). See Siddiqi (1991: 6–30).

[37] "Pertoendjoekan Derma", *WW*, 7 July 1925.

[38] "Wajang orang derma", *WW*, 30 Sept. 1925.

education, health care and poverty relief.[39] The matter of education in the Indies was radically different in the Philippines, where the colonial government, aided by the Americans, sponsored education at all levels. The urge to emancipate in absence of colonial support, resulted in the colonised in Indonesia giving popular culture new social significance.

Philanthropic Fans

Between the mid-1920s and early 1930s, it was customary for prominent Malay opera companies to stage one or more benefit shows during their season in a city. In fact, without such shows, it was as if a Malay opera company had no legitimate existence.[40] Malay opera fans assumed a pivotal role in fundraising. Wealthy Malay opera patrons, millionaires (*hartawan*), mostly peranakan Chinese businessmen and Chinese social organisations would hire a company for one or more nights. Hiring (*borongan*) a troupe was a secure and often lucrative arrangement for Malay opera companies and actually dates back to the early days of Komedie Stamboel.[41] Benefit performances increased the chances of a full house. The patrons-cum-benefactors invited family, friends and business acquaintances and attracted people connected to charity institutions. The

---

[39] Many Chinese businessmen were displeased by the fact that the colonial authorities taxed expenses on charity if they were tracked in the company books. See "Belasting atas keamalan", *Sin Jit Po*, 11 July 1927.

[40] "Pertoendjoekan Derma Komedie 'Opera Setia of Singapore'", *WW*, 7 July 1925. This performance was held for poverty relief in Semarang; Chinese strikers in Shanghai received financial aid from Chinese in Semarang who staged an "Opera derma", see "Opera Derma", *WW*, 22 July 1925; in early January 1926, Malay opera troupe Komedie Constantinopel donated half of its proceedings to the Surabaya branch of the Federation of Chinese Associations. "Banjak trima kasi", *SP*, 8 Jan. 1926; in May 1926, Malay opera company Union Dalia Opera donated 30 per cent of its proceedings to the Young Girls Islamic School in Ampel, Surabaya and the same month also donated for poverty relief among the Chinese of Surabaya. See "Union Dalia Opera", *SP*, 28 and 31 May 1926. In July 1926, Malay opera company The Comet of Java staged "Tjelorong dan Tjeloreng" in Semarang to raise funds in support of the victims of an earthquake in West Sumatra, see *WW*, 20 July 1926. In August 1927, Dalia Opera donated 10 per cent of the proceedings from a performance in Surabaya to a local Chinese association. Throughout its existence, this latter opera company engaged in benefit performances, see "Miss Inten moentjoel lagi", *Sin Jit Po*, 15 Aug. 1927; "Boengah Roos dari Tjikembang Dalem Dalia Opera", *WW*, 24 Oct. 1927; "Derma dari The Union Dalia Opera", *Djawa Tengah*, 31 Oct. 1927; "Pertoendjoekan amal", *WW*, 4 Feb. 1929; "Pendapatannja Dalia Opera", *Perniagaan*, 11 Mar. 1929; "Dalia-Opera dan Amal", *Sin Jit Po*, 9 Dec. 1929; "alia Opera perkoempoelan Tionghoa", *Perniagaan*, 27 Jan. 1930.

[41] Cohen (2006: 91) relates that, in 1891, on its first tour in Semarang, Komedie Stamboel, the troupe who gave its name to this type of theatre, was hired by a wealthy Chinese resident from the city.

Chinese social organisations brought their members to the venue. The Chinese, Indonesian or Eurasian benefactors covered all costs, including losses from empty seats. In advertisements and reviews in the Sino-Malay press, the Malay opera patrons-cum-benefactors were referred to in Malay as *penderma* or *dermawan* (benefactors). These Malay opera patrons were also referred to in Malay and Javanese, respectively, more generally as *sobat-sobat* or *kontjo-kontjo*, literally meaning "friends".[42]

Within a few months after her first appearance in Surabaya, several peranakan Chinese millionaires (*hartawan*) had turned into Riboet fans, and she herself proved a willing charity object. Throughout the six-month Surabaya season, different Chinese individuals and social associations hired, on and off, Malay opera company Orion for hosting benefit performances. One of the philanthropists named in the newspapers was Tjan Kiem Tjong, who, as Kwee Thiam Tjing witnessed in May 1926, was mocked by Miss Riboet during a performance. And in March 1926, a group of wealthy peranakan Chinese from Surabaya, announced as "friends" and "loyal spectators" of the company, organised a show before a packed house. By then, benefit performances sponsored by Chinese social and religious associations, such as the local Chinese orphanage Thay Tong Bong Yan, occurred with such frequency that a reporter of one of Surabaya's Sino-Malay dailies cynically indicated that people were getting tired of supporting such associations and would rather give Miss Riboet the money. And this seemed to have happened.[43] Another more frequent beneficiary of Miss Riboet's Malay opera was the Surabaya branch of the Federation of Chinese Associations (Tiong Hoa Hwee Koan).[44] The high number of benefit performances and the discussions they evoked, inspired Riboet to create a dongeng titled: "Miss Riboet dapet derma" (Miss Riboet receives a donation).[45]

Malay opera proved an attractive vehicle for affluent middle-class fans to display their social status, wealth as well as compassion for poorer sections of society, enhancing the benefactor's social status as wealthy yet altruistic individuals. Malay opera drew mass audiences across class, gender and ethnicity, enabling the opera companies and their benefactors to raise substantial amounts of money. The print press also played an important role announcing events and its sponsors, as well as informing the public about the allocation of proceeds from

---

[42] Ad "Orion", *SP*, 21 Nov. 1925.

[43] "Miss Riboet dapet derma", *Soeara Publiek*, 18 Mar. 1926.

[44] Ad "Orion", *Sin Jit Po*, 17 Dec. 1925; "Komedie Orion", *SP*, 26 Nov. 1925; ad "Orion", *SP*, 31 Dec. 1925.

[45] Ad "Orion", *SP*, 19 Mar. 1926.

benefit performances.[46] Beneficiaries would often publicly express their gratitude for the generous donations, thus reaffirming the benefactor's respectable social status. Crucially, financial accountability was given in the print press in order to avoid accusations of embezzlement; in other words, financial transparency was designed to uphold the social prestige of those involved and to quell disputes over allocations.

Compassion for fellow humans was appreciated and encouraged. That said, fundraising was sometimes problematic and altruistic intentions were publicly questioned now and then. Surabaya's *Soeara Publiek*, for instance, both praised and scrutinised philanthropic activities. In September 1926, the paper lamented the difficulties in raising money for a Chinese children's educational fund in Surabaya. Many of the cities' Chinese millionaires were reported to have remained passive.[47] *Soeara Publiek* did not hesitate to portray millionaires who were slow or reluctant to engage in charity as selfish people, for whom the Hokkien adjective *kokati* was reserved.[48] In these matters, *Soeara Publiek* assumed the role of a moral compass and watchdog.

And even those who did stimulate compassion and participated in philanthropic practices were not always safe from critique. A good example is the altruistic behaviour of fans of Miss Riboet, but also her own philanthropic activities, which evoked suspicions about the benefactors' intentions. In 1926, *Soeara Publiek* reported critically on a Riboet fan from Surabaya, Hadji Drachman bin Mohamad Hie Soen, who was sufficiently affluent that he could make the costly pilgrimage to Mecca. Progressive intellectuals and journalists such as Kwee Thiam Tjing were sceptical of millionaires like Hie Soen and their benevolent behaviour. The Chinese Muslim had made his fortune in the notorious business of money lending. The wealth accumulated from this controversial trade suggested "dirty money" and, therefore, in the eyes of *Soeara Publiek*, this benefactor was a second-rate Miss Riboet fan.[49] It should be recalled

---

[46] Lists of benefactors, amounts of individual donations, expenditures or the total net amounts are given in, for instance: "Verslag lengkep dari pertoendjoekan Opera-Derma T.H.H.K. jang dimaenken oleh Vereeniging 'Hak Yoe Hwee' Solo pada 25–26 Juni 1927", *WW*, 16 Aug. 1927; "Pemborongan Orion", *Sin Jit Po*, 8 Oct. 1927. Similar financial accounts are given in "Verslag Polikliniek Tionghoa Dalem boelan October 1927", *WW*, 25 Nov. 1927; "Pendapetan Dalia Opera boeat Tung Chih Hui", *Perniagaan*, 7 Feb. 1930.

[47] "Studiefonds Boeat Anak Tionghoa", *SP*, 28 Sept. 1926.

[48] "Kokati", *SP*, 11 Dec. 1926.

[49] "Hadji Drachman 'bin Hie Soen'", *SP*, 28 Apr. 1926. It is particularly ironic that Hie Soen, a Muslim who had made the pilgrimage to Mecca (*hajj*), a sign of religious devotion, acquired his wealth through moneylending. According to Islam, interest on loans is forbidden (*riba*). It is, of course, possible that Hie Soen made money through other trades.

that, in 1926, Kwee was charged with inciting violence against moneylenders in one of his provocative columns.

Miss Riboet's altruistic behaviour also came under public scrutiny. An early example of suspicions about her altruistic intentions occurred in December 1926, when Orion's management announced that it would donate the net profits from a show to the victims of a fire in the Pasar Senen area of Batavia. Three weeks after the announcement, residents from Pasar Senen complained to the local newspaper *Bintang Timoer* that they had not yet seen a penny.[50] Another, more telling example, revealing tensions between popular culture and compassion, concerns the football team employed by the opera company. In July 1928, we first hear of a soccer team by the name of Miss Riboet's XI. Like Luis Borromeo's marriage of boxing with vod-a-vil, a soccer team was another novel way of drawing audiences to Orion's opera shows. The team initially consisted of members of the opera cast who played barefoot, but they were later replaced by semi-professional players, the latter travelling along the touring opera company. These soccer players paved the way for professional soccer in Southeast Asia. During the company's tours across Java, Sumatra, the Straits and the Federated Malay States, Riboet's XI met local teams.[51] The competitions drew hundreds up to thousands of paying spectators. The local print press often announced and reviewed these games.[52] Like Malay opera performances, Orion's management also used the soccer games to raise funds for charitable purposes. For example, in October 1929, Miss Riboet's XI was challenged in Batavia by a team of officials from the Department of Justice to a charity game. Proceeds from the ticket sales were partly allocated for poverty relief of Eurasians, and partly channelled to two hospitals run by native Indonesians and local Chinese, respectively.[53]

---

[50] Ad "Miss Riboet's Maleisch Operette Gezelschap 'Orion'", *Bintang Timoer*, 7 Dec. 1926; "Bagimana itoe derma di Senen?", *Bintang Timoer*, 27 Dec. 1926.

[51] Ad "Orion", *Java Bode*, 13 July 1928; "AFSCHEID VAN MISS RIBOET", *Java Bode*, 16 July 1928.

[52] For example, a game during the 1930 season of Riboet in Penang was announced as: "Big football match at Dato Kramat Ground. Miss Riboet's Football team, which has won 25 matches out of 27 in whole Sumatra, will meet Champion of Penang: the well-known Darul Aisham Football club". Ad "Kronchong Night/Big Football Match", *The Straits Echo*, 19 Jan. 1930.

[53] In this particular case, public attendance of this charity game was said to have been disappointing. The Eurasian association concerned was the poor relief department of the Indo Europees Verbond (IEV). The two hospitals were: Boedikemoelian and Jang Seng Ie. "Voetbal. 'Miss Riboet's XI'", *Het Nieuws voor den Dag van Nederlandsch-Indië*, 6 Oct. 1928; "Justitie-Miss Riboet's XI", *Bataviaasch Nieuwsblad*, 19 Aug. 1929; "Voetbal te Batavia", *Bataviaasch Nieuwsblad*, 21 Aug. 1929.

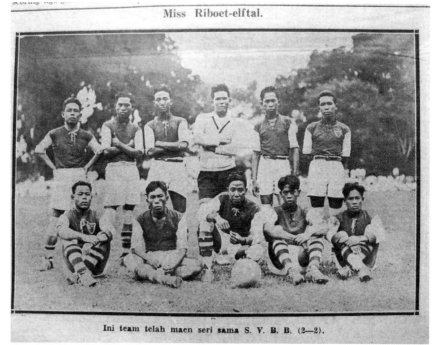

Illus. 9.1 Miss Riboet's XI, pioneers of professional soccer in Indonesia and Malaysia. *Sin Po*, 11 Nov. 1931.

In July 1929, a reporter from *Warna Warta*, a Sino-Malay newspaper from Semarang, questioned Riboet's unselfish motives, arguing that the purpose of the soccer team was simply commercial, that is to draw audiences and to make money. Insulted and outraged by the insinuations, a written response followed, signed by the Riboet's XI captain and published in *Warna Warta*. The letter's content and its articulate language strongly suggests that Tio Tek Djien Jr., and not the captain, was the author.[54] Some journalists, however, applauded the Malay opera diva for her "amazing commercial instinct to find the ultimate means to reach out to the masses by bringing in Miss Riboet's soccer team".[55] Distrust did not discourage Riboet and Tio. Up to early 1941, shortly before the

---

[54] "SEDIKIT ... KETRANGAN", *WW*, 16 Jan. 1929.
[55] "Het Miss Riboet elftal", *De Sumatra Post*, 27 Aug. 1929.

Japanese occupation of the East Indies, they continued to financially support voluntary organisations across ethnic, religious and political divides.[56]

The intertwining of ethics and popular culture was not restricted to Miss Riboet's Malay opera company. The company found a rival in opera company Dardanella that also developed a particularly social relevant theatre and attracted its own and distinct intellectual fandom with an undercurrent of Indonesian nationalism, very different from Miss Riboet's devotees.

Dardanella: Mirror of Life

In May 1930, newspaper *Pewarta Menado*, published in the town of Menado, North Sulawesi, was thrilled by a Malay opera show staged in the city. The reporter related: "As the stage opened it reminded me of 'La Gaité Lyrique', 'Scala, Casino', and other theatres in Paris. The orchestra beautifully played Jazz songs, Charleston and Javanese songs with great feeling. I think there is no other Opera in Indonesia as good, compared to this one."[57] Obviously, this reporter was impressed and pleased by the professional, modern and cosmopolitan outlook of this Malay opera company. He concluded that, in the ten years he had refrained from attending a show, this group had managed to modernise Malay opera. The reporter had witnessed Dardanella, one of colonial Indonesia's major innovative troupes, next to that of Miss Riboet's.

Dardanella was established in Sidoarjo, East Java in June 1926 by the Penang-born Piedro Klimanoff, who was of Russian ancestry. The Klimanoff family had been working as professional dancers and acrobats in between "Colombo and Java" since the turn of the century. As itinerant artists, they had joined travelling circuses and bangsawan troupes, such as the pioneering and famous Wayang

---

[56] For example, throughout the 1930s, Orion supported the following organisations: the children's department of Jang Seng Ie Hospital and the hospital's anti-opium programme; the Chinese Unemployment Fund; the General Support Fund for Native Poor (Algemeen Steunfonds voor Inheemsche Behoeftigen, ASIB) in Surabaya; an orphanage in Surabaya; the Red Cross in China; the outpatient clinic of the Islamic association Moehammadijah, Malang branch; see *Sin Po*, 16 Aug. 1934; *Nieuws van den Dag van Nederlandsch-Indie*, 19 Aug. 1935; "Miss Riboet dan Amal", *Sin Tit Po*, 9 Sept. 1936; "Miss Riboet's Orion", *Pelita Andalas*, 14 Jan. 1938; "Malang. Miss Riboet dan Moehammadijah", *Sin Tit Po*, 18 Jan. 1940; "Miss Riboet dan VORO", *Sin Po*, 21 Feb. 1941.

[57] "Iseng2 ka Opera Dardanella", *Pewarta Menado*, 31 May 1930.

Kassim from Penang.[58] In August 1927, Dardanella debuted in Surabaya, coinciding with Miss Riboet's second season in the harbour city.[59] At this early stage, Dardanella's undisputed leading actor and star (*bintang*) was peranakan Chinese singer-actor Tan Tjeng Bok (c. 1900–85). He was announced as "Si Item" (blacky), referring to his dark complexion, and as "Kampioen Krontjong" (Kroncong Champion), referring to the title he had once won in an East Java kroncong singing contest.[60] German record company Beka also recognised his vocal qualities and his commercial potential. While working for Dardanella, Tan recorded for Beka in 1927, 1928 and, likely, 1931.[61] In 1928, newspaper *Warna Warta* described Tan's vocal style as "njaring dan terang" (loud and clear), an important asset for the Malay opera stage, where electric audio amplification was only introduced in 1934, and likely sparingly, due to the high costs that came with the new microphone technology.[62]

Tan had joined Dardanella in 1927. Up to that date, he had gone through a rather tumultuous career from janitor in a cinema theatre, indentured estate worker (coolie) on the East Coast of Sumatra, stage hand for peranakan Chinese opera company Swie Ban Lian in Batavia to actor on the Malay opera stage.[63] Tan Tjeng Bok excelled as an actor in action plays such as "The Three Musketeers" in which he took the leading role as D'Artagnan, or, for example, in "Don Q the

---

[58] "Did Not Report 1903 Birth", *The Straits Times*, 26 Sept. 1936; "Ott's Circus", *Eastern Daily Mail and Straits Morning Advertiser*, 13 Apr. 1907; ad, *The Singapore Free Press and Mercantile Advertiser*, 21 Nov. 1908; see "Untitled", *The Straits Times*, 14 Feb. 1910; ad, *The Singapore Free Press and Mercantile Advertiser*, 14 Oct. 1911. On Piedro's father, Adolf Klimanoff, and his artistic involvement with Wayang Kassim, see also Tan (1993: 40).

[59] Ad, *Sin Jit Po*, 8 Aug. 1927; "Opera Dardanella", *Sin Jit Po*, 9 Aug. 1927.

[60] Ad, *Sin Jit Po*, 6 Aug. 1927; "The Malay Opera 'Dardanella'", *WW*, 31 Oct. 1928; "Kabar Kota", *WW*, 17 Nov. 1928.

[61] "Acteurs dan actrices Dardanella boeat Grammafoon", *WW*, 24 Nov. 1928; 4 Nov. 1931. According to an ad by toko Tan Tjin Giok in newspaper *Sin Tit Po*, 2 Sept. 1932, Beka released another batch of Dardanella recordings, including a duet of Tan with Miss Riboet II: "Krontjong Akrek", Beka no. 997.

[62] From a surviving Beka recording entitled "Stamboel Marayap" (Stamboel on the move) (Beka B. 15789-II), we can infer that Tan's singing style was inspired by Western baritone opera singing. On Dardanella's musical repertoire, see "Tjang", *Bahagia*, 23 Apr. 1934. Faroka cabaret, a Malay opera company sponsored by local cigarette manufacturer Faroka, was said to have been the first to use loudspeakers, especially employed to accommodate spectators in the rear seats. "Het Faroka-Cabaret", *Het Nieuws van den dag voor Nederlandsch-Indië*, 8 Sept. 1934.

[63] "Tan Tjeng Bok (Douglas Fairbanks van Java)", *Doenia Film dan Sport* Speciaal "Dardanella Nummer", 15 Nov. 1930; "Sekedar riwajat Tan Tjeng Bok", *Pertjatoeran Doenia Film* no. 7. Th. 1, 1941; "Tan Ceng Bok dari ngamen sampai ke dunia film", *Citra Film*, no. 19, Mar. 1982.

Illus. 9.2　Malay opera actor and singer Tan Tjeng Bok, c. 1931. This publicity picture is one of a series of postcards of Dardanella's prominent artists that came with the purchase of a Beka phonographic record of one of these Malay opera stars. KITLV 182527. Leiden University Libraries, Digital Collections.

Son of Zorro".[64] As early as 1928, Tan earned the name of "the Douglas Fairbanks of Java" as a result of a series of roles in locally-produced silent films, starting with *The Thief of Bagdad* in 1928.[65] This latter story was also on Dardanella's play repertoire. Between 1932 and 1934, however, Tan associated with Miss Riboet's Orion Malay Opera Co.[66]

During Dardanella's early existence, the company's leading lady was Miss Riboet II, or the "second Miss Riboet". Like the original Miss Riboet, she also acquired a peranakan Chinese fan base in Surabaya.[67] Her stage name gave rise to a dispute between Tio Tek Djien Jr. and the Dardanella management that was settled in 1928.[68] From 1931, Dardanella's Miss Riboet II was surpassed in popularity and fame by Dardanella's new leading teenage female star, Soetidja or Miss Dja, also known as "Dardanella's Sweet Seventeen".[69]

Dardanella's fame as an exciting novel and modern Malay company rocketed as fast as that of Miss Riboet's Orion. In 1928, the troupe toured the Outer Islands, receiving acclaim and being awarded medals and certificates by government officials and local rulers (*raja-raja*).[70] That same year, Semarang Sino-Malay newspaper *Warna Warta* praised the company for representing "Modern Opera". Like Riboet's Orion, Dardanella's repertoire was initially firmly rooted in the Stamboel/bangsawan play repertoire, including Sino-Malay stories and Malay adaptations of European novels. For example, during its 1927 Surabaya debut, Dardanella staged the classic Sino-Malay story of "Sam Pek Eng Tay". The following year Alexander Dumas's "The Three Musketeers" (Tiga Panglima

---

[64] "The Malay Opera 'Dardanella'", *Bintang Hindia*, 18 May 1929; ad "Dardanella", *Sin Po*, 25 Oct. 1930.

[65] Ad movie "The Thief of Bagdad", *Sin Jit Po*, 17 Oct. 1928.

[66] "Dalia Opera", *Perniagaan*, 4 Jan. 1930; ad "Dr Samsi Dardanella", *Sin Po*, 21 Oct. 1931; "Miss Riboet's Orion"; ad "Miss Riboet", *Bintang Borneo*, 21 June 1932; "Destiny atawa takdir Allah", *Sinar Sumatra*, 27 Aug. 1934.

[67] "Dardanella", *Sin Jit Po*, 17 Aug. 1927; "Opera Dardanella", *Sin Jit Po*, 9 Aug. 1927; "'Indonesia'. Opera Dardanella Oendjoek actie", *WW*, 24 Jan. 1929; "The Malay Opera 'Dardanella'", *Bintang Hindia*, 18 May 1929.

[68] A birth certificate ascertained that Dardanella's Miss Riboet was indeed her true and not only a stage name used to capitalise on the popularity of Orion's prima donna. "Directie Miss Riboet", *WW*, 22 Nov. 1928; "Miss Riboet Orion dan Miss Riboet Dardanella", *WW*, 23 Nov. 1928; "Iseng-iseng malem Minggoe", *WW*, 24 Nov. 1928; "Apa nama orang bisa digedeponeerd", *WW*, 24 Nov. 1928; *Doenia Film dan Sport* Speciaal "Dardanella Nummer", 15 Nov. 1930.

[69] Ad "Dr Samsi Dardanella", *Sin Po*, 21 Oct. 1931; *Sin Tit Po*, 8 Aug. 1932; *Sin Tit Po*, 27 Aug. 1932.

[70] "The Malay Opera 'DARDANELLA'", *WW*, 17 Oct. 1928. As a form of indirect rule, the Dutch retained local hereditary rulers across Indonesia.

perang), also staged by Miss Riboet's Orion, was a big hit, particularly because of Tan Tjeng Bok's acting.[71]

Dardanella's breakthrough as a popular and modern Malay opera came in 1930, when the ambitious journalist Abisin Abas alias Andjar Asmara joined the troupe as publicity man and playwright. Like Tio Tek Djien Jr., Dardanella owner-manager Klimanoff attempted to wrest the company from the Stamboel stigma of a repertoire of ghost and fairy tales; it was only after Asmara had come on board that the troupe successfully claimed it offered something novel and, important to note, a socially relevant theatre. Dardanella presented its plays as a mirror of life ("Tjermin penghidoepan").[72] Working for the Batavia-based newspaper *Bintang Timoer*, Asmara had first come into contact with the company in 1929 after being invited by Klimanoff to watch a show. The young Soetidja especially impressed Asmara, in whom he recognised more artistic potency than the then leading lady Miss Riboet II.[73] In 1930, Klimanoff employed the journalist with, as would turn out, artistic aspirations.[74] Between 1929 and 1931, Asmara conducted an aggressive publicity campaign in a series of articles in *Bintang Hindia* and other periodicals promoting Dardanella, in a way never done before by any Malay opera company.[75]

Like Miss Riboet, Dardanella also drew an ethnically diverse lower middle- to upper-class audience.[76] For example, a show staged in Yogyakarta in 1929, was said to have drawn spectators from "all races" (*segala bangsa*), including "well-known Europeans", presumably estate owners, local government officials and white-collar workers.[77] Dardanella was also committed to charity and, following the example of Miss Riboet's Orion, employed a soccer team.[78]

---

[71] "Opera Dardanella", *Sin Jit Po*, 17 Aug. 1927; "The Malay Opera 'Dardanella'", *WW*, 31 Oct. 1928.

[72] Ad "Dardanella", *Sin Po*, 4 Nov. 1930.

[73] On Dja's social background and career as a dancer, see Cohen (2010: 179–208).

[74] "Kenang-kenangan kepada Miss Dja. Oleh Andjar Asmara", *Pertjatoeran Doenia Film*, no. 2 th. I, 1 July 1941.

[75] In 1930, now also working for Dardanella, Andjar Asmara published a special Dardanella issue in the periodical *Doenia Film dan Sport* (The World of Cinema and Sports) of which he was editor-in-chief. Moreover, he announced a monthly under the name of *Dardanella Revue*, published in the city of Medan to be published in January 1931. See ad "Dardanella", *Sinar Deli*, 11 Jan. 1931.

[76] "Dardanella", *Sin Jit Po*, 17 Aug. 1927; "Indonesia. Opera Dardanella oendjoek actie", *WW*, 24 Jan. 1929; "Annie van Mendoet di Dardanella", *Sinar Deli*, 15 Jan. 1931.

[77] "Indonesia. Opera Dardardanella oendjoek actie", *WW*, 24 Jan. 1929.

[78] On 29 May 1934, Dardanella gave a benefit performance at the Thalia Theatre in Batavia for the Jang Sie Eng Hospital and the Committee for the Support of Unemployed Chinese in Batavia.

Thus, from 1927 to 1929, Dardanella followed an artistic and commercial trajectory very similar to that of Malay opera company Orion. Unlike Tio Tek Djien Jr., who remained ambiguous and reluctant about Malay opera as an art form, Asmara was far more explicit about and active in transforming Malay opera into *toneel* (Dutch for theatre or *tonil*, a Malay corruption of the Dutch term). He associated *tonil* with high-class European theatre, and juxtaposed it with lowbrow theatrical forms, such as Stamboel and ketoprak, the latter also out of reach for most Indonesians and, therefore, in Asmara's view, not suitable as a model for a modern Indonesian theatre.[79] Significant from a social perspective was that Asmara's vision of a modern Indonesian theatrical form was shared and followed with great interest by a small, but articulate group of peers from theatrical, literary and emancipatory and nationalist circles in the capital Batavia. As Sino-Malay newspaper *Sin Po* observed in 1931, after decades of neglect, native Indonesian and peranakan Chinese journalists and intellectuals had started to take Malay opera "seriously".[80] By this time, Miss Riboet's Orion and Dardanella became the yardsticks for measuring other Malay opera troupes artistically and in terms of social significance.[81]

The Spirit of Today

The making of a popular modern Malay opera by Riboet's Orion and by Dardanella was paralleled by discussions among intellectuals in Batavia regarding a "new culture" (*keboedajaan baroe*). Among those most vocal in promoting this new hybrid culture of interconnected music, theatre and literature was a small group of writers and journalists at a literary periodical *Poedjangga Baroe* (New Writer), founded in 1933.[82] They could be ranked among a wider group of Indonesian nationalist intellectuals-cum-activists in Batavia, some with roots in the pergerakan movement of the 1910s, many of whom had a professional background in journalism. These intellectuals promoted independence but, with some exceptions, did not reject collaboration with the colonial government per se. They also did not envisage a narrow, inclusive cultural nationalism as model for a modern Indonesia, but rather a cosmopolitan nationalism. When, in 1934, young Indonesians, attracted by the new alien-inspired modern culture, came

---

[79] "Berbitjara dengan toean A. Abas", *Pandji Poestaka*, 25 May 1934.

[80] "KOTA. Perhatian pada Dardanella", *Sin Po*, 13 Nov. 1931.

[81] For instance, reviewers compared Miss Riboet and Dardanella to Miss Alang Opera, see, "Dardanella Opera", *Oetoesan Sumatra*, 16 Dec. 1930; "Miss Alang Opera", *Pergaoelan*, 10 Nov. 1931; "Kunst. Miss Alang", *Pergaoelan*, 8 Dec. 1931; "Tentangan Tooneel Melajoe", *Sinar Sumatra*, 29 May 1931.

[82] Sutherland (1968: 107); Frederick (1996: 54–89).

under attack from cultural purists, Takdir Alisjahbana, one of *Poedjangga Baroe*'s founders, came to their defence: "Allow them to choose whatever they like. From all the corners of the world there is something that can be taken to develop something new, something more noble and grand than the old. Why would we wish to prevent those among our youngsters to be interested in Western culture, in the arts, and literature."[83]

While acknowledging Miss Riboet's contribution to modernising Malay opera, and appreciating her many talents, the Batavia-based intellectuals came under the spell of Dardanella. According to Armijn Pane, writer and co-founder of *Poedjangga Baroe*, Dardanella was the "mouthpiece of today's spirit".[84] What this writer meant with "today's spirit" was a synthesis of modernity and cosmopolitanism compatible with the spirit of Indonesian nationalism as propagated by the pergerakan.[85]

Like Kwee Thiam Tjing, alias Tjamboek Berdoeri, before him, Pane seemed to sense the excitement and the social potential of the new culture, not yet regarded as "popular culture", which was disputed as the basis for a modern national Indonesian culture. A bone of contention, for instance, was whether the modern popular music genre of kroncong could serve as Indonesian national music.[86] Pane was very likely conscious of the mass audiences modern Malay opera could reach. *Poedjangga Baroe*'s subscriptions were confined to a happy few in the colony, only around 150 during its entire existence.[87] By comparison, travelling Malay opera troupes, like Riboet's Orion and Dardanella, attracted tens of thousands of spectators across the archipelago during a single season, many of them barely educated or even literate.

We learn more about the social significance attributed by nationalist-intellectuals and others to Malay opera company Dardanella through play reviews. "Annie van Mendoet", staged by Dardanella in Medan in 1930, is a good example. The drama was a great hit with native Indonesians and even more so among the intellectual sections. The story of "Annie van Mendoet" conveyed a strong moral message and, as such, was a typical example of the new modern drama repertoire with realism and ethics at its core, as spearheaded by Tio and Riboet. The tale warned spectators for the dangers of Westernisation, particularly those Indonesians who sought intimacy with Dutch culture and society. The "reality" portrayed in this story is that of a young Javanese woman, Annie,

---

[83] "Menghadapi keboedajaan Baroe", *Poedjangga Baroe*, th. I, no, 12, 1934: 358–63.

[84] "Pemandangan Pers. Dardanella", *Poedjangga Baroe*, th. I, no. 12, 1934.

[85] Frederick (1996: 60).

[86] See Frederick (1996), on the controversy over kroncong as "national music".

[87] Sutherland (1968: 106–27).

daughter of a Javanese official of aristocratic origins. Annie marries a Javanese man, Andogo, who takes a law degree in the Netherlands. During his study abroad, this student, Andogo, drifts away from his own people (the Javanese) and his wife. He speaks with contempt about native Indonesians, avoids them, and no longer acknowledges the child he has with Annie. Andogo marries a Dutch lady. Annie is left desperate, but with the little money she receives from her husband she successfully starts a tailoring business. Meanwhile, as Annie expands her business and recovers from the emotional strain, Andogo is abandoned by his Dutch wife and descends into misery.

Reviewing the play, Malay newspaper *Sinar Deli* exclaimed: "The play Annie van Mendoet is truly one full of meaning, deep symbolic significance and learning. Our Indonesian youngsters with their heads full of Western ideals will be cursed by Indonesia if they do not become conscious by this instructive play staged by Dardanella."[88] And Malay newspaper *Oetoesan Sumatra* concluded: "'Annie van Mendoet' is a story of interest, a reminder to those who wish to study in Europe."[89] *Pemberita Makassar* concluded about the audience: "It could not have been foreseen that this play has become a mirror [of life, PK] and is so much appreciated by those who witness it, especially [native] Indonesian intellectuals (*kaoem intellectuelen Indonesiers*)."[90]

In spite of "Annie van Mendoet's" anti-Dutch undercurrent, neither Dutch audiences, nor the colonial authorities took offence; some Dutchmen even appreciated the play, but for different reasons than most Indonesian nationalists. Having staged "Annie van Mendoet" in Medan in 1930, Dardanella's management was approached by the Secretary of a local section of the Kunstkring, a Dutch-dominated art association in the Netherlands East Indies. The art-loving Secretary spoke highly of the company in terms of Dutch theatre (*toneel*) and not Malay opera. Rather ironically, given the message of the play, he associated Dardanella with high art and successful Westernisation. He invited the troupe to perform before the Kunstkring's Bogor chapter, West Java, and even suggested inviting the Governor General of the Netherlands-East Indies, the colony's highest-ranking

---

[88] "Betoellah lakon Annie van Mendoet soeatoe tjerita jang banjak mengandoeng arti, ibarat dan pengadjaran, penoeh dalamnja. Pemoeda Indonesier kita jang kepalanja penoeh angan ke-Baratan, aken tjoema soempah tanah Indonesia djika tidak mengambil insjaf dari lakon pengadjaran jang dioendjoekkan Dardanella itoe". "Annie van Mendoet di Dardanella", *Sinar Deli*, 15 Jan. 1931.

[89] "Tontonan. Dardanella", *Oetoesan Sumatra*, 8 Dec. 1930.

[90] "Tooneel gezelschap 'Dardanella'". "Annie van Mendoet", *Pemberita Makassar*, 28 Mar. 1933.

official.[91] Whether Dardanella's management, Klimanoff and Asmara, accepted the invitation remains unclear. What we do know, as will become clear in the next chapter, is that, in contrast to Miss Riboet and her husband, Dardanella's management was not eagerly waiting for approbation from a Dutch upper-class audience. In fact, Dardanella was, as Armijn Pane articulated so concisely, the "mouthpiece of today's spirit", the spirit of Indonesian nationalism that the majority of Dutchmen, including many Eurasians, in the colony despised.

Regarding cultural borrowing and hybridity, Asmara took a contradictory cultural nationalist stand. On the one hand, his ideas on developing Malay opera into high-class theatre were very much on par with the Kunstkring's conception; on the other, he denounced Westernisation. Asmara shared with the Kunstkring a belief in "progress" and both perceived theatre as an educational means to uplift the masses and to bridge "East and West" through "highbrow art". During its 1932 Surabaya season, Dardanella made its mission explicit: to elevate the standard of Malay theatre (Asmara purposely avoided the word opera).[92] While he engaged in creating a cultural hybrid form of theatre, and borrowed European and American theatrical and musical elements, Asmara also advocated the removal of these same elements. In December 1934, during a lecture in Padang, West Sumatra, on invitation of a branch of the nationalist-oriented *Persatoean Djoernalis Indonesia* (Perdi, The Association of Indonesian Journalists), Asmara claimed to have been active in an organisation in Batavia with the purpose of "exterminating Americanism".[93] This "extermination" remained a dead letter as far as Dardanella was concerned. The troupe continued to stage its intermissions, so called "extras", of modern Western dances and music, and continued its adaptations of Western novels and films. It should also be noted that the name of the company itself was very likely borrowed from the same global American popular culture Asmara denounced; Dardanella was probably named after the title of the jazzy hit song, a foxtrot performed by Selvin's Novelty Orchestra and recorded by Victor Talking Machine Company in 1919. The song, initially published by Tin Pan Alley producer Fred Fisher, who, in 1920, had also

---

[91] "Tontonan. 'Annie van Mendoet'", *Oetoesan Sumatra*, 6 Dec. 1930. The newspaper reiterated that the Governor General "loved to watch Western-style theatre (tooneel) and not bangsawan".

[92] Ad "Dardanella", *Sin Tit Po*, 10 Sept. 1932.

[93] Perdi was established in 1931 in Surakarta, Central Java. See Poeze (1988: 348). On Asmara's Padang lecture, see "Kabar kota dan daerahnja. Lezing toean Abisin Abbas (samboengan kemaren)", *Sinar Sumatra*, 8 Dec. 1934.

distributed Luis Borromeo's foxtrot "Jazzy Jazzy Sound in Old Chinatown", went global in the early 1920s.[94]

Recapitulating, Miss Riboet's novel stardom was connected with commerce and consumerism, but also with compassion. In addition to these traits, the belief of intellectuals that modern Malay opera served progress, infused the new popular culture with a distinctive social and ethical dynamic that fitted the struggle for emancipation. There is more to say. Armijn Pane's "today's spirit" contained broader meanings than progress or nationalism. This spirit or mindset also implied new notions of society (*pergaoelan hidoep*) and, as such, formed another significant indicator of the social meaning attributed to the new popular culture represented by Dardanella. And while a select group of nationalist intellectuals associated this latter Malay opera troupe with social change and emancipation, Miss Riboet would alienate herself from this particular group.

---

[94] The song "Dardanella" was composed by Felix Bernard and Johnny S. Black, see http://adp. library.ucsb.edu/index.php/talent/detail/20058/Selvins_Novelty_Orchestra_Musical_group. It was available on shellac in the Netherlands as early as June 1920 and released by Columbia Grafonola and Records as "The Foxtrot Dardanella, Currently Highly Popular in America", ad "K.K. Knies", *Bataviaasch Nieuwsblad*, 25 June 1920.

Chapter 10

Approbation and Alienation

Between 1929 and 1935, the face of popular culture in the East Indies transformed significantly, as it did in the Philippines. Artistic interaction and experimentation as well as the social potency of vernacular theatre began to wane. In the early 1930s, intellectuals from the Indonesian emancipatory and nationalist movement were still exploring the aesthetic and social dimension of popular arts. This would change by the mid-1930s. This social aspect will be examined in the first two sections of this chapter, when discussing the Malay concept of *pergaoelan* (*pergaulan* in modern Indonesian and Malay) and an aspect of participatory pop: fan gatherings. A small group of Batavia-based intellectual nationalists approbated Malay opera company Dardanella as a model, as a promise for the future, as socially relevant, modern Indonesian theatre. According to these intellectual fans of Malay opera, this form of theatre presented a new type of social affinity, referred to using the term pergaoelan. Dreams of a modern Indonesian theatre, however, evaporated when the troupe disbanded in 1936, ending the "marriage" between modern Malay opera and social and political progress.

Miss Riboet's Malay opera troupe survived managerial and financial troubles that plagued many troupes. But, in contrast to Dardanella, as I will discuss in the closing sections, Riboet never attracted a nationalist intellectual fandom. In fact, the opposite occurred. Between 1929 and 1935, a reactionary Dutch middle-class audience embraced Riboet and her Malay opera as a safe and acceptable form of colonial entertainment. In this process, Riboet and her husband Tio alienated themselves from the emancipatory and nationalist movement.

These processes of approbation and alienation marked the end of the cultural dynamics of modern Malay opera as it had developed since Miss Riboet's debut in Surabaya in late 1925. By 1936, Malay opera's social relevance had broken down completely. Its social demise should, however, not simply be understood as a definite or complete downfall of popular culture. Like vaudeville in the Philippines, Malay opera was also one of the artistic sources for the local cinematic and record industry. Already in the early 1930s, Malay opera people connected to the film and record industry, channelling their artistry and ideas into them. Films and records might have attracted masses, but compared to the development of modern Malay opera in the preceding decade, the capacity to connect arts, promote ethics, progress and enhance community and society remained latent or dormant.

Community and Society: Pergaoelan

Between 1931 and 1932, terms such as *pergaoelan hidoep* and *pergaoelan bersama* came to the fore in the print press, suggesting the term became current in this period.[1] Taken from the root *gaul* (to mix, socialise) the term stood variably for "social intercourse", "community" and "society". Significant for our understanding of popular culture is that the term was frequently linked to modern Malay opera. For instance, in 1931, a newspaper with the telling name *Pergaoelan*, published in Kota Radja (Aceh), reviewed a show of Malay opera troupe Miss Alang, named after its leading star. The paper reported on the troupe's repertoire: "Its stories are interesting, they provide a lot of advice as how to live together (*pergaoelan bersama*)."[2]

In 1932, Sino-Malay newspaper from Surabaya, *Soeara Oemoem* praised Miss Riboet's acting and play repertoire in similar terms: "[…] among her plays are some that very much serve society (pergaoelan hidoep bersama), especially as Miss Riboet often subtly comments on rotten situations […]".[3] These "rotten situations" could be interpreted as immoral human behaviour, or, for those with anti-colonial and nationalist inclinations, the social injustices of the colonial system. In 1932, the new women's emancipatory magazine *Pedoman Isteri* (est. January 1932), led by moderate Indonesian nationalists, gave an explicit explanation of the meaning of the term pergaoelan hidoep. The magazine editors used the allegory of the household and the Dutch equivalent of society, *maatschappij*: "If we have a family, we have to be aware beforehand, that a household is like a small society (*pergaoelan hidoep ketjil*) that is part of larger society (*pergaoelan hidoep doenia*) […]."[4]

Pergaoelan became a buzzword in connection with the social significance of Malay opera troupe Dardanella. For example, the play "Dr. Samsi", written by

---

[1] A Hokkien equivalent to *pergaoelan*, and also a term for "community" or "society" in relation to Dardanella's social significance, which I came across in Sino-Malay newspaper *Sin Po* is *shiahwee*. "Kota. Perhatian pada Dardanella", *Sin Po*, 13 Nov. 1930.

[2] "Kunst. Miss Alang", *Pergaoelan*, 8 Dec. 1931.

[3] "Miss Riboet", *Soeara Oemoem*, 12 Jan. 1932.

[4] "Erti Bergaoel", *Pedoman Isteri* no. 5, May 1932.

Asmara, was reviewed as a realistic and appropriate moral warning for the youth. It is a story of a respected medical doctor who descends into the darker side of life.[5] He keeps a young woman as his mistress; she is dishonoured, ostracised and, in the end, Dr. Samsi turns to manslaughter. The press regarded the story a moral lesson that pointed out the dangers of free social intercourse (*pergaoelan jang vrij*) of current times (*waktoe sekarang*).[6] Another review, a few years later, stressed the drama's core message—the unjust nature of human life. The play was reported as being "[…] a mirror of life, of social intercourse (pergaoelan)…."[7]

Dardanella's management explicitly referred to the concept of pergaoelan hidoep in relation to dramas staged. This social aspect came, for example, to the fore, in 1931, when several local Sino-Malay and Malay papers from Sumatra took offence about Asmara's demeaning portrayal of native journalists in the drama "Medan by Night".[8] In defence of, and emphasising the company's social engagement, Asmara responded: "It is not only the responsibility of you gentlemen to remove disparity in society (pergaoelan hidoep), but also our responsibility."[9]

The line between addressing societal and political issues was thin, as in "Haida", written by Andjar Asmara and performed in the early 1930s. The company advertised the play as: "An issue of current interest to society in Indonesia (Satoe soal jang actueel dalam pergaoelan hidoep di Indonesia)."[10] "Haida" is the story of a young, modern, educated woman (performed by Miss Dja). She marries happily, but things take a turn when her husband, according to Islamic custom, takes a second wife. A political dimension is added to the story; the husband is exiled to Boven Digoel, the place for political exiles in New Guinea, indicating

---

[5] "Dr. Samsi" was partly autobiographical. Pressed by his parents, who had arranged a marriage, Asmara returned to Padang from Bogor, ending a relationship with a woman from which a son was born. He never saw them again. This tragic personal experience inspired Asmara to write the story. Information courtesy of Jaap Erkelens, 29 Dec. 2016.

[6] "Miss Dja dari Dardanella", *Kaoem Moeda*, 28 Nov. 1931.

[7] "Dokter Samsi. Gadis jang tergoda … Lelaki jang moelia …", *Sinar Sumatra*, 4 Dec. 1934.

[8] "Medan by Night" tells the story of a native concubine who is first abandoned by her Dutch master, and subsequently by a native aristocratic patron "Dardanella dengan Ind Romannja. Selaloe mempertoendjoekkan tjerita jang berarti di kalangan pergaoelan", *Tjaja Soematra*, 2 June 1931.

[9] "Soerat terboeka", *Tjaja Soematra*, 31 May 1931.

[10] Ad "Dardanella 'Haida'", *Sin Po*, 6 Nov. 1931. The play had been staged previously in Padang, West Sumatra, in July 1931, under a different title "Isteri Kedoea" (the second wife) and was staged later in Singapore in 1938 under the provocative title "Boven Digoel".

he was supporter of independence or a communist (or both).[11] The reviews of "Haida" are silent on the political background of the drama, apparently a form of self-censorship.

Boven Digoel was a sensitive and risky topic for Malay opera companies, one that could invite attention from the intelligence service and the police. This happened to Miss Riboet's Orion in 1932, when the company staged a play in Surabaya provocatively entitled "Boven Digoel". Like so many of Orion's stories, Boven Digoel was a comedy about the hardships of life. It is possible that Tio was inspired by the success of Kwee Tek Hoay's *Drama di Boven Digoel*, published as a short story serial in periodical *Panorama* between 1928 and 1932.[12] Like writer Kwee Tek Hoay, Tio was keen to touch upon such sensational stories, without necessarily addressing Dutch colonial surveillance or articulating communist or nationalist sympathies. In Orion's play, the leading character, a young man, is arrested and exiled to Digoel prison camp. He manages to escape from "*tanah-Noraka*" (the land of Hell), but luck is short-lived. The escapee is reunited with his child, but finds out his wife has abandoned him; the authorities recapture the fugitive and return him to Digoel.[13]

Although Orion had already staged the play in late 1931, it was in early 1932 that the authorities in Surabaya became suspicious about its content.[14] Sino-Malay newspaper *Pewarta Soerabaia* probably best summarised the political sensitivity surrounding Boven-Digoel as staged by Orion in the following understatement: "It is really very difficult to direct a play that is connected to politics."[15] The reviewer refrained from referencing the political situation, instead emphasising the entertaining character of the play, the clowning, songs and

---

[11] The title of Asmara's play and the character of "Haidi" bear a striking resemblance to the famous opera *Aida*, written by the Italian composer Guiseppe Verdi (1870). The scenery and periods of the plays might differ, Asmara's "Haida", however, suggests a similar struggle faced by Verdi's *Aida*. Against the backdrop of a war between Egypt and Ethiopia, a young female slave, Aida, is torn between her patriotism and her lover, an Egyptian army leader, and eventually dies with him. Asmara might have cleverly placed his "Haida" within the context of modern times and Dutch oppressive colonialism (Boven Digoel), de-emphasising politics by stressing the issue of polygamy as a key theme. Ad "Haida", *Sin Po*, 1 June 1934; "'HAIDA'. Dardanella poenja pertoendjoekan amal", *Sin Po*, 6 June 1934; "DJA's DARDANELLA. Haida", *Sinar Sumatra*, 3 Dec. 1934; "Dja's Dardanella Opera", *Pemandangan*, 6 June 1934; ad "HAIDA", *Pelita Andalas*, 2 Nov. 1935.

[12] See Chandra (2013: 248–57).

[13] Ad "Boven Digoel", *Pewarta Soerabaia*, 8 Jan. 1932.

[14] "Miss Riboet's Geschelschaps 'Orion'", *Kiauw Po*, 21 Nov. 1931.

[15] "Kabar Kota. Tjerita 'Boven-Digoel'. Dapat perhatian dari politie dan publiek Europa", *Pewarta Soerabaia*, 11 Jan. 1932.

dances.[16] The reviewer, however, did note that the show had drawn the attention of the Political Intelligence Service (PID, Politieke Inlichtingen Dienst). The PID had summoned Tio Tek Djien Jr. to the office, and he politely explained to the intelligence officers that the play was not intended "to annoy the government nor intended to insult one or another racial group (*golongan bangsa*)", likely meaning the Dutch. The play went on, but apparently the PID was not satisfied with Tio's reassurance. During the first two performances, police officers appeared; the second night, the PID chief himself was present. And it is not unlikely that these guardians of the colonial state enjoyed the allegedly subversive show. There is no evidence the show was banned.

In spite of the social significance attributed to Miss Riboet, the political loyalties of her and her husband remained implicit. No evidence of anti-colonial, nationalist or communist sympathies, not even vaguely, can be detected in their work or in public statements. Nor are such sympathies found among sections of their audience. This was very different from Malay opera company Dardanella and its fans who stressed pergaoelan. The troupe did not, obviously given the repressive climate, openly sympathise with the nationalist movement or with communism for that matter. Such explicit sympathies would have meant the end of the troupe. The troupe and its fans, however, did indirectly or covertly convey the message of Indonesian nationalism committing itself to removing inequality in society (pergaoelan hidoep), and by propagating cultural nationalism.

Fan Gatherings

Although Tio and Riboet could not be denied social engagement, and even though educated Indonesian and peranakan Chinese took an interest in them, they never drew the intellectual nationalist fandom that surrounded Dardanella. Dardanella's most vocal fans originated from the ranks of the emancipatory and nationalist movement in Batavia, many with links to the print press as journalists and novelists. As with the loose network of Filipino playwrights, poets, composers, entertainers and social activists, these people gravitated towards each other boosting a new hybrid urban popular culture that crossed the borders of literature, journalism, music, theatre, film and social activism. For the Batavia-based intellectuals, Dardanella formed a new nexus bringing different arts and people together; a group of socially kindred spirits and devotees of modern Malay opera, who participated in and promoted a new Indonesian culture.

---

[16] Ad "Boven Digoel", *Bintang Borneo*, 9 June 1932. "Kabar Kota. Tjerita 'Boven-Digoel'. Dapat perhatian dari politie dan publiek Europa", *Pewarta Soerabaia*, 11 Jan. 1932.

Among the kindred spirits we find some of the people introduced in previous chapter, such as Njoo Cheong Seng, peranakan Chinese novelist and playwright who had worked for Miss Riboet's Orion, but who traded his services for Dardanella, and Armijn Pane, nationalist, writer and co-founder of literary periodical *Poedjangga Baroe*. There are, however, also a number of individuals that we usually would not associate with popular entertainment: Haji Agoes Salim, nationalist, one of the leaders of Partai Sarekat Islam Indonesia and labour movement activist; Pieter Frederick "Frits" Dahler, an Eurasian, colonial official, editor of Malay newspapers and among the pioneers of the Indonesian nationalist movement; Kwee Tek Hoay, peranakan Chinese newspaperman and novelist; Parada Harahap, a nationalist journalist and film playwright; Saeroen, nationalist journalist, trade unionist and film playwright; Miss Rangkajo Datoek Toemenggoeng, nationalist and editor of *Pedoman Isteri* (The Wife's Guide).[17] These people publicly expressed their appreciation for Dardanella and emphasised its social significance. For example, political and religious leader Haji Agoes Salim praised Dardanella's dramas as "obvious steps of progress" (Langkah kemadjoean jang njata). Taking Asmara's drama "Dr. Samsi" as example, Salim emphasised Dardanella's successful modernisation of Malay opera.[18]

In 1934, to honour and promote the troupe, these fans organised a tea party in Batavia covered by the local press. Present were several of the above-mentioned people and others from the nationalist movement and vernacular print press. Among them, we find trade unionist and journalist Saeroen of *Pemandangan*, who, it should be emphasised, was also an outspoken devotee of Miss Riboet.[19] Haji Djoenaedi, *Pemandangan*'s director; Ang Jan Goan, director of Sino-Malay newspaper *Sin Po*; Frits Dahler; and two ladies active in the field of Indonesian women's emancipation movement, the earlier mentioned Miss Rangkajo Datoek Toemenggoeng and Miss S.Z. Goenawan, editor of periodical *Dewan* and president of an Islamic Orphanage Foundation in Batavia.[20] Two

---

[17] Some of the other Dardanella fans named were: Adi Negoro, Djauhari Salim and Hassan Noel Ariffin; see ad "Dardanella", *Sinar Deli*, 11 Jan. 1931. They were all contributors to Asmara's periodical *Dardanella Revue*.

[18] Ad "H.A. Salim", *Soeara Oemoem*, 25 Aug. 1932; "'KOTA'. H.A. Salim tentang 'Tjang'", *Pemandangan*, 5 June 1934.

[19] In 1929, Saeroen was editor of Sino-Malay newspaper *Keng Po* (Batavia) and also leader of the Association of Chauffeurs in Jakarta (Perserikatan Sopir Jacatra), see Poeze (1983: 22). In 1933, he was editor-in-chief of *Siang Po* (Batavia), and President of Association of Indonesian journalists, see "Javanese Editor. Speaks Several European Languages", *The Malaya Tribune*, 22 Feb. 1933.

[20] "Perdjamoean thee pada Dardanella", *Pemandangan*, 8 June 1934; "Kota. Tea party boeat Dardanella", *Sin Po*, 8 June 1934.

years earlier, in *Pedoman Isteri*, Goenawan had praised Dardanella for offering society (pergaoelan) a socially significant theatre that contributed to progress (*madjoe*) and high culture of a people (*cultuur tinggi satoe bangsa*).[21] These were the recurring terms used by prominent nationalists, giving weight to the companies' social and cultural significance.

Dahler, co-editor of *Penindjauan* opened the tea party with a speech.[22] Since the early 1920s, and unlike most Eurasians who passively or actively supported the colonial status quo, Dahler advocated equality of all races and independence from the Netherlands.[23] He was one of the founding fathers of the Nederlandsch Indische Partij, and had been member of the Municipal Council of Batavia. In 1932, Dahler headed the Language Section of the Department of People's Literature (Taaltechnische afdeeling bij Volkslectuur) and was leader of the Indische Sociaal-Democratische Partij (ISDP, East Indies Social Democratic Party, est. 1917). The ISDP promoted Indonesian independence, kept close contact with several nationalist associations and encouraged native Indonesians to join trade unions.[24] In May 1932, a local newspaper spotted Dahler in Batavia while he was addressing a large crowd at the first congress of one of the largest Indonesian nationalist organisations, Partai Indonesia (Partindo). Partindo had been established in April 1931 in response to the court ruling and exile of nationalist leader Soekarno, which subsequently led to the demise of Soekarno's Partai Nasional Indonesia (PNI).[25] On this particular occasion, Dahler spoke fervently in support of achieving Indonesian independence "with the people" (*dengen rajat*), "for the people" (*oentoek rajat*) and "by the people" (*oleh rajat*). The assembled throng reacted enthusiastically to his proclamations.[26]

At the Dardanella tea party, however, Dahler proved more restrained and politically subtle. Nothing of the radical nationalism could be detected at this event. He gently praised the evolution of Malay opera and summed up Dardanella's social relevance:

> When discussing theatre, [we can say] that within [the last] thirty years Indonesia has already achieved progress. From a meaningless bangsawan company [Dardanella] has turned into an organised theatre company. In

---

[21] "Kiriman", *Pedoman Isteri* no. 11, Nov. 1932.

[22] In October 1934, *Penindjauan* announced a merger with Malay periodical *Pedoman*. See *De Indische Courant*, 28 Sept. 1934.

[23] Dahler held the motto "Down with the race criteria!" (Weg met het rascriterium!), quoted in Meijer (2004: 67).

[24] Poeze (1982: xxxii, 82, 89, 142, 279, 305–6).

[25] Poeze (1988: xiv–xx).

[26] Ibid., pp. 165–6.

brief, from being held in contempt it currently is regarded as exalted. This standard in theatre has to be kept up with determination, as this art is like a picture of a people, developing their country (*negri*) and society (pergaoelan hidoep).[27]

Newspaper *Pemandangan* reported that the party hosts had stated that: "[...] Dardanella has caused a revolution within theatre circles, one that could offer a lesson for society in general". Klimanoff, the troupe's director, in response to his distinguished fans, expressed his delight that Malay opera had developed from something despised in society, to something that was currently at the centre of society (*ditengah2 pergaoelan oemoem*).[28]

According to devotee Ang Jan Goan, director of the China-oriented Sino-Malay newspaper *Sin Po* and representative of the Chinese Hospital Foundation in Batavia (Jang Seng Ie Hospital), Europeans were also fond of Indonesian art, including Dardanella.[29] Piedro Klimanoff found the European fandom for Dardanella rather puzzling as when it came to politics and social intercourse (*pergaoelan sosial*) these same Europeans did not like things Indonesian.[30] He not only meant to say that Europeans avoided socialising with non-Europeans, but also that Europeans (read: Dutchmen and Eurasians) had little sympathy for the nationalist political aspirations of intellectual native Indonesians and peranakan Chinese. Director of Malay newspaper *Pemandangan*, Djoenaedi, expressed a desire for the press to work together with Indonesian theatrical arts (*tooneel-kunst Indonesia*), especially with Dardanella, to achieve "meaningful progress" (*kamadjoean jang berarti*).[31] This collaboration was already in effect, as demonstrated by the composition of Dardanella's fan group and the press coverage given.

Two weeks later, the same fans again assembled in downtown Batavia, this time to celebrate Dardanella's eighth anniversary. Among those present were peranakan Chinese journalist, novelist and Malay opera playwright Kwee Tek Hoay, Sumatran journalist Parada Harahap and Frits Dahler.[32] Kwee Tek Hoay was the author of the earlier mentioned *Drama di Boven Digoel* and the best-selling novelist and author of *Boenga Roos dari Tjikembang* which was published

---

[27] "Kota. Tea Party Boeat Dardanella", *Sin Po*, 8 June 1934. In Sept. 1934, Dahler was one of the directors of weekly *Penindjauan* together with Indonesian nationalists Amir Sjarifoedin and Sam Ratulangi, see "Weekblad Penidjauan", *De Indische Courant*, 28 Sept. 1934.

[28] "Perdjamoean thee pada Dardanella", *Pemandangan*, 8 June 1934.

[29] "Kota. Tea Party Boeat Dardanella", *Sin Po*, 8 June 1934.

[30] "'Penindjauan dalam negeri'. Dja's Dardanella (3)", *Penindjauan*, 12 June 1934.

[31] "Kota. Tea Party Boeat Dardanella", *Sin Po*, 8 June 1934.

[32] "Jubileum 8 tahoen Dardanella", *Pemandangan*, 22 June 1934.

in 1927. This book was already in reprint in 1930.[33] This writer was very much part of the group of vernacular writers and journalists who were excited by modern Malay opera, attested by the fact that, somewhere between 1928 and 1930, he was playwright for Malay opera company Miss Inten.[34] In turn, several Malay opera companies adapted Kwee Tek Hoay's popular novels, such as *Boenga Roos dari Tjikembang*, for the stage. In March 1927, apparently with Kwee's permission, Malay opera company Dalia Opera was the first to stage the latter story during its season in Batavia.[35] *Boenga Roos dari Tjikembang* is a dramatic story of intimate inter-ethnic relationships and concubinage.[36] In 1928, Dardanella compensated Kwee for a stage adaptation of the story. Many years later, in March 1934, he was with Dardanella preparing the cast for a stage show of *Boenga Roos dari Tjikembang*. By then, he actively participated in modernising Malay opera using modern stories, modern props and electric light effects on stage. Equally significant, according to Kwee, was Dardanella's use of ordinary or low Malay on stage, a language on par with Sino-Malay. This low Malay stood in contrast to the high Malay (*Melajoe Atas*) from the Riau Archipelago, which had been commonly used in Malay opera in the past. Melajoe Atas might have fitted the conventional Malay opera drama repertoire of kings, queens and genies, it proved too formal and stiff to fit the realistic stories of modern Malay opera. Kwee stressed that formal, high Malay fell short of the conciseness, sharpness and precision that characterised low Malay. Manager Klimanoff praised Kwee for developing Malay. Klimanoff emphasised that this language had contributed significantly to Dardanella's glory, as well as to that of Miss Riboet's.[37] In sum, in the views of Kwee Tek Hoay, Tio Tek Djien and Klimanoff, low Malay was the modern language understood by the urban masses. This form of Malay, the hybrid language spoken in the bustling port cities of the East Indies and the Straits Settlements, and not Dutch or English, proved the key to the modern world and age.

---

[33] On Kwee Tek Hoay's literary output, including *Drama di Boven Digoel*, see Sumardjo (1989).

[34] Gunadharma (1989: 270). It is doubtful whether Kwee co-managed a troupe by the name of Miss Inten Malay Opera Co before 1928, as at that time, Miss Inten had not founded her own Malay opera company. In 1927, she was leading lady (*sri panggoeng*) of Union Dalia Opera (see "Pridato hari Saptoe", *SP*, 20 Aug. 1927).

[35] Ad "Dalia", *Sin Po*, 23 Feb. 1927. The play "Boenga Roos di Tjikembang" was also staged by Dalia Opera later that year in Semarang, ad "Dalia Opera", *WW*, 24 Oct. 1927.

[36] Sidharta (1989: 291–2).

[37] "Tooneelgezelschap Dardanella poenja Bahasa Melajoe", *Moestika Romans*, June 1934.

Peringatan Dardanella 8 tahoen.

cliche „Sin Po"

Sebagaimana kemaren telah dikabarkan, Dardanella soedah rajakan hari tahoen jang ke 8. Dalam gambar ini kelihatan dibarisan depan dari kiri ke kanan Toean-toean Kwee Tek Hoey, Panangian Harahap, berdiri Mrs. Tjoan Hin Hoey, doedoek anak dan njonja Kwen Tek Hoey, njonja S.Z. Goenawan, Miss Dja, Miss Suratna, Parada Harahap, F. Dahler, Mohamad Noer, Pedro dan Andjar Asmara.

Illus. 10.1 Fan gathering to celebrate Dardanella's eighth anniversary attended by several prominent people from the emancipatory and Indonesian nationalist movement of Batavia, also active in the vernacular press and literary circles. *Pemandangan*, 22 June 1934.

In 1935, another "tea party" was held in Medan, Sumatra, to honour Dardanella; it would be the final one. The event was organised by a local art association (Kunstvereeniging Ratu Timur) to celebrate the fifth anniversary of the play "Dr. Samsi", which had been staged over 400 times across Indonesia and the Straits Settlements. Journalist and writer, Hasbullah Parindurie (pen name Matu Mona), editor of *Pewarta Deli*, was the association's chairman. The Medan fans lauded playwright, Andjar Asmara, for his achievements.[38] Within six months of the fan gathering in Medan, however, Dardanella's fans would be shocked when, the following year, the troupe disbanded, evaporating its intellectual fandom and dreams of a modern Indonesian theatre.

---

[38] "Jubileum 5 tahoen Dr Samsi. Tea party Kunstvereeniging Ratu Timur oentoek Andjar Asmara", *Pewarta Deli*, 5 Nov. 1935. On Matu Mona, see Poeze (2001) and also Horton (2016: 61–3).

Fragile Marriage

Andjar Asmara and Piedro Klimanoff had ambitious plans for Dardanella. In 1934, the management decided to tour the world and to make a movie.[39] For this purpose, the big company was temporarily divided into a dance group that would go abroad and a larger group that would remain in Indonesia.[40] At the end of January 1935, Miss Dja, now known as Ratu Idja, was one of the leading dancers of the Royal Balinese Dancers appearing in Singapore. From February to May 1935, the group toured Hong Kong, Shanghai and other places in China.[41] In May 1935, the complete Dardanella cast reassembled in Singapore, including a new female star Fifi Young, staging Indonesian dances, Malay opera plays, special kroncong nights, sometimes advertised as vaudeville shows. The Theatre Royal, one of the cradles of Malay opera in Singapore, served as Dardanella's permanent venue.[42] In November 1935, the troupe returned to Medan for a short season, where they were invited for the aforementioned fan gathering.[43] Later that month, the group returned to Singapore on its way to Penang, Rangoon and British India.[44]

By June 1936, intellectual dreams and hopes of Dardanella's Malay opera as modern Indonesian popular art with social relevance were shattered. The troupe "imploded" due to financial and managerial troubles, a common feature of many Malay opera companies. Manager Klimanoff had refused to pay part of the cast during their season in British India and he had failed to provide medical care for a disease-struck member. Stranded in Bombay, due to insufficient financial means, the disbanded members had to pawn their jewellery and called for financial aid from the Dutch consul in the city. The Malay press lamented Dardanella's unfortunate and humiliating end. Klimanoff was blamed for mismanagement, even neglect of his *anak wayang* (cast).[45] Andjar Asmara filed a report with the Dutch consul in Bombay and with the Labour Office in Batavia.

---

[39] "Kabar Tontonan", *Soeara Oemoem*, 3 Mar. 1934.

[40] "Dardanella Opera. Aken pergi ka Asia Timoer", *Sin Tit Po*, 16 Aug. 1934.

[41] "Balinese Dancers in Singapore. Clever Young Girls. First and Only World Tour", *The Malaya Tribune*, 14 Jan. 1935; "Dja's Dardanella akan datang di Medan", *Pewarta Deli*, 3 Sept. 1935.

[42] "Balinese Dancers Return; with Dardanella Co at Theatre Royal", *The Malaya Tribune*, 30 May 1935.

[43] "Dja's Dardanella. 'Fatimma', de Balineesche Tempeldanseres", *Pewarta Deli*, 2 Nov. 1935.

[44] Ad, *The Singapore Free Press and Mercantile Advertiser*, 12 Nov. 1935.

[45] "Keterangan. Riwajat Dardanella", *Tjaja Timoer*, 3 June 1936.

He also declared his return to journalism.[46] The former fans were silent, at least in the print press.

In 1936, after Dardanella's break up, Andjar Asmara established his own Malay opera troupe, Bolero, but it lacked the intellectual appeal and popularity of Dardanella. Miss Dja and some of the remaining company members continued as Dja's Dardanella, touring the Federated Malay States and the Straits Settlements throughout the second half of 1936 and the first half of 1937.[47] In 1938, Dja was in Europe with a dance group, followed by the US in 1939.[48] Only many decades later would she return to Indonesia briefly and, against her wish, would find her last resting place in California.[49]

In 1942, the Japanese invasion of Southeast Asia was ongoing and Indonesia was about to be occupied by the Japanese army and navy. Andjar Asmara looked back on the success of Dardanella and its leading actress Miss Dja.[50] His retrospect reminds us of that of Filipino artist and playwright Eliseo Carvajal. Both Carvajal and Asmara discussed the rise and fall of modern vernacular theatre in their respective countries. Asmara credited Dardanella with moving Indonesian theatre away from the world of kings and genies of the Stamboel theatre into "the age of modern theatre" (*zaman toneel modern*). With Dardanella's demise, the evolution of Indonesian theatre (*tooneel Indonesia*) had come to a standstill. To use Asmara's words, Indonesian theatre was in a state of "crisis".[51]

Carvajal and Asmara documented the decline of vernacular theatre, the end of an era of dynamic cultural developments in which they had fully participated. What both cultural producers, and many other contemporaries, could not yet foresee was how the local cinematic and the phonographic industry would develop. There was also a marked difference between Eliseo Carvajal and Andjar Asmara. The former regarded the cine as the vernacular theatre's silent assassin,

---

[46] "Impresario Andjar Asmara berhenti dari tooneelgez. Dardanella. Akan kembali kedoenia journalistiek. Mengalami keroegian di India", *Pewarta Deli*, 18 May 1936; "Javaansche artiesten in Britsch-Indie. Schandelijke exploitatie van Dardanella-personeel", *Indische Courant*, 26 May 1936.

[47] "21 Juni 1926–1936. Sepoeloeh tahoen 'Dardanella'; 'Dardanella' telah tjoekoep 10 tahoen", *Dagblad Radio*, 6 July 1936. Dardanella was reported to have reappeared in Indonesia, in the city of Cirebon, in late November to December 1937. "De Dardanella-Opera", *Nieuws van den Dag van Nederlandsch-Indië*, 25 Nov. 1937. This was likely an error made by the Dutch newspaper, mixing up Dardanella with Pagoda, the new Malay opera company established by Njoo Cheong Seng and his wife Fify Young.

[48] Cohen (2010: 175–208).

[49] On Miss Dja's American journey, by then rebaptised Devi Dja, see Cohen (2010: 175–201).

[50] "Kenangan-kenangan kepada Miss Dja", *Pertjatoeran Doenia Film*, no. 2 (1941).

[51] "Crisis tooneel Indonesia", *Pertjatoeran Doenia Film*, no. 8 (1942).

while, already in 1936, Asmara seized cinema as an artistic and commercial opportunity, during Dardanella's fatal season in British India. Featuring the Dardanella cast, Asmara adapted "Dr. Samsi" to the screen.[52] Produced by Radha Film Co. from Calcutta, the film premiered in Singapore on 9 February 1937, followed by Penang in April and Batavia in June.[53] The film was received well, at least in Penang and Batavia.[54]

The "Malay Talkie" *Dr. Samsi* was a success, but it did not reach the heights of the huge box office hit, the Malay musical movie *Terang Boelan* (Bright Moon), also released in 1937 in Indonesia and British Malaya. The screenplay was written by nationalist, journalist, trade union leader and Malay opera fan Saeroen.[55] Building on the hybrid pop cosmopolitanism tradition of 1920s Malay opera and connecting it to social issues, Saeroen was among the people who moved the infant local cine industry slowly and cautiously in a new direction.

Bright Moon

Since 1928, local film companies in Indonesia were struggling with insufficient capital resources, limited technical know-how and competition from imported films.[56] A good example of the then infant industry is the ambitious cinematic venture undertaken by Miss Riboet and her husband. Although very successful in Malay opera, Riboet and Tio Tek Djien Jr. envisaged a bright future for the cinema in Indonesia. As early as mid-1928 they had drawn up plans to retreat from Malay opera to move into the local cinematic industry as independent film producers. A film company was founded, a former *singkong* (cassava) factory in Bandung was purchased to be turned into a film studio. Tio assumed the film companies' directorship; Riboet was shareholder and would continue as film actress. The venture was capitalised at f. 50.000. A separate Miss Riboet Foundation was co-established to provide for the care of relatives, the tending of family graves, the education of their children and for charity.[57] In October 1928, anticipating their departure from Malay opera and entry into the film industry, Riboet and Tio launched what they announced as a series of unforgettable

---

[52] "Opera Dardanella. Di Bombay terpetjah belah", *Darmokondo*, 28 May 1936.

[53] "Malay Talking Picture At the Theatre Royal From Tuesday", *Sunday Tribune*, 7 Feb. 1937.

[54] Ad, *The Straits Echo*, 4 Aug. 1937; "Cinema-Palace: Dr. Samsi", *Bataviaasch Nieuwsblad*, 11 June 1937.

[55] Terang Boelan was produced by Algemeen Nederlandsch-Indisch Filmsyndicaat (ANIF), see Biran (2009: 164–82).

[56] Nio (1941: 398–9).

[57] "Miss Riboet poenja filmfabricage", *Tjaja Timoer*, 10 Dec. 1928.

souvenir performances across Java to honour their Malay opera fans.[58] It took another two years for them to announce their first film project: *Destiny* "[…] a Sketch of life of an Indo-Chinese girl in Java, her adventures, her struggle against fate, her efforts to save her wrecked brother, the sport of destiny…!"[59] For his film endeavour, Tio had sought the advice and assistance of A. Boellaard van Tuijl, former owner of the Orion cinematic theatre in Bandung, and Nelson Wong from Shanghai. Although Wong had been working for Miss Riboet's Orion as a cashier, he was actually an experienced cameraman.[60] Film shooting was planned to take place in Surabaya, Kediri, Malang and Medan. In spite of their foresight about the prospects of cinema in Indonesia, and the expertise assembled, the cinematographic venture failed. According to Misbach Yusa Biran, who interviewed Tio Tek Djien Jr. in the early 1970s, the endeavour faltered because Riboet's screen appearance turned out to be disappointing.[61] This was likely only a partial explanation for the failure. It is equally possible that Tio and Riboet were forced to return to Malay opera as the result of financial uncertainties following the economic crisis caused by the 1929 Wall Street Crash. In spite of the setbacks, Tio proved patient and determined. In 1933, while touring British Malaya, he cordially invited investors to put their money in "Miss Riboet movies" of Java/Malayan pictures. Already in 1930, and again in 1938, Tio launched the plan to turn the successful Malay opera drama "Black Sheep" (Kambing Hitam) into a movie.[62] It would take over a decade, in the 1950s when Indonesia had gained its independence, before Tio's dream of making a movie would be realised. By then, Miss Riboet had retired from an active stage career and was sinking into oblivion.

While Tio and Riboet tried their luck unsuccessfully, prospects for the local cinematic industry improved from 1937. This was a combination of the recovery from the global economic crisis, technological developments (the introduction and acceptance of the talkie) and people eager to channel their money and artistry into commercial filmmaking. It is under these conditions, in 1937, that the film musical *Terang Boelan* (Bright Moon) was released, a film that would mark the renaissance of a local cine industry in terms of artistic content, number of films produced and the number of film companies.[63]

---

[58] Ad "Orion", *Perniagaan*, 27 Oct. 1928; ad, *SP*, 17 Nov. 1928.

[59] Ad "Miss Riboet", *The Malaya Tribune*, 11 Apr. 1930. "Destiny" was also the name of a play staged by Orion, possibly an adaptation by Tio of the book that he hoped would be turned into a screenplay.

[60] "Chineesche film-industrie", *De Indische Courant*, 8 Sept. 1928.

[61] See Biran (2009: 81–2).

[62] Ad, *The Straits Times*, 10 Apr. 1933; ad, *The Malaya Tribune*, 11 Apr. 1933; "Maleisch in Films. Praktische Moeilijkheden", *Sumatra Post*, 27 Aug. 1938.

[63] Nio (1941: 399–402).

Terang Boelan tells of a couple, Kasim and Rohaya, who elope to Melaka to escape an arranged marriage for Rohaya with a wealthy, yet crooked man, Moesa, an opium dealer. The latter tracks the couple down, but Kasim manages to seek help from the locals and fights Moesa successfully. The film featured the then still relatively unknown Malay opera actress and singer Roekiyah. The story was written by journalist Saeroen, whose journalistic career and political position in many respects show striking similarities with that of the provocative journalist Kwee Thiam Tjing, aka Tjamboek Berdoeri. Apart from both being explicit Miss Riboet fans, they actively supported Indonesian independence; they wrote witty controversial pieces under pseudonyms. Like Kwee, Saeroen was locked up. The colonial authorities detained him in 1939, not for seditious writings, but for allegedly undermining the colonial government.[64]

Terang Boelan was also a box office success in British Malaya.[65] The Indonesian Javanologist and philologist Raden Ngabei Poerbatjaraka, however, scrutinised the story as ethnologically unsound: "Persons wearing kain batik for large part, and thus remind us of Java, and for other part [dressed] as heathens wearing nothing but a loin cloth, and in addition persons in Hawaiian make up [...], who offer kroncong-ditties and jazzband-like music, but not native music at its best."[66] The Dutch newspaper editors supported the views of this authority on Javanese customs. The *Bataviaasch Nieuwsblad* assured its readers that "it would be very useful for the infant cine industry, next to the expressions of the primitive mass, also to take into consideration the criticism of the intellectual part of the native world". Poerbatjaraka and the editors thus implicitly defined *Terang Bulan* as banal entertainment designed for and claimed by the native masses. Saeroen paid no heed to such racialist and elitist criticism. He would continue to write screenplays and did so successfully until 1942.[67] In spite of the kitsch and lack of authenticity observed by Poerbatjaraka, other Dutch reviewers judged the film stories written by Saeroen as socially relevant. This might not have been so in the case of *Terang Boelan*, but especially the film *Asmara Moerni* (Pure Love), released in 1941, was praised for addressing realistically the issue of the urban–rural divide as a key theme.[68] Like the Malay opera playwrights and Sino-Malay novelists before him, Saeroen assumed a cultural brokerage role. Through the medium of film, he conveyed to mass audiences the challenges of modern life.

---

[64] On Saeroen, and particularly his contribution to Indonesian cinema, see Woodrich (2015: 36–7).

[65] Barnard (2010: 51–2).

[66] "Men schrijft ons: 'Terang Boelan'", *Bataviaasch Nieuwsblad*, 13 Dec. 1937.

[67] Woodrich (2015: 40–2).

[68] "Iets over de Maleische film. En de Moeilijkheden welke zij te overwinnen heeft in den Strijd om de Realiteit", *Bataviaasch Nieuwsblad*, 8 May 1941.

In 1940, Njoo Cheong Song teamed up with Oriental Film Coy as screenwriter and director for the film *Kris Mataram* (Mataram Dagger). His wife and Malay opera actress, Fifi Young, formerly with Dardanella, debuted as film singer-actress. The film's cast included several renowned kroncong singers and recording artists.[69] And from 1940, we find Andjar Asmara as film critic and, a year later, as film director in the burgeoning Indonesian film industry of Batavia, "Batawood".[70] That same year, Malay opera actor and recording artist Tan Tjeng Bok also tried his luck as a film actor, and with great success.[71] In short, popular culture had developed away from one of its major sources, modern Malay opera, and taken a new turn into film and recorded music.

Paralleling the cine industry was the development of local popular music and commercial recording. In particular, the kroncong genre developed as an important commercial asset for foreign phonographic record companies. In spite of its appeal, the style remained disputed as both art and national music, and this became an issue in 1940.[72] Kroncong singers from the screen were also active for the phonographic industry and for radio broadcasting station NIROM (Netherlands East Indies Radio Broadcasting Society), which began operating in 1934. For example, in 1939, the popular, blind, female kroncong singer Annie Landouw appeared in the film *Fatimah*, a musical romance also written by Saeroen. This film was reported to have been an even bigger success than *Terang Boelan*.[73] In *Fatimah*, Landouw was accompanied by kroncong singer Louis Koch, who himself had carved out a recording and radio career.[74] Many of these artists, like Landouw and Koch, recorded for His Master Voice (HMV), the first foreign phonographic company to establish a permanent recording studio in

---

[69] "Sampoerna. Kris Mataram", *Soerabaijasch Handelsblad*, 9 July 1940. "Kris Mataram" was produced by Oriental Film Co and it marked Fifi Young's first film appearance. See "Sampoerna. Kris Mataram", *Soerabaijasch Handelsblad*, 9 July 1940. The kroncong singers were recording artists Netty, Lee and Soerip.

[70] On Asmara's film critique see, for example, "Deradjat films Indonesia", *Poestaka Timoer*, 15 May 1940; "Koendjoengan pada Java Industrial Film", *Poestaka Timoer*, 1 Sept. 1940.

[71] Tan Tjeng Bok's first film appearance was in Srigala Item, see "Srigala item", *Pertjatoeran Doenia dan Film*, 1 June 1941.

[72] Frederick (1996); Keppy (2008).

[73] "Fatimah. Tan's 2e maleische film", *Soerabaijasch Handelsblad*, 6 July 1939.

[74] Both recorded songs for HMV and they appeared live on radio throughout February and March 1940. Louis Koch was a lead singer of kroncong orchestra Lief Java, which featured in the film *Fatimah*. Koch was also recording artist for both HMV and Columbia records. Lief Java, including Koch and Miss Roekiyah, performed for NIROM-radio, Bandung branch on 1 Feb. 1940. *Soeara Nirom* no. 4 (28 Jan. 1940): 20. Annie Landouw recorded for Columbia, see Yampolsky (2013: 153). She also appeared on NIROM-radio Bandung, see for instance, on 6 Feb. 1940. *Soeara Nirom* no. 5 (4 Feb. 1940): 14.

Singapore in 1934, and the first of its kind in Southeast Asia. HMV's Singapore-based recording director and talent scout was Zubir Said, a musician who hailed from West Sumatra. Said, a former Malay opera band leader, actively recruited talent from Java and Sumatra as well as from Penang and Kuala Lumpur.[75] In 1938, Andjar Asmara and his wife also went to Singapore to record for HMV, likely on Said's invitation.[76] Zubir Said is primarily remembered as the originator of the national anthem of Singapore, composed in 1958, obscuring his earlier role as cultural broker for HMV and as pioneer of a hybrid popular music in the colonial Malay world.[77]

Miss Riboet failed to catch up with the new developments. After 1934, she did not appear in films, nor did she record on shellac. Moreover, from the late 1920s, a significant shift occurred within her spectatorship, which would come to a climax in 1935. With this transformation of her audience, the social potency that had marked her performances in the late 1920s was lost.

New Audiences

In 1935, just before she was about to perform on the radio in Batavia, nationalist journalist Saeroen interviewed Riboet in the studio. Their relationship was cordial and an informal conversation developed between the two. Relating this encounter in newspaper *Pemandangan*, Saeroen explained Riboet's appeal in terms of her unique and charismatic personality that sent audiences into rapture.[78] Saeroen was one of those spectators, who, he confessed, had turned into one of her fans. His fandom can be compared with that of Riboet's first self-confessed devotee Kwee Thiam Tjing, alias Tjamboek Berdoeri. After 1927, however, Kwee's admiration of Riboet appears to have faded completely. His tributes in print to the Malay opera diva had run dry. How Kwee perceived developments in popular theatre and music in the early 1930s is therefore unknown.[79] There is, for instance, no evidence that Kwee showed any interest in Dardanella as a modern form of Indonesian theatre. What is known is that, by the early 1930s, his views about the injustices of Dutch colonialism had become a conviction that Indonesia should be freed from the Dutch. In 1932, Kwee had become politically active, co-founding with his colleague and friend Liem Koen Hian

---

[75] Oral History Interviews. National Archives of Singapore. Zubir Said. Accession no. 000293.

[76] "Ratna Asmara, Andjar Asmara ke Singapore", *Pemandangan*, 23 May 1938.

[77] For Said's disassociation from popular culture in the late 1950s, see Johan (2014: 139–41).

[78] "Dengan Miss Riboet di studio B.R.V.", *Pemandangan*, 1 Aug. 1935.

[79] Kwee had left *Soeara Publiek* in 1929. In the early 1930s, he had moved to the town of Jember, East Java. He was editor of a weekly there, *Pembrita Djember*, which began publication in 1933. See for example *Pembrita Djember*, 20 Mar. 1934.

the pro-independence Persatuan Tionghoa Indonesia (The Indonesian Chinese Association), an inclusive nationalist association.[80] His former object of devotion, Miss Riboet, was not the kind of subversive popular star that he had in mind when producing his poetry for newspaper *Soeara Publiek* in 1926. In fact, as we can see from the venues Riboet and her husband played and the audiences that Riboet started to attract, the opposite had occurred. From 1929, she was caught in a slow process of approbation from a reactionary spectatorship, a process that came to completion around 1935.

By 1934, it had become perfectly acceptable for high-ranking Dutch officials and so-called native self-governing rulers to visit a Miss Riboet show as a form of leisure. Unlike previous decades, these upper-class people regarded her Malay opera as a legitimate form of entertainment. For example, *Sinar Deli* in Medan noted on the opening night in Medan's Hok Hoa Theatre the presence of the Dutch governor of Sumatra, the Dutch mayor of Medan, the Sultan of Deli and other prominent local native aristocrats and Europeans at the show.[81]

In contrast to this reactionary audience were radical sections of the nationalist movement who were appalled by Miss Riboet's repertoire. The play "Kambing Hitam" (Black Sheep) may serve as a good example. In 1934, Orion staged this play in Padang, West Sumatra, where it evoked a controversy with distinct ethnic and political undertones.[82] "Malay" journalists in Padang were offended by the famous singer-actor Tan Tjeng Bok, who, in his stage role stereotyped Indonesian journalists as people of low professional and moral standards. The journalists from Padang claimed that the opera company insulted their profession and the Indonesian race. The Padang branch of the nationalist association of Indonesian journalists, Perdi, sided with the journalists and protested.[83] A controversy was born. The daily *Persamaan* (Padang) joined the protesters. On the whole, the press in Sumatra, however, remained divided over the issue.[84] As with the play "Boven Digoel", Tio, sensitive to sensation, cleverly exploited the controversy for publicity purposes. He underscored "Kambing Hitam's" dramatic content and social and political significance, reporting that the play had caused a riot between Indonesian newspapers ("bikin riboet […] dalem pers Indonesia") in Padang. Tio

---

[80] *Orang-orang tionghoa jang terkemoeka di java* (1937: 198–9). Kwee (2010: 65–6, 69).

[81] "Pertoendjoekan pertama dari Miss Riboet", *Sinar Deli*, 1 Nov. 1934.

[82] "Miss Riboet dan Perdi", *Sinar Sumatra*, 20 Aug. 1934.

[83] "Fikiran Oemoem. Kambing Hitam", *Pewarta Deli*, 24 Aug. 1934.

[84] "Tooneel Miss Riboet contra Journalisten Indonesiers", *Persamaan*, 21 Aug. 1934. See for instance *Sinar Sumatra* editors who opined that Perdi's protest was exaggerated. "Miss Riboet dan Perdi", *Sinar Sumatra*, 20 Aug. 1934. The same for daily *Radio* (Padang), see "Lantaran Kambing Hitam. 'Perdi' digoenaken sebagai sendjata tjoema boeat membalas sakit hati pada Miss Riboet's Orion?", *Radio*, 21 Aug. 1934.

went as far to suggest that the controversy had revealed a political schism between "cos" and "non-cos" ("cos", or the moderate Indonesian nationalists willing to collaborate with the colonial government; "non-cos", the radical nationalists who refused such cooperation).[85] From this case, we can infer that Tio could not be accused of being political ignorant or naïve.

The year 1935 was a turning point in the career of Miss Riboet. That year, the colonial elite and the European middle class accepted Riboet as a legitimate artist. Since 1928, she and her husband had actively sought the approbation of the European establishment, asking the municipal council of Batavia permission to play the city's Schouwburg, the European controlled bastion of high art. In 1935, this ambition materialised.

In 1935, the municipal board of Batavia offered Riboet and her company the privilege of playing the Schouwburg. It was the first and last Malay opera company ever to be given this honour. One Dutch-language newspaper suggested the privilege was simply given due to the Schouwburg's dire financial situation.[86] Another Dutch paper argued that it was quite legitimate to offer Orion the opportunity. After all, this Malay opera troupe was among the best companies native theatre had to offer. And to support this claim, the same paper added that the last time Riboet performed in the city, four years previously, "many prominent individuals from Batavian society" had patronised her shows.[87]

On 1 August 1935, the Schouwburg was packed with an "Asian audience" (*publiek Azia*), among many well-known Indonesian officials and aristocrats, Indo-Arab businessmen and prominent Indonesian Chinese. Among the spectators were the Regent of Garut, Raden A.A. Soerianata Atmadja; the *Kapitan Cina* of Batavia, Lie Tjian Tjoen (the Kapitan China was the officer representing the Chinese community of a city); Mohamad Husni Thamrin, delegate of the nationalist faction in the People's Council; Ariffin, judge of the native court of Justice (Landraad) of Meester Cornelis (Batavia); and Mohamad Alatas, owner of a construction company. Being staged was a tragedy in three parts, "Gagak Solo" (The Crow of Solo). It tells of a female court dancer (*serimpi*), Soelasti, who is involved in palace intrigues in the sultanate of Solo, central Java. Soelasti falls in love with a prince and bears his child, but her minor social status prevents a

---

[85] "Satoe Indische Roman jang telah bikin 'riboet' di Padang, jang bikin orang dari 'Co' bisa berobah djadi 'Non' atau dari 'Non' berbalik djadi 'Co'", *Pelita Andalas*, 11 Nov. 1934; ad, *Sin Po*, 3 Aug. 1935.

[86] "Miss Riboet. Na vier jaren weer terug", *Bataviaasch Nieuwsblad*, 1 May 1935.

[87] "Miss Riboet in den Schouwburg", *Het Nieuws voor den dag van Nederlandsch-Indië*, 29 July 1935.

marriage with a higher status aristocrat. Her pet, a crow (*gagak*), is released from captivity when Soelasti dies.

Saeroen, present in his capacity as Riboet's fan and journalist, reviewed the play and documented the audience response. He wrote that the drama "sketched sufficiently clearly the state of our aristocracy, not only within the royal palace, but also within others groups in society [pergaoelan hidoep]". What Saeroen meant to say, without seeking direct confrontation with incumbent Sultans and, by extension, with the colonial government, is that feudalistic practices of social exclusion on basis of birth, hampered emancipation and progress. Spectators were excited about the revue, which included kroncong music, Javanese songs, Javanese court dancing and the funny acts of the "clowns" Semar, Gareng and Petruk, characters from the Javanese *wayang* stories. And Saeroen registered nationalist Mohamad Husni Thamrin's claim that "Miss Riboet is number one!"[88]

Two weeks later, on 15 August 1935, Malay Opera Company Orion proudly celebrated its ten-year jubilee in Thalia in Mangga Dua, downtown Batavia. Riboet again staged "Gagak Solo", and this time before the families of the highest-ranking Dutch officials of the colony, who, as explained in Chapter 8, usually avoided Thalia Theatre. The special guests included the wife and children of Governor General Bonifacius Cornelis de Jonge, in office since 1931, and the wives of other prominent colonial officials and Dutch businessmen and their families.[89] The Governor General himself did not attend the show. The previous month, as if to revive the spirit of the ethical policy of uplifting the native, the Governor's wife had taken the initiative to establish the General Support Fund for Native Poor (ASIB).[90] Ironically, her husband was not in favour of the ethical policy of his predecessors, had been less than enthusiastic about the initiative of his wife and, moreover, pressed by the economic crisis, had cut government expenditure, particularly on education.[91] It should be noted that Governor de Jonge took a staunch anti-independence position. He was responsible for the arrest of leading nationalist Soekarno in 1933 for having published his brochure "Mentjapai Indonesia Merdika"

---

[88] "Miss Riboet di schouwburg tadi malam", *Pemandangan*, 2 Aug. 1935.

[89] "Koendjoengan loear biasa bagi Miss Riboet", *Pemandangan*, 17 Aug. 1935.

[90] "Steunfonds voor inheemse behoeftigen", *Bataviaasch Nieuwsblad*, 24 July 1935. "Miss Riboet in 'Gagak Solo'. Voorstelling ten bate van het ASIB", *Het Nieuws dan den Dag van Nederlandsch-Indie*, 17 Aug. 1935. Members of Batavia's ASIB chapter included prominent Indonesian, Indonesian-Chinese and Dutch women, who announced the show and called for support in one of the Dutch newspapers. "Plaatselijk Comité", *Het Nieuws van den dag voor Nederlandsch-Indië*, 14 Aug. 1935.

[91] Van der Wal (1968: 79, 87, 100, 138–40).

(Achieving an Independent Indonesia).[92] De Jonge was also eager to go after Thamrin, but failed to make a case against this nationalist, whom he labelled in his memoirs "the worst of them all, skillful and clever".[93] In 1932, Thamrin and Soekarno had given the divided nationalist movement new impetus by closely collaborating and establishing the Persatoean Perhimpoenan-Perhimpoenan Politik Kebangsaan Indonesia (PPPKI).[94]

For the special occasion at Thalia, the theatre owner, W.T. Tio, offered Orion the venue for free.[95] In the established tradition of charity, Miss Riboet's Orion held a benefit show for the Chinese hospital Jang Seng Ie and for ASIB. Orion's existence for over two decades was a landmark itself, given the fact that most Malay opera troupes often perished within a decade or less due to the previously mentioned financial and managerial problems. Writing for *Pemandangan* and articulating his fandom for Riboet, Saeroen summarised the show as an achievement; a step forward (*madjoe ke depan*) by a courageous woman who showed that "natives" could wrench themselves free from an inferiority complex. He argued that Riboet set an example for those active in art, journalism and commerce.[96] Saeroen thus publicly regarded Riboet as a person who actively contributed to progress and the emancipation of native Indonesians. His intellectual compatriots from the emancipatory and nationalist movement— Thamrin a probable exception—many of whom had gathered around Dardanella, did not join him in this view. They simply remained silent on Miss Riboet's social significance, at least in the print press.

By 1935, the politically conservative Eurasian and European community had embraced Riboet as their darling of the Malay opera stage. They, unlike Saeroen, did not necessarily regard Riboet as a courageous woman who contributed to the emancipation of native Indonesians. As one newspaper summarised, Europeans simply wanted to have an "entertaining evening".[97] Deeper social critique, moral guidance and emancipatory aims were lost on them. Dutchman Willem Walraven, a journalist for a Dutch-language Batavia newspaper, who was married

---

[92] Poeze (1988: 310).

[93] Van der Wal (1968: 191). Soekarno was arrested in front of Thamrin's house after having visited the latter. On the political significance of Husni Thamrin and on the events leading to Soekarno's arrest, see Hering (1996: 156–203).

[94] Poeze (1988: 162).

[95] "KOTA. Jang Seng Ie", *Sin Po*, 19 Aug. 1935. W.T. Tio was probably heir to Tio Tek Kang, the founder and first owner of Thalia who had died on 25 Mar. 1931, see "Tio Tek Kan", *Utrechts Nieuwsblad*, 26 Mar. 1931.

[96] "Madjoe ke depan", *Pemandangan*, 17 Aug. 1935.

[97] "Een gezellige avond Bij Miss Riboet", *Soerabajasch Handelsblad*, 14 Jan. 1942.

to a native Indonesian woman, is a good example. He wrote to his kin in the Netherlands:

> [...] Miss Riboet (and especially her mates and assistants) set me off laughing tremendously. Native girls pretending to be able to dance ballet, or *chanteuse-a-voix*; Natives assuming to be able to play romantic scenes. One gets weak from laughter [...] This is all swallowed by Indonesians and taken seriously.[98]

Illus. 10.2 A glimpse of Miss Riboet's middle- to upper-class audience during the show at the Thalia Theatre, August 1935. The lady seated in the front row, in front of the small table and flowers is the wife of Governor General de Jonge, accompanied by her two daughters. *Sin Po*, 17 Aug. 1935.

Such derogatory assessments were not unique, as we have seen in the opening of Chapter 5, when Englishman Hubert Banner judged Malay opera as a poor form of theatre and as preposterous mimicry of Europeans. Walraven voiced what was a general feeling among the Dutch in colonial Indonesia: Riboet represented light entertainment.

Riboet's quest for approbation continued. On 31 August 1935, she performed live on radio before the Bandung branch of NIROM for the occasion of the

---

[98] Walraven (1992: 588).

public celebration of Queen Wilhelmina's anniversary.[99] NIROM had started broadcasting the previous year as the first professional radio broadcasting station in the colony, and was closely monitored by the colonial government.[100] The special radio show was entitled "Around the Archipelago with Miss Riboet", an anthology of condensed popular songs (*lagu*) from different locations in the Malay world, ranging from Singapore in the west to Ambon in the east.[101] As NIROM broadcasts were normally never relayed to the Netherlands, Riboet's 1935 live studio performance was a rare and unique occasion for Dutch radio listeners to get an impression of Malay opera and one of its divas. According to the radio "We, on the occasion of the anniversary of our honoured Queen, would like to offer you something that expresses the simple sentiments of those tens of millions [...] subjects in different regions of the Indies living a peaceful and quiet life."[102] Putting the radio broadcast in the socio-political context of the mid-1930s, NIROM, as a government-controlled media, preached the paternalising colonial mantra of peace and order in the colony. In this colonial reading, Miss Riboet was a popular actress adored by a mass of simple-minded apolitical natives. Obviously, not a single word was uttered in the broadcast about the nationalist movement, its encounters with the colonial government, Boven Digoel and the exile of prominent political activists. This was the colonial way of

---

[99] Riboet had performed on local radio before. In 1931, she was invited to appear on a small privately-owned radio broadcasting station in Batavia. In 1934, she appeared live on a private radio station in Medan. "Bataviasche Radio-vereeniging", *Bataviaasch Nieuwsblad*, 28 Oct. 1931. "Boeal. Omong omong dengan Miss Riboet", *Sinar Deli*, 31 Oct. 1934.

[100] In the course of 1935 to 1937, NIROM would seek closer collaboration with a number of smaller, private radio stations owned and managed by well-to-do native Indonesians and peranakan Chinese in Java and Sumatra. By doing so NIROM aimed at reaching a larger group of listeners, that is "natives" and peranakan Chinese. Eventually, this led in 1937 to the founding of the Perikatan Perhimpoenan Radio Ketimoeran (PPRK, Federation of Eastern Radio Associations). In return for a subsidy from NIROM, these radio stations programmed music, lectures and radio plays for non-Western listeners. See Yampolsky (2014: 58–9).

[101] This broadcast was recorded and is one of the few instances that we can actually hear Riboet's great talent for mimicry in both language and singing styles. Backed by an ensemble of piano, violin, a few wind instruments and possibly one or two guitars, Riboet performed songs in different Malay dialects and singing styles current from Singapore to Ambon (De Radiovereniging 17-04-1990 – Indische Radio – (De NIROM deel 1 & 2). VPRO Radio CC).

[102] (De Radiovereniging 17-04-1990 – Indische Radio – (De NIROM deel 1 & 2). VPRO Radio CC). Dutch newspaper *Bataviaasch Nieuwsblad* criticised NIROM's assumption that listeners in the Netherlands would find Miss Riboet entertaining; the paper even argued that those unfamiliar with the Indies would find her appalling, see "De Radio", *Bataviaasch Nieuwsblad*, 12 Sept. 1935.

informing those in the motherland. The revue show was repeated at the Dutch Club in Singapore in 1938, this time to celebrate the Queen's 40-year jubilee.[103]

It is reasonable to assume that the 1935 Schouwburg performance and the radio broadcast in honour of the Dutch Queen made clear to Indonesian nationalists and Dutch reactionaries that Tio and Riboet wanted to be associated with Dutch colonial power and the status quo. There is no evidence that Riboet or her husband objected to such political interpretations. There is evidence that, in the mid-1930s, they increasingly demonstrated their political loyalty to the Dutch. For example, of symbolic significance is that, in 1936, Riboet and Thio chose the Dutch national anthem, and not the banned Indonesian national anthem "Indonesia Raya", to close a show during the Surabaya season of that year.[104] And three years after the Schouwburg show, in 1938, with no sign of any regret, Tio recalled the event in an advertisement as a "milestone" in Orion's history.[105] There is also no evidence that they sought a political middle way, supporting the Dutch publicly while covertly backing the nationalist movement.[106]

By 1935, Riboet was no longer causing the excitement for which she was known in the 1920s. A striking example of this is that, in 1931, she had started to slowly abandon her signature dongeng singing act, explaining to the press that "she had other things to sing about" and that "the public demanded something novel".[107] This artistic change is illustrative of the "new" audience she was serving and the new docile direction she had taken in the popular realm. Her new "European" middle- to upper-class audience did not appreciate the moral messages, and often hardly understood her dongeng delivered in Javanese and hybrid low Malay. At the other extreme, Indonesian nationalists, with a few notable exceptions, like Riboet's admirer Saeroen, had lost the spirit of progress and pergaoelan in relation to Malay opera.

---

[103] "All-Java Non-Stop Revue", *The Straits Times*, 6 Sept. 1938.

[104] "Miss Riboet. Singapore lepas tengah malam", *Soeara Oemoem*, 1 Sept. 1936. Sympathy with the Dutch was also expressed in late 1941, when the Netherlands was under German occupation. Orion published a song "bendera Olanda" (the Dutch Flag), in support of Dutch resistance against the German occupier "dedicated to all fighters against defeatism". It was modelled after an English popular song with lyrics adapted by Tio Tek Djien Jr. Spectators were called to join the singing during the performance, see ad "Miss Riboet", *Soeara Oemoem*, 19 Dec. 1941.

[105] Ad "Miss Riboet", *Sinar Deli*, 8 Jan. 1938.

[106] The innovative Burmese actor-singer Po Sein, for example, chose such a "middle way", supporting the British publicly and financing the Burmese independence movement secretly, see Maung and Whitney (1998: 77).

[107] "Miss Riboet", *Preangerbode*, 22 May 1931.

Artists Not Politicians

In August 1935, Riboet was invited to perform at the studio of the Bataviaasche Radio Vereeniging, a private radio station. During a break, Riboet-fan Saeroen took the opportunity to interview her and members of the cast, two Filipino entertainers from Manila, Eddy Mendieta and Frank Martinez. Mendieta was artistically rooted in Manila's Hispano-Filipino zarzuela and vaudeville stage of the late 1910s. Like many of his generation, he developed a long-lasting relationship with Malay opera. As a teenager in 1925, Mendieta had been a member of the Iberia Vaudeville Co. from Binondo, Manila, which had played Singapore's amusement park, the New World.[108] In 1932, he was choreographer and dancer for the Rose Opera of Singapore.[109]

As an Indonesian nationalist taking great interest in politics and the independence issue in the Philippines, Saeroen approached the two Spanish-speaking artists in a garbled Castilian. He asked them what they thought of Filipino political leader Manuel Quezon and the prospect of Philippine independence. Saeroen was referring to the Tydings-McDuffie Independence Act, approved in March 1934 by President Franklin D. Roosevelt. In June 1934, Nacionalista leader Manuel Quezon had won the Philippine legislative elections with a majority vote. In August 1934, he headed the newly established Partido Nacionalista Democrata and his name circulated as the first Commonwealth President. Pro-independence Indonesian nationalists, including Saeroen, followed political developments in the Philippines closely, particularly since 1932, when Quezon renewed activity to achieve political freedom from the United States. The two might even have met when, in September 1934, Quezon visited the Association of Indonesian Academics in Batavia, a nationalist organisation.[110] Among the Indonesian nationalists, who were most certainly present at that particular occasion, was Mohamad Husni Thamrin, Miss Riboet devotee and leader of the nationalist faction of the People's Council. Thamrin would send Quezon a cable the following year, congratulating the Filipino leader on behalf of the Indonesian political parties with the inauguration of the Philippine Commonwealth.[111] During his brief visit to Batavia in 1934, and in the presence

---

[108] "New World Shows", *The Straits Times*, 10 June 1925. After the Second World War, Mendieta picked up a career as actor in the Indonesian film industry and changed his name to Abdul Hadi.

[109] Tan (1993: 44–5).

[110] Poeze (1988: 158). "Perdjamoean teh kepada pembesar Pilipina", *Penindjauan*, 12 Sept. 1934; "Het oog naar de Philippijnen", *Soerabaijasch Handelsblad*, 5 Sept. 1934. On his trip to Indonesia, Quezon was accompanied by Mr. J.B. Vargas and Mr. J.S. Estrada.

[111] Hering (1996: 187).

of the local press, Quezon was careful with his words. He diplomatically stated to his Indonesian hosts that he "hoped that this country will receive the best for what is necessary".[112] Saeroen met a similar diplomatic response from the two Filipino vaudeville artists he interviewed. Regarding the forthcoming autonomy and independence of their home country, Saeroen reported that the two literally said they "know of nothing". And he also reiterated that, in response to his queries, the Filipinos had emphasised that they were "artists not politicians".[113] It should be noted that, as early as the mid-1910s, Filipinos were aware that "[t]here is little of no talk of independence among the Javanese, and even to hint at it is regarded as seditious".[114] Given the arrest and exile of Soekarno and other leading Indonesian nationalists in 1933, and Dutch suspicions concerning Philippine independence (the Dutch feared this would produce a precedent for the East Indies), Mendieta and Martinez, like Quezon, appear to have been extremely cautious in venting their political opinions in public.

Compared to the colonised in Indonesia, the situation in the Philippines in 1935 was almost the complete opposite. This was perhaps unsurprising given the prospect of Philippine independence. Louis Borromeo's artistic and commercial endeavours may serve as a good example. In 1935, he celebrated the new status of the Philippines as a commonwealth nation and the inauguration of its first president, Manuel Quezon, in a musical composition: "Philippine Commonwealth Hymn". Borromeo advertised the hymn as something to be "conveniently sung in schools and colleges and civic gatherings. It appeals to the patriotic feelings of all Filipinos [...]" and the old vaudeville director was proud to mention that "[i]mmediately after its playing, His Excellency complimented the author by autographing the original of the piece [...]".

In retrospect, Saeroen's encounter with the Filipino Malay opera artists in a Batavia radio studio sums up perfectly the relationship between society and popular culture in colonial Indonesia in the mid-1930s: the chances of a coming together of nationalist grass-roots politics and popular art were gone for good. By 1936, popular culture in colonial Indonesia had lost its social relevance and with it its vitality.

---

[112] "Quezon's bezoek", *De Indische Courant*, 5 Sept. 1934.
[113] "Dengan Miss Riboet di studio B.R.V.", *Pemandangan*, 1 Aug. 1935.
[114] "Are You Afraid of Japan? If so, Read This", *PFP*, 6 Mar. 1915.

Illus. 10.3 Cover of "Philippine Commonwealth Hymn" composed and co-published by Luis Borromeo, 1935.

Epilogue

The adventures of Luis Borromeo and Miss Riboet in vaudeville and Malay opera in the 1920s show that a brief eruption of creative and artistic activity occurred in the Philippines and Indonesia, one that took the shape of a previously unknown secular popular culture marked by stardom and fandom. Linking to peers in theatre, music, literature, journalism and even sports, the two protagonists consciously crossed artistic borders to create something new and exciting. The innovative theatre was rooted in local cultural conventions as well as inspired by modern Western culture; moreover, it proved socially relevant. Borromeo and Riboet assumed roles as cultural brokers, opening up a popular modernity and popular cosmopolitanism for the working to middle classes. It did not produce an *avant garde* cosmopolitan art for elites.

The emergent new culture remained situated in-between low and high culture and moving between tradition and modernity. This socially relevant popular culture started to wane in the early 1930s, due to an increasingly exclusive nationalism, a global economic crisis and the introduction of sound motion pictures. By the mid-1930s, the popular art had lost its artistic potency and social appeal. The eruption, the cultural acceleration, had gradually begun to slow.

The nexus of this vibrant new culture was an innovative vernacular theatre. It evolved at a time when the activities of the emancipatory and nationalist movement gained momentum, and at a time of economic prosperity that fell in-between two major global economic crises. Active supporters and sympathisers of the emancipatory and nationalist movements overlapped with an increasingly self-conscious, consumer-oriented, multi-ethnic urban working to middle class. These people recognised political, social and ethical relevance in the work of Luis Borromeo and Miss Riboet. These audiences did not consist of merely passive consumers; some actually participated fully in the new culture, offering artists venues and organising social events, blurring the distinction between consumers and cultural producers. The new, popular vernacular theatre represented and promoted progress and also drifted on the undercurrents of emancipation, nationalism and anti-colonialism; yet, it was not outspokenly progressive in social or political terms. The theatre was particularly moralising in nature and remained rather reactionary in political terms. In sum, the theatre produced by Boromeo and Riboet cannot simply be reduced to escapist entertainment, to an instrument of elites for manipulating the masses, or to an instrument for channelling anti-colonialism.

Compared to Indonesia, the evolution of a popular art in the Philippines offers a complex picture of both non-elite and elite participation in the popular realm. For the greater sake of nation-building and as a civilising project, Filipino political and economic elites put their stamp on popular culture with the consent and collaboration of the American regime. By contrast, popular entertainment in Indonesia developed relatively autonomously from the colonial state and elite involvement was absent. The Dutch colonial government showed very little interest in popular entertainment as an instrument for civilising the native. In contrast to this disinterest, people with strong sympathies for the Indonesian emancipatory and nationalist movement seized popular cultural institutions as vehicles to transform society into a more just social order. Grassroots activities in the popular realm ranged from engaging in charity to more abstract goals such as forging social solidarity and community in the face of the social inequalities created by Dutch colonialism. Such social purposes were not evident in the case of a more top-down and elitist-driven popular culture in the colonial Philippines.

How should we assess developments in the popular realm after 1936? As the new, socially relevant popular culture had been on the wane since the mid-1930s, the Second World War did not mean an abrupt break with developments within the cultural realm. Rather, the Japanese occupation seems to have enhanced a trend that had already set in years earlier. Under the Japanese, space for cultural experimentation and cultural borrowing became officially restricted. The Japanese military occupation administration in Indonesia, and the Japanese-sponsored Philippine puppet government after 1943, geared the arts, from literature to music, towards war propaganda, and to rather essentialist and equally ambiguous ideas about pan-Asianism and nationalism. American popular culture and its iconic jazz, became extremely suspect, and were officially banned. After the war, as independence had been achieved, the few remaining Malay opera and Filipino vaudeville companies in the 1950s were reduced to playing small and obscure venues, vanishing completely somewhere in the 1960s. In the 1950s, the local film industries blossomed, and the first local record companies were founded that were independent from the handful of large foreign corporations who had monopolised the music industry prior to the Second World War. In the wake of the Cold War, nation-building and the search for new national identities, new controversies arose in the late 1950s, over a new, popular youth culture marked by jeans, rock 'n' roll and electric guitars, disputes that recall pre-war debates on morality, modernity, cosmopolitanism and cultural nationalism.[1]

---

[1] Day and Liem (2010); Barendregt, Keppy and Schulte Nordholt (2017: 39–52).

Legacies?

February to March 1945 was a period of great confusion and human suffering in Manila. To break Japanese military resistance, the Americans shelled the city heavily for weeks. The American barrages combined with Japanese scorched earth tactics, and Japanese atrocities committed against civilians, turning Manila into a ruin as well as into an open graveyard. Luis Borromeo, his family and one of his brothers were there. Luis survived the war, but somewhere in 1946, not long after the war had been terminated, he succumbed to a severe illness around the age 66.[2]

Luis's whereabouts during the war are opaque. In both the Philippines and Indonesia, the Japanese authorities banned jazz and vaudeville as American imperialist cultural forms. The Japanese cultural policy likely forced Luis into unemployment. It is certain that he was not among the artists who had gathered around the Filipino National Theatre, based at the Metropolitan Theatre, the centre of nationalist cultural activity in Manila, sponsored by the Japanese and the Philippine puppet regime. In fact, none of the prominent vodavilistas of the 1920s and 1930s are found as patrons of the National Theatre.[3] This absence is in line with the National Theatre's highbrow policy of promoting European classical music and "national" Filipino music and theatre. During the war, Luis was probably already seriously ill and was taken care of by his brothers.[4] After he died in 1946, his family took his remains to the family's crypt at the Basilica of Cebu, the home of the Santo Niño. While to this day the Santo Niño continues to receive hundreds of thousands pilgrims annually, the Philippine King of Jazz, who once drew tens of thousands of Filipino spectators, is largely forgotten.[5] His memory, however, lives on in the hearts and minds of members of the extended Borromeo family.

---

[2] In 1946, Luis was evicted from his house in Manila which indicated he was still alive in 1946. See Republic of the Philippines SUPREME COURT Manila EN BANC G.R. No. L-131, 30 Mar. 1946. NARCISA DE LA FUENTE y su esposo JOSE TEODORO, demandantes y apelados, vs. LUIS BORROMEO, demandado y apelante; Personal communication with Fritz Schenker, 23 Mar. 2014. One of Luis's brothers was killed during the battle of Manila and his body was never found.

[3] The only exception is Atang de la Rama, who is on the National Theatre's list, see *The Filipino National Theater Souvenir Program season 1943–1944*, Manila.

[4] Testimonies from members of the Borromeo family are contradictory on the nature of the disease, with tuberculosis sometimes being mentioned. Nonetheless, the stories leave little doubt that Luis was seriously ill and eventually died from whatever condition he suffered from.

[5] In 2012, when my research for this book was still ongoing, I found that employees of the Music Museum in Cebu, which claims to immortalise Cebu's musical heritage, had absolutely no clue about who Luis Borromeo was.

On 19 April 1965, an austere ceremony took place at the Kebun Jahe Kober cemetery, Tanah Abang, Jakarta. Since the late 18th century, this had been the last resting place for Batavia's well-to-do Europeans, including many Eurasians. The ceremony was held for Miss Riboet who passed away that same day. Apart from an announcement in newspaper *Warta Bhakti*, placed by her husband Tio Tek Djien Jr., Indonesian newspapers paid no attention to the death of the former Malay opera diva.[6] Maybe the papers were preoccupied with the profound economic crisis and the political tensions building between President Soekarno, the army and the Indonesian Communist Party. Four months after Riboet's passing, an alleged communist coupe d'état was staged on 30 September 1965, which would eventually lead to the mass killing and imprisonment of hundreds of thousands alleged communists. In 1967, President Soekarno stepped down, heralding President's Suharto's authoritarian New Order regime. The new leader focused on developing Indonesia economically with the aid of Western countries, including its former coloniser, which had been antagonised by Soekarno. In this new spirit of economic development, Mayor Ali Sadikin of Jakarta embarked on modernising the capital in the mid-1970s, replacing historical sites with concrete buildings and highways. In 1977, following this process of urban renewal, the Kebun Jahe Kober cemetery was, however, saved from destruction and partly transformed into open air Museum Taman Prasasti. A number of tombstones of people considered significant in the capital's history were preserved, including Riboet's original headstone. Riboet's husband Tio Tek Djien had died two years earlier, in December 1975, and thus had not been able to witness this symbolic token, honouring the local cultural significance of his wife.[7]

During the Japanese occupation, Riboet had been working in Solo, central Java. She was based in Jakarta during the violent episode of the Indonesian revolution (1945 to 1949), and presumably also during the transfer of sovereignty in 1949, when the colony passed hands from the Dutch to the United States of Indonesia.[8] In the early 1950s, Tio Tek Djien's long unfulfilled dream of making

---

[6] "Berduka Tjita", *Warta Bakti*, 23 Apr. 1965.

[7] "Tio Tek Djien Suami Miss Riboet Meninggal Dunia", *Sinar Harapan*, 19 Dec. 1975. Present at Tio's funeral in late 1975 was a certain Rosilawaty, reported to have been one of Riboet's nieces. The former head of the State Police, Hoegeng Imam Santoso, was also mentioned attending the ceremony. Santoso was a Hawaiian music and *kroncong* fan and produced a number of kroncong records in the early 1970s.

[8] "Kunst. Miss Riboet", *Java-Bode*, 9 May 1955.

motion pictures finally came true. He produced, wrote and directed three films.[9] Riboet continued with theatre, albeit low profile and back-stage, focusing on dance revues.[10] To make ends meet, she and her husband rented out part of their house. Riboet had turned into a relic of the past only rarely appearing in the print press. In 1960, a newspaper briefly mentioned her in connection with a benefit dance show in Bogor. Her picture was taken with one of President Soekarno's wives, Hartini, who had patronised the show and who had personally congratulated the former diva.[11] In 1975, on the occasion of being publicly honoured by Jakarta's Mayor Sadikin for his cultural achievements, Tio confessed to a newspaper that he had made it his "hobby" to visit the cemetery where his beloved wife rested almost every day.[12] Four months after this confession, Tio died at the age of 80. A few Jakarta newspapers covered his passing, and this time they did not fail to mention his wife and their pre-war artistic achievements.

In the mid-1980s, with Suharto's New Order regime at its height, a theatre company already active since 1977, Teater Koma, led by prominent theatre maker Norbertus Riantiarno, became immensely popular among Jakarta's middle class. In 1985, one of its musical black comedies, "The Cockroach Opera", was a box office hit. Mary S. Zurbuchen noted that this was not political theatre in response to the political repressive climate under Suharto. She explained that Riantiarno's work "reminds one of traditional theatre forms that weave together drama, music, and humour, forms where expression of social criticism provides an outlet for social tensions".[13] In the 1920s, Luis Borromeo and Miss Riboet actively engaged in what Zurbuchen observed as "weaving together". Such processes of connecting, innovating and transformation explain why Borromeo and Riboet made it as a first generation of trans-local popular stars. They eventually and unintentionally contributed significantly to the emergence of a popular, modern cosmopolitan culture widely enjoyed in the 1920s Philippines and Indonesia.

---

[9] These films were *Topeng Besi* (1953), reported to have been produced by Tio, and *Musim Melati* (1950) and *Melarat tapi sehat* (1954), both written and directed by him. See "Almarhum Tio Tek Djien Bikin Sandiwara Dengan Miss Ribut", *Terbit*, 25 Feb. 1980. See also Kristanto (2005: 15, 35).

[10] "Kunst. Miss Riboet", *Java-Bode*, 9 May 1955; "Djakarta Club herdenkt Onafhankelijksdag", *De nieuwsgier*, 20 Aug. 1956.

[11] No title, *Warta Bogor*, 16 Oct. 1960.

[12] "Tio Tek Djien Penerima Hadiah Dari Bang Ali", *Sinar Harapan*, 30 Aug. 1975.

[13] Zurbuchen (1990: 130–1). Cohen (2010: 225), asserts that Riantiarno was actually inspired by Miss Riboet's Orion and Dardanella.

Bibliography

Special Collections

Bañas Collection, Special collections, National Library of the Philippines, Manila.
H. Otley Beyer Ethnographic Collection, National Library of the Philippines, Manila.
Atang de la Rama Collection, Cultural Center of the Philippines, Manila.
Filipinas Heritage Library Photo Collection, Makati, Metro Manila.
Digital Collections, Leiden University Libraries.
Oral History Interviews, National Archives of Singapore.
Collection Nederlands Instituut voor Beeld en Geluid, Hilversum.
Jaap Kunst Collection, Special collections, University of Amsterdam.

78rpm Recordings

"Manila's Jazzy Scandal – Foxtrot". Por Benito Trapaga. Orchester Dobbri. Parlophon, B 33594. Carl Lindstrom AG. (Courtesy of Fritz Schenker)
"Stamboel. Orion Jazz". Ternjanji oleh Miss Riboet v/h Maleis Operette Gezelschap Orion. Miss Riboet Records. Beka B 15103 – II. (Private collection of Jaap Erkelens)
"Ah, Ah, Ah, Ah (Lagoe Turki)". Ternanji oleh Miss Riboet v/h Maleis Operette Gezelschap Orion. Miss Riboet Records. Beka 27788. (Private collection of Jaap Erkelens)
"Stamboel 1927 Baboe ndie Lombok-se (Bananas-leloetjon)". Ternanji oleh Miss Riboet v/h Maleis Operette Gezelschap Orion. Miss Riboet Records. Beka 27820 (Private collection of Jaap Erkelens)
"Bapak Poetjoeng (extra)". Jazz Orkest dengen di njanjiken oleh: Miss Riboet. Miss Riboet Records. Beka B 15802 – I. (Private collection of Jaap Erkelens)
"Nasibnja Kambing Item (matinja Karno tjrita Black Sheep)". Jazz orkest dengen di njanjiken oleh: Miss Riboet v/h Maleis Operette Gezelschap Orion. Miss Riboet records. Beka. B. 15812-1. (Private collection of Jaap Erkelens)
"Stamboel Marayap". Orkest dengen di njanjiken oleh Tan Tjeng Bok alias Si Item dari Opera "Dardanella". Beka B. 15789-II. (Private collection of Peter Keppy)

Home Recordings by Fritz Schenker (piano) Performed from Original Scores, 2015

"Tristezas" (Amelia Hilado), late 1910s/early 1920s
"Jazzy Jazz in Chinaland" (Luis F. Borromeo), c. 1920
"My Beautiful Philippines" (Luis F. Borromeo), 1920

"Dodge Me Daddy" (Luis F. Borromeo), 1922
"Manila Mia" (Luis F. Borromeo), 1922
"Jazz Electrico" (Francisco Buencamino), 1922

Periodicals

Algemeen Dagblad de Preangerbode (*Preangerbode*), Bandung
Bag-ong Kusog, Cebu
Bahagia, Semarang
Bataviaasch Nieuwsblad, Batavia
Bintang Borneo, Banjarmasin
Bintang Hindia, Weltevreden (Batavia)
Bintang Pranakan, Singapore
Bintang Timoer, Batavia
Boemi Melajoe, Palembang
British North Borneo Herald, Sabah
Cambridge Chronicle, Cambridge, Massachusetts
Citra Film, Jakarta
D'Oriënt, Weltevreden (Batavia)
Darmokondo, Solo
De Indische Courant, Surabaya
De Locomotief, Semarang
De Malanger, Malang
De Nieuwe Vorstenlanden, Solo
De nieuwsgier, Jakarta
De Preangerbode, Bandung
De Sumatra Post, Medan
De Volksstem, Batavia
Deli Courant, Medan
Djåwå, Weltevreden (Batavia)
Djawa Tengah, Semarang
Doenia Film dan Sport, Weltevreden (Batavia)
Doenia Istri, Surabaya
Dramatic Mirror, New York
Eastern Daily Mail and Straits Morning Advertiser, Singapore
Elegancias, Manila
Excelsior, Manila
Fotonews, Manila
Graphic, Manila
Het nieuws van den dag voor Nederlandsch-Indië, Batavia
Java-Bode: nieuws, handels- en advertentieblad voor Nederlandsch-Indie (Java-Bode), Batavia
Kansas City Times
Kaoem Moeda, Bandung
Kemadjoean, Semarang
Keng Po, Batavia

Kiauw Po, Bandung
Liwayway, Manila
Makinaugalingon, Iloilo
Manila Nueva, Manila
Malayan Saturday Post, Singapore
Medan Doenia, Semarang
Midden Java, Yogjakarta
Moestika Romans, Batavia
Nieuwe Soerabaja Courant, Surabaya
Nueva Fuerza, Cebu
Oetoesan Sumatra, Medan
Official Gazette, Manila
Pandji Poestaka, Weltevreden (Batavia)
Pantjadjania, Solo
Pedoman Isteri, Batavia
Pelita Andalas, Medan
Pemandangan, Batavia
Pemberita Makassar, Makassar
Pembrita Djember, Jember
Penindjauan, Batavia
Pergaoelan, Kota Raja
Perniagaan, Batavia
Persamaan, Padang
Pertjatoeran Doenia Film, Batavia
Pewarta Deli, Medan
Pewarta Menado, Menado
Pewarta Soerabaja, Surabaya
Philippine Free Press (PFP), Manila
Philippine Magazine, Manila
Pinang Gazette and Straits Chronicle, Penang
Poedjangga Baroe, Batavia
Poestaka Timoer, Yogjakarta
Progress, Cebu
Radio, Padang
Sinar Deli, Medan
Sinar Harapan, Jakarta
Sinar Sumatra, Padang
Sindoro-Bode, Pekalongan
Sin Jit Po, Surabaya
Sin Tit Po, Surabaya
Sin Po, Batavia
Soerabaijasch handelsblad, Surabaya
Soeara Oemoem, Surabaya
Soeara Nirom, Batavia
Soeara Publiek (SP), Surabaya

Sumatra Bode, Padang
Sunday Tribune, Manila
Terbit, Jakarta
The Independent, Manila
The Manila Times (MT), Manila
The Malaya Tribune, Singapore
The Music Trades, New York
The New York Times, New York
The Philippines Herald, Manila
The Philippine Herald Year Book, Manila
The Singapore Free Press and Mercantile Advertiser, Singapore
The Straits Echo, Penang
The Straits Times, Singapore
The Sunday Tribune, Singapore
The Sunday Tribune Magazine, Manila
The Tribune, Manila
Tjaja Timoer, Batavia
Tjaja Soematra, Padang
Variety, New York
Warta Bakti, Jakarta
Warta Bogor, Bogor
Warna Warta (WW), Semarang

Books and Articles

Abalahin, A.J. "Prostitution and the Project of Modernity: A Comparative Study of Colonial Indonesia and the Philippines, 1850–1940", PhD dissertation, Cornell University, 2003.

Alexander, Jennifer and Paul Alexander. "Protecting Peasants from Capitalism: The Subordination of Javanese Traders by the Colonial State", *Comparative Studies in Society and History* 33, no. 2 (1991): 370–94.

Almario, Virgilio S. *Art and Politics in the Balagtasan*, UCLA Center for South East Asian Studies (2003), http://escholarship.org/uc/item/23b7f9h6.

Alzona, Encarnacion. *The Filipino Woman: Her Social, Economic, and Political Status 1565–1933*. Manila: University of the Philippines Press, 1934.

Anderson, Warwick. *Colonial Pathologies. American Tropical Medicine, Race and Hygiene in the Philippines*. Quezon City: Ateneo de Manila University Press, 2007.

Atkins, E. Taylor. *Blue Nippon: authenticating jazz in Japan*. Durham: Duke University Press, 2001.

Ballerino Cohen, Colleen et al., eds., *Beauty Queens on the Global Stage: Gender, Contests, and Power*. New York: Routledge, 1996.

Bañas, R.C. *The Music and Theater of the Filipino People*. Self-published, 1924.

―――. "The Tagalog Theater and the Future of Our Music". *The Music Lover* (January 1932): 11, 21.

―――. *Pilipino music and Theater*. Quezon City: Manlapaz Publishing Co., 1975.

Banner, Hubert S. *Romantic Java as it was and is: a description of the diversified peoples, the departed glories and strange customs of a little known island, remarkable both for its arts, decorative and dramatic, for is natural beauty and the richness of its resources*. London: Seely, 1927.

Barendregt, Bart, Peter Keppy and Henk Schulte Nordholt. *Popular Music in Southeast Asia: Banal Beats, Muted Histories*. Amsterdam: Amsterdam University Press, 2017.

Barnard, Timothy P. *Contesting Malayness: Malay Identity Across Boundaries*. Singapore. Singapore University Press, 2004.

_____. "*Film Melayu*: Nationalism, modernity and film in a pre-World War Two Malay magazine", *Journal of Southeast Asian Studies* 41, no. 1 (2010): 47–70.

Bhabha, Homi K. *The location of culture*. London and New York: Routledge, 1994.

Biran, Misbach Yusa. *Sejarah film 1900–1950. Bikin film di Jawa* [Film history 1900–1950. Making film in Java]. Depok: Komunitas Bambu, 2009.

Bosma, Ulbe and Remco Raben. *Being "Dutch" in the Indies. A History of Creolisation and Empire, 1500–1920*. Singapore: NUS Press, 2008.

Brechin, Gray. "Sailing to Byzantium: the architecture of the fair", in *The anthropology of world's fairs: San Francisco Panama Pacific International Exposition of 1915*, ed. Burton Benedict. Berkeley: Lowie Museum of Anthropology; London: Scolar Press, 1983, pp. 94–113.

Briones, C.G. *Life in old Parian*. Cebu City: University of San Carlos, 1983.

Camasura, A.R. *Cebu-Visayas Directory. Volume 1*. Manila, 1932.

Castle, Vernon. *Modern dancing*. New York: World Syndicate Co., 1914. http://memory.loc.gov/ammem/dihtml/dihome.html.

Castro, C.A. *Musical Renderings of the Philippine Nation*. Oxford/New York: Oxford University Press, 2011.

Chandra, E. "Women and Modernity: Reading the femme fatale in Early Twentieth-century Indies Novels", *Indonesia* 92 (2011): 1–26.

_____. "From Sensation to Oblivion: Boven Digoel in Sino-Malay Novels", *Bijdragen Taal-, land en Volkenkunde* 169 (2013): 244–78.

Cohen, Matthew Isaac. "Border crossings: Bangsawan in the Netherlands Indies in the nineteenth and early twentieth centuries", *Indonesia and the Malay World* 30 (2002): 101–15.

_____. *The Komedie Stamboel. Popular Theatre in Colonial Indonesia, 1891–1903*. Leiden: KITLV Press, 2006.

_____. *Performing otherness: Java and Bali on international stages, 1905–1952*. Basingstoke: Palgrave Macmillan, 2010.

Cooper, F. *Colonialism in Question. Theory, Knowledge, History*. Berkeley: University of California Press, 2005.

Cressey, Paul Goalby. *The taxi-dance hall: a sociological study in commercialized recreation and city life*. Chicago: The University of Chicago Press, 1932.

Cruz, Denise. *Transpacific femininities: the making of the modern Filipina*. Durham, N.C.: Duke University Press, 2012.

Cullinane, M. "The changing nature of the Cebu urban elite in the 19th century", in *Philippine social history*, ed. A.W. McCoy and Ed. C. de Jesus. Quezon City: Ateneo de Manila University Press, 1982, pp. 251–96.

_____. *Ilustrado Politics. Filipino Elite Responses to American Rule, 1898–1908*. Quezon City: Ateneo de Manila University Press, 2003.

Cultural Center of the Philippines. *Union catalog on Philippine culture. Music*. 3 volumes. Manila: Cultural Center of the Philippines, 1989.

_____. *Encyclopedia of Philippine Art. Vol. VI. Philippine Music*, 1994.

Curaming, R.A. "Filipinos as Malay: Historicizing an Identity", in *Melayu: The Politics, Poetics and Paradoxes of Malayness*, ed. Maznah Mohamad and Syed Muhamad Khairudin Aljunied. Singapore: NUS Press, 2011, pp. 241–73.

Daftar dari namanja plaat Odéon Malajoe dan Tjina [Odeon Malay and Chinese Records Catalogue]. N.p., c. 1912.

Day, Tony and Maya H.T. Liem. *Cultures at War. The Cold War and Cultural Expression in Southeast Asia*. Ithaca, NY: Cornell University, Southeast Asia Program, 2010.

Dery, Luis C. "Prostitution in colonial Manila", *Philippine Studies* 39 (1991): 475–89.

Dick, Howard W. *Surabaya, City of Work: A Socioeconomic History, 1900–2000*. Athens, Ohio: Ohio University Press, 2002.

Doeppers, D.F. *Manila, 1900–1941: Social change in a late colonial metropolis*. New Haven, Conn.: Yale University Southeast Asian Studies, 1984.

Doran, Christine. "Spanish and Mestizo Women of Manila", *Philippine Studies* 41 (1993): 283–4.

Elson, Robert E. "International Commerce, the State and Society: Economic and Social Change", in *The Cambridge History of Southeast Asia. Volume Three. From c. 1800 to the 1930s*, ed. Nicholas Tarling. Cambridge: Cambridge University Press, 1999, pp. 127–89.

Enriquez, Elizabeth L. *Appropriation of colonial broadcasting: a history of early radio in the Philippines, 1922–1946*. Quezon City: The University of the Philippines Press, 2008.

Evans, Nicholas M. *Writing jazz. Race, Nationalism and Modern Culture in the 1920s*. New York/London: Garland Publishing Inc., 2000.

Fernandez, Doreen G. *The Iloilo Zarzuela: 1903–1930*. Quezon City: Ateneo de Manila University Press, 1978.

The Filipino National Theater. *The Filipino National Theater Souvenir Program season 1943–1944*. Manila: Musical Philippines Inc., n.d.

Frederick, William H. "Dreams of freedom, moments of despair; Armijn Pané and the imagining of modern Indonesian culture", in *Imagining Indonesia: Cultural politics and political culture*, ed. Jim Schiller and Barbara Martin-Schiller. Athens, Ohio: Ohio University Center for International Studies. Monographs in International Studies, Southeast Asia Series 97, 1996, pp. 54–89.

Frijn, Maya. "Introduction", in *Jaap Kunst. Traditional music and its interaction with the west*, ed. Ernst Heins et al. Amsterdam: Royal Tropical Institute/University of Amsterdam, 1994, pp. 51–5.

Gardinier, David E. and Josefina Z. Sevilla-Gardinier. "Rosa Sevilla de Alvero and the Instituto de Mujeres of Manila", *Philippine Studies* 37 (1989): 29–51.

Garrett, Charles Hiroshi. *Struggling to Define a Nation. American Music and the Twentieth Century*. Berkeley/Los Angeles/London: University of California Press, 2008.

Gennari, John R. "Recovering the 'noisy lostness'. History in the Age of Jazz", *Journal of Urban History* 24, no. 2 (1998): 226–34.

Gleeck, Lewis E. *The Manila Americans (1901–1964)*. Manila: Carmelo & Bauerman, 1977.

Go, Julian. *American empire and the politics of meaning; elite political cultures in the Philippines and Puerto Rico during U.S. colonialism*. Durham, NC: Duke University Press, 2008.

Golay, Frank. *Face of Empire. United States-Philippines relations 1898–1946*. Madison, WI: Center for Southeast Asian Studies, University of Wisconsin-Madison Monograph no. 14, 1998.

Gorsuch, Anne E. "The Dance Class or the Working Class. The Soviet Modern Girl", in *The Modern Girl Around the World. Consumption, Modernity and Globalization*, ed. Alys Eve Weinbaum et al. Durham & London: Duke University Press, 2008, pp. 174–93.

Govaars, Ming. *Dutch colonial education: the Chinese experience in Indonesia, 1900–1942*. Singapore: Chinese Heritage Centre, 2005.

Groenendael, V.M.C. *Java en Madura in de uitvoerende kunsten. Th. G. Th. Pigeauds Javaanse volksvertoningen en latere studies 1817–1995* [Java and Madura and the Performing Arts. Th. G. Th. Pigeaud's Javanese folk arts and later studies 1817–1995]. Leiden: KITLV, 1995.

Gunadharma, Visakha. "Riwayat Hidup Kwee Tek Hoay" [Biography of Kwee Tek Hoay], in *100 tahun Kwee Tek Hoay. Dari Penjaja Tekstil sampai ke Pendekar Pena* [100 years of Kwee Tek Hoay. From Textile Peddler to Master of the Pen], ed. Myra Sidharta. Jakarta: Pustaka Sinar Harapan, 1989, pp. 257–83.

Hall, Stuart and Paddy Whannel. *The Popular Arts*. London: Hutchinson Educational Ltd, 1964.

Harper, Timothy N. *The End of Empire and the Making of Malaya*. Cambridge: Cambridge University Press, 1999.

Hawkins, Michael C. *Making Moros. Imperial Historicism and American Military Rule in the Philippines' Muslim South*. DeKalb, IL: Northern Illinois University Press, 2013.

Heins, Ernst. "Jaap Kunst and the rise of ethnomusicology", in *Jaap Kunst. Traditional music and its interaction with the west*, ed. Ernst Heinz et al. Amsterdam: Royal Tropical Institute/University of Amsterdam, 1994, pp. 13–23.

Hering, Bob. *M.H. Thamrin and his quest for Indonesian nationhood 1917–1941*. Edisi Khusus Kabar Seberang, Sulating Maphilindo 26/27, 1996.

Hernandez, Tomas C. *The emergence of modern drama in the Philippines (1898–1912)*. Honolulu: University of Hawaii, 1975.

Hills, Matt. *Fan cultures*. New York: Routledge, 2002.

Hoogervorst, Tom and Henk Schulte Nordholt. "Urban Middle Classes in Colonial Java (1900–1942). Images and Languages", *Bijdragen tot de Taal-, Land en Volkenkunde* 173 (2017): 442–74.

Horton, William Bradley. "History Unhinged: World War II and the Reshaping of Indonesian History", PhD dissertation, Waseda University, 2016.

Hutari, Fandy. *Para Penghibur. Riwayat 17 Artis Masa Hindia Belanda* [The Entertainers. The Histories of 17 Artists from the Dutch East Indies Era]. Yogyakarta: Penerbit Basabasi, 2017.

I. Beck Inc. Recording Expedition. *I. Beck Inc. Recording Expedition. Columbia Filipino Records. Recorded in Manila* (c. 1930).

Irving, David R.M. *Colonial Counterpoint. Music in Early Modern Manila.* Oxford: Oxford University Press, 2010.

Jacobs, Aletta H. *Reisbrieven uit Afrika en Azië. Benevens eenige brieven uit Zweden en Noorwegen* [Travel letters from Africa and Asia. And some letters from Sweden and Norway]. Almelo: W. Hilarius Wzn, 1915.

Jedamski, Doris. "'… and then the lights went out and it was pitched-dark': from *stamboel* to *tonil* – theatre and the transformation of perceptions", *South East Asia Research* 16, 3 (2008): 481–511.

Jenkins, Henry. *Fans, Bloggers and Gamers. Exploring Participatory Culture.* New York/London: New York University Press, 2006a.

_____. *Convergence Culture. Where Old and New Media Collide.* New York & London: New York University Press, 2006b.

Joaquin, Nick. "Pop culture: the American Years", in *Filipino heritage: the making of a nation*, ed. A.R. Roces et al., Vol. IX. Manila: Lahing Pilipino Publishing, 1978, pp. 2732–44.

Johan, Adil. "Disquieting Degeneracy: Policing Malaysian and Singaporean Popular Music culture from the Mid-1960s to Early-1970s", in *Sonic Modernities in the Malay World. A History of Popular Music, Social Distinction and Novel Lifestyles (1930s–2000s)*, ed. Bart Barendregt. Leiden/Boston: Brill, 2014, pp. 135–61.

Jones, Andrew F. *Yellow Music. Media culture and colonial modernity in the Chinese jazz age.* Durham/London: Duke University Press, 2001.

Jones, Russell, ed., *Loan-words in Indonesian and Malay. Compiled by the Indonesian Etymological Project.* Leiden: KITLV Press, 2007.

Jurriens, Edwin and Jeroen de Kloet, eds., *Cosmopatriots: on distant belongings and close encounters.* Amsterdam: Rodopi, 2007.

Kahn, Joel. *Modernity and exclusion.* London/Thousand Oaks/New Delhi: Sage, 2001.

Kalaw, Teodoro M. *Spiritual Register. The news columns of Teodoro M. Kalaw in La Vanguardia, 1926–1927.* Translated from the Spanish by Nick Joaquin. Pasig City: Anvil, 2001.

Kanahele, George S. *Hawaiian Music and musicians. An illustrated history.* Honolulu: The University of Hawaii, 1979.

Kartomi, Margaret. "Indonesian-Chinese Oppression and the Musical Outcomes in the Netherlands East Indies", in *Music and the racial imagination*, ed. Ronald M. Randano and Philip V. Bohlman. Chicago: The University of Chicago Press, 2000, pp. 271–317.

Keppy, Peter. "Keroncong, concours and crooners. Home grown entertainment in twentieth-century Batavia", in *Linking Destinies. Trade, towns and kin in Asian history*, ed. Peter Boomgaard, Dick Kooiman and H. Schulte Nordholt. Leiden: KITLV Press, 2008, pp. 141–58.

_____. "Southeast Asia in the age of jazz: Locating popular culture in the colonial Philippines and Indonesia", *Journal of Southeast Asian Studies* 44 (2013): 444–64.

Kerkvliet, Benedict J. *The Huk rebellion: a study of peasant revolt in the Philippines.* Lanham, MD: Rowman & Littlefield, 2002.

Kinkle, Roger D. *The Complete Encyclopedia of Popular Music and Jazz, 1900–1950.* Volume 2 A through K. New Rochelle, NY: Arlington House Publishers, 1974.

Kramer, Paul. "Making Concessions: Race and Empire Revisited at the Philippine Exposition, 1901–1905", *Radical History Review* 73 (1999): 74–114.

Kristanto, J.B. *Katalog Film Indonesia 1926–2005* [Indonesian Film Catalogue 1926–2005]. Jakarta: Nalar, 2005.

Kwee Thiam Tjing. *Menjadi Tjamboek Berdoeri. Memoar Kwee Thiam Tjing* [Becoming Tjamboek Berdoeri. The Memoirs of Kwee Thiam Tjing]. Depok: Komunitas Bambu, 2010.

Larkin, John A. *Sugar and the Origins of Modern Philippine Society.* Berkeley: University of California Press, 1993.

Lasker, Bruno. *Filipino Immigration to Continental United States and to Hawaii.* Chicago: The University of Chicago Press, 1931.

League of Nations. *Commission of Enquiry into Traffic in Women and Children in the East: Report to the Council. Series of League of Nations Publications, IV. Social. 1932. IV. 8.493.* Geneva. League of Nations, 1933.

Leppert, Richard. "Introduction", in Theodor W. Adorno, *Essays on Music. Selected, with introduction, commentary, and notes by Richard Leppert. New translations by Susan H. Gillespie.* Berkeley/Los Angeles/London: University of California Press, 2002, pp. 1–82.

De Leon, Felipe P. "Manila Welcomes the Opera", in *Filipino heritage: the making of a nation*, ed. A.R. Roces et al. Vol. IX. Manila: Lahing Pilipino Publishing, 1978, pp. 2340–6.

Lewis, Lisa, ed., *The Adoring Audience. Fan Culture and Popular Media.* London/New York: Routledge, 1992.

Lewis, Su Lin. *Cities in Motion: urban life and cosmopolitanism in Southeast Asia, 1920–1940.* Cambridge, UK: Cambridge University Press, 2016.

Lumbera, Bienvenido and Cynthia Nograles Lumbera. *Philippine Literature. A History & Anthology.* Revised edition. Pasig City: Anvil, 1997.

Maier, Henk. "From Heteroglossia to Polyglossia: The Creation of Malay and Dutch in the Indie", *Indonesia* 56 (1993): 37–66.

_____. *Maar geluk duurt nooit lang. Maleise verhalen vol bitterheid* [Happiness never last long. Malay tales of bitterness]. Leiden: KITLV, 2002.

Manchester, William. *American Caesar. Douglas MacArthur 1880–1964.* Boston: Little, Brown & Company, 1978.

Maters, Mirjam. *Van zachte wenk tot harde hand. Persvrijheid en persbreidel in Nederlands-Indië, 1906–1942* [From soft hint to hard hand: Press freedom and press censorship in the Dutch East Indies 1906–1942]. Hilversum: Verloren,1998.

McCoy, Alfred W. "Zarzuela and welga: vernacular drama and the growth of working-class consciousness Iloilo city, Philippines, 1900–1932", in *Society and the writer: essays on literature in modern Asia*, ed. Wang Gungwu, M. Guerrero & D. Mar. Canberra: The Australian National University, 1981, pp. 35–66.

Meijer, Hans. *In Indië geworteld. De twintigste eeuw* [Rooted in the Indies. The Twentieth Century]. Amsterdam: Uitgeverij Bakker, 2004.

Middleton, Richard. "Articulating Musical Meaning/Re-Constructing Musical History/ Locating the 'Popular'", *Popular Music* 5 (1985): 5–43.

Mobini-Kesheh, Natalie. *The Hadrami Awakening. Community and identity in the Netherlands East Indies, 1900–1942*. Ithaca, NY: Cornell University Studies on Southeast Asia no. 28, 1999.

Möller, Allard J.M. *Batavia A Swinging Town. Dansorkesten en jazzbands in Batavia 1922–1949* [Batavia A Swinging Town. Dance orchestras and jazz bands in Batavia 1922–1949]. Den Haag: Moessoen, 1987.

Montesano, Michael and Patrick Jory, eds. *Thai South and Malay North: Ethnic Interactions on a Plural Peninsula*. Singapore: NUS Press, 2008.

Moon, Kristen. *Yellowface: Creating the Chinese in American Popular Music and Performance, 1850s–1920s*. New Brunswick, NJ: Rutgers University Press, 2005.

Mrázek, Rudolf. *Engineers of happy land. Technology and nationalism in a colony*. Princeton: Princeton University Press, 2002.

van den Muijzenberg, Otto. *The Philippines through European lenses*. Quezon City, Manila: Ateneo de Manila University Press, 2009.

del Mundo, Clodualdo A. *Native resistance: Philippine cinema and colonialism, 1898–1941*. Manila: De La Salle University Press, 1998.

Nas, Peter J.M. "The Early Indonesian Town: Rise and Decline of the City-State and its Capital", in *The Indonesian city. Studies in urban development and planning*, ed. Peter J.M. Nas. Dordrecht, Holland: Foris Publications, 1982, pp. 18–36.

Nio Joe Lan. "De vestiging van een Indische filmindustrie" [The establishment of a Dutch East Indies film industry], *Koloniale Studien* (1941): 386–403.

Njoo, Tjiong Sing Jr. *Sair dan Pantoen. Krontjong trang boelan. Sair sindir menjindir nona manis* [Syair and Pantun. Bright Moonlight Kroncong. Sweet lady's satirical poetry]. N.p., 1922.

Nguyen-Marshall, Van. *In search of moral authority: the discourse on poverty, poor relief, and charity in French colonial Vietnam*. New York/Oxford: Peter Lang, 2005.

Nyuda, Doris G. *The Beauty Book*. Manila: MR. & MS. Publishing Company, 1980.

Orang-orang Tionghoa. *Orang-orang Tionghoa jang terkemuka di Djawa* [Prominent Chinese in Java]. Solo, 1937.

Pagayon Santos, Ramon. *Tunugan: four essays on Filipino music*. Quezon City: University of the Philippines, 2005.

Perret, Geoffrey. *Old Soldiers Never Die: The Life of Douglas MacArthur*. New York: Random House, 1996.

Philippine Commission of Independence. *Beautiful Philippines: A handbook of general information*. Manila: Philippine Commission of Independence, 1923.

Pigeaud, Theodoor. "Over den huidigen stand van de toneel- en danskunst en de muziekbeoefening op Java" [On the current state of theatrical and dance arts and musical practice in Java], *Djåwå* (1932): 155–65.

Pinches, Michael. "Cultural relations, class and the new rich of Asia", in *Culture and Privilege in Capitalist Asia*, ed. Michael Pinches. London: Routledge, 1999, pp. 1–55.

Poeze, Harry A. *Politiek-politionele overzichten Deel I, 1927–1928* [Political intelligence reports Part I, 1927–1928]. The Hague: Martinus Nijhoff, 1982.

_____. *Politiek-politionele overzichten van Nederlandsch-Indië. Deel II 1929–1930* [Political intelligence reports Part II, 1929–1930]. Dordrecht-Holland: Foris Publications, 1983.

_____. *Politiek-politionele overzichten van Nederlandsch-Indië. Deel III 1931–1934* [Political intelligence reports Part III, 1931–1934]. Dordrecht-Holland: Foris Publications, 1988.

_____. "Kata Pengantar" [Foreword], in Matu Mona, *Pacar Merah Indonesia. Buku Pertama. Tan Malaka: Petualangan Buron Polisi Rahasia Kolonial* [The Indonesian Scarlet Pimpernel. First Book. Adventures of a Fugitive of the Colonial Secret Police]. Yogyakarta: KITLV and Jendela, 2001, pp. xxi–xxxii.

Post, Peter. "The Oei Tiong Ham Concern and the change of regimes in Indonesia, 1931–1950", in *Chinese Indonesians and Regime Change*, ed. Marleen Dieleman, Juliette Koning and Peter Post. Leiden/Boston: Brill, 2011, pp. 169–99.

Quirino, Carlos. *Who's who in Philippine history*. Makati City: Tahanan Books, 1995.

Quirino, Richie C. *Pinoy Jazz Traditions*. Pasig City: Anvil, 2004.

Rafael, Vicente L. *White Love and other events in Filipino history*. Quezon City: Ateneo de Manila University Press, 2008.

Rahmann, Rudolf and Gertrudes R. Ang. *Dr. H. Otley Beyer: Dean of Philippine Anthropology (a commemorative issue)*. Cebu City: University of San Carlos, 1968.

Ramamurthy, Priti. "All-Consuming Nationalism. The Indian Modern Girl in the 1920s and 1930s", in *The Modern Girl Around the World. Consumption, Modernity and Globalization*, ed. Alys Eve Weinbaum et al. Durham & London: Duke University Press, 2008, pp. 146–73.

Reid, Anthony. *Southeast Asia in Age of Commerce 1450–1680. Volume One: The Lands below the Winds*. New Haven and London: Yale University Press, 1988.

Robb, Walter. *Filipinos: pre-war Philippine essays*. Rizal: Araneta University Press, 1963.

Roces, Mina. "Is the Suffragist an American Colonial Construct? Defining 'the Filipino Women' in Colonial Philippines", in Louise P. Edwards and Mina Roces, *Women's Suffrage in Asia: Gender, Nationalism and Democracy*. London & New York: RoutledgeCurzon, 2004, pp. 24–58.

Rosenstock, C.W. *Rosenstock's Manila City Directory 1924–1925*. Manila, 1925.

Rustopo. *Menjadi Jawa: orang-orang Tionghoa dan kebudayaan Jawa di Surakarta, 1895– 1998* [Becoming Javanese: Chinese and Javanese culture in Surakarta, 1895–1998]. Jakarta: Yayasan Nabil, 2007.

Sabanpan-Yu, Hope. *Institutionalizing Motherhood in Cebuano Literature*. Cebu City: University of San Carlos Press and Cebuano Studies Center, 2011.

Salmon, Claudine. *Literature in Malay by the Chinese of Indonesia: a provisional annotated bibliography*. Paris: Editions de la Maison des Sciences de l'Homme, 1981.

Schenker, Frederick J. "Empire of Syncopation: Music, Race and Labor in Colonial Asia's Jazz Age", Doctoral dissertation, University of Wisconsin-Madison, 2016.

Sein, Maung Khe and Joseph A. Whitney. *The Great Po Sein*. Bangkok: Orchid Press, 1998.

Shiraishi, Takashi. *An age in motion. Popular radicalism in Java, 1912–1926*. Ithaca, NY: Cornell University Press, 1990.

_____. "The Phantom World of Digoel", *Indonesia*, no. 61 (1996): 93–118.

Siddiqi, Mohamad Nejatullah. "The Role of the Voluntary Sector in Islam: a conceptual Framework", in *The Islamic Voluntary Sector in Southeast Asia*, ed. Mohamad Ariff. Singapore: ISEAS, 1991, pp. 6–30.

Sidharta, Myra. "Njoo Cheong Seng: a Peranakan novelist, playwright, director, poet, editor", in *Southeast Asian Chinese : the socio-cultural dimension*, ed. Leo Suryadinata. Singapore: Times Academic Press, 1995, pp. 273–89.

_____. "Sinopsis Buku-buku Bunga Roos Dari Cikembang, Drama Dari Merapi dan Drama Di Boven Digoel" [Synopsis of the books Bunga Roos Dari Cikembang and Drama Di Boven Digoel], in *100 tahun Kwee Tek Hoay. Dari Penjaja Tekstil sampai Pendekar Pena* [100 years of Kwee Tek Hoay. From Textile Peddler to Master of the Pen], ed. Myra Sidartha. Jakarta: Pustaka Sinar Harapan, 1989, pp. 291–8.

Siegel, James. *Fetish, Recognition, Revolution*. Princeton, NJ: Princeton University Press, 1997.

Skinner, William G. "Creolized Chinese Societies in Southeast Asia", in *Sojourners and Settlers. Histories of Southeast Asia and the Chinese in Honour of Jeniffer Cushman*, ed. Anthony Reid. St Leonards, NSW: Allen & Unwin with Asian Studies Association of Australia, 1996, pp. 51–93.

Slide, Anthony. *The encyclopedia of vaudeville*. Westport, Conn: Greenwood Press, 1994.

Spottswood, Richard K. *Ethnic music on records: a discography of ethnic recordings produced in the United States, 1893–1942*. Urbana: University of Illinois Press, Vols. 4–6, 1990.

Stagg, Samuel W. *Teodoro R. Yangco. Leading Filipino Philantropist and Grand Old Man of Commerce*. Manila: University of Manila Press, 1934.

Stanley, Peter W. *A nation in the making. The Philippines and the United States, 1899–1921*. Cambridge, Mass: Harvard University Press, 1974.

Stein, Charles W. "Introduction", in *American vaudeville as seen by its contemporaries*, ed. Stein, Charles W. New York: Alfreda A. Knopf, 1984, pp. 3–6.

Storey, John. *Inventing Popular Culture. From Folklore to Globalization*. Oxford: Blackwell Publishing, 2003.

Sumardjo, Jakob. "Kwee Tek Hoay Sebagai Sastrawan" [Kwee Tek Hoay as a Writer], in *100 tahun Kwee Tek Hoay. Dari Penjaja Tekstil sampai Pendekar Pena* [100 years of Kwee Tek Hoay. From Textile Peddler to Master of the Pen], ed. Myra Sidartha. Jakarta: Pustaka Sinar Harapan, 1989, pp. 89–121.

_____. *Teater modern dan sastra drama Indonesia* [Modern theater and Indonesian drama literature]. Bandung: Penerbit PT Citra Aditya Bakti, 1992.

Sutherland, Heather. "Pudjangga Baru: Aspects of Indonesian Intellectual Life in the 1930s", *Indonesia*, no. 6 (1968): 106–27.

Suryadinata, Leo. *Prominent Indonesian Chinese. Biographical sketches*. Singapore: ISEAS, 1995.

Svinth, Joseph R. "The Origins of Philippines Boxing, 1899–1929", *Journal of Combative Sport*, July 2001. http://ejmas.com/jcs/jcsart_svinth_0701.htm

Talusan, Mary. "Music, Race and Imperialism: The Philippine Constabulary Band at the 1904 St. Louis World Fair", *Philippine Studies* 52, 4 (2004): 499–526.

Tan Sooi Beng. *Bangsawan. A social and stylistic history of popular Malay opera*. Singapore: Oxford University Press, 1993.

_____. "The 78rpm record industry in Malaya prior to World War II", *Asian Music* 1 (1996–97): 1–42.

Tan, Arwin Q. "Reproduction of Cultural and Social Capital in Nineteenth Century Spanish Regimental Bands of the Philippines", *Humanities Diliman* 11 (July–December 2014): 61–89.

Teitler, Gerke. "The mixed company: fighting power and ethnic relations in the Dutch colonial Army, 1890–1920", in *Colonial Armies in Southeast Asia*, ed. Karl Hack & Tobias Rettig. London & New York: Routledge, 2006, pp. 154–68.

Terami-Wada, Motoe. "Karayuki-san of Manila, 1890–1920", *Philippine Studies* 34 (1986): 287–316.

Termorshuizen, Gerard. *Realisten en reactionairen. Een geschiedenis van de Indisch-Nederlandse pers 1905–1942* [Realists and reactionaries. A history of the Dutch East Indies press 1905–1942]. Amsterdam/Leiden: Nijgh & van Ditmar/KITLV, 2011.

Tiongson, Nicanor G. "Atang de la Rama. The once and future star", in Cultural Center of the Philippines, *The National Artists of the Philippines*. Pasig City: Anvil Publishing, 1998, pp. 97–109.

Tjamboek Berdoeri. *Indonesia dalem api dan bara* [Indonesia in fire and embers]. Jakarta: Elkasa, 2004.

Todd, Frank Morton. *The Story of the Exposition*. 5 vols. New York: G.P. Putnam's Sons, Vols. 2 & 3, 1921.

Tofighian, Nadi. "José Nepomuceno and the creation of a Filipino national consciousness", *Film History* 20 (2008): 77–94. http://www.academia.edu/15675402/Jos%C3%A9_Nepomuceno_and_the_creation_of_a_Filipino_national_consciousness

Touwen, Jeroen. *Extremes in the archipelago. Trade and economic development in the Outer Islands of Indonesia, 1900–1942*. Leiden: KITLV, 2001

Tsou, Judy. "Gendering Race: Stereotype of Chinese Americans in Popular Sheet Music", *Repercussions* 6, no. 2 (1997): 25–62.

Valenzuela, Jesus Z. *History of journalism in the Philippine islands*. Manila, 1933.

Van der Wal, S.L. *Herinneringen van Jhr. Mr. B.C. de Jonge met brieven uit zijn nalatenschap* [Reminiscences of Jhr. Mr. B.C. de Jonge and letters from his endowment]. Utrecht: Uitgave van het Historisch Genootschap, 1968.

Walraven, Willem. *Brieven Aan familie en vrienden 1919–1941. Biografische inleiding van F. Schamhardt* [Letters to family and friends 1919–1941. Biographical introduction by F. Schamhardt]. Amsterdam: Van Oorschot, 1992.

Wan Abdul Kadir. *Budaya popular dalam Masyarakat Melayu bandaran* [Popular culture among urban Malays]. Kuala Lumpur: Dewan Bahasa dan Pustaka, 1988.

Weinbaum, Alys Eve et al., eds. *The Modern Girl Around the World. Consumption, Modernity, and Globalization*. Durham & London: Duke University Press, 2008.

Wertheim, Arthur Frank. *Vaudeville wars; how the Keith-Albee and Orpheum circuits controlled the big-time and its performers*. New York: Palgrave MacMillan, 2006.

Wilson, Andrew. *Ambition and Identity. Chinese Merchant Elites in Colonial Manila, 1880–1916*. Honolulu: University of Hawaii Press, 2004.

Woodrich, Christopher A. "Between the Village and the City. Representing Colonial Indonesia in the Films of Saeroen", *Social Transformation* 3, no. 2 (2015): 33–55.

Yamamoto, Nobuto. "The Chinese Connection; Rewriting Journalism and Social Categories in Indonesian History", in *Chinese Indonesians and Regime Change*, ed. Marleen Dieleman, Juliette Koning and Peter Post. Leiden/Boston: Brill, 2011, pp. 93–116.

Yampolsky, Philip. "Kroncong Revisited: New Evidence from Old Sources", *Archipel* 79 (2010): 7–56.

————. "Music and media in the Dutch East Indies: Gramophone records and radio in the late colonial era, 1903–1942", Doctoral dissertation, University of Washington, 2013.

————. "Music on Dutch East Indies radio in 1938: representations of unity, disunity, and the modern", in *Sonic Modernities in the Malay World. A History of Popular Music, Social Distinction and Novel Lifestyles (1930s–2000s)*, ed. Bart Barendregt. Leiden/Boston: Brill, 2014, pp. 47–112.

Yeatter, Brian L. *Cinema in the Philippines. A History and Filmography, 1897–2005.* Jefferson: McFarland & Co, 2007.

Zurbuchen, Mary S. "Images of Culture and National Development in Indonesia: The Cockroach Opera", *Asian Theatre Journal* 7, no. 2 (1990): 127–49.

Index